D0166950

Stephanie James is a pseudonym for bestselling, award-winning author **Jayne Ann Krentz.** Under various pseudonyms—including Jayne Castle and Amanda Quick—Ms. Krentz has nearly thirty million copies of her books in print and has been a *New York Times* bestselling author at least twenty-seven times. Her fans admire her versatility as she switches between historical, contemporary and futuristic romances. She attributes a "lifelong addiction to romantic daydreaming" as the chief influence on her writing. With her husband, Frank, she currently resides in the Pacific Northwest.

JAYNE ANN KRENTZ

writing as
Stephanie James

CARRIED AWAY

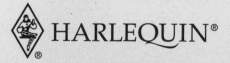

HARLEQUIN®

TORONTO • NEW YORK • LONDON
AMSTERDAM • PARIS • SYDNEY • HAMBURG
STOCKHOLM • ATHENS • TOKYO • MILAN • MADRID
PRAGUE • WARSAW • BUDAPEST • AUCKLAND

ISBN 0-373-83540-X

CARRIED AWAY

Copyright © 2002 by Harlequin Books S.A.

The publisher acknowledges the copyright holder of the individual works as follows:

GOLDEN GODDESS
Copyright © 1985 by Jayne Ann Krentz

CAUTIOUS LOVER
Copyright © 1986 by Jayne Ann Krentz

GREEN FIRE
Copyright © 1986 by Jayne Ann Krentz

Visit us at www.eHarlequin.com

Printed in U.S.A.

CONTENTS

GOLDEN GODDESS

One

By the time Hannah Prescott realized there was an intruder in her hotel room, it was too late to scream. In the light of the pale Hawaiian moon filtering through the window she saw a small, blunt object in the stranger's hand. A gun?

"Come in and close the door. Quietly." The man's voice floated across the room to her in tones of darkness and dominance, reaching her with the impact of an uncoiling whip.

Frozen in the doorway, Hannah stared, trying to discern his features in the shadows. Her first reaction after the initial fear was bewilderment. "I know you," she heard herself whisper shakily. "You were on the plane yesterday."

"Close the door, Miss Prescott." The man had been crouching beside one of her suitcases. He got to his feet with slow intent as she continued to stand like a startled doe in the doorway.

His right hand moved in the dim light, and Hannah's fear-induced trance broke long enough for her to decide that the odds were just as good if she ran for her life as they were if she stayed and awaited her fate. She whirled to flee.

He was upon her before she could get back out through the door. A hard palm clamped fiercely across her mouth and a sinewy arm wrapped around her waist.

"Damn it, you're soaking wet!" the man complained gruffly as the outline of her still-damp swimsuit was imprinted on his shirt. "Just my luck. The first time I get my hands on you, you're fresh out of a pool!"

Hannah struggled wildly, feeling horribly vulnerable in her brilliant purple bikini. The suit had been bought expressly for the South Pacific tour and covered a good deal less of her rounded curves than the more prosaic one-piece she had left at home.

In her frantic efforts to free herself, the small, triangular patches of fabric that covered her breasts began to shift disastrously. Hannah was unaware of the precarious position of the bikini bra. All she knew was the superior strength in the large hands of the man who was half dragging, half carrying her toward the bed. He held her with an efficient, professional grasp that left her unable to find her balance or do any real damage in return.

"Stop struggling," the intruder ordered roughly. "Don't make me hurt you."

She wanted to scream and couldn't because of the hand across her mouth. It was like a dark, perverted nightmare, Hannah realized in panic. This was the man she had fantasized about yesterday on the airplane; the one who had caught her attention even as he'd casually walked down the aisle to take a seat a few rows behind her. It had been such a harmless, gentle fantasy. A feminine daydream. Never in the course of that daydream had she imagined this kind of violence. How could a fantasy go so darkly awry?

She fought desperately, using her sandal-clad feet to kick at him and her nails to rake his arm, but she fought inefficiently and unskillfully. The stranger seemed to realize that her frantic efforts to free herself weren't going to stop at his command. Ruthlessly he pinned her to the bed, his palm still sealing her mouth.

Hannah was terrifyingly aware of the heavy weight of the hard body anchoring her to the beige bedspread. He was using his strength to crush her into submission.

"Calm down, you little hellcat. I won't hurt you if you'll just behave yourself. I'm here for the goddess!"

The goddess? He wasn't merely an intruder, Hannah realized, he was an insane intruder. How did one handle a crazy man bent on assault? Eyes wide and fearful, she stared up at him in the moonlight, temporarily ceasing her struggles. She must remain calm, she told herself, encourage him to at least release her mouth. Perhaps then she could manage a scream for help. He didn't seem to be using the object she had assumed was a gun. Maybe he was unarmed after all. She might have a chance. The possibility gave her the first ray of hope she'd had since she'd entered the room.

"That's better," the man growled as she went quiet beneath him. He made no immediate effort to move, continuing to let his hard weight sprawl across her softness. "You'd think I was trying to rape you, the way you're struggling. Such a fierce little thing. But you're much too soft for this kind of battle. A man only has to put his hands on you in order to either crush you or make love to you."

Hannah saw the way his eyes moved from her panic-stricken gaze, down the length of her throat to the area where her purple bikini should have been covering her breasts. It was then that she realized how the bra cups had slipped, exposing the rounded, high-crested globes. The tension in her body reached an even higher level. In the moonlight she could see the way his gaze lingered. The silent menace in the room was palpable.

Then, very slowly, the man moved one hand from her wrists to the scraps of purple fabric lying alongside her breasts. With care and a curious precision, as if he didn't quite trust himself to do the job properly, he slipped the bra back into position. Hannah's eyes closed briefly in silent relief. Surely if he had been bent on rape he wouldn't have made such a concession to modesty.

"I don't want to hurt you," the man stated quietly.

Trapped as she was beneath him, Hannah didn't believe the words, and her reaction showed in her eyes. A strange smile flickered around the edge of his mouth and then disappeared.

"I mean it, Hannah Prescott. I don't want to have to use force. And I'm not here to rape you." His hand moved with almost casual interest across her stomach and then went back to anchoring her wrists. "Although I have to admit that the idea of making love to you is rather intriguing. I wonder how you'd feel if you were clinging to me instead of struggling," he added whimsically. "Are you soft all the way through, or is it only on the surface? Have you ever needed a man, Hannah, or do you just use them?''

Crazy. Hannah continued to stare up at him with bewilderment, anger, and fear. The man was absolutely crazy. God help her; she had fallen into the hands of a madman.

''Are you going to behave?'' he asked calmly.

She nodded at once. Her assailant looked skeptical, as well he might. Hannah fully intended to scream her head off as soon as he released her mouth. In the shadows she could make out the harsh lines of his face as he studied her. Eyes that were almost the color of gun-metal in moonlight watched her intently for a moment longer as if trying to read her mind, and then he slowly removed his hand.

''One false move, Miss Prescott, and I'll put a gag in your mouth and tie you to the bed with my belt. Understood?'' he asked just before he freed her lips.

Hannah reconsidered her decision to scream. There was something about the cold, threatening way he spoke that convinced her he meant what he said. Perhaps it would be better to obey him for the moment. After all, he was giving her a certain amount of freedom. And one could never tell with crazies. He might calmly wring her neck after she screamed. Hannah lay on the bed, unmoving except for the fine tremor of fear that gripped her body.

''Okay, I think we understand each other.'' The intruder sat up warily, clearly ready to pounce if she tried anything suspicious. ''Like I said, I'm not here to hurt you. I just want to know where you fit into the scheme.''

''Wh—what scheme?'' Her voice was a weak whisper, as if it had been a long time since it had been used.

''Look, honey, I suggest we don't waste a lot of time playing games. It's almost midnight already. I know about the goddess. What I want to know is where you fit into this. I thought the Clydemores worked alone.''

''The Clydemores!'' Hannah stared at him, dumb- founded. ''John and Alice?''

''Who else?'' The man shrugged as he continued to study her. ''If it will help speed this up a bit, you can rest assured I'm not a Customs agent.''

Hannah blinked in bewilderment. "I didn't think you were." She sat up very carefully, anxious not to provoke him into grabbing her again. As she moved she saw in his hand the object that she had mistaken for a weapon. It was a small wooden statue that hadn't fit into her souvenir suitcase. She had stashed it in her bag with some lingerie. The realization that this man had been going through her panties and bras made her distinctly uncomfortable.

"Ah, then you know who I am?" A flickering smile edged the man's mouth.

"You...you were on the plane with our tour group yesterday when we flew here to Hawaii from that last island."

"You handled yourself beautifully going through Customs. An incredible performance. I was very impressed. Where did you learn that delightfully scatterbrained, exhausted tourist effect? Worked like a charm. They didn't even give your bags more than a cursory glance, did they?"

In spite of her predicament, Hannah flushed in the moonlight. "That was not an act," she declared huffily, then realizing that made her sound even more scatterbrained. "I just don't happen to be a very sophisticated traveler. This ten-day South Pacific tour is my first trip out of the continental U.S."

"Beautiful," he murmured.

"Who? Me?"

"No, the act."

Hannah nodded. "I didn't think you meant me. Would you mind telling me what this is all about? Are you here to steal something?"

"You've already done the stealing. I'm here to get the stolen merchandise back for its rightful owner." The man rose from the bed and moved across the hotel room to switch on a light. "Now that we've established my reason for being in your room, I don't think you'll resort to screaming. You don't want the attention of the authorities any more than I do."

Hannah stared at him as he dropped down beside her suitcase again. "I don't?" she asked blankly. She didn't sense any immediate threat in his action. The stranger seemed totally concerned with the suitcase full of souvenirs. He was idly flicking the combination lock.

"It would be a little difficult to explain the goddess, wouldn't it?

And if you force me into it, I'll tell the authorities about her. I'm willing to handle the whole thing quietly if you'll cooperate, but otherwise..." He let the sentence trail off significantly while glancing at her over his shoulder.

"I see." Hannah swallowed uncertainly, frowning at his hard, lean frame as he crouched beside the case. A thought struck her. "Are you a cat burglar?"

"No. I'm just not particularly fond of Customs agents and related types. What's the combination of the lock, Miss Prescott?"

"Why? There's nothing but souvenirs in that suitcase."

"I'm a great collector of souvenirs."

"If you'll leave my room, you can take the whole bag full of them!" she snapped, regaining some of her composure as she realized she didn't seem to be in any personal jeopardy. Yet. The man didn't really look crazy. He looked determined, but not irrational. But then why was he so concerned with a suitcase full of souvenirs collected on a ten-day whirlwind tour of the South Pacific?

Actually, if she'd been asked to guess his occupation yesterday when he'd boarded the plane, she would have said he wasn't the type to break into hotel rooms and pry into suitcases.

But then, Hannah Prescott always tended to believe the best of everyone until something happened to prove her wrong. And in this case, when she had actually found herself strangely aware of the man as he'd walked down the center aisle of the jet to take his seat, she definitely would not have wanted to believe him a criminal. She had sat in her seat and fantasized about him surreptitiously watching her just as she was watching him. Hannah was practical enough to realize that was a highly unlikely possibility, but she was enough of a dreamer to let herself spin a quick fairy tale. She rarely saw men about whom she wanted to dream.

What an idiot she had been! He probably *had* been watching her, but not because of any instantaneous chemical attraction. He had been plotting to steal her bulging bag full of souvenirs.

"Why?" she asked in growing confusion. "I mean, you're welcome to them, but why would you want them? You don't really look like the kind of man who takes home a lot of souvenirs when he travels.

"The combination, Miss Prescott?" He tapped the lock meaningfully.

"Five-four-three," she mumbled.

He nodded. "Thank you. That will save us some time." He quickly spun the dials.

"You seem to know my name," Hannah began carefully.

"If you want to know mine, it's Jarrett Blade." He didn't seem to care one way or the other, but he glanced up briefly to see if there was a flash of recognition on her face. He smiled again as she frowned. "You really are very good at the dumb tourist bit. If I didn't know better, I would have bought the act myself."

"I am not a dumb tourist!" she felt obliged to declare. "I may look a bit frazzled, but I'm at the end of a very full tour. Hawaii is the last stop before I go home to Seattle. In the past week I've been to New Zealand and so many islands I've forgotten the names of half of them. You'd look a little dumb and scatterbrained too if you'd been on the hectic schedule I've been on for the past week."

That wasn't precisely true, she realized. There wasn't much that would ever make this man look dumb or scatterbrained. Jarrett Blade had a cool, restrained aura of self-control that bordered on raw power. Yesterday she had only seen him for a few moments, time enough to notice the compelling gray eyes and the somber brown hair with its flecks of gunmetal gray. He had walked down the aisle of the plane with a strong, graceful stride, and she had dared to stare for a few seconds at the hard profile.

Blade was a good name for him, she decided now. A man of tempered steel. A man with a cutting edge that could slice a woman or an enemy to ribbons. How could she have been even briefly attracted to someone as cold and alien as this man?

As he deftly manipulated the lock of the suitcase, Hannah knew a sense of wry wonder at her initial fantasies about Jarrett Blade. Look at him, she thought. He looks as if he's spent his life totally alone. The kind of man who simply doesn't need anyone else. There was no suggestion of charm in the unhandsome, bleakly carved features, no hint of warmth or compassion in those strange gray eyes. Dressed in khaki slacks and a cotton shirt of the same color, Jarrett Blade looked at home here in Waikiki. He was the kind of man who would look assured and in control anywhere he chose to be.

While she looked frazzled and scatterbrained.

What a silly fantasy she had indulged in yesterday on the return flight to the States. Imagine having had even the briefest of daydreams about a man like this. Definitely not her type.

"Be careful!" she yelped as the last digit of the combination fell into place.

Her instinctive cry of warning came too late, however. The suitcase, which had been packed to the brim and shut with great effort, sprang open as the catch was released. The contents seemed to leap out of the bag as it flew open. A bundle of cloth printed in a wild, exotic pattern, several clay statues of various island gods, a heavy Tahitian dancing skirt, a bunch of shell necklaces, and a grotesque little purse trimmed in beads and shells fell out on the floor. There was a great deal more of the same still inside the suitcase.

"Quite a collection," Jarrett Blade observed, reaching out to pick up one of the small clay statues. "You must have spent most of the trip in the various island markets. It looks like you've got every bit of junk manufactured on every island in the Pacific."

"It's not junk! Those are souvenirs of a trip I'll always want to remember. I may never get to the South Pacific again. I almost didn't make it this time."

"No?" He sounded skeptical as he studied the small statue in his hand.

"I lost my job just before I was scheduled to leave ten days ago," Hannah explained sadly. "I should have cashed in my ticket and saved the money until I found another position, but I'd been looking forward to the trip for so long I just couldn't bring myself to do it."

"I'll bet you couldn't." He spoke almost absently, his attention still on the small clay god. Then, as Hannah watched with horrified eyes, Jarrett lifted the statue high in the air and brought it down sharply against the tile floor of the room. The little object shattered into several pieces.

"Hey! What do you think you're doing?" she squeaked. "That cost me three and a half dollars!" Maybe he really was crazy!

"You didn't really intend to drag all this junk back from Hawaii, did you? You only needed it as a cover to get through Customs."

"No! Wait a minute!" Hannah gasped as he picked up a small statue of a laughing creature with a huge tummy. Jarrett ignored her, rapping the second statue sharply on the tile. It, too, shattered.

Maybe she could edge toward the door and make her escape while he was methodically smashing her souvenirs, Hannah thought on a rising note of hysteria. Her pulse pounding as she acknowledged that she must, after all, be dealing with a maniac, she skittered a couple of inches across the bed.

"Don't get any ideas. You're not going anywhere." Jarrett didn't even bother to glance in her direction. He was reaching for the next statue.

"Mr. Blade," Hannah managed, trying for a soothing, placating tone, "I'm very sorry if you have something against little clay statues. You're welcome to smash all of them, if you like, but you really don't need me around while you do it. Take the lot of them. Wouldn't you really rather smash them in privacy?"

"You could save me some time by pointing out which one is the goddess," Jarrett told her calmly as the third statue disintegrated beneath his hands.

"The goddess? Yes, well, uh, perhaps the little doll with the tapa cloth skirt?" she suggested weakly, indicating one of the remaining souvenirs. It was a wild guess, of course. The doll, as far as Hannah knew, was not meant to represent a goddess. It was merely a toy. Dear Lord, she thought frantically, which of her souvenirs looked most like a goddess? And what in the world would this man want with such a thing? Crazy. Jarrett Blade was out of his mind.

"The little island-girl doll? Okay." He picked it up and promptly rapped the small plastic toy against the tile. It didn't shatter, but it did crack along the length of the body. Jarrett pulled it apart to reveal a hollow interior.

"There! Now she's destroyed. Your mission is accomplished," Hannah announced, trying for a bright voice. "She's quite dead. You can leave now. Go back to your room. Rest assured that the goddess will never bring bad luck again to anyone." Was that the right sort of patter for soothing an escaped mental patient who had a thing against island gods and goddesses? Maybe she should take another approach. She could try telling him that the goddess had escaped from the suitcase during the day....

"It's a matter of opinion whether she brings bad luck," Jarrett said coolly, pawing through the remaining souvenirs. "Some women may have thought so, of course, but generally speaking, most people probably held her in reverent awe. Ancient primitive people had a different view of childbirth. They knew that bringing forth children wasn't a casual matter to be taken for granted. It was an act of powerful magic. The goddess would have been wooed with sacrifices and much reverence, I imagine."

Feeling as if she had been caught in a degenerating wonderland, Hannah watched Jarrett through widening eyes. "Yes, yes, of course," she agreed faintly. "Uh, perhaps she escaped from the suitcase, Mr. Blade. After all, a powerful goddess would have found it easy to pick that lock and get out, don't you think?"

"Not without a bit of help, and I've been watching this room all day. She didn't get any assistance."

"Oh." Hannah found herself stumped for a more intelligent response. He'd been watching the room all day? And to think that yesterday she had been indulging in romantic fantasies of having him notice her! Right now she'd sell her chance at another job back in Seattle if it meant being free of this man.

Tonight, his gaze was deeply disturbing, especially when it settled on the too-small purple bikini! Her cognac-brown hair was in its usual braided coronet, making it appear that the only thing she had on beside the skimpy bathing suit was a crown. But Hannah felt very underdressed for any regal occasion.

The crown of hair framed an attractive face that was kept from any dramatic beauty by a scattering of freckles and a sweetly wholesome look. Hannah had assumed that the disgustingly healthy, wholesome look might disappear as she neared thirty, and she had hoped the freckles would follow. But she was twenty-nine now, and neither attribute showed any sign of fading.

Intelligence and a faintly amused, good-natured appreciation of life were apparent in her aqua-green eyes. Hannah smiled readily, and there was blazing warmth in the expression when she did so, a warmth that filled her life with friends, if not lovers.

The basic warmth in her smile seemed to be echoed in the soft, full curves of her body. Hannah was not really plump, but there was an appealing roundness to her that held a certain attraction for some men. With one dramatic exception, however, Hannah had rarely been attracted in turn.

She had spent her adult years coming to the conclusion that whatever it was she had been looking for in a man, it was either exceedingly rare or didn't exist at all. She had long since decided she was probably being far too choosy, but somehow she couldn't bring herself to settle for less. The strange part was that she was unable to put into words exactly what it was that she sought. Hannah only knew that she had never been lucky enough to find it.

And time was slipping past. In another year she would be thirty. Even though she hadn't yet reached the symbolic age, Hannah had already consciously accepted the fact that she might never marry. And even if she did, it might be far too late to risk starting a family. The freckles on her nose contained no magic power to keep her young until the right man came along.

Men like Jarrett Blade never had freckles, Hannah found herself thinking gloomily as she watched him going through her bags. Even if they were crazy. How old was he? she wondered. She estimated his age at somewhere over thirty-five and less than forty. Had he spent his life in mental institutions, or had he only recently developed this problem with goddesses?

It seemed distinctly unfair that the one man who had called to her senses in years was demented and potentially violent. What hostile fate had put her in Jarrett Blade's path?

"We're wasting time," Jarrett pointed out, interrupting her thoughts. "It would be a whole lot easier if you just told me which one was the goddess."

"Well, I'm, uh, not exactly sure, you see," Hannah began awkwardly, frantically trying to think of a way to handle this bizarre situation. "Perhaps you'd like to take the whole suitcase full of souvenirs back to your room and go through each item at leisure? That way you could be certain you got the right goddess."

"Are you so willing to give me all this junk because the goddess isn't in here?" he asked, arcing one dark brown brow. "Is she in another case after all? I assumed she was mixed in with the rest of these trashy souvenirs, but..."

"They are not trashy!" Dammit, why did she feel compelled to defend her taste in souvenirs?

"Quit playing games, Miss Prescott. I'm not leaving without the goddess." Jarrett went back to smashing items from the suitcase.

"Please...I really don't know what you're talking about. Take anything you want, but just leave!" Hannah broke off abruptly, a startled frown crossing her features as Jarrett lifted a new item out of the suitcase. It was a clay statue, not unlike those he had smashed earlier, but she honestly didn't remember buying this one. Of course, she had picked up so many last-minute things during the past several days it was entirely possible she had forgotten this ugly little creature.

"Now this one feels about right," Jarrett murmured, staring at the clay object with an intensity that made Hannah more nervous than ever.

Things were bad enough with his looking for the mysterious "goddess," but what was he liable to do when he found it? That unnerving question flashed into Hannah's mind just as Jarrett very gently fractured the badly modeled souvenir.

"Ah!" The soft, indrawn sigh came from Jarrett as the clay shards fell away to reveal something that gleamed richly in his hands.

Hannah stared, transfixed, as her midnight visitor carefully flicked off the remaining bits of clay. "A statue within a statue?" she whispered.

"Not a particularly novel way of disguising her, but then, who would think of going through all these other damn souvenirs to get to her?" Jarrett remained where he was, crouched on the floor. He turned the small, gleaming object over and over in his hands with a reverence that made Hannah chew nervously on her lower lip.

She had thought him cold and alien until now, but in this moment Hannah realized that Jarrett Blade had another side to him, a side that breathed a soul-stirring intensity and hinted at deep passions.

And he had saved it all for the gleaming object cradled in his palms.

Hannah shuddered. Just her luck that the only interesting man she'd seen on the entire trip had a souvenir fetish.

That thought brought another, more disturbing realization. How had the object of Jarrett Blade's strange desire gotten into her suitcase?

"I....I really don't know where that came from," she began earnestly.

"I do."

"Well, you're certainly welcome to it," Hannah went on quickly.

"You're very generous," he drawled, tearing his fascinated gaze away from the gleaming thing in his hand long enough to send her a derisive glance.

"What's one souvenir more or less?" she tried to say heartily. "Take it. Do whatever you want with it. Just get out of here and leave me alone."

Slowly Jarrett got to his feet, ignoring the array of broken souvenirs on the floor. Holding the gleaming object in both hands, he sank down into a chair and continued to study it intently. "She's magnificent. Absolutely magnificent."

In spite of her precarious situation, Hannah found herself following the direction of his gaze. Jarrett was holding his treasure up to the light, and she could see that it was another little statue. But it wasn't made out of clay or wood. If she hadn't known better, Hannah would have said that the object was made out of gold. Deep, burnished, ancient gold.

"Not very attractive, is she?" Hannah said with an attempt at humor as she studied the golden statue. It appeared to be a representation of a woman crouched on her haunches, giving birth. There was a round fullness to every aspect of the statue. Clearly, it had been modeled by an artist who understood femininity in fundamental terms. The power of the female body as it brought forth life was in every line of the straining form.

"She wasn't meant to be beautiful," Jarrett said simply. "She was meant to induce fertility, to create new life. That sort of power transcends mere beauty. Whoever created this understood that."

Hannah cleared her throat, at a loss as to what to do or say next. "How...how did you know she was in among my souvenirs? What are you going to do with her? Is that real gold? Where is it from? How did it get in my bag?''

Folding his hands carefully around the birth deity, Jarrett looked at Hannah as she sat stiffly on the edge of the bed. Her wet swimsuit had left a damp spot on the bedclothes, and she felt increasingly uncomfortable as the suit dried on her body.

''I was going to ask you a few of those questions,'' Jarrett said far too gently. ''Some of them I can answer myself, of course. Yes, the gold is real, but you already know that. You must know where she came from, too. South America. Peru, to be exact. She belongs to a friend of mine, and that's who I'll be giving her back to eventually. Now, suppose you answer the other questions?''

''I don't understand,'' Hannah gasped. ''Is she stolen? Are you from the police?''

''Yes, she's stolen, as you very well know. And I've already told you I'm not from Customs or any other policing agency. Like you, I prefer not to deal with such folk any more than is absolutely necessary. I must congratulate you, Miss Prescott. You almost made it back to Seattle with her. If it weren't for the fact that I know about the Clydemores and their rather extensive interest in South American antiques, I would never have guessed you might be involved. You really don't look the type.''

''The type for what?'' Hannah demanded.

''The type to smuggle such things as this little goddess.'' Jarrett shrugged mildly. ''It's amazing. With that sincere expression in those blue-green eyes and that charmingly bedraggled, beaten tourist air about you, I'll bet you could get the Mona Lisa through Customs undisguised. I watched your whole act yesterday as we went through the formalities. Very impressive.''

''There's no call to sit there and insult me! *You* appear to be the thief around here, not me!''

''I'm merely going to return some stolen property. But first I'd like to know exactly where you fit into the picture, Miss Prescott. I can't quite figure you out. I was so sure the Clydemores worked alone....''

''Why do you keep bringing John and Alice Clydemore into this? They're a very nice couple I met in Tahiti. They've been wonderful to me!'' As she talked, Hannah began once more to edge across the foot of the bed toward the door. If she were quick enough, she might be able to get the door open and run out into the hall before he could get across the room.

"Are you going to pretend you didn't know that the Clydemores' current world tour included a stay in South America?" Blade looked lovingly down at the gold birthing goddess. It was probably the only thing he looked at lovingly, Hannah told herself. "We all know how difficult it is now to get this sort of thing across the Mexico–U.S. border these days. Much easier to reroute stolen antiquities through other countries. Who would look for pre-Columbian art in the bags of tourists returning from the South Seas? The Clydemores are professionals."

"You sound quite admiring!"

"I'm capable of appreciating a good scheme to get items like this into the U.S. art market. I understand the lure of such objects," he added softly.

Hannah stared at him. He did seem to be enthralled with the little gold goddess. She found herself wondering if Jarrett Blade had ever been that enthralled with a real live woman. Well, perhaps it would work in her favor. If he continued to study the object so intensely, he wouldn't notice her slipping to the very edge of the bed.... Hungrily she cast a quick glance at the door.

"The Clydemores were smart to latch on to someone with your charmingly naive expression," Jarrett went on thoughtfully. "In spite of their cleverness, it's better not to take unnecessary chances. Letting you carry the goddess through Customs was a wise move. Who would suspect you of being capable of smuggling?"

"You, apparently!"

"Only because I've observed how close you've been to the Clydemores since yesterday. You sat next to them on the plane, had dinner with them last night, and breakfast with them again this morning. I overheard you planning an excursion into downtown Honolulu with them today. It was obvious you were probably working with them."

"I am not working with anyone! I'm not working at all, in fact! I don't even have a job to go back to!"

"The proceeds from this little lady would keep you for quite a while. There wouldn't be any need to take a nine-to-five job, would there?"

"I wouldn't know about that! If you want my opinion, it's not a pleasant sort of statue. Not at all the kind of thing I'd want sitting on my coffee table. Who'd buy it?"

"I would. If it didn't already belong to a friend of mine who wants it back," Jarrett said simply.

"Look, take the dumb thing. I don't want it, and I honestly don't know how it got into my suitcase. I just want to be left alone, okay?"

"I'm afraid I can't do that." Blade sounded genuinely regretful. "My curiosity is aroused, you see. I really do want to figure out your role in the current smuggling market. We might run into each other again, you see."

"Not if I can help it!" At her wit's end, Hannah leaped for the door. Her single advantage, she knew, lay in the fact that Jarrett Blade seemed compelled to treat the gold goddess with reverence. He wouldn't be able to just toss it aside in order to pursue her. She would gain precious seconds while he carefully set it down.

"Oh, no, you don't!" he snapped behind her as she flung open the door and raced out into the hotel hall. But he was several steps behind.

There was someone at the far end of the hall, Hannah realized. She would scream for help, call for a security guard. She ran barefoot down the corridor for several paces, opening her mouth to shout for assistance. The words were on the tip of her tongue when the breath went out of her lungs. Jarrett Blade had thrown an arm around her midsection, yanking her still-damp body back against his hard one.

Desperately Hannah gasped for breath, determined not to let her chance of escape go down the drain. But even as her mouth opened once more, her lips were crushed beneath those of her captor.

Hannah was paralyzed by the totally unexpected assault. She had expected to be physically restrained, to have a palm clamped across her mouth, even to be knocked unconscious. She hadn't expected to be kissed into submission. Indeed, if anyone had asked her about it before the event, she would have stated unhesitatingly that it is physically impossible to be kissed into submission.

Now she knew differently.

Jarrett crowded her soft body back against the corridor wall, his mouth fastened on hers with an intensity that literally left her breathless. His hands locked into the neat coil of braids on her head, forcing her to hold still for the overwhelming embrace. With ruthless intent, his leg pushed between her bare thighs, leaving Hannah feeling ravished and helpless.

Her fingers dug into the fabric of his khaki shirt in an instinctive movement of defense. But if he felt the punishment of her nails on his shoulders, he gave no sign.

Barely able to breathe, her body completely captive in the grip of Jarrett's superior strength, Hannah endured the endless, silencing kiss. Dimly she heard the passing of other people in the hall. She knew they must have smiled to themselves and turned politely away from the scene Jarrett was creating, but she was incapable of appealing for assistance.

Hannah's body shuddered beneath the force being unleashed against her. Her head spun with the kaleidoscope of sensations that poured over her and through her. The kiss was meant to silence and punish. Jarrett demanded no other response but surrender. Out of some primitive female instinct of self-protection, Hannah gave in to him. She allowed her body to go limp and acquiescent, and she parted her teeth for the invasion of his tongue.

Jarrett seemed to crowd even closer as she gave ground before his assault. He seized the territory she yielded, conquering and claiming until Hannah felt she had given him everything she had.

It was only as she stopped fighting him that she began to sense that Jarrett Blade was not unaffected by the scorching embrace. When her body softened against his, she realized just how hard and urgent his own was. When her mouth yielded to his, she became conscious of more than mere dominance in his kiss. For a blinding moment Hannah thought she was experiencing a fragment of the deep passion she had sensed in Jarrett Blade when he had cradled the birthing goddess in his hands.

That was impossible, of course. The man was only trying to restrain her in the most effective way he could devise. But just for an instant she could have sworn she experienced something else in his arms: a frighteningly heady emotion that she could only be grateful was not totally released.

How long she stood locked against him, Hannah never knew. But when Jarrett finally lifted his mouth from hers, she was panting as if she had just run a marathon. Wide-eyed and wordless, she looked up at him. His face was an unreadable mask, although she was still fiercely aware of the tension in his body.

"If you run from me again," he grated, "I'll turn you over to Customs. I'll tell them how I found the statue in your bag, and i'll leave you to talk yourself out of the situation. Do you understand? You will do as I say, Hannah Prescott, or I'll see to it you wind up explaining everything to the authorities."

"But I haven't done anything!" she wailed, feeling trapped.

"You think they'll believe you after I've shown them the goddess?" He clamped his hands around her bare shoulders, giving her a small shake.

"You...you're threatening me!" she gasped.

"You're very perceptive!"

"But I'm innocent!" How could she have gotten herself into such a situation? She'd never come close to a brush with the law in her entire life. Her aqua-green eyes shimmered with bewildered anxiety and her bruised mouth trembled. "I didn't steal that stupid statue! I've never stolen anything in my whole twenty-nine years!"

"Are you trying to tell me the Clydemores used you? That you had no notion of what was going on?" he rasped.

"Yes!"

There was a tense pause as he stared down at her upturned face. Hannah felt as if her whole future was suddenly hanging in the balance. This man held her in the palm of his hand, just as he'd held the statue.

"Prove it," Jarrett finally whispered.

She blinked uncomprehendingly. "Prove what?"

"That you're not involved with the Clydemores."

"But how?" Her plea was a cry of helpless frustration. How could she prove anything with that damaging bit of evidence in her suitcase?

"I'll set up a way for you to show me you're not working with the Clydemores," he told her evenly. "But it won't work unless you're telling me the truth."

"How can I prove anything?"

"Leave the how of it to me." He stepped away from her, taking her elbow firmly and guiding her back to her room.

Hannah caught her breath as a realization dawned on her. "You don't really want to turn me over to the authorities, do you? You want that statue for yourself!"

"What I want doesn't come into it at the moment," he retorted coolly. "Believe me, I won't hesitate to hand you over to Customs if you try to escape again. Are we very clear on that point?"

She slanted him a sullen, seething glance. "You've made yourself very clear, Mr. Blade."

"Good. With a woman it's always best to have everything on the table, I've found. Never allow any loop-holes. Women will find loop-holes in a relationship faster than the IRS will find mistakes on a tax form."

"We don't exactly have a relationship!" Hannah bit back, stung.

"But that's just exactly what we do have, Hannah," he murmured as he pushed her into her hotel room. "Beginning tonight, you and I have a relationship. And after that kiss in the hallway, I'm inclined to think it won't be platonic, either."

Two

"**D**on't look so shocked, Hannah." Jarrett dropped lightly back into the chair he had occupied earlier. The little gold goddess sat on the table beside him, light gleaming from its time-smoothed surface. The statue's gaze seemed to be focused on Hannah as she moved uneasily around the small room. "Our 'relationship' is the way I'm going to keep track of you while you prove you're not involved with the Clyde-mores. We have to have some way of accounting for my constant presence in your vicinity, don't we? We'll let John and Alice think you're having a vacation fling. How much longer are you due to stay in Hawaii?"

"Four more days," she muttered.

"That doesn't give us much time, does it? You may have to extend your visit."

"That's impossible. I have responsibilities back in Seattle. I can't stay away any longer than the time I originally planned!"

"What responsibilities? You told me you lost your job just before you left." Jarrett gave her a cold smile. "Is there a man waiting for you, Hannah?"

Angrily she looked away from him. "I have no intention of explaining my whole life to you. Just tell me how I'm supposed to prove I'm innocent of stealing your friend's statue, and let's get on with it."

Jarrett studied her for a moment as she moved restlessly about the room. "If you're not involved in the theft and if the Clydemores planted the statue in your bags so that you could take the risk of smuggling it through Customs for them, then we have to assume they'll want to retrieve the goddess before you go home to Seattle."

Hannah frowned. "Well, yes, I suppose so. The Clydemores told me they live in San Diego."

"They do. Soon you'll all be going your separate ways. That means that sometime in the next few days the Clydemores will have to find a way of getting the statue out of your luggage. It will be interesting to see what they do when they discover it's not there."

Hannah licked her lower lip. "And if they don't make an attempt to steal the statue from my luggage?"

"Then we'll have to assume that you are working with them and that they plan on letting you carry it all the way back to the mainland. If they allow you to take it home, then I'll have to believe they intend seeing you again, won't I? That you are, in fact, a partner in their little scheme."

"You're saying that the only way I can convince you I'm innocent is if the Clydemores make an attempt to get that statue back before I leave for Seattle. What if they don't make the attempt? You're just going to assume that's evidence I'm working with them?"

"Makes sense, don't you think?"

"But that leaves me at the mercy of fate. Maybe the Clydemores won't make an attempt to steal the goddess back. Maybe they weren't the ones who put it in my luggage in the first place. Maybe they're innocent too! Have you thought of that?" she demanded wildly.

"Then you're going to look like the only guilty party, aren't you?" he drawled. "But to tell you the truth, I already have some doubts about you in the role of smuggler. There's something about you that doesn't fit the image."

"I thought you'd decided my frazzled tourist act was just that—an act!"

"It probably is," he agreed too easily. "But there's just a chance you're for real. And if you are, I'm willing to be convinced of your innocence."

"Thank you very much!" she snapped scathingly. "Are you always so distrustful of other people?"

He looked at her. "Yes. Especially women. Women are so very good at deceit, you see."

"No, I don't see! Of all the prejudiced, bigoted, chauvinistic attitudes!"

"I learned my lesson the hard way, but I learned it well, Hannah. Most modern women don't seem to need a man; they just use men for various and assorted reasons."

"Meaning men don't use women?" she snapped back.

He shrugged. "It happens."

"Gracious of you to admit it. A case of self-defense, I suppose?"

"Things weren't meant to be that way, Hannah," Jarrett said intently.

"No?"

"No." He nodded toward the little goddess. "Ancient civilizations such as the one that produced that lady understood the real nature of women. And the danger in them. Women, in turn, understood that they needed men. Men protected them, provided them with homes, fathered their children, assumed the responsibilities of economic support...and kept the magic in them under control."

"In other words, the men kept the women barefoot and pregnant!" Hannah interrupted scathingly. "How perfectly ridiculous to romanticize the kind of master-slave relationship that existed between men and women in ancient times. Typical of a man to look back on such things with nostalgia. Don't expect modern women to share your point of view!"

"I'm well aware that they don't," he assured her quietly.

Hannah gave him a startled glance. "My God," she breathed with perception. "Some woman really worked you over good, didn't she?"

"I'm grateful to her. She taught me a lesson I'll never forget."

"I'll bet you don't have a lot of female friends! I can't see many intelligent women putting up with your antiquated philosophies of how a relationship between the sexes should work."

His mouth curved wryly as he acknowledged the insight. "No, I don't have a lot of female friends. At the moment I don't even have a lover. Are you interested in applying for the position?"

"Not on your life!" Hannah stormed. "Besides, if you distrust and dislike modern women so much, I'm surprised you're even interested in having one for a lover. Or are you just in the market for someone you can use the way that woman who taught you a lesson once used you?"

Jarrett's gunmetal-gray eyes hardened briefly, and he made a visible effort to relax. "I have all the normal male instincts."

"Including a few left over from primitive times?"

"Perhaps," he acknowledged.

"It's no wonder you can't find yourself a modern-day love!" A misfit, Hannah decided morosely. What a quirk of fate. The one man who had attracted her in years, and he turned out to be some kind of throwback, alienated from his own world in a fundamental way. Maybe that was why the little golden goddess held such fascination for him. She was from his era. Hannah shivered.

"I haven't led a completely celibate life, if that's what you're assuming, Hannah. But I'm damn careful what role I allow a woman to play in my life."

"In other words, you're willing to let one into your bed so that you can satisfy your physical needs, but that's as close as she can get, right?"

"That's pretty damn close," Jarrett pointed out with amusement.

"Two people can go to bed together and still be a thousand miles apart. Or a thousand years, in your case," Hannah protested, wondering how on earth she had ever gotten into such an intimate discussion with this man.

"You sound like an authority on the subject," Jarrett mused, gray eyes glittering. "What happened? Did some man invite you into his bed and then refuse to let you manipulate him? That's very frustrating for a woman, isn't it? Women prefer to be the manipulators in a relationship. At least modern women do."

It was a stupid discussion, she decided. "I didn't want to manipulate him," Hannah sighed. "I only wanted to love him and to have him love me. I only wanted a family.... He was the one who used me, if it makes you feel any better," she concluded abruptly. With the ease of long practice, Hannah pushed the bitter memories of her twenty-fourth year to the back of her mind. She certainly had problems enough at the moment. Coming to a halt in the middle of the room, she swung around to face her unwelcome visitor and found him studying her broodingly. "I think you've done enough damage this evening, Mr. Blade. It's about time you left. Take that dumb little statue with you and get out of my room."

Jarrett rested his chin on a propped hand for a moment longer, as if he were trying to analyze something he saw in her face. Then he appeared to abandon the attempt. He got to his feet with a slow, easy movement that spoke of a strong, coordinated body. Reaching down to pick up the goddess with both hands, he walked deliberately across the room to the closed connecting door. Casually he opened it and then paused in the doorway.

"Don't look so stunned, Hannah," he said gently. "I made sure that you were assigned this room yesterday and that I got the one next to you. The desk clerk was only too happy to accept a small tip for doing me the favor of putting me next to the frazzled lady tourist with the little crown of braids."

Hannah glared at him. "That door is supposed to be locked at all times. From both sides!" He'd been right next door to her last night. An unnerving thought.

"Not while you and I are involved with each other." Jarrett held up a key and then dropped it into his pocket. "Good night, Hannah. Don't worry about the goddess. I'll take good care of her."

"Better make sure she doesn't cast any magical female spells over you!" Hannah hissed. "After all, she is a goddess, remember? A golden lady with power. You'd better be careful."

Suddenly a wide, very male grin appeared on Jarrett's harshly carved face. It startled Hannah. For an instant he looked almost likable. "You're the one who should exercise caution, Hannah. She's a fertility goddess. Her specialty was ensuring that women got pregnant. And you've been carrying her around in your suitcase for several days."

The slipper Hannah aimed at her tormentor's head struck the door instead.

Fertility goddess! So Jarrett thought that amusing, did he? That was because he believed in the old adage about keeping women barefoot and pregnant. Hannah stormed into the bathroom and turned on the shower. She wondered just what that other woman had done to him to make him so distrusting of the female sex. Was it after the fateful lesson he had learned at her hands that Jarrett had begun pouring his passion into pre-Columbian art? Because there was passion in the man. She had seen more than one hint of it tonight.

Hannah shivered beneath the warmth of the shower and stopped herself from pursuing that line of thought. No, she was most definitely not going to allow herself to dwell on the implications of Jarrett Blade's passions. If the man chose to bury himself amid the artifacts of another age, that was his problem. She was certainly not going to allow herself to feel any compassion for a man who distrusted women the way Jarrett did. He'd made his own damn bed, apparently, a long time ago.

"Let him lie in it. Alone." Hannah grimaced at herself in the steamed mirror as she stepped out of the shower. In the meantime, what was she going to do? She was in an unbelievable mess. A smuggler? Her? Only a man as cynical as Jarrett Blade could actually believe such a thing!

What now? Should she confront the Clydemores? Warn them that somebody by the name of Blade thought they were involved in a smuggling ring? If they weren't guilty of having stashed that little goddess in her suitcase, then presumably they would be safe. Jarrett could prove nothing against them. After all, he'd found the statue in her own luggage. Frowning, Hannah dried herself quickly and went back into the bedroom.

On the other hand, what if John and Alice *were* smugglers? Jarrett seemed so sure of his facts. Of course, he was also sure that all women were out to conquer and control men, too!

The guy is a first-class nut case and he's in the adjoining room! Hannah slid a nervous glance toward the closed door between the rooms. What if she simply slipped out of the hotel and headed for the airport?

No, if she fled the scene, Jarrett would be certain she was guilty. And somehow she wanted to convince him she'd known nothing about the gold goddess. It would be satisfying to have Jarrett Blade eat his accusations and suspicions.

But her only chance of proving herself innocent lay with the Clydemores. What if they made no move to retrieve the stolen figurine?

Well, Jarrett probably wouldn't turn her over to the authorities. She'd sensed he really didn't want anything to do with Customs. Apparently he was acting for a friend and preferred to keep the whole shady matter quiet.

"So what does that make you, Jarrett Blade?" Hannah whispered into the darkness as she slid into bed. "Are you a smuggler yourself? Are you a thief? A private agent dealing in pre-Columbian art? Where the hell do you fit into this whole picture?"

In the adjoining room Jarrett lay in bed listening as Hannah showered and climbed into bed. The small gold figure was on the nightstand beside him, and as he listened he absently reached out a hand and stroked it. This statue was fantastic. Early Chavín goldsmithing from ancient Peru. Probably around 250 B.C. A magnificent example of the fine artistry of the Chavín culture. God, he'd give a fortune to add it to his collection.

And Hannah Prescott seemed genuinely unconcerned with it. To her the priceless statue had simply been placed in her overstuffed souvenir bag by accident. Hannah Prescott, in fact, seemed remarkably genuine all the way around. But you could never be sure with a woman.

Still, was it really possible for someone with eyes like Hannah's to lie? Jarrett's fingers tightened briefly around the body of the goddess and his thumb moved on the gold surface in an unconsciously sensual motion. He wondered what Hannah's eyes would look like filled with desire.

"Christ," he grated softly to himself. "I must be going out of my mind to even consider the possibility that she's an innocent bystander caught up in all this."

But she had felt startlingly good against him when he'd captured her and kissed her in the hall. Gentle and soft and warm. He couldn't recall being so aware of the gentleness and softness of a woman before. Certainly not during a kiss meant to threaten and control.

She was dangerous, a creature of magic and power because she gave out signals of sweet, womanly softness when he knew her to be a hard, accomplished smuggler.

At least, Jarrett corrected himself with a frown, all the evidence indicated she was a smuggler. But there was just a chance she wasn't guilty. He'd been watching her since yesterday, and for some reason he couldn't quite bring himself to believe she was a hardened thief. Dammit, he wanted her to prove herself innocent. He wanted her to be merely an unsuspecting pawn of the Clydemores. He wanted the honesty in those aqua eyes to prove genuine and he wanted the softness in Hannah Prescott to include more than just her body.

If she was an innocent victim she was going to need him to protect her from the Clydemores. And the notion of Hannah needing him was very satisfying, Jarrett decided.

Very early the next morning Hannah sat in the hotel coffee shop, gloomily stirring her coffee and trying to convince herself that the strange man who had paid her such a frightening visit in the middle of the night was only a bad dream. Unfortunately there were all those bits of broken souvenirs still lying on her floor this morning to argue otherwise.

There was no denying the fact that the small golden statue had been in her bag, and Hannah honestly could not remember having purchased the souvenir statue that had concealed it. Could Jarrett Blade possibily be right about the Clydemores? They had spent a great deal of time with her since Tahiti and they were world travelers. They knew their way around airports, Customs, and foreign hotels. Could they possibly be genuine smugglers? Had she been used by them to take the risks of getting that golden goddess through U.S. Customs?

"Good morning, Hannah."

With a wary expression Hannah lifted her eyes to find Jarrett standing at her table, about to seat himself. Jarrett Blade embodied a good lesson on the subject of wishful thinking: he proved out the old admonition about being careful what one wished for because one might get it. She appeared to be stuck with him.

"I don't suppose there's any point in my saying you're not particularly welcome to sit down and join me?" she said.

"None at all. I heard you leave the room a few minutes ago. You should have waited for me." Jarrett slid easily into the seat across from her. In the bright morning light that illuminated the terrace café he looked every bit as hard and dangerous as he had at midnight. His somber brown hair was ruthlessly combed into place and the cotton slacks and shirt he wore looked as if they had just come back from the cleaners.

"You like to control everything in your life, don't you, Mr. Blade?" Hannah was as surprised as he was to hear the comment come from her lips.

"What makes you say that?" he asked casually as a waitress poured coffee.

Hannah lifted one shoulder uncomfortably, wishing she'd kept her mouth shut. The shoulder was bare, as were her legs. The flower-spattered island dress she was wearing left a lot of her bare this morning. "Your hair's too short, as if you're afraid it might get out of line if you let it grow longer. Your clothes look as if they were just pressed, even though you're in Hawaii where that sort of thing isn't important. Even your shoes are shined. You look as if you're here on business."

"I am." He sipped his coffee and eyed her watchfully. "You're my business."

"Look, Mr. Blade, I've done a lot of thinking since last night," Hannah said earnestly, "and I have the impression you really don't want to mess with the authorities any more than I do. You've got your precious statue. Why not take it and leave me alone?"

"Because I want to know where you fit into all this."

"But why?" she demanded helplessly.

"I don't like unknown quantities. I've been aware of the Clydemores' activities for years. But you're new on the art smuggling scene. I want to know who you are and where you fit in. You're too much of a mystery lady to be left alone. I want answers."

Hannah narrowed her eyes. "I assure you the answers are going to be exceedingly dull."

"Maybe. Maybe not." He glanced up, and a satisfied expression tightened the small lines around his gray eyes. "Here come the Clydemores. Maybe we'll start getting a few of those answers now."

Hannah glanced up nervously. What should she do? Warn John and Alice that there was a crazy man in their midst? On the other hand, if the middle-aged couple were innocent they didn't need the warning, did they? Where would that leave her, though? Shouldering the entire blame for the theft of that damn fertility goddess?

As if he sensed her uncertainty and anxiety, Jarrett slanted her a chilling glance. "Just follow my lead, Hannah. That's an order."

"I didn't sign anything that says I have to take orders from you," she shot back under her breath, and she at least had the satisfaction of having had the last word. In the next instant John and Alice Clydemore descended on the table.

"Good morning, Hannah!" Alice gushed happily, her cheerful blue eyes going rapidly from Hannah's face to Jarrett's. Alice Clydemore was a handsome woman in her early sixties with a still-trim figure and stylishly silvered hair. She wore expensive resort-style clothing from a leading designer and there were several gold chains at her throat and on her wrist. "And who's this?" she asked pertly, smiling at Jarrett as she sat down.

"Richard Adams," Jarrett announced smoothly, rising to his feet politely.

Hannah nearly choked on her coffee as she heard him blithely lie about his name. She glanced up with startled eyes as the man she knew as Jarrett Blade shook John Clydemore's hand.

"Adams, hmmm?" John clarified genially, taking the seat opposite his wife. His middle-aged, patrician features matched those of his wife, handsome and politely bespeaking wealth. "Don't recall having met you. Not part of Hannah's tour group, are you?"

"No. I just happened to be on the same plane yesterday." Jarrett smiled affectionately at Hannah, who stared back at him in consternation. "I followed her through Customs and then lost her. But last night I located her at this hotel. It wasn't hard. All I had to do was ask around until I found someone who knew where her tour group had been booked."

"I smell a romance," Alice Clydemore decided in satisfaction. "How exciting! Poor Hannah's had a very dull trip so far."

"Things are livening up quite a bit," Hannah muttered into her coffee. She wished Jarrett Blade, or whatever his name was, hadn't chosen to pretend he was romantically interested in her.

"Never too late for a vacation romance," John Clydemore chuckled. "You've still got—what?—four more days in Hawaii before you go back to the mainland."

"I'll have to work fast," Jarrett drawled.

"You're also going to have to work around a few obstacles," John Clydemore said with a grin, glancing across the room to where a small family of three sat eating breakfast.

Jarrett's gaze hardened. "Other men?" Hannah didn't care for the ominous note in his voice, even if it was a faked attempt at jealousy.

Before she could answer, John was grinning even more broadly. "You could say that. One in particular, I'm afraid. Hannah has already spent several evenings with him, and he's not likely to give her up easily."

"I'll reason with him," Jarrett said coolly. "I'm sure he'll see things my way."

"From what I've seen of this young man, he's fairly stubborn. However, he's smaller than you, so..."

"So there should be no problem." Jarrett nodded as if the matter was settled.

His ridiculously possessive attitude was too much for Hannah to bear. She got to her feet. Let the Clydemores and Jarrett play silly games. She had other things to do in Hawaii.

"If you'll excuse me, I'm going down to the beach," she announced bravely, not glancing at Jarrett for his approval.

"Of course," Alice Clydemore said quickly. Then she hesitated, "Oh, by the way, Hannah, dear, I wonder if I might stop by your room this afternoon."

Hannah tilted her head uncomprehendingly. "Well, of course. Was there something you wanted to speak to me about?"

"I just wanted to take a quick look through your suitcase full of souvenirs, if you don't mind," Alice said easily. "I seem to have misplaced one of the items I picked up in Tahiti. Do you remember the night we compared purchases?"

Hannah's mouth went dry. She didn't dare look at Jarrett now. "Yes, Alice, I remember." Her fingers whitened on the back of her chair as she waited for Alice to finish incriminating herself.

"Well, I think we may have gotten a few things mixed up. I seem to have a lovely piece of tapa cloth in my suitcase that I don't remember buying and I also realized I'm missing a little clay statue I planned to take back to my granddaughter. Nothing valuable, really, but a rather cute little doll. I'm sure you wouldn't have much use for her. Do you suppose it might have gotten into your bag by mistake that evening? As I recall, we had souvenirs lying all over the hotel room that night, and it's just possible.''

"It's just possible.'' Hannah felt unaccountably shaky. She had to get out of the restaurant. ''I'll, uh, see you later, then....'' Without glancing back, she hurried toward the door. En route she remembered to wave to the Tylers, the small family seated near the window, and then she was free.

Desperately she tried to think as she collected her beach bag and a towel from her room. The little doll Alice Clydemore seemed to think she had ''misplaced'' matched the description of the one that had concealed the golden statue. Could Jarrett be right? Were the Clydemores smugglers?

No, they might be victims too, just like herself. Perhaps there was someone else manipulating all three of them. She had been traveling with the Clydemores for several days now and felt she knew them. The one person in the whole situation whom she barely knew at all was Jarrett Blade. Or Richard Adams, or whoever he was. Was he the one doing the manipulating? He said he'd just gotten on the plane at the last stop, but who knew how long he'd been trailing the tour.

It was all so damn confusing, Hannah decided as she stretched out on the beach twenty minutes later. And if she guessed right, she wasn't going to have long to consider the problem. Jarrett Blade would probably be wandering along any minute now. She had the impression he wasn't going to leave her alone for long. Even as the thought crossed her mind his voice cut through her short-lived privacy.

"When did you get that swimsuit? When you were twelve years old?''

"It's brand-new!'' Hannah said in angry defense of the purple bikini. She refused even to glance at Jarrett as he casually spread a towel out beside her on the sand. But out of the corner of her eye she could see he'd changed into a snug-fitting pair of swim trunks that revealed the flatness of his stomach and the muscled shape of his thighs. Hannah was appalled to find that her mind insisted on embellishing the original fantasy it had begun the day before yesterday on the plane.

"It looks as though it was designed for a scrawny twelve-year-old. You're not the scrawny type, Hannah.'' He stretched out beside her, critically surveying the shape of her rounded hips and breasts in the purple bikini. "I think you ought to get another suit." The final pronouncement was flat and autocratic.

Hannah's eyes flared. Enough was enough! "I really don't give a damn what sort of suit you think I ought to wear. You may be living in the past, but I'm not. This happens to be my vacation you're ruining, you know. I'd appreciate it if you'd keep your opinions to yourself. I find your threats and accusations bad enough as it is."

Jarrett considered her, leaning on one elbow as he studied her defiant expression. "You do realize that suit makes you look as though you're trolling for men?"

"So what? Maybe I am! After all, this is a vacation."

"It ceased to be a vacation the minute you got involved with the Clydemores. And you don't need to cast out any lures for strange males. You've got me now."

"A *really* strange male," she agreed in heartfelt tones.

He ignored that. "Who's this guy on the tour you've been seeing in the evenings?"

"You'll meet him tonight if you stick around," Hannah retorted with a certain relish.

"You're spending the evening with me. I'm not letting you out of my sight. Especially not after Alice Clydemore gets around to finding out that her little souvenir is no longer in your bag."

"I'm spending the evening with Danny Tyler," Hannah returned firmly. "If you insist on joining us, I suppose there's not much I can do about it. You'll probably be quite bored, however."

"Break the date."

"I can't."

"The hell you can't! You've gotten yourself mixed up in a smuggling ring, lady. If you want to prove yourself innocent, you'd better do as I say. Besides, this Tyler guy can't be very interesting if the Clydemores claim the trip has been dull for you."

"That's my business," Hannah gritted.

Without any warning, Jarrett stretched out a hand and flattened it against the gentle swell of her stomach. His eyes gleamed in the sunlight, revealing an iron will he was bent on enforcing. Hannah sucked in her breath at the touch of his fingers, every nerve in her body suddenly, throbbingly aware of him in a way she didn't wish to recognize. Mutely her eyes met his.

"Break the date, Hannah."

"What is it with you?" she whispered starkly. "Do you always have to be in charge? Do you always have to give orders? Couldn't you try making *requests*?"

His hand pressed a little harder on her bare skin, letting her know the physical strength behind the touch but not actually hurting her. He was using raw intimidation, Hannah realized angrily. And it was highly effective. She shivered.

"I told you last night that I don't want you to be in any doubt about who's in charge. Until I know for certain you're not involved with the Clydemores, I'm not taking any chances. I'm giving orders, not making requests. And you're going to obey, Hannah, aren't you?"

"If you're ever finally convinced of my innocence, am I going to get an apology? Will you give me the satisfaction of groveling at my feet?" she taunted, calling on every ounce of courage she had. It took courage to defy this man.

To her surprise, he actually considered the question. "No," Jarrett said at last. "No apology. If you aren't involved, then you should be thanking me. I'm keeping an eye on you for your own good. Who knows what the Clydemores might decide to do when they realize that statue is no longer in your souvenir bag?"

Hannah stirred beneath his touch, her uneasiness generated more by the feel of his casually intimidating hand than by any thought of what the Clydemores might do. "All right," she scoffed, "I won't hold my breath waiting for the apology. In the meantime, however, would you mind removing your hand? I'd rather you didn't touch me."

His eyes narrowed. "I like touching you. And if you're going to insist on wearing minuscule swimsuits like that one, you have to expect a certain amount of touching. Doesn't your friend Tyler put his hands on you?"

"Not frequently," she said dryly.

"Because you won't allow him to get close? Are you in control of that relationship, Hannah?"

"I make an effort to be in control, yes!" she snapped.

"Maybe you can manage the Danny Tylers of this world, but I'm different.'' Jarrett leaned closer, a lazily intrigued expression on his face.

Hannah caught her breath. She could smell the clean, musky scent of his body as the sun began to warm it, and she didn't like the way it sent her other senses skittering. He was going to kiss her, and Hannah was suddenly very nervous. "Jarrett, no, I don't..."

"Yes, you do. I can see it in your eyes. You have very expressive eyes, Hannah Prescott.'' His mouth hovered a tantalizing inch above her own. "I'm becoming more convinced by the hour that you're not a very accomplished liar.''

"You, on the other hand, seem very adept at the business. You rattled off the name of Richard Adams without blinking an eye!" she accused, her body stiff and tense in the shadow of his.

"I was afraid they might recognize my real name," he said casually.

"Why? Are you also in the smuggling game?''

"Hush, Hannah.'' He brushed her mouth lightly.

"I don't want you kissing me or touching me or...or anything else!''

"You really are a very poor liar, honey.'' His mouth closed over hers.

"Hannah! Hannah, I've been looking all over for you!''

Jarrett's head came up swiftly as he glared at the six-year-old, tow-headed boy who was skipping eagerly across the sand. Hannah turned her head, grateful for the interruption.

"Hello, Danny,'' she said quickly. "How are you this morning?''

The child came to a halt, eyeing Jarrett curiously. "I'm fine,'' he said politely. "Who's this?''

Jarrett looked at the boy for a moment. "My name is Jarrett. And yours is Danny?''

"Danny Tyler. Hannah's my friend,'' the boy added with a touch of aggression.

"So I hear. She's been telling me about you.'' Jarrett's voice, sounding unexpectedly reassuring, surprised Hannah. "She likes you.''

Danny appeared to relax slightly. Then he sent an uncertain glance at Hannah. "Is he your friend, too?''

"Not nearly as good a friend as you are, Danny,'' Hannah declared roundly.

"Good enough to spend the evening with her, just as I hear you're going to do," Jarrett corrected mildly. "Are those your parents?" He glanced briefly at the young couple waving from several yards away.

"That's Mom and Dad. They're going out to dinner tonight. That's why I'm staying with Hannah. You're going to be there too, huh?"

"Do you mind?"

Danny paused while he came to a decision and then shook his head. "No, it's okay. See you later, Hannah." Danny took off in the direction of his parents, turning to wave frantically a couple of times.

Hannah sat up as Jarrett slowly pulled away. There was a thoughtful, faintly derisive expression in his eyes.

"So the mystery of Danny Tyler is solved. How long did you plan to keep stringing me along about his true role in your life?"

"As long as I could get away with it. Anything to annoy you," she added sweetly, staring fixedly out to sea.

"That's a dangerous game, Hannah."

"Annoying you? Maybe, but it's the only one in town at the moment."

"Much safer to play the game of placating me, honey." But he was smiling, she realized as she caught the curve of his mouth out of the corner of her eye. Jarrett was actually smiling. He had a weird sense of humor, she decided. "How did you get stuck baby-sitting for a six-year-old on your vacation?" he went on conversationally.

"Danny's parents had originally planned to leave their son with his grandmother, but at the last minute she got sick and couldn't take him. They had to bring him along. They were all on the same tour schedule as I was, so I got to know them. It seems that his parents had planned this trip as a second honeymoon. Having little Danny along has put something of a damper on that."

"So you let them impose on you? You've been baby-sitting for them?" he mocked.

"My evenings have hardly been full of activities on this trip. Everyone else on the tour is either married or over sixty. I haven't minded staying with Danny a few evenings so that his parents could salvage something from the trip," she shot back defensively.

"That's ridiculous," Jarrett said evenly. "You let his parents use you. Didn't you pay every bit as much for the tour as they did?"

"Well, yes, but..."

"But nothing. They had no right to corral you into baby-sitting for them. You've been used."

"You know nothing about the matter!" Hannah hissed furiously.

"It's obvious." He shrugged dismissingly. "And it's beginning to look as if the Clydemores used you, too. Does this happen a lot to you, Hannah?"

"Does what happen?"

"Do you let people use you frequently?"

"I thought you'd already decided I was a scheming, conniving user of other people," she muttered, not meeting his eyes.

"I'm beginning to wonder about you, Hannah Prescott. I'm beginning to wonder."

"Gee, thanks for that tiny vote of confidence," Hannah returned waspishly, "but it really doesn't mean much when you consider it's coming from the one person in my life who's really trying to use me—you!"

To her surprise, Jarrett's gray gaze widened in startled protest. "I am not trying to use you."

"Sure you are," she scoffed. "You're using me to prove your theories about who stole that dumb statue."

"I'm just keeping tabs on you until I know for certain what the story is," he muttered, sounding almost defensive.

"You're trying to intimidate and control me. That's another way of saying you're trying to use me. Your arrogance has to be seen to be believed, Jarrett Blade. Now would you mind shutting up for a while? I'm going to read."

It proved something of a surprise to her when he did exactly as she requested. Perhaps, Hannah decided, the trick to dealing with a man like Jarrett Blade was to take a very firm hand.

Three

She didn't understand, Jarrett decided as he lay watching Hannah smear suntan lotion on her rounded calves and thighs. He was only making certain that he stayed in control of a potentially dangerous situation. If she was an innocent victim of the Clydemores' manipulation, then his actions would also serve to protect her.

Women, in his experience, were generally not innocent victims, however. Elaine had been so beautiful and had claimed to love him so much that he had been unable to see the ruthless ambition in her until it was far too late. What a fool he'd been about her. But never again. Now he made certain he was always in control of himself. He never let a woman get to him in any way except the physical.

Hannah Prescott was very different from Elaine as far as looks went, Jarrett mused, his eyes continuing to follow Hannah's fingers as she stroked the lotion on her legs. Elaine had the clean, sleek lines of a thoroughbred, all long legs and elegant throat and slender body. But Hannah was soft-looking, round and full in places he found himself wanting to touch. Like the top of her legs, for instance....

"Do you want some help putting on that lotion?" he heard himself ask.

Hannah sent him a scathing glance. "No, thanks." She continued applying the suntan cream, her fingers slipping up to her bare stomach. Her skin gleamed under the fragrant oil.

Jarrett gazed at the delicate curve of her stomach and remembered how it had felt under his hand a few moments earlier. Then he followed her fingers as they moved up to anoint the upper slope of her breasts. Round and round her hands moved in smooth, sweeping patterns that left the skin glistening in their wake. Shoulders, breasts, the upper part of her arms, all seemed soft and curved and infinitely feminine. Like the utterly feminine shape of the little fertility goddess he had carefully locked away in his room, Jarrett realized.

With that realization came another. His body was hardening with alarming urgency, and the snug bathing trunks he was wearing weren't providing much concealment.

"Damn!" The short, impatient oath came from between clenched teeth as he abruptly rolled over onto his stomach.

"What's the matter?" Hannah stopped stroking her skin long enough to glance at him with a small frown.

"Nothing. Hannah, I'm serious about that bikini. I want you to wear some other suit from now on." He didn't look at her, cradling his chin on his crossed forearms. Grimly he focused on Danny Tyler, who was building a ditch together with some other children.

"Go to hell, Jarrett Blade," Hannah said lightly.

He couldn't stop himself. He knew he ought to ignore the provocation, but something in him refused to obey common sense. With a deceptive laziness Jarrett moved, shifting onto his side and angling his body very close to Hannah's. She was so startled she dropped the bottle of suntan oil. Jarrett could feel the slickness of her skin as he deliberately let his thigh come into contact with hers. Hannah's eyes opened very wide and she went quite still as she felt the heaviness of his aroused manhood through the fabric of his suit.

"Now do you understand?" he rasped, a little surprised at just how husky his voice was.

Hannah rallied quickly. "I can't help it if you have no self-control."

"You'll wear another swimsuit in the future?"

"If it will keep you from assaulting me, yes."

With a coolness he was far from feeling, Jarrett willed himself to relax. Slowly he pulled away. It took more willpower than he had anticipated to return to his own towel. But he thought he managed the feat with commendable masculine casualness. It had to look casual. The last thing he wanted Hannah to think was that he couldn't control himself at all.

"Have you ever been pregnant, Hannah?" he asked abruptly, thinking of the goddess.

She turned a faint shade of pink at the very personal question. "It's none of your business, but no, I've never had a child."

"You'd look good pregnant," Jarrett told her almost absently.

Hannah felt the embarrassed flush spreading. "Don't get any ideas where I'm concerned. I don't plan to leave Hawaii carrying your kid."

Jarrett rolled over onto his side, gray eyes meeting hers with lazy aggression. "What would you do if you went home pregnant with my baby, Hannah Prescott?"

She sucked in her breath, her whole body tensing at the cool challenge in him. Don't panic, she told herself silently. Above all, you must not panic. Don't let him rattle you. That's exactly what he's trying to accomplish. Keep your head and don't let him get away with it.

"Cry a lot," she finally suggested sarcastically. "And then file a paternity suit."

To her chagrin, Jarrett's face relaxed into a wide grin. "Make me pay through the nose, hmmm? But you wouldn't have to go to court to get me to acknowledge my responsibilities, Hannah," he added softly.

"I'll bet I would," she contradicted fiercely. "Given your distrust of women, I don't expect you'd believe any female who claimed she was pregnant by you! My God! Why am I having such a stupid conversation? Excuse me, Jarrett, I've had enough sun for today. I'm going back to the hotel!"

Leaping to her feet, she whisked her towel into her beach bag, picked up the paperback she had planned to read, and started back along the beach with a brisk, determined stride. Dammit, why had she let him goad her into such an inane discussion! Jarrett Blade had fertility goddesses on the brain.

"Hannah!"

She didn't look around as he moved smoothly to join her, but she sensed his anger.

"Hannah, don't walk away from me like that."

"Is that the only way you know how to talk, Jarrett? One order after another? One intimidating comment after another? I'll bet your social life is very limited. You make a lousy date, do you know that?"

"Unless you want to face Alice Clydemore alone when she discovers that her 'souvenir' is missing, you'd better not ditch me, lousy date though I may be," he grated, taking her arm in a grip of steel.

Hannah started to protest and then bit her lip in vexation. He was right. The last thing she wanted this afternoon was to handle Alice Clydemore alone. "Just stop talking to me as if I were some kind of female slave you have to keep in line!"

A ghost of a smile crossed his face. "I might make a lousy date, Hannah, but I have a feeling you'd make a very nice little slave girl."

She didn't smile. There was nothing at all humorous in his small joke. Resolutely she continued through the sand to the hotel entrance.

Alice Clydemore's knock came on Hannah's door just as she stepped from the shower twenty minutes later. Hastily she toweled dry and reached for a muu-muu.

"I'm coming."

The door between Hannah's room and Jarrett's opened, and she glanced up to see him standing there, his expression grim. His gray eyes glittered with anticipation. "Let her in and act as if absolutely nothing is wrong."

Hannah cast him a fulminating glance as she hurried to the door to greet Alice Clydemore. Everything was wrong, couldn't he see that? And it was all his fault!

"Hi, Alice. I just got in off the beach."

Alice smiled charmingly, nodding at Jarrett as she handed Hannah a small bundle of fabric. "I'm sorry to bother you, dear, but I decided I'd better return your tapa cloth and take a look for the little doll while I remembered it. I'd hate to get home and have to confront my granddaughter with no present! Five-year-olds aren't very understanding about such matters, you know. Hello, Richard. Did you meet your competition yet?"

"Danny and I had a little chat on the beach. We agreed to share Hannah this evening. I'm banking on the fact that I can outlast him. With any luck he'll be asleep by nine o'clock." Jarrett moved idly into the room. He was still barefoot, wearing only a pair of neatly creased slacks. He could have put on a shirt at least, Hannah thought irritably. Half naked like this, he looked far too at home in her room. What would Alice think?

"Here's the souvenir bag, Alice," she said hastily, dragging out the heavily loaded suitcase and opening it. "Take a look. I've got so much stuff in here that I'm not sure I know what's mine and what isn't. After a while all these souvenirs start to look alike, don't they?"

"You're so right, but I rather think I can remember this particular clay doll," Alice said, coming forward to begin searching through the chaos of mementos. "A fat little thing with a Tahitian skirt, as I recall..." Her hands moved more and more quickly through the jumble of items in the suitcase. A small frown began to etch her face as she failed to locate the doll. "I could have sworn I must have gotten it mixed up with your things that night we compared purchases, Hannah. Is this the lot? Any souvenirs in your other case?" She flicked a glance at the remaining suitcase.

Obligingly Hannah stepped forward to open the bag, but her palms were damp as she did so. Was Alice Clydemore really looking for that statue? Or just a missing souvenir? What was the truth of the situation? Perhaps Alice had also been duped. How did Jarrett know so much about the Clydemores? Awkwardly, her fingers trembling with nervousness, Hannah succeeded in undoing the catch.

"I don't see anything else, Alice. Want to take a look?"

Alice moved up beside her, frowning down into the case. "Well, I don't see it," she said slowly. "It must have gotten lost somewhere along the line. Are you sure this is everything? What about your beach bag?"

The beach bag, too, was opened, revealing no clay doll. Jarrett sat watching the whole process, coolly sipping from a glass of ice water he'd poured for himself. His gray gaze hovered on Alice Clydemore with something akin to satisfaction.

"It looks as though you'd better pick up something else for your granddaughter, Mrs. Clydemore,'' he finally drawled. ''Pity to disappoint a kid.''

''Yes, it certainly would be.'' Alice's frown cleared miraculously as she smiled at Jarrett. ''I shall have to run down to one of the local souvenir shops and find something else, as you say. Well, thank you, Hannah. Sorry to bother you. You're quite sure that's everything?''

''V-very sure, Alice.'' Hannah didn't look at the older woman as she relatched the suitcase. ''I'm sorry we couldn't find it,'' she offered lamely.

''No problem,'' Alice declared airily, heading for the door. ''I'm sure I'll be able to find something else that will do. See you later. Uh, you're having dinner with Richard here, did you say?''

''And Danny,'' Hannah added, not quite meeting Alice's eyes. This is so awkward! she told herself.

''As I said, Danny and I will be sharing Hannah this evening,'' Jarrett murmured.

''I see. Well, have a lovely time. John and I are going to one of the restaurants on the other side of the island. We'll see you in the morning, then, right?''

''Right. Good-bye, Alice.'' Hannah shut the door behind the older woman with a shaky sense of relief and leaned back against it to stare at Jarrett. For a long moment she could think of nothing to say. Then she burst out, ''Don't look so pleased with yourself! I think she's just as innocent as I am!''

''An interesting theory.'' He smiled. ''Just another duped victim, hmm?''

''Yes, dammit!''

''You're forgetting I know something about John and Alice Clydemore.''

''Such as?''

''Such as the fact that they've been involved in shady art deals for the past ten years. They've bought stuff from poor African museums, bribed border guards and museum officials, and brought it back to sell for a fortune on the U.S. art market. They've paid a few bucks to Peruvian farmers to rob ancient graves of priceless artifacts and then they smuggled the stuff out of the country and sold it for thousands.

John Clydemore even got caught three years ago trying to bring illegal pre-Columbian art in through Customs in Washington D.C.''

"What happened?" Hannah demanded, startled.

"Not much. He got slapped with a fine for failing to make a proper Customs declaration, and the artifacts got shipped back to the Peruvian government. Many of the emerging nations are being systematically stripped of their heritage by this kind of smuggling. They've all enacted strict laws forbidding artifacts to be exported from the country, but laws like that tend to get ignored and they're hard to enforce. Collectors are careful not to inquire too closely into the background of a particular piece of art being offered for sale. Not if they want it badly.''

"You seem to know a lot about it," she charged tightly.

"I do. I have an excellent pre-Columbian collection." Jarrett bared his teeth in a brief, humorless smile.

"Then you're no better than the Clydemores," she accused.

He lifted a hand in denial. "Wrong. I'm reformed. I'll admit there was a time when I didn't inquire any more closely into the background of certain pieces than any other collector who was determined to get his hands on a certain object. And I knew where to go and who to see to get what I wanted. But I never slipped into outright smuggling. Frankly, there were easier ways of obtaining what I wanted. But now I don't even use those methods. I'm cleaner than newly fallen snow these days. I only buy pieces offered for sale by reputable dealers who have acquired them from long-standing collections.''

"Don't sound so damn virtuous. I'll bet you're planning to keep that little gold fertility goddess all for yourself, aren't you?" It was a shot in the dark, but Hannah thought she detected a flicker of guilt in Jarrett's hard eyes. It was gone an instant later.

"I'm going to return that goddess to a friend of mine. I told you that. It was stolen from his collection in Peru.''

"Uh-huh." She didn't bother to hide the skepticism she was feeling.

"Dammit, don't you dare accuse me of shady dealing. You're the one who's still not in the clear," he growled, surging to his feet with a restless movement. "Put your shoes on. We're going browsing or something. I don't want to sit around this hotel room all afternoon." He stalked back to his own room.

Shopping with Jarrett Blade in the countless gift and souvenir shops of Waikiki proved to be a trying experience. Hannah soon learned that the only way to keep her temper was to ignore him completely when she spotted something she wanted to buy. Jarrett simply did not share her taste in souvenirs, and he let her know it.

"Why on earth do you want that ridiculous statue of King Kamehameha?" he demanded, frowning as she selected one from the ranks of a hundred similar such carvings.

"It's made out of genuine lava!" Hannah protested, clutching the king.

"That's like saying it's made out of genuine rock. There's nothing rare or priceless about lava in Hawaii. And there's nothing rare or priceless about that statue. It was churned out on an assembly line."

"I like it and I'm going to buy it," she declared stoutly.

"It's a waste of money," Jarrett grumbled.

"Maybe, but it's legal to take back with me, unlike some of the stuff you've collected in the past!" Feeling as though she'd definitely had the last word, Hannah marched to the cashier to purchase the statue.

Matters did not improve, however. Half an hour later when she hovered over several jars of macadamia nuts, Jarrett again interfered.

"You can buy macadamia nuts back on the mainland. Why weigh down your suitcase with them?"

"Because when I get them home and eat them I'll remember that I actually bought them here in Hawaii. The same with those Maui potato chips. I'm going to take back as many bags as I can pack," Hannah informed him aggressively. "It's really none of your business, is it?"

"You're being idiotic." Jarrett surveyed the three artificial flower leis, the two hula dolls which actually did the hula when wiggled, the Kamehameha statue, and the bottle of Hawaiian flowered perfume she was already carrying. "If you want a worthwhile souvenir of the trip, let's go take a look in some of the local art galleries."

"I can't afford that sort of thing," Hannah informed him regally as she selected a bottle of the nuts.

"Well, I can, and I'm tired of browsing through all this junk. Buy the damn nuts and let's go find some good galleries."

"You go. I'd rather browse through junk."

"I'm not leaving you alone," he told her flatly.

"Then you're stuck with me and my taste in junk, aren't you?" she said, smiling kindly. "At least," she added coolly, "until you learn how to say please."

There was a distinct pause. Then Jarrett said very quietly, "Please, Hannah?"

She blinked, looking as astonished as she felt. She honestly hadn't expected him to do that. "I didn't think you'd lower your masculine ego long enough to try being civil."

Something moved in his eyes. She couldn't decide if it was annoyance or amusement. But he said nothing.

"Oh, all right," she managed rather ungraciously. "Just let me buy these nuts and I'll go with you to the art gallery."

For the next two hours she tramped around with him as he wandered through several galleries specializing in watercolors, pottery, and, to her surprise, quilts.

"Quilting? In Hawaii?" she asked, pausing before a beautifully designed coverlet.

"Umm. The missionaries taught the island women how to quilt. The women came up with their own patterns and designs. Beautiful work." Jarrett spoke almost absently as he examined the specimen in front of them.

"Hey, that's even nicer than my Kamahameha statue," Hannah decided, reaching for the price tag. "Six hundred dollars! Good grief! I could buy four hundred Kamehameha statues and a bunch of macadamia nuts for that price!" Hastily she dropped the tag and went on to the next item on display. Jarrett lingered for a while, studying the quilt.

"Look at this, Jarrett," Hannah called eagerly as she fingered some small napkin rings carved out of teak.

He glanced across the room and smiled almost indulgently. "You can buy those anywhere, honey. Besides, when was the last time you actually used napkin rings?"

"Spoilsport." She sighed and let the rings cascade back into the glass bowl that displayed them. "It's tough shopping with an art collector."

"No appreciation for the finer forms of junk, hmmm?" Jarrett laced his fingers through hers and led her through the rest of the gallery.

"Exactly." The intimate contact of his hand disturbed her. She ought to shake it off. After all, they were hardly lovers or even friends! "Souvenir hunting is an art form in and of itself, you know. You have no proper understanding of it. You've been dealing in the world of exotic art too long."

"Perhaps," he agreed, to her surprise. He paused at the cashier's desk and nodded at the woman seated behind it. "I'll take that quilt. Item number two sixty-five. Please have it wrapped and boxed for shipping by air."

"Of course, sir." The young woman beamed at him and got to her feet.

"What are you going to do with that quilt?" Hannah whispered loudly.

He slanted an unreadable glance down at her. "Make love on it," he said outrageously.

Instantly Hannah freed her hand and stepped away from him. "Well, I hope you can find a woman to share it with you," she retorted smartly. "You'll have to stop giving orders and trying to control people, though, if you expect to lure a female onto that quilt with you. Unless you're not particularly interested in a female with any intelligence, that is."

"We'll see," he said, drawing out his slim, calfskin wallet and flipping through it for a charge card.

Hannah refused to spend any more time in art galleries with him after that. Ruthlessly she insisted on going back to the souvenir stalls, and since it was getting late in the afternoon, Jarrett apparently decided not to protest.

Dinner that evening gave Hannah an oddly wistful sensation that took her by surprise. It was strange to sit at a table with a man and a small boy. She felt as if she were playing wife and mother. Most of the other guests in the hotel dining room undoubtedly assumed that the three were a family, and Jarrett and Danny did little to counteract the impression.

Hannah was amazed at Jarrett's willingness to talk with the child, letting the youngster chat eagerly about his experiences during the day.

Danny, in turn, seemed quite happy to accept Jarrett in the role of substitute father for the evening.

"Can I watch TV?" Danny demanded as he polished off dessert. "One of my favorite shows is on tonight, and I haven't seen it since we left home."

"I think that can be arranged," Jarrett agreed, glancing at Hannah with a smile. "Unless Hannah has other plans?"

"No, not really. I thought a walk on the beach might be nice after dinner, though. Would either of you be interested? I'm so stuffed after all those pineapple fritters!"

"I think that's a fair trade-off for a television show, don't you, Danny?" Jarrett inquired seriously.

"Sure. I can look for some more shells," Danny agreed enthusiastically.

"So can I," Hannah murmured, ignoring Jarrett's mocking eyes. What did she care if he didn't appreciate shells as souvenirs? The man was too wrapped up in ancient art for his own good.

It was still light out by the time the three of them had taken off their shoes on the beach and begun strolling along the waterline. Danny darted hither and yon searching out the best specimens, and Hannah wasn't far behind. She collected so many, in fact, that she wound up having to twist the skirt of her muu-muu into a makeshift sack. As eagerly as Danny, she hunted along the beach while Jarrett watched them both with a faintly indulgent expression.

"You're going to have to buy another suitcase to carry all those," he commented as she added another shell to her collection. "What are you going to do with them when you get home?"

"I think I'll decorate my plant containers with them," Hannah decided.

"Charming," he sighed.

"Here," she announced, holding out a large, tapering shell to him. "This one's for you. A souvenir of your little 'business trip' to the South Pacific." She regretted the impulsive gift almost immediately, and her chin came up with a touch of defiance as she waited for him to reject the shell.

Jarrett stared at it for a long moment until Danny came along and peered into his hand.

"That's a great one, Mr. Blade," the boy said enthusiastically. "If you don't want it, I'll take it."

"No," Jarrett said slowly, his eyes meeting Hannah's, "I think I'll keep it."

Hannah caught her lower lip between her teeth and gnawed on it for a moment, feeling strangely uneasy under his unreadable regard. "Of course, it's not as good a souvenir as that damn fertility goddess, but it won't cause you any legal trouble, either," she announced aggressively.

"What's a fertility goddess?" Danny demanded before Jarrett could respond.

That got to Hannah's sense of humor. "Go ahead, Jarrett, explain it to the boy," she said with a grin and then went off in search of more shells.

Hannah had half expected Jarrett to retreat to his own room once they returned to the hotel, but he didn't. He endured what passed for prime time television together with Hannah and only began glancing at his watch as ten o'clock approached.

"Aren't you getting sleepy, Danny?"

"Nope. I never get to stay up this late at home!"

"I'll bet," Jarrett said dryly. "When are his parents due back, Hannah?"

She frowned. "I don't know. I didn't put them under a schedule!"

Jarrett's eyes darkened, but he said nothing. Danny eventually went to sleep in the middle of Hannah's bed, and she turned down the television. Its tube continued to flicker through the room, and in the ghostly glow she glanced at Jarrett, who was sitting beside her.

He reached out and caught her hand, saying nothing. But his eyes never left hers as he drew her fingers slowly to his lips.

"Jarrett, please don't," she whispered anxiously, trying to retrieve her fingers.

"Quiet, or you'll wake Danny." Deliberately he kissed each fingertip. She felt his warm breath on her palm; then he turned over her wrist and kissed the sensitive skin there. "You still smell a little like suntan lotion. I wanted to help you put that lotion on today, Hannah. I wanted to have an excuse to touch you. There's something very intriguing about you."

"E-even if I do have lousy taste in souvenirs?" she tried to say lightly. She knew it didn't quite come off. The whole situation was about to get out of hand, and she should be taking steps to control it before Jarrett did the controlling for her. The easiest thing would be to "accidentally" awaken Danny and let him play chaperone. If she could keep him awake!

"You might have lousy taste in art, but I think you yourself will taste very good," Jarrett murmured. His tongue touched the inside of her forearm experimentally.

"Jarrett, stop that. What's the point of seducing me? I'm already doing everything you want me to do, aren't I? I let you set up poor Alice Clydemore this morning. What more do you want?"

"You," he said simply. "I've been wanting you all day, Hannah."

"You just want to seduce me because it will make you feel even more in control of me," she protested violently.

"Can a man control you with sex, Hannah?" he whispered starkly. His eyes burned suddenly into hers. "Would you give yourself so completely to a man that he could actually control you that way?"

She gasped, frantically trying to yank her arm back. "I'm certainly not about to let you experiment and find out!" Something told her that going to bed with Jarrett Blade would be the riskiest thing she had ever done in her life.

With unerring, primitive feminine instinct, Hannah prepared herself to draw away from the man beside her. She freed her hand with an abrupt movement and jumped to her feet, eyes wide and heart beginning to race.

"Leave me alone, Jarrett Blade. Don't touch me!"

"You're really afraid of me, aren't you?" he asked in a surprised tone. "There's only one reason for that, Hannah..."

She was about to silence him with a wild protest when a knock sounded on her door. Feeling as if a life preserver had just been thrown to her while she struggled in deep water, Hannah ran to the door and flung it open.

"Hi. We're a little late." Annie Tyler smiled apologetically. "Is Danny asleep?"

"Yes, yes he is," Hannah said quickly, vividly aware of Jarrett coming up behind her. He had the sleeping boy in his arms, and he handed him over to his father.

"A nice kid," Jarrett said coolly. "But I'm afraid Hannah won't be able to do any more baby-sitting. She's going to be busy for the remainder of her trip."

Ralph Tyler nodded quickly. "Sure, I understand. We really appreciate all you've done for us, Hannah."

Annie Tyler didn't look quite so enthusiastic over the prospect of losing the free baby-sitter, but she had the grace to smile and nod agreeably. "You've been great with Danny. He'll miss you."

"Oh, he's welcome to—"

"No, I'm afraid he's not welcome. Not in the evenings," Jarrett cut in smoothly. "The hotel offers a baby-sitting service, though. Perhaps you'd like to look into that."

Annie flushed. "Of course. It's just that Danny doesn't like strangers, and..."

"Come on, Annie, it's late." Ralph Tyler nodded down the hall in the direction of their hotel room. "Good night, Hannah, and thanks again. We'll see you in the morning."

"Good night," Hannah said with a touch of desperation as Jarrett firmly closed the door. Then she took refuge in her temper. "Honestly, Jarrett, you had no right to be so rude to the Tylers! I was perfectly happy looking after Danny. It's not as if they asked me to baby-sit him every night or anything, and I..."

"Honey, they were using you. They should never have asked you to baby-sit in the first place. You're on vacation too! And hotels the size of this one always have baby-sitting services available."

"You don't know what you're talking about!" she fumed.

Jarrett reached out and caught her defiant chin in his hand. "Hannah, let's get something straight," he said a little roughly. "If anyone's going to take advantage of you, it's going to be me!"

His mouth came down on hers with such dominating intensity that she stumbled against him. An instant later she was locked in his arms.

Four

It was like being caught up in a whirlwind. Hannah wanted to free herself and couldn't think of any way to do it. She couldn't really think at all, not with Jarrett's mouth controlling hers with a sensual command unlike anything she had ever experienced. Hannah found herself clinging when she knew she should have been pushing herself away from the intense demand of his body.

"Hannah, honey," Jarrett muttered against her lips, "I'm going to take you tonight. I'm going to lay you down and find out just how soft and warm you really are. Don't fight me, sweet Hannah, just give yourself to me and I'll take care of you. I'll make you happy tonight, I swear it."

His words continued to pour over her like warm honey, sweet and tantalizing and full of masculine promise. Hannah shivered beneath them, fiercely aware of a wild new recklessness moving within her.

On one level she was frightened of this man, but on another she was inexplicably drawn to him. From the first moment that she had allowed herself to fantasize about him aboard the plane, she had been aware of him in a way that was entirely new to her.

Now he had declared that he wanted her. The wild fantasy in which she had indulged had come true. The attraction was there, waiting to be acted upon. All she had to do was surrender....

But surrender was a dangerous thing to give Jarrett Blade. It was exactly what he wanted, but what would he do with it when he had it? How would he use it against her? It was too risky by far to even contemplate giving herself to this man. He was quite capable of taking the gift, *but what would he do with it?*

"Leave everything to me, Hannah. I want to learn all there is to know about your softness. I'll take care of everything."

Then his mouth closed on hers again, his tongue pushing warmly between the barrier of her teeth as he began to explore the prize he intended to take completely.

It was her chance, Hannah told herself, her one chance in a lifetime to learn the nature of passion and sensual excitement. Once before she had given herself in lovemaking to a man who had no respect for her or desire for love. The experience had been a disaster, leaving her crushed and unfulfilled and alone.

She had never been tempted to repeat it until tonight.

But tonight she would have an element of safety, Hannah assured herself as her arms stole around Jarrett's neck. Tonight there was no possibility that she was in love. How could there be? She had only known him a couple of days, and he had hardly been courting her during that time!

Jarrett Blade would probably be incapable of courting any woman, Hannah thought fleetingly. He had no use for gentleness or tender persuasion. He would not make himself vulnerable to a woman.

And this was the man with whom she was contemplating a brief vacation affair? But his very lack of loving desire was one of the elements which gave her safety, Hannah tried to tell herself. He would make no emotional demands on her, and she could keep her heart free even as she indulged her crazy fantasy.

"Oh, Jarrett, it's all so confusing," she whispered into his shirt as he lifted his mouth from hers. Unable to meet his eyes, she clung to him, trembling.

"No, it's not," he growled huskily, his hands roaming down her back to the curve of her hip. "Between you and me it's all very simple. I want you tonight and I think you want me. Relax, honey, and let it happen."

"But there's no love between us," Hannah said bleakly, her words muffled by his shirt. She felt his hands tighten on her waist.

"Don't you think you could learn to love me tonight?" he asked deeply. "Just a little, Hannah?"

Startled that he should even want such a response from her, Hannah's head came up sharply and her wide, anxious eyes searched his gaze. "Is that what you want, Jarrett? Really?"

"I want you completely. If you have love to give, even a little, then I want that, too."

She shivered, unable to comprehend the meaning behind his words. Dare she take them at face value? "It's so dangerous, Jarrett." *For me*.

"Not if you're honest with me, honey. Not if you surrender with no ulterior motives. I'll be as honest with you as you are with me. Fair enough?"

"It sounds crazy. All wrong somehow. Jarrett, I don't understand you or myself tonight."

"You don't have to understand. Leave everything to me," he soothed. Then he gently twined his fingers into the coiled braid of her hair and pushed her face against his chest so that she could not speak.

Oh, God, she wanted him, Hannah thought over and over again. She wanted him in a way that was so new to her. His fingers began to loosen the coronet of twisted hair and she heard his soft sigh of pleasure when the fine mass of cognac-brown came free in his hands, cascading down her back.

"I knew it," Jarrett rasped softly against her throat as he tangled his hands in her hair. "You don't really belong in the twentieth century at all, do you? With your hair down like this you look as if you stepped out of another world. And when I have you completely naked in my arms I think you are going to seem even more primitive."

Hannah took a deep breath, aware of how significant the act of taking down her hair had been. It left her feeling as if he'd already moved to claim her, as if he'd exerted a right over her that she hadn't been aware of giving him.

Dangerous. Primitive and dangerous. And irresistible.

With a sigh of surrender, Hannah let her body soften against Jarrett's lean strength. This was what she wanted, regardless of what the morning brought in the way of regrets. Tonight she would let herself experience the mystery that was Jarrett Blade.

"Sweet Hannah," he growled, sensing her unspoken surrender. "There's nothing left to think about tonight. Just let yourself feel. Just give yourself to me." He held her a little distance away, intently searching her face for a long moment.

Wordlessly she returned his searching gaze, knowing her growing desire must be showing in her eyes. Then he moved a hand from her waist and deliberately fitted it to her breast. Another small act of possession, she realized, just as taking down her hair had been. Was that what making love with Jarrett would be like? Nothing more than being possessed?

"Jarrett..."

He lifted his hand from her breast to lightly touch her lips. "No more words, honey. We've both made our decisions."

Then he bent to lift her into his arms, striding effortlessly through the connecting door. Hannah found herself being set down on a bed that had already been turned back, and the first thing she saw was the golden statue of the ancient fertility goddess on the nightstand.

"I took her out of hiding earlier when I turned back the bed," Jarrett said quietly as his eyes followed hers. "Something about her makes me think of you."

Before Hannah could respond he was sitting down on the bed beside her, his fingers finding the fastening of the muu-muu she was wearing. Hannah sucked in her breath as he deliberately lifted the dress from her body, leaving her in only a small bra and matching panties.

"Round and soft and womanly," Jarrett breathed, gray eyes gleaming in the shadows as he let his hand glide up her thigh to her stomach. "You were made for making love and making babies."

Hannah shook her head even as her body responded to his touch. "I'm not sure I like the sound of that. A bit limited as careers go." She tried to keep the words light in an attempt to ward off the certainty in his voice.

He didn't smile. Instead his expression became even more intent. "A thousand years ago you wouldn't have needed any other career."

"Jarrett, I think you're the one living in the wrong century," Hannah whispered as she touched his shoulder. A tiny smile curved her mouth and her eyes were soft and inviting in the pale light of the tropical moon.

"I think you may be right," he agreed huskily. Then his fingers freed the catch of the bra. Instantly the banked fires in his eyes flamed into full, glorious life. His palm grazed across one nipple as he bent down to kiss her. "Come alive for me tonight, Hannah. Let me have all you can give."

She cried out softly as her breast seemed to tighten and swell beneath his touch. His palm moved back and forth until the nipple firmed. In a small, convulsive spasm of mounting excitement, Hannah's leg flexed.

"Oh, Jarrett!" Fumbling, her fingers groped for the buttons of his shirt. She felt him tense as she began to free him of the garment. Then he pulled away.

Rising to his feet, Jarrett finished undressing himself in the shadows, peeling off the shirt and unclasping the belt of his slacks. In a moment or two he was naked in the moonlight, his body proudly, fiercely, aroused.

Hannah stared up at him, a little fearful now of the masculine power which was about to overwhelm her. He must have seen the uncertainty in her face, because he came down beside her with muttered words of reassurance and command.

"It's too late to change your mind, honey. You want me and you know it. Stop thinking about it." He flattened his hand on her stomach and then eased his fingers beneath the elasticized edge of her panties. He felt Hannah stiffen momentarily as the final barrier was breached and he folded his hand warmly against the melting core of her femininity. "Far too late to change your mind," he repeated with deep satisfaction. "Your body would betray you if you tried."

It was true. Hannah whimpered softly with desire, turning her face into his shoulder. Never had she been at the mercy of her own passion before. The experience was heady and frightening, and it left her breathless. Wonderingly she inhaled the intoxicating scent of Jarrett's body, her hand slipping down his chest to shape the hard line of his hip.

"Do you like the feel of me?" He caught her trailing hand and moved it to his thigh. "Touch me, Hannah." Deliberately he moved her trembling fingers to the thrusting evidence of his manhood.

"You seem so...so strong," she whispered. "Jarrett, you frighten me a little."

"A little fear won't hurt. And it will soon be gone," he assured her.

Slowly, deliberately, he stroked her body into full arousal. Never had Hannah guessed she was capable of such burning desire. It seemed to engulf her, causing her legs to twine with Jarrett's and her hands to pull at him. She wanted him to quench the fire that had begun to rage inside her. Instinctively she pressed herself closer, enticing him with the ancient wiles of womanhood.

But Jarrett refused to be pulled too quickly into the vortex of the passion he was creating. Slowly it dawned on Hannah that he was determined to set the pace. It was as if he meant her to know that even in this he would be the one in command.

"Jarrett, oh, Jarrett, *please!*" she begged, clinging to him as he rained kisses across her full breasts. "I need you."

"I know," he breathed triumphantly. "I can feel your need."

But he would not satisfy it completely. Instead he drew patterns in the soft hair at the juncture of her legs while he nipped gently at the tight buds of her nipples. His heavy leg pushed between her soft thighs, the roughness of it sending thrills along her nerves. Hannah was soon a twisting, curling bundle of aching feminine desire.

Yet when she could stand the sensual tension no longer and tried to push him onto his back so that she herself could complete the union, Jarrett caught her wrists and pinned her back against the mattress.

"No," he vowed, gunmetal eyes blazing with his own fiercely checked desire, "not yet."

"Oh, Jarrett, I can't stand it any longer!"

His mouth curved faintly in satisfaction. "I like you this way, Hannah. You're all woman and you're all mine, aren't you?"

She didn't know what he meant, but if it would serve to hurry him toward the shimmering conclusion of this encounter, she would agree with anything he said. "Yes, Jarrett. Yes! Please take me now. I'm going out of my head. I've never felt like this!"

Slowly, as if he would savor every second of the joining, Jarrett lowered himself along the length of her body. "Put your legs around me," he groaned.

Willingly she did as he commanded, although obeying him left her feeling more physically vulnerable than she had ever felt in her life. Eyes squeezed shut, she clung to him. Then he was pushing against her, probing slowly.

Hannah gasped as she felt the full extent of his masculine strength at the gate of her passion. And although she ached for him as she had never ached for a man in her life, Hannah was suddenly gripped with a wholly unexpected tension.

Jarrett must have felt it immediately. He paused, and when she opened her eyes he was lying very still, watching her. For a long moment they stared at each other.

Jarrett's expression was rigid with sensual intent, his eyes like molten silver in the moonlight. "It's all right, Hannah," he ground out carefully. "Relax. Give yourself to me."

"Jarrett, I'm afraid," she confessed in a tiny, ragged voice.

"I can taste your fear," he whispered, bending to run the tip of his tongue along her parted lips. "It's because you don't know where it will all end. You don't know how much of you I'll take. But I've already told you, sweetheart, I'm going to take all you have to give."

He waited no longer, entering her with a slow, firm power that made Hannah's breath catch in her throat. She closed her eyes tightly once more, her fingers clenching into the muscles of his back. Her body shivered in response to the steady, deliberate invasion and then it welcomed the invader completely.

"Ah, Hannah!" Her name was a throaty cry of triumph as Jarrett reacted to the acceptance of his body by hers. He began to move, driving into her with steady, pulsing strokes that sent Hannah into a whirling, spiraling climb.

Nothing else mattered except this moment and this man. Nothing else in the whole world. The little fertility goddess on the nightstand gleamed in the moonlight as Hannah learned the full extent of her own sensuality. When the pulsating climax gripped her, sending wave after wave of convulsive ripples into the deepest regions of her body, Hannah gave herself up to it completely. And in the process she gave herself up to the man who had commanded such an incredible response from her.

Jarrett took her gift with savage delight, his own cry of satisfaction a hoarse shout muffled against her breast.

Long moments later Jarrett stirred slowly, lifting his head to look down into Hannah's love-softened face. She could feel the cooling perspiration on his body as well as her own as reality filtered back.

"We have a lot to talk about in the morning, honey," Jarrett whispered huskily.

"Do we?" Hannah looked up into the face of the man to whom she was very much afraid she had just given her heart. Hope flared in her breast.

"Yes, but it can all wait until morning. God! I feel so good right now." Jarrett stretched luxuriously, keeping her body covered with his own. "So good."

Hannah smiled tremulously. "So do I. I've never felt anything like that before in my life, Jarrett," she confessed softly.

"Are you still frightened of me?"

Was she? she asked herself. "I don't know you very well. In fact, I can hardly believe I'm lying here with you tonight. I know so little about you, Jarrett." It was a plea for communication, for reassurance. It came from her heart.

"You'll be safe with me as long as you're honest with me," he told her quietly.

"Honest with you?" Bewildered, Hannah tried to read his eyes.

"I think you will be now, won't you, honey?" Jarrett drawled with easy certainty as he rolled off her and onto his back in a satisfied sprawl. "Tell me about your relationship with the Clydemores, Hannah. The whole truth."

"The Clydemores!"

"Are you working with them?" He turned his head to pin her with his gaze.

"Jarrett, I've already told you everything I know. Why bring it up now?"

"Because now I'm sure you can't lie to me," he said simply. His eyes held such masculine assurance that Hannah wanted to claw at them.

"Now you're sure!" The beginnings of dismay and shock brought Hannah to a sitting position, her gaze darkening as she stared down at him. Hastily she clutched the sheet to her breast, suddenly very conscious of her nakedness. "Was that what this was all about, Jarrett? Was making love to me some sort of bizarre test?"

The brackets around his mouth tightened, but he kept his voice calm and even. "You told me a lot by the way you made love. I don't think you realized just how much you revealed about yourself."

A flame of seething, purely feminine anger began to burn deep in Hannah's soul. She stared at the man lying at his ease beside her. "I don't believe this!"

"Tell me about the Clydemores, Hannah," he ordered softly.

Hannah's eyes narrowed as she succumbed to her fury. "You want to know about the Clydemores? Okay, I'll tell you about them. I'm working with them. We set you up with that damn fertility goddess! She's a fake, Jarrett! A fake, do you hear me? We knew you'd come out of the woodwork to get her back for your friend and in the process try to seduce me. I'm going to pretend to be so mesmerized by your phenomenal sexual talents that you'll want a full-scale affair with me. Once I'm in your home, I'm going to be able to rip off your entire pre-Columbian collection. The Clydemores are going to market it and split the profits with me! There! How's that for a grand scheme! Does that suit your distrusting, paranoid view of reality and of women?"

"Hannah, stop it," he gritted as she scrambled off the bed, taking the bedspread with her to cover herself. "Come back here and stop acting like a child. You just told me the sex was good for you. Why are you so mad?"

She whirled beside the bed, her breasts heaving with the force of her anger. Aqua eyes flashed with blue fire. "The sex might have been good, but it wasn't anywhere good enough, you bastard. I want a man who can give a little of himself while he's taking from me, but you can't do that, can you?"

"Now calm down and listen to me. And forget about that wild tale you just told me. I know damn well you made it up on the spur of the moment. Just tell me the truth."

"The truth," Hannah gasped, seizing the golden goddess in both hands and raising it high over her head, "is that I never want to see you or this stupid goddess again!"

"Hannah!" Clearly horrified by the prospect of her hurling the goddess halfway across the room, Jarrett leaped from the bed. "Give me that. Don't you dare throw it at the wall! It's priceless!"

"Then I'll throw it at you!" She slung the rounded figure at him, heedless of whether or not he had time to catch it. He managed, just barely, but Hannah didn't stick around for another attempt. She fled, naked, from the room. As she passed through the open connecting door, she shoved wildly at it, slamming it closed and locking it in one swift motion. She was almost unable to see what she was doing because of the burning tears filling her eyes.

Dashing the back of her hands across her eyes, Hannah fled into the bathroom and turned on the shower full force. She needed a bath. Nothing made a woman feel so unclean as when a man used her.

"Hannah!" The shower curtain was shoved aside to reveal Jarrett. The key to the connecting door was the only thing he was wearing. He tossed it down on the sink and confronted her with his hands on his lean hips.

"Get out of here, Jarrett. I'm taking a shower. I want to get rid of the feel of you!"

He smiled grimly. "You'll never succeed in doing that." Then he glanced at the wet strands cascading down her back. "You're going to have to sleep on wet hair. Why didn't you put on a shower cap?"

"The wet hair is my problem. Leave me alone."

"It's my problem, too, since you'll be sleeping with me," he told her evenly, stepping into the shower with her.

Hannah backed against the tile wall, holding up her hands as if to ward him off. "Jarrett, I'm warning you..."

He captured her hands and pulled her against his body, a faint smile touching his mouth. "Just tell me the truth about the Clydemores."

"I've already told you the truth!" she cried, frantically trying to free herself.

"You know them only as fellow tourists? You had nothing to do with stealing that statue?"

"No, I had nothing to do with it! But why ask me? You're going to believe exactly what you want to believe anyway!"

"I believe you now," he said gently, stroking his hands along her back beneath the curtain of her hair. "You really can't lie, can you? I was almost sure of it because of your eyes. But now I'm positive. In my arms you give me everything, including the truth. I think you gave me some love, too, didn't you, sweetheart? That's why you're so angry at the moment. But you don't have to worry. I'm not going to throw it back in your face."

She blinked uncomprehendingly. "What are you saying? That you...that you love me a little, too, Jarrett?" Her heart beat erratically as she waited tensely for his response. She could tolerate almost anything from him, even his ancient philosophy on how to handle a woman if he actually loved her. Philosophies could be changed, but the existence of love or the lack of it was another matter.

"I didn't say that, sweetheart," he murmured. He continued to stroke her back as if she were a high-strung mare. "I said I wouldn't throw your love back in your face. I'll take good care of it and of you, Hannah. You won't have cause to regret loving me."

"I regret it already! My God, Jarrett, I want a man who knows how to love, not one who just knows how to take that emotion from a woman!"

"Love is a woman's emotion, honey," he soothed. "It suits you. It makes you even softer and warmer than you already are. But a man who is in love is weakened by it. And there's no surer way for a man to lose his woman than to have her discover that he's weak. I won't let you make me weak, Hannah. But rest assured that I'll only use my strength to protect you and take care of you. That's what a woman needs from a man: strength and protection. All I demand of you in return is honesty and loyalty."

"Oh, is that all?" she quipped angrily, unable to believe what she was hearing.

The corner of his mouth kicked up whimsically. "Well, maybe not all."

"Do go on, I don't want to miss anything on the list! What else am I expected to provide in exchange for your masculine strength and protection?"

"The love and affection you need to bestow on a man, for starters," he suggested softly. "It's there inside you, honey, and you have to give it to someone."

Her chin tilted defiantly. "I get it. I'm supposed to love, honor, and obey and in return you're willing to provide nothing!"

The amusement faded from his eyes. "I'll keep my part of the bargain."

"But I don't happen to need what you're offering. This is the modern age, Jarrett. Raw strength doesn't come in very handy in an era of computers. As for protection, I pay my taxes like everyone else, and one of the things the money buys is a police force. Do I make myself clear? I don't need what you're offering! I'll save my love for a man who knows how to return it! Why are we even discussing the matter? You act as if there were some future for us, and you know damn well there isn't. This is what's known as a vacation affair."

Jarrett's hands went to her shoulders as his eyes hardened. Water cascaded down his chest, making him glisten. "You know as well as I do that what we just had together isn't going to end when you go back to Seattle."

"How do I know that?" she stormed. But she did know it, and the knowledge was terrifying in its implications. She would never be totally free of this man now that he had claimed her.

He shook his head, his eyes suddenly gentle. "I can see you're as aware of the future as I am. I've waited a long time to find a woman I can trust, Hannah, and I'm not about to let her go now that I've found her."

She looked up at him helplessly, feeling as if she were caught in a deep patch of quicksand. "What do I have to do to prove you can't trust me?"

"Well, you'll have to do better than that story about a fake fertility goddess and a plot to steal my collection." He grinned, leaning down to brush his lips across her nose. "But, frankly, you haven't got much of a chance. I told you last night I didn't think you could lie very well. Tonight I'm sure you can't."

"I did okay lying to Alice Clydemore today! I can lie just like anyone else!"

"I didn't say you couldn't try to lie, I merely said I'd always know if you were making the attempt. Alice Clydemore was probably much too rattled about losing the goddess to waste time studying your eyes. If she had, she would have seen the uneasiness you were radiating. Or perhaps she wouldn't have seen it," Jarrett decided musingly. "Maybe I'm the only one who really understands you."

"You don't begin to understand me," Hannah wailed helplessly.

He shook his head. "Something about you attracted me the moment I saw you on the plane, even before I decided you might be working for the Clydemores. Yesterday I spent hours watching you, studying you..."

"You didn't!" She was honestly shocked.

"I did. Why does that surprise you? After all, I had to know where you fit into the scheme of things. And I liked watching you. Even if you hadn't been involved with the Clydemores, matters would have ended the same way between us. I want you, Hannah. You're soft and gentle and there's something so deeply feminine about you..."

"That's a ridiculous thing to say," she squeaked, stunned by the insistent urgency in his words. It frightened her all over again. "All women are feminine by definition."

"No, not all. Some are as hard and cold and ruthless as any man when it comes to getting what they want."

"And you don't think I could be?" she demanded furiously.

Jarrett smiled again, his mouth a curve of certainty and satisfaction. "If anything, you're not hard and tough enough. Look at the way the Clydemores used you. And the way the Tylers took advantage of you as a free baby-sitter. My guess is those two instances are probably indicative of the way you live your whole life. How did you lose your job in Seattle, honey?"

She stiffened, alarmed at his flash of perception. "I got laid off. There was a reduction in the work force due to the economic situation, and I..."

He bent to shush the flow of words with his mouth. Then he lifted his head again. "You're lying. See how easily I can tell?" he asked tenderly. "Tell me the truth. Did you lose your job because you were the weak one in a power struggle? Or because someone used you somehow?" He gave her a small shake. "Tell me, Hannah. I want to know if I'm right. Did your innate softness get you into trouble?"

Hannah glared up at him. "Well, you can just keep wondering. I'm not about to discuss my entire personal life with you just because you're curious to know if you're right!''

Which he was, she thought dismally. How had he guessed? Was he really able to read her so well? Had he really been able to draw such conclusions about her based on knowing her for only a couple of days. It was unnerving and very unsettling. She felt far too vulnerable around this man, both physically and emotionally.

"I'm not going to push you about it tonight, honey, so you can relax," Jarrett assured her as if he genuinely wanted to soothe the rising turmoil in her. "You can tell me about how you lost your job some other time."

"Don't hold your breath," she muttered fiercely.

"I'd rather hold you." He pulled her closer against his water-slick body, letting her know the returning sensual power in him.

"Let me go!" Hannah began to struggle with the wild, useless, frantic fluttering of a small, trapped bird. "Jarrett, please let me go!"

To her surprise, he released her. But his voice was stern when he spoke. "Hannah, calm down. There's no need to have hysterics about this."

"Why not? It's part of my deeply feminine, soft, weak personality!" she yelped, shoving at his chest. "If I want to have hysterics in the shower, I'll have hysterics!"

He frowned. "It's obvious you're not in any condition to be rational about the situation tonight."

"How perceptive of you!"

"So I'll leave you alone. Go to bed, Hannah. We'll talk this over in the morning when you've had a chance to calm down." He stepped out of the shower, grabbed one of the towels from the rack, and turned to glance over his shoulder as he started out the door. "If you get lonely between now and morning, honey, you're welcome to come back to my bed."

"Gosh, thanks," she gritted scathingly. "Your generosity overwhelms me! I'd advise you not to stay awake waiting for me, though. I'm going to try to be real strong and tough and make it through the night all by myself!"

"Sarcasm doesn't become you, Hannah."

Speechless at the overbearingly superior note in his voice, Hannah was unable to think of a fitting last word as Jarrett left the bathroom. When he had gone, she whirled around and turned off the shower. The wet length of her hair made her grimly aware of the fact that she was going to have to spend the next half hour with the blow dryer. Stupid. Why hadn't she thought to put it under a shower cap as Jarrett had suggested?

Because she hadn't been thinking at all when she'd fled his bed. She'd reacted with the emotional side of her nature instead of the intellectual side. But, then, if she'd been acting intelligently she never would have allowed herself to be seduced by that damn chauvinist in the first place!

What an idiotic way to wind up an expensive vacation. Miserably Hannah plugged in the blow dryer and began the long process of drying her wet hair. How had she ever gotten into such a humiliating mess?

Since her painful experience with Ned Ferris the year after she'd graduated from college, she had been so careful of involvement. She'd had male friends, but she had never allowed them to become lovers.

But all the while she had been protecting herself from shallow relationships, she had been longing for the real thing. A part of her would never stop seeking the love and commitment she needed to give and to receive. Long ago Hannah had made up her mind to wait until she found the right man before she again risked her heart. Until tonight it had been surprisingly easy to resist the overtures of the men she knew. For four years she had been content with casual dating relationships.

How could she have let everything go to pieces tonight? And with a man like Jarrett Blade, of all people.

"If you were going to have a vacation fling, why didn't you at least pick someone handsome and charming and polite?" she demanded of herself in the mirror. "Why did you have to pick a dangerous, uncharming bastard like Jarrett Blade?"

How had he slipped so easily past all her defenses? she wondered with a sad sigh. One thing was for certain. She had to leave as soon as possible in the morning. Hannah knew she couldn't risk another day of Jarrett's persistent company.

Willing herself not to give in to tears, Hannah turned out the light and climbed into bed, her hair still slightly damp. With any luck she would be safely back in her own bed tomorrow night.

The last image she had as she drifted off to sleep was of the rounded, golden body of the ancient fertility goddess crouching beside the bed during their dangerous voyage of sensual discovery.

A troubling realization hit Hannah just as she was about to surrender to sleep: She had been far too enthralled with the wonder of having Jarrett make love to her to worry about getting pregnant.

Surely she wouldn't...she *couldn't*...not by a man she had only known two days! A man who had thought her a smuggler and who had seduced her to satisfy his ego and his questions about her role in a theft!

Hannah lay awake a while longer trying to convince herself that over the centuries that damn goddess had lost her power.

Five

Hannah awoke with the suddenness that indicates underlying tension. It was barely dawn. As she sat up in bed and gazed out at the pearl-colored ocean, it occurred to her that it was indeed time to go home.

"One island morning is beginning to look a lot like another," she mumbled to herself as she pushed back the covers.

A quick glance at the connecting door assured her that the entrance to Jarrett's room was still closed. She winced as the memory of what had happened on the other side of that door the previous evening returned. Feeling depressed and uneasy, she began to dress quietly.

There was no point in trying to go back to sleep and it was far too early to have breakfast or call the airline company about changing her reservations. What she needed was an invigorating walk on the beach. At this hour she would have the long stretch of sand to herself.

There was no sound from Jarrett's room as Hannah pulled on one of her new flower-splashed muu-muus and slipped into a pair of sandals. Out of long habit she took the time to braid her hair and twist it into the familiar coronet. Maybe she'd cut it when she got back to the mainland. If it were very short she might forget the way Jarrett had wound his hands through it so possessively.

The crisp dawn air felt good and the beach was pleasantly deserted as Hannah made her way out through the hotel lobby to the waterfront.

The sweep of Waikiki beach was ringed with elegant hotels, but they all looked curiously silent at this early hour.

She was tired, Hannah realized. The tour had been a grueling one, and she had been determined to take advantage of everything offered. Until last night the growing exhaustion had been rather pleasant, a sign of having enjoyed herself.

But this morning the tiredness had a depressing, restless aspect to it.

"Hannah!"

She turned at the familiar voice and found John and Alice Clydemore on the beach behind her. Surprised that they should be up so early, she paused and managed a smile. Their pace was brisk as they approached and the usual geniality seemed to be missing from their expressions. For the first time that morning Hannah suddenly found herself wishing the beach weren't quite so deserted.

She also found herself remembering something Jarrett had said about not knowing what the Clydemores might do when they discovered the statue was missing. But, then, she didn't really believe the Clydemores were guilty of the theft in the first place, did she?

"We saw you leave the hotel, Hannah," Alice began coolly as she and her husband came to a halt. The older woman's blue eyes were hard this morning, completely lacking in the usual warm charm Hannah had come to expect. "We've been waiting for a chance to see you alone. That Adams character who's been hanging around has monopolized you completely lately, hasn't he?"

"I don't know what you mean," Hannah began awkwardly, her mouth going dry just as her palms began to grow damp. There was no kidding herself now. The Clydemores were angry, which meant they must be guilty of having stolen that damned statue.

"Let's not beat around the bush," John Clydemore ordered flatly. "We want the statue back, Hannah. I don't know what kind of game you're playing or who you're working with, but it's over. The statue belongs to us."

"Then you shouldn't have let me run the risk of carrying it through U.S. Customs!" Hannah flared, deciding there was no point pretending ignorance now. What could they do to her here on the beach? Soon other people would begin filtering out of the hotels. As soon as someone else appeared, Hannah decided, she would call for help.

"I'm afraid we're becoming a bit too familiar to certain Customs officials," John Clydemore drawled. "Your naive, wholesome little face was exactly the sort we needed. I'll admit you had us fooled as well as Customs!"

"Who would have thought you were in the business?" Alice asked in tones of great disgust. "All that sweetness and light, taking care of the Tyler brat, buying all those junky souvenirs from every vendor with a sales pitch..."

"They aren't junky!"

Alice Clydemore ignored the interruption. "Gathering shells along every beach like a little kid, reading all those romances set in the South Seas as 'research,' helping every little old lady on the tour with her luggage and her problems. It's a hell of an act, Hannah, I'll give you that. Even had John and me fooled. But the game's over. Where's the statue?"

Hannah licked her lips and took a deep breath. A male figure dressed in khakis had emerged from the hotel entrance and was moving up the beach with a steady, strong stride. He was too far away to allow Hannah to see his features clearly, but there was something very familiar about his smooth, gliding pace. A sensation of relief swept through her. Jarrett was approaching.

"Mr. and Mrs. Clydemore," she began firmly, "I did not steal your stupid statue. I suggest you take the matter up with the gentleman who is coming toward us. I believe the three of you will have a lot to discuss, if I'm not mistaken. I, however, am not involved, so if you will excuse me..."

"Hold on, Hannah," John Clydemore said smoothly. "You're not going anywhere."

"Who's going to stop me?" she demanded, feeling more hostile than she had ever felt in her entire life. How dare all these people use her as a pawn in their smuggling games? "I've about had it with all three of you, do you hear me?" she went on aggressively as Jarrett came within listening distance. She sent him her most ferocious frown, a part of her thinking that this wasn't the most romantic "morning after" a woman had ever experienced. And it was all Jarrett's fault.

"Jarrett, tell your friends here to leave me alone. You three can squabble about that damn statue as long as you like. But count me out!"

"That's exactly what we're going to do," Jarrett agreed easily. One dark brow arched in a gesture of command. "Go back to the hotel and wait for me, Hannah. I'll be along as soon as the Clydemores and I have sorted this out."

"Stop giving me orders!" Hannah yelped, even though going back to the hotel was exactly what she intended to do. "You should have been a drill sergeant, the way you're always giving orders!"

"Now see here, Adams, or Jarrett, or whatever your name is..." John Clydemore began, only to be interrupted by a glowering Hannah.

"His name is Jarrett. Jarrett Blade."

To her astonishment, that brought an immediate halt to Clydemore's words. Actually it brought a lot more than that, Hannah realized belatedly as the Clydemores turned to stare at Jarrett, who smiled sardonically. Alice had gone rather pale beneath her fashionable tan and John looked as if he'd been punched in the stomach. Breeding showed, however, Hannah admitted to herself. The Clydemores recovered quickly.

"Mr. Blade," John Clydemore said icily. "How interesting to meet you at last. I've heard of you, of course."

"And I've heard of you and your wife, Clydemore," Jarrett retorted. "Hannah, you can go now. I'll handle this."

Perversely Hannah stood her ground. "Actually, I'm getting a little curious. I think I'll stay for a while."

John Clydemore swung on her before Jarrett got a chance to issue another order. "So you're working with Blade here, is that it? That explains a lot."

"Like how a naive, scatterbrained tourist like myself could pull off the coup of stealing that statue?" Hannah returned sweetly, her eyes glittering with resentment.

"That's enough, Hannah," Jarrett cut in with a tone that did not encourage further defiance. "I told you to go back to the hotel. Move, woman."

For a moment longer Hannah debated the wisdom of ignoring him. The Clydemores were curiously silent, their attention on Jarrett. Jarrett concentrated the full force of his willpower on Hannah, and she found herself weakening. Jarrett Blade, she discovered, was not an easy man to defy. His gray eyes were hard and unyielding as he waited for her to obey.

"What in the world would make me want to hang around the three of you any longer than necessary?" Hannah asked rhetorically. Chin tilted regally, she took a few steps past the small group of intense people on the beach. They had their backs to her, but even so, she could hear John Clydemore's opening words to Jarrett.

"So, Mr. Blade. You couldn't resist taking the goddess for your own collection. I had heard you no longer operated in the international market. What made you decide to come out of retirement?"

"You made the mistake of taking the goddess from Jorge Valesquez's collection. Señor Valesquez is a friend of mine," Jarrett said quietly.

"And what will you tell your 'friend' when you are unable to return the goddess?" Alice Clydemore interjected sharply. "Because we all know that statue will never make it back to Señor Valesquez, don't we? It's going to disappear into the private collection of one Jarrett Blade."

Hannah didn't wait to hear anything else. She broke into a run and made her way swiftly back to the shelter of the hotel. It sounded as if Jarrett and the Clydemores understood each other very well. Was Jarrett really going to keep the statue for himself? Was he no better than the Clydemores?

Dammit! Why was she torturing herself with thoughts like that? It was obvious Jarrett Blade was in the same league as her ex-friends John and Alice. After all, if he'd been playing it straight, he would have called in U.S. Customs.

And she would have been in very hot water.

That last realization was a sobering one. Like it or not, she supposed she owed Jarrett some gratitude for not having turned her over to the authorities. But apparently the only reason he hadn't was that his own background was somewhat shady. So shady that the Clydemores automatically assumed he would keep the goddess for himself.

When she reached her room Hannah began throwing her belongings into a suitcase. Working frantically, she tried to stuff the Hawaiian souvenirs in with the others. If Jarrett hadn't destroyed a few of them that first night, she thought, she wouldn't have been able to get the shells into the bag. There wouldn't have been room. As it was, she'd have to carry the Maui potato chips on her lap.

A knock on her door came just a few moments before she was ready to leave. Hannah panicked and then realized that it had been a timid little knock. Not at all the kind of knock Jarrett Blade would use, if he bothered to knock at all. Nervously she answered.

"Oh, hi, Danny." She smiled in relief as she opened the door. "What are you doing here?"

"I came to see if you and Mr. Blade want to go swimming before breakfast. Mom and Dad said that if you did, I could go with you. They're still in bed," the boy added disgustedly. "They never want to do anything."

Hannah sighed. Poor Mom and Dad. They had wanted a second honeymoon. And poor Danny. He'd been dragged along on a trip that really hadn't been all that much fun for him. "Oh, Danny, I'm so sorry," she murmured, crouching in front of him and trying to smile. "I would love to take you swimming this morning, but I can't. I have to go home today."

Danny looked at her, perplexed. "I thought you'd be going home when we did. Why are you going early?"

"Because I have to." No point going into lengthy explanations with a kid, Hannah decided wryly. "I have lots of responsibilities at home. I've been away a long time."

He looked interested. "Have you got kids like me at home?"

"Well, no, but I do have some other creatures who will be missing me."

"Like what?"

"Let's see, there's Erasmus and Siegfried, Herbie, Yolanda and Ludmilla..."

"Those don't sound like kids!" Danny observed wonderingly.

"They're not. Erasmus is a dog and Siegfried is a bird. Herbie is a turtle and Yolanda and Ludmilla are a couple of plants. I have a few other plants, too. Want to hear their names?"

Danny shook his head. "I don't like plants much. But I like animals. I'd like Eras-rasmus and Sieg-whatever his name was. And Herbie, too. Maybe I could see them someday?"

"Maybe," Hannah agreed slowly, knowing what the odds were on that score. She got to her feet, ruffling Danny's light-colored hair affectionately. "Take care of yourself, Danny. It's been nice meeting you. I hope you enjoy school this fall."

"Good-bye, Hannah," the boy said wistfully. "Will Mr. Blade be going with you?"

"No, Danny. He won't." Hannah turned back into the room, took a last glance around, and picked up her overstuffed suitcases. "Could you close the door for me, Danny?"

"Sure." The boy obliged and then hesitated. "Want me to say good-bye to Mr. Blade for you?"

Hannah stiffened. "There's no need, thank you, Danny."

"But I think he likes you, Hannah," Danny objected.

"Mr. Blade likes his women with a little age on them," Hannah told him dryly. "Like a few centuries. Mr. Blade does not like me at all. He only wanted to use me for a while! Good-bye, Danny." Eyes burning with unshed tears, Hannah clutched her cases and hurried down the hall.

A good many hours later Hannah finally turned the key in the lock of the small house she rented in a friendly Seattle neighborhood. Instantly a cacophony of noise went up, a combination of welcoming barks and scolding squawks. It was good to be home.

"Erasmus!" Happily Hannah let go of her suitcases to go down on her knees in front of the large, enthusiastic dog that was doing his utmost to leap into her arms. Erasmus was really much too big to be leaping into anyone's arms, but he apparently still thought of himself as a puppy in some ways. His background might have been in doubt, but his joyous greeting was not. "You missed me!" Hannah exclaimed. "Did Jimmy remember to take you out twice every day? You don't look like you're starving. He must have remembered to feed you! How're Siegfried and Herbie?"

The squawking from the direction of the parakeet cage in the corner of the living room confirmed that Siegfried, too, had survived her vacation. The little yellow bird was racing back and forth on his perch, shrilly demanding attention. Herbie the turtle was a more staid creature by nature, not given to displays of affection, but even he stuck his head out to acknowledge Hannah's return. And Yolanda, Ludmilla, and the other plants all looked healthy and green.

By the time Hannah had greeted everyone, kicked off her shoes, and poured a glass of white wine for herself, she was feeling almost relaxed at last.

Almost, but not quite. Frowning at her drink while she absently scratched Erasmus's ears, Hannah considered her newfound restlessness. It would disappear in time, she promised herself. She would find another job soon and settle down into another routine that would be pleasant and satisfying.

After all, she liked her life the way it was, didn't she? Why should she be feeling so restless and uneasy? "Must be the vacation," she told Erasmus wisely. "There's always a letdown after a vacation, you know."

Erasmus snuffled intelligently and adjusted his head for a better scratching angle. He ignored the bird, which was hopping about in its cage beside the chair. He also ignored the turtle, which dozed happily on its island. He could afford to ignore them all because he was bigger than they were and he knew it.

Hannah glanced around her cozy living room, idly noting that everything looked much the same as when she had left ten days before. The hothouse window was filled with plants and herbs that had all stayed green with the help of a neighbor. The old-fashioned wing-backed chairs and pillow-covered sofa looked comfortable and inviting. The white area rug in front of the fireplace provided a pleasant focal point for the pastel color scheme of the room. Against the soft yellows and beiges, the green plants had a sculptured effect.

Hannah liked the house. She had been renting it for two years now, and it provided the backyard that Erasmus needed. But it wasn't cheap. She frowned at the thought.

"A lot of mouths to feed in here," she announced to the occupants of the room. "Looks like I'd better get cracking on finding another job."

There was silent agreement. No one else in the room was particularly worried, it seemed. Hannah smiled to herself. Dog, turtle, bird, and assorted plants were all blissfully content in the knowledge that they would be taken care of by her. They were, after all, the recipients of a deep and abiding affection. They had a home with Hannah.

Hannah finished her wine, notified her neighbor she was home a couple of days early, covered Siegfried's cage, and said good night to Herbie and Erasmus. Then she went to bed, exhausted. But her dreams that night were filled with dark fantasies of a man with somber brown hair and cold, lonely eyes. Lonely?

Yes, lonely, Hannah realized somewhere in the farthest recesses of her sleeping mind. Lonely. Jarrett Blade was a lonely, alienated man who would probably never learn what love was all about. At least she knew what it meant to love.

Hannah spent the next day unpacking and adjusting to being at home again. Regardless of how soothing it was to get back into her familiar routine, the restlessness did not fade. Would she always carry these annoying images of Jarrett Blade around in her head?

"I never even learned where he lived!" she complained to Herbie when she changed the water in his terrarium. "Not that I care. And you don't either," she added wryly as Herbie paddled blithely about, "do you? I suppose it doesn't matter to any of you that I had a mad fling while I was on vacation. That I actually let myself be seduced?" Hannah glanced at the dozing dog and the chattering parakeet. Neither bothered to respond. "How about the fact that I almost got myself arrested for smuggling? That news shake anyone here? No?"

Was it really a bad sign to find yourself carrying on extended conversations with pets and plants? No, Hannah decided resolutely, it was not.

As she arranged her collection of shells in Yolanda's and Ludmilla's pots, Hannah found herself remembering the evening she had gathered them. "I suppose he threw away the one I gave him," she confided to the rubber tree plant. "He only likes treasures made of gold that have been buried for a thousand years."

Hannah postponed the evil task of job-hunting until a couple of days after her return. A glance into the eyes of her pets on the second morning convinced her she could put it off no longer. The extravagance of her trip to the South Pacific demanded that she find work soon now that she was home. She had used up a sizable portion of her savings on the tour. The little statue of King Kamahameha became a paperweight as she began overhauling her résumé. Every time she glanced at it she remembered Jarrett's mockery of the purchase.

"I hope he's home now enjoying his precious pre-Columbian artifacts," she told the cheap lava carving. "Old artifacts are about all he's capable of enjoying. And you know why? It's because they don't demand real love in return. The man doesn't know how to love." She frowned seriously at Siegfried, who was perched on the tip of her pen. "The funny part was that he had the nerve to tell me I was free to love *him*! I just wasn't supposed to expect anything in return! Talk about raw nerve! Oh, Lord. I really do have to find a job. I'm starting to talk to you and Erasmus and Herbie far too much."

"Love you. Love you. Love you," Siegfried chattered reassuringly.

The phone rang the next morning just as Hannah was licking her twentieth stamp and attaching it to the twentieth résumé-containing envelope. The voice on the other end of the line was cheerfully familiar. And pleasantly human.

"Charlotte! I'm so glad you called. How are things at the office?" Charlotte had been her co-worker in the information storage retrieval department of the large corporation where Hannah had worked. Together they had indexed and stored in a computer the countless documents, plans, and drawings produced by the manufacturing firm. The other woman was older than Hannah by about five years and married with three children. Hannah had missed hearing about the day-to-day adventures of the three Pomeroy kids.

"That's exactly why I'm calling," Charlotte announced grandly. "I'm so glad you're back. I couldn't remember exactly which day you were due to return. Have I got *news,* friend!"

"I'm sitting down." Hannah chuckled.

"You'd better be for this. Scoville got caught in a clinch with Jessica Martin in the supply room. Gossip is that Benson himself found them and this time he lost his temper."

"Benson found them?" Ronald J. Benson was the president of the company. "What on earth was he doing within fifty yards of a supply room? He never leaves the executive suite!"

"Hannah," Charlotte interrupted irritably, "you're seizing on the least important aspect of the situation. Apparently Benson's secretary was temporarily out of the office and he needed a new pen or something. Who cares why he happened to walk in when he did? The point is, he found them in a most compromising situation. And according to Harry Shaeffer, who happened to come along at just the right moment to hear *everything*...''

"Harry always did have a talent for overhearing *everything*," Hannah observed.

"Well, the upshot of the whole thing was that Scoville has been asked to submit his resignation," Charlotte finished in triumph.

"You're kidding!"

"Nope. Knew that would get your attention. Benson reportedly told his vice-president that Scoville's name had cropped up one too many times in compromising circumstances and that this particular instance was the last straw. He wants Scoville out. By the end of the month.''

"Well, it's about time," Hannah murmured. "Jessica Martin, hmm? Poor kid. I'll bet she was devastated.''

"Didn't handle it nearly as well as you did," Charlotte giggled delightedly.

"I don't know about that. Has she still got her job?''

"Oh, yes. Benson didn't blame her at all. In fact, Hannah, now that the truth about Scoville's harassment is out, everyone's talking about how you should never have been let go. I'm positive you can get your old job back. I think you should phone Personnel today and reapply.''

"Do you really think so, Charlotte? it was all so horribly messy...''

"Listen, everyone knows now what kind of turkey Scoville was. Benson is a married man, remember? A happily married man. He expects a certain kind of behavior from his management staff. And he's setting the tone of office opinion. Everyone is firmly against Scoville now and in favor of the women who've complained about his harassment. Hannah, you need a job, right? Information storage and retrieval positions aren't exactly lying around on the ground right now. Please come back. I'd love to work with you again. We all miss you.''

"I'll think about it," Hannah offered slowly. After all, it had been a good job except for Doug Scoville's obnoxious advances. He had been her boss, and he had been accustomed to using his position to take advantage of any female employee who caught his eye. A few had cooperated willingly enough, it was true. Scoville was a handsome, self-assured man who promised much and delivered nothing. He was also a married man. Even if Hannah had wanted to believe his promises of advancement and love, she would never have allowed herself to become involved with a married man.

Scoville's persistent demands had become increasingly difficult to deal with. Personnel didn't want to have to confront him with accusations of harassment. He was too powerful, and many of the men in Personnel took the attitude that it was the fault of the women involved anyway. The situation had come to an embarrassing conclusion when Hannah was politely asked to leave.

"I hope you'll do more than think about it, Hannah. Believe me, things have really changed. Personnel got chewed out for not having paid attention to previous complaints about Scoville. Those guys will probably bend over backward to get you back on the staff."

"I'll give it some thought, Charlotte. Really. Now tell me, how are the kids?"

Charlotte laughed at the familiar question. "Oh, they're all running true to form. Scott fell out of the swings at day care yesterday and cut his arm. Had to rush him to Emergency. Corrie tried to find out if her pet goldfish can breathe air and Jimmy has a cold. Same old story. You haven't missed a thing. You know, Hannah, you ought to have some kids of your own. You're nearly thirty and you really shouldn't put it off much longer. I'm not sure it's healthy for you to be wasting all that love and affection on that menagerie and arboretum you maintain. Find yourself a nice man and have some kids, friend. Misery loves company."

"Gosh, thanks, Charlotte." Hannah laughed.

"Anytime, Hannah, anytime. Well, I've got to run. Mac McDonald is taking over this department until a replacement is found for Scoville. I've got to give him a rundown on how we operate. Promise me you'll reapply?"

"I promise. Good-bye, Charlotte. And thanks." Thoughtfully Hannah hung up the phone and reached for another envelope. She addressed it to the Personnel department of her old firm. Nothing to lose, and it had been a good job.

That evening she curled up after dinner with a novel—a spy thriller. Erasmus lounged on the rug in front of her and Siegfried played with his mirror. Herbie, as usual, wasn't terribly active, but he looked content investigating a shell Hannah had put in his terrarium.

Hannah was just coming to the conclusion of a particularly hair-raising chase sequence when the front doorbell chimed. Instantly Erasmus leaped to his feet, his shaggy body tense, ears cocked. He issued his standard warning bark and strode aggressively to the door ahead of his owner.

"Who is it?" Hannah called, her hand on the knob.

"It's Doug, Hannah. Let me in. I have to talk to you."

Hannah backed away from her side of the door as if it had grown alarmingly hot. Doug Scoville? Here at this hour? "What do you want?"

"Hannah, please let me in. I just found out you were back in town. We have to talk. I'm sorry about what happened. I came by to apologize for that incident at the office. That's the only reason I'm here, Hannah. I just want to say I'm sorry."

With a sigh of resignation and irritation, Hannah opened the door to reveal the good-looking man with the chestnut-brown hair and green eyes who had been directly responsible for causing her to lose her job.

It wasn't until she saw the strange glitter in his gaze and the too-steady way he held himself that she realized he'd been drinking.

Erasmus growled.

Six

By the time Jarrett had rented a car at Sea-Tac airport, found Interstate 5 into Seattle, and gotten lost three times after exiting the Interstate onto surface streets, he was not in the best of moods.

Damn town must have been laid out by a drunk, he decided, not knowing that local legend supported that theory. Eventually he found his way into the pleasant north Seattle suburb where the address he held seemed to fit the numbering system.

When he finally discovered the right block and the right house, it was after nine o'clock in the evening and even the late summer light had faded to deep dusk. Jarrett switched off the ignition and sat for a moment behind the wheel of the rented Chevrolet, staring at the warmly lit cottage.

The place looked like Hannah, he decided. The light seeping through the curtains had an inviting, golden quality. Somehow it reminded him of the cognac shade of her hair. There was a slightly overgrown but obviously cherished yard in front that seemed to extend around to the back of the house.

A garden would be nice, Jarrett was surprised to find himself thinking. He'd never bothered with one. But Hannah would look right at home planting seeds and picking vegetables. Yes, he'd have that terraced rockery at the back of his house torn out and replaced by a garden. She'd like that.

Thoughts of having Hannah safely established in his own home sent a ripple of anticipation through him. Jarrett's fingers tightened momentarily on the wheel, and then he drew a long breath. Why was he hesitating?

He'd come all this way just to find Hannah and take her back with him, and here he was sitting outside her house like a nervous high school kid trying to get up the nerve to pick up his first date.

There was nothing to be nervous about. Oh, sure, Hannah would probably put up a small battle, but it would be a token protest at best. All he had to do was start making love to her and she would melt in his arms. She might not even put either of them through that much trouble. After all, Jarrett reminded himself, she was half in love with him already. It wouldn't take much to secure her love completely.

It was a decidedly pleasant notion, the idea of being loved by Hannah Prescott. She would make a comfortable addition to both his home and his life. With a cool resolve, Jarrett opened the door and got out. Deliberately he headed toward the brick walk that led to the front door.

He would take good care of Hannah. She needed someone to shelter her, whether she realized it or not. He'd keep the Clydemores and the Tylers and Lord knew who else away from her. Hannah's sweet, naive nature led too many people to take advantage of her. He would protect her and give her a focus for all the warmth and passion she had locked inside. Jarrett had been telling himself he was the man to take care of Hannah ever since he had arrived back at his hotel room and found her gone. All the way home from Hawaii he had tantalized himself with pleasant pictures of Hannah in his home and in his bed.

It would be a good relationship for her. He'd see to it.

He was just about to sound the knock on the door when he caught the faint drone of a man's voice from inside the cottage. Jarrett frowned, glancing at the sleek Datsun sports car parked at the curb. Who the hell was visiting Hannah at this hour? Damn, he'd only given her a few days alone and already some creep in a snappy car was bothering her.

His frown intensifying, Jarrett rapped sharply on the door. Instantly a dog's loud, warning bark responded. The voices inside stilled. A moment later the door was flung open and Jarrett found himself staring hungrily down into Hannah's sweetly freckled face.

But there was no sign of welcome in the startled aqua eyes that lifted to meet his. In fact, he realized grimly, Hannah looked harassed and upset. And that could only be the fault of whoever was inside the cottage.

"Jarrett! My God! What on earth are you doing here?"

Dammit, she didn't have to look *that* astonished to see him. "I think the answer to that question is obvious. I came for you." Jarrett had fully intended to take her into his arms the moment he saw her again. But clearly other matters were going to have to come first. He clamped a hand around each of her nicely rounded shoulders, allowing himself an instant to savor the feel of her, and then firmly moved her aside. "What's going on in here, Hannah? You look upset." He pushed his way into the hall.

"Finding you at my door is not doing anything to improve my mood! Jarrett, please, I don't know why you're here, but I'm busy at the moment and I wish you would just go away."

He ignored her request. She obviously was too agitated to realize what she was saying. Now was the time to be soothing but steadfast, he told himself. Dammit, he wasn't going to make any more mistakes handling Hannah. He'd learned his lesson the night he'd made love to her and then brought up the subject of the Clydemores. She was a romantic at heart, and a man would do well not to force the harsh realities of life on her.

"Honey, what's the matter? Is someone bothering you?"

"A couple of someones are bothering me!" she snapped irritably, "and they're both male. I wish I'd had the sense to send Erasmus to attack-dog school!"

"Erasmus? Oh, the dog. Hello, Erasmus." With the sure instinct of a man who'd never in his life owned a dog but who saw no reason why they shouldn't be dealt with rather like people, Jarrett put out his hand. Erasmus whimpered gently and thrust his damp nose politely into the extended palm. An instant bond was established, and Hannah glowered down at the dog.

"Men!"

"Honey, I don't know what's wrong, but whatever it is, I'll take care of it. Just tell me—"

"Hannah?" The interruption was caused by the masculine voice Jarrett had heard just before he'd knocked. "Hannah, what's going on? Who is this?" the stranger demanded as he moved into the hall behind Hannah.

Jarrett draped an arm around Hannah's shoulders with lazy possession, pulling her against his side. He paid no attention to the stiffness in her as he studied the other man. Good-looking but weak. The kind who would take advantage of a woman like Hannah. "I'm the one who should be asking the questions," Jarrett drawled. He felt Hannah stiffen further, but he didn't release her. "Who the hell are you?"

The other man regarded him with a hint of aggression. "I'm a friend of Hannah's."

"Hannah's friends all have to be vetted by me, and I get the feeling I'm not going to approve of you."

"Jarrett, stop it!" Hannah struggled briefly within the curve of his arm, but he paid no attention. "Both of you cut it out this minute. I will not have my home turned into a back alley."

"Who is he, Hannah?"

"I'm Doug Scoville. I'm Hannah's boss."

"Not anymore," Hannah interjected quickly.

"Last I heard, Hannah had just lost her job," Jarrett murmured coolly. "If you were her boss, maybe you know something about that? Maybe you were responsible?"

"Now hold on just a minute, Mr...." Scoville began blusteringly.

"The name's Blade. Jarrett Blade. And I think that's about as close as our association is ever going to get. It's time you were gone, Scoville. Hop into that little car of yours and get lost."

"Dammit, I'm not going anywhere until Hannah and I have had a chance to talk. I don't know who you think you are, but..."

"I'm the man who looks after Hannah now. People like you will learn to stay away from her in the future," Jarrett explained calmly. "And I might as well tell you that you're only going to get one warning."

Hannah made another effort to extricate herself from the circle of his arm, but once again Jarrett ignored it. His hold wasn't enough to silence her tongue, however, and he heard the flare of temper in her words.

"If both of you don't stop acting like a couple of alley cats I'm going to scream until the police arrive, do you understand? I've had it with both of you. I want each of you to get into your car and leave, do you hear me? Just leave me alone!"

"Scoville, you're the one who's upset her like this," Jarrett gritted. "I don't allow other men to upset Hannah. Get out, before I throw you out."

"Dammit, you're not going to give me orders!"

Jarrett released Hannah and took a menacing step forward. He had no qualms at all about using force, and that fact must have shown. Scoville flinched, and then after an angry glance at Hannah's anxious face, he edged quickly toward the door. Erasmus barked good-bye, clearly glad to see him gone.

Jarrett moved to slam the front door shut just as Scoville gunned the accelerator of his Datsun. Then he turned to confront Hannah. "It's all right now, honey. He's gone." Soothing and gentle. That was the ticket now. He wouldn't give in to his own fury and demand a full explanation of Doug Scoville's presence in Hannah's home. With a great effort of will he told himself he would be tender and calming until Hannah relaxed and explained everything. No more mistakes, he vowed for the hundredth time.

"Well," Hannah began assertively as she faced him with her hands on her hips, "this is certainly turning into an eventful evening. What are you doing here, Jarrett?"

He eyed the way her sweet rear filled out her snug, faded jeans. There was a strong temptation to put out a hand and cup the soft shape, but Jarrett valiantly resisted. Nevertheless, the fullness of her breasts beneath the plaid shirt she was wearing and the roundness of her thighs brought back memories that he could hardly wait to relive. But he'd take this one step at a time.

"Stop glaring at me like that, honey," he muttered softly, stepping forward to assess the living room with an appreciative eye. "Your house looks just like you. Cozy and comfortable and inviting. Who's that?" He walked over to the birdcage and looked down at the yellow, feathered creature sitting on the swing.

"That's Siegfried. And I wish you would explain yourself, Jarrett. You had no right to barge in here and threaten my visitor." Hannah stormed into the room behind him just as Siegfried hopped onto Jarrett's extended finger. "Put him down. He bites."

"He'll only bite me once, won't you, Siegfried?" Jarrett traded stares with the bird for a moment.

"Don't you dare threaten my bird!"'-

"I'm not threatening him. We're coming to an understanding." Siegfried was apparently content with the "understanding," because after a moment's close assessment of the alien human on whose finger he was sitting, he calmly began to preen his already perfectly aligned feathers. Gently Jarrett deposited him back on his swing and glanced around. "Anyone else I should meet? Ah, here we go. A turtle. I'll bet he's a real comfort on a cold night, hmm? And look at all these plants. It looks as if you're trying to re-create the Amazon jungle in here. So! That's what happened to all those shells you collected, hmm?" He peered at the way they were artfully arranged in the various pots. "Wait until you see how the quilt looks in my bedroom."

"There's not a chance in hell I'll ever see how the quilt looks in your bedroom," Hannah sputtered in outrage.

He might as well lay his cards on the table. Jarrett straightened from studying the placid turtle and turned to face her, reminding himself to take it slow and gentle. "Of course you're going to see that Hawaiian quilt, honey. I've come to take you home with me."

She stared at him, her lips parted in astonishment. "Take me home with you!" she finally squeaked. "Are you out of your mind? I wouldn't go across the street with you."

"There's plenty of time to talk it all over," he assured her. "It's been a long trip. Have you got a drink?"

"No!"

"Are you sure? Scoville looked as if he'd had a couple." Jarrett heard the harshness creeping back into his voice and deliberately tried to suppress it.

"Doug had had a couple before he even showed up here tonight. Stay away from my kitchen, damn you!" She hurried after him as he walked into the other room.

With sound instinct Jarrett began exploring Hannah's kitchen. It was as cheerful and comfortable as the rest of the cottage. God, she was going to be pleasant to have around. Visions of his own home being turned into a cozy, warm environment flashed into his head just as he found the liquor cabinet.

"Jarrett, you have no right..."

Deftly he removed the whiskey bottle and located a couple of glasses. "Here you are." He handed her a glass with a small amount of whiskey and a large amount of ice and soda in it. Then he poured himself a rather large amount of whiskey over ice. "Take a few sips and calm down. We have a lot to talk about."

"I'm not in a conversational mood!" she warned vengefully as he pushed the glass into her hand.

"That's okay. I can do most of the talking." Taking her arm, he guided her back into the living room and pushed her gently onto the couch. She glared up at him and then took a long swallow of her drink. "If you hadn't run off that morning in Hawaii we could have had this little discussion then. And I wouldn't have had to chase after you like this."

"I'm terribly sorry you were put to so much trouble."

"I've told you before, honey, sarcasm doesn't become you. Now just settle down and listen." He ignored her outraged expression and plugged on determinedly, striving for a calm, controlled manner. "Hannah, it's obvious you need someone to look after you. You need a man."

"Oh, my God," she mumbled indistinctly, taking another swallow of whiskey.

"You're too soft and naive for your own good. Every time I see you, someone is trying to take advantage of you. The Clydemores used you to smuggle that goddess, the Tylers used you as a free baby-sitter, your ex-boss is clearly trying to get you into bed..." He broke off as a pink flush stained the cheekbones beneath her freckles. He knew he'd been close to the mark, but having this confirmation of it enraged him. It took a tremendous effort to control his temper. "Just what is the story with Doug Scoville? What happened to make you lose your job? And what was he doing here tonight?" Dammit, he'd intended to wait before he brought up that topic.

"It's none of your business," she informed him sullenly.

"You want me to track down Scoville and ask him?" Jarrett suggested far too mildly. He left no doubt in his tone that he'd do exactly that. The hint of menace was successful.

Hannah's lips tightened for a moment; then she attempted a cool little shrug.

"I'll tell you if it will speed up this 'discussion' we're having." She sighed. "Scoville was my boss. He had a nasty habit of sexually harassing the female employees who worked for him. I was one of the unlucky ones. He kept pestering me, making life very difficult on the job. I complained to Personnel, but they simply assumed it must be my fault. Scoville got worse after that, as if he knew he was safe. He was so sure..." She trailed off awkwardly, but Jarrett knew what came next.

"He tried to push you into an affair, and you refused." His fingers were like bands of steel around the whiskey glass now. He absently hoped it wouldn't fracture. It would be nice if the glass were Scoville's neck. He should have throttled the guy while he'd had the chance.

"It all came to a grand, humiliating conclusion the day he followed me home from work and tried to...to..." She licked her lower lip nervously.

"Tried to rape you?" Jarrett couldn't even feel the glass now. His eyes never left Hannah's face. All he could think about was going after Scoville.

Hannah made a wry expression. "I'm sure he thought of it as an attempted seduction," she muttered. "It, uh, failed. But Scoville's wife had become suspicious, apparently. She walked in just as things were getting very unpleasant. She was furious and blamed me. She then demanded that Scoville see to it I was fired. I resigned first. End of story. Satisfied?"

"Satisfied!" Jarrett exploded. "Are you crazy? I won't be satisfied until I take him apart piece by piece! Lady, you really do need a keeper, don't you? What the hell was he doing here tonight, as if I need to ask?"

"As long as you've obviously got it all reasoned out, why are you asking?" she snapped moodily.

"Because I want to hear all the gory details! I want you to spell it out so we'll both hear the words. Come on, Hannah, tell me exactly what he was doing here and then tell me you don't need me!''

"He came here to apologize," she said recklessly.

Jarrett grimaced, knowing at once that she was glossing over the truth. "Tell me exactly what sort of apology he wanted to make," he bit out. The little fool. Didn't she know enough not to open her door to men like Scoville? A babe in the woods.

"He said he really was sorry for what happened," Hannah persisted defensively. Jarrett narrowed his eyes and said nothing. After a moment her nerve broke, just as he had known it would. "And to tell me his wife was divorcing him," she concluded in a low mumble.

Jarrett closed his eyes in disgust and swore with soft violence. "To tell you his wife was leaving him. Let me see if I can finish this, shall I? He was very upset and wondered if you'd let him stay here for the night, right? It was really you he'd wanted all along. He'd only been staying with his wife for the kids' sake, and now that she had taken the initiative and filed for divorce he was free to come to you at last.''

Hannah was staring at him in bewilderment. "How did you know about the kids?" she asked, tacitly agreeing to the rest.

Jarrett stifled another rough oath and surged to his feet. "A wild shot in the dark," he told her derisively. "Oh, hell, Hannah. That tale's as old as the hills. Don't tell me you were on the verge of buying it. You can't want a man like that!''

"I never said I wanted him!''

Restlessly Jarrett got to his feet and began pacing the room. He mustn't lose his control. That would really frighten her. He must remember to keep everything calm and deliberate. Gentle. Tender. Sensitive. It was time to exercise all those fine qualities he'd never had occasion to use before. But lack of use had a penalty that was becoming obvious.

He wasn't proving to be very good in the role of gentle, tender, sensitive, understanding protector. Dammit, he'd keep trying.

"Hannah, you need me. You'll come home with me tomorrow. We can take the pets with us and see about having the rest of your things moved at a later date," he began carefully.

"Damn you, Jarrett Blade, what makes you think I have any intention at all of letting you take over my life like this?" Hannah gulped another sip of the whiskey and watched him as he stalked back and forth in front of her.

He ran his hand through his hair, fighting for control. "It's obvious that you need me to look after you. I'll treat you well, Hannah. I'll keep you safe from all the people in the world who use women like you, and I'll give you everything you need and most of what you want."

"Does that mean you'll decide which of the things I want are really good for me?" she drawled from behind him.

If she didn't cut out the sarcasm, Jarrett decided resolutely, he really couldn't be responsible for his actions. "Hannah, you're going to have to trust me."

"Why?" she asked simply, taking another long swallow of the whiskey. Maybe he shouldn't have poured her quite so much, Jarrett thought with a frown.

"Because I say so!" At once he realized how irrational that sounded. "Look, honey, stop trying to bait me and just let me explain how it's going to be between the two of us."

"Ah, yes. The famous bargain you tried to make in Hawaii." She nodded wisely. "I'm supposed to love, honor, and obey, and in return I get security and a brick wall built around me to keep out the rest of the world. Big deal. I'm not interested, Jarrett. Try your fine bargain on some other unsuspecting female. I'm not that naive or that soft in the head, in spite of what you think. I don't need you or your great bargain." She took another swallow of the whiskey.

Jarrett felt his control slipping. This wasn't going at all the way he'd planned it. Tossing back the remainder of his own drink, Jarrett set the glass down on the nearest end table with due care. He was fully aware that he wasn't functioning with his usual controlled precision.

"Hannah, whether you realize it or not, you do need me." He called on reason. "Look at the mess you'd have been in with the Clydemores if I hadn't come along."

"No mess at all, as far as I can see," she said flippantly. "Alice Clydemore would have collected her stray 'souvenir' and we would have gone our separate ways."

"Doesn't it bother you that they used you?" Jarrett asked furiously.

"They aren't that much different from you, are they, Jarrett?"

It was too much. Jarrett forgot all his good intentions and decided to revert to Plan B. *Take the woman to bed and make love to her until she can't do anything except surrender,* he heard a small, primitive voice in his head advise. With a groan he paced forward, yanked Hannah's half-empty glass out of her hand, and pulled her to her feet.

"I'm not using you," he ground out. "You need me, Hannah Prescott."

"I don't need you or anyone else!"

"You're lying. And I'm going to prove you're lying," he vowed. He brought his mouth close to hers, and his eyes locked with her stormy ones. "We'll start with the most basic area in which you need me and we'll work up from there. I'm going to take you to bed, Hannah Prescott, and show you just how much you need me there. Then we'll see if you can't be a little more reasonable."

"Reasonable!" she gasped. "*Reasonable!* You call that reasonable? I won't—"

He cut off her next words by crushing her mouth beneath his own. The tremor that went through her body seemed to flood him with desire. It also flooded him with triumph and relief, because he knew instinctively it was a tremor of more than just anger.

"Hannah," he muttered against her mouth. "Honey, you want this as much as I do. How can you deny it?" Instead of giving her a chance to answer, he filled her mouth with his tongue. The soft moan that came from deep in her throat was all the answer he needed, Jarrett told himself. God, she was soft. And when her fingertips found their trembling way to his shoulders he remembered that there was more than an inviting softness in Hannah. There was a deep passion in her, too.

He wanted to be the only one to set that passion free.

"That's it, sweetheart, let me feel your need. Don't be afraid of it or of me, Hannah. Just give yourself to me. I'll make it good for you." He only half heard the low rumble of the reassuring words which he ground out against her mouth and throat. He only knew he meant them.

"Jarrett, please, no. Don't do this to me. I don't want this..."

Jarrett stifled the plea by kissing her again. With a rough groan of desire he slid his hands down her body, shaping the delightful curves of breast and thigh.

"You were made for me, honey," he breathed as he cupped the rounded contour of her buttocks and pulled her intimately close. "You need me and you want me. Why are you fighting me?"

"Jarrett, you don't understand. It's not enough!" Hannah whispered. But the words were spoken on a note of surrender as her head sank down on his shoulder.

"I'll make it enough. I'll make it everything you need," he vowed. Jarrett moved, sweeping her up into his arms. By God, he would make it perfect. He'd show her she didn't need anything or anyone else except him. With Hannah in his arms he glanced around impatiently and spotted the hall that must lead to the bedroom.

He felt a little light-headed, but he also felt incredibly strong. Hannah was a satisfying weight as he carried her down the carpeted hall to a room that was filled with plants. The bed in the center looked as if it were in the middle of a jungle bower. Huge ferns cascaded over the headboard and tall palms swayed around the flower-printed comforter. Ruffles and flounces had been used everywhere. Underneath the jungle setting was a deep, emerald-green carpet.

Jarrett grinned with a savage pleasure as he surveyed the very feminine, yet surprisingly primitive, room. "A man could disappear into a room like this and never emerge again. The goddess would look right at home here."

"The goddess..." Hannah broke off dazedly, lifting her head from his shoulder with an uncertain frown as if she were trying to make sense of a situation that had gone beyond her control. "Jarrett, we have to talk."

Jarrett hushed her gently, setting her down on the fluffy, flowered comforter. "We'll talk later." He sat down beside her, curving an arm around her thighs to make certain she didn't try to escape. With his other hand he reached down to deliberately begin undoing the buttons of the shirt she wore. At the first touch of his fingers on the bare skin of her throat Hannah went very still. Her eyes wide with apprehension and desire, she stared up at him.

"Why did you come here tonight?" she said thickly.

Jarrett shook his head once, unable to comprehend the question. Didn't she understand that she belonged to him now? Hadn't she guessed that he would follow her? "Why did you run from me?" he countered, sliding his fingers from one button to the next. "You knew I'd come after you."

"No." She shook her head, eyes closing briefly and then opening very wide once again. "No, I didn't know you'd follow me. It makes no sense. You got what you wanted. You got the goddess."

"And every time I look at her I think of you," he confided huskily. "She's pure female, just like you." His fingertips trailed lightly between the gentle hills of her breasts, and he felt her responsive shiver. It echoed through his own body, hardening it and sending a wave of reckless wonder along his nerve endings.

Hannah wanted him; he could feel the desire in her. It gave him a heady sense of masculine power to be able to make this one particular woman respond, even against her will. Jarrett realized vaguely that he'd never taken such pleasure in a woman's response. But with Hannah it fed something deep and primitive in him. Tonight he would make her acknowledge the desire she felt and the underlying need.

"Tell me about it, honey," he growled as he pulled her shirt free of the snug jeans.

"A-about what, Jarrett?" she asked shakily.

His mouth tilted slightly at the corners and he slowly spread the opening of her shirt until he could see the crest of one rose-tipped breast. Jarrett bent his head and nipped the tightening bud with exquisite care. "Tell me what you're feeling. Tell me about the heat that's building in you. Tell me you need me, Hannah."

"You seem to have everything figured out for yourself," she managed with faint defiance, although she gasped as he let her feel the edge of his teeth on the other nipple.

"But you don't, apparently. I want you to figure it out too, sweetheart. Tell me what it means; what it feels like when your breasts harden like this. Tell me what those little shivers mean. Don't fight it, Hannah. Just give in to it. Surrender. You're safe with me." Jarrett kept talking softly as he found the fastening of her jeans. Hannah stiffened again as he unsnapped them, her hand coming down protestingly on top of his. "No, sweetheart. You don't want me to stop. And it would be beyond my ability now, anyway. I'm aching for you, honey. I don't think I'll ever be able to get enough of you. Something about you makes me want you more than I've ever wanted any other woman in my life. I want to take you until you can't do anything except respond. And I'm going to do just that. Now talk to me, Hannah. Tell me what I want to hear.''

"Jarrett, please!''

His own fingers were shaking a little now as he pushed the tight-fitting jeans down over her hips. The scrap of lacy panties came with them, revealing the dark, curling triangle at the juncture of her legs. The promise of her complete nudity destroyed some of his methodical intent. Jarrett let his fingers brush through the alluring tufts that shielded the heart of her femininity. He felt, rather than heard, the small moan that shook her.

"Can you tell me yet? Let me hear you say the words, honey.'' Gently he encouraged her as he pushed the jeans and the panties completely off her legs. Slowly he let his palm glide back up her calf to the sensitive inner part of her thigh. Dammit, he would make her tell him. She was trembling with the force of her desire, and sooner or later she would have to admit it aloud.

"Oh, Jarrett!''

She twisted on the comforter, her fingers clenching into the fabric. Her eyes were closed now, and Jarrett could see the way her mouth glistened as she dipped her tongue along her lower lip. That small evidence of her heightening need was almost too much for his self-control. Grimly he forced himself to slow down.

But his body was threatening to betray his willpower, Jarrett acknowledged ruefully. His slacks were suddenly far too confining and he wanted to feel her fingertips prowling through the hair on his chest. With one hand stroking her warm body, Jarrett began stripping off his own shirt. Then he stood up briefly beside the bed to unfasten his slacks. A moment later he was naked, and he looked down to find Hannah watching him with feverish eyes. Part of the fever was desire and part of it was apprehension.

"Don't be afraid of me, honey,'' he murmured as he came down beside her and gathered her close. "Don't be afraid of needing me.'' Deliberately he stroked the length of her back down to her hip. Then he bent his head to kiss her with slow passion. When he felt the involuntary arching of her lower body he had to fight down an overwhelming rush of desire.

His head was beginning to spin. He couldn't think coherently any longer and he wasn't sure exactly what he was saying. He only knew he kept up a low, reassuring, encouraging pattern of words meant to draw Hannah more tightly into the web he was weaving.

"That's it, honey. Yes...touch me. Touch me, darling." Impatient with the uncertain exploration of his body, Jarrett took her hand and forced it gently lower. When her fingers at last cupped his manhood, he groaned. Then he began to stroke the pulsing bud between her legs until she cried out and clung to him.

"Jarrett, Jarrett, please. Take me now. Make love to me, Jarrett."

"Do you need me, Hannah?" God, if she didn't admit her need of him soon he would not be able to hold back. His body was throbbing with demand, his senses clamoring for the final coupling.

"Yes, Jarrett. Yes, I need you." The words were a sigh against his shoulder.

"Ah, sweetheart, that's all I wanted to hear. Hold on to me. Hold on tight."

The heat in his own body was a flame now, and it could only be extinguished in the liquid warmth of Hannah. Urgently Jarrett pushed her deep into the softness of the comforter. Then he lowered himself onto the greater softness of her body.

Her legs parted for him, and he knew a sense of burning triumph and pleasure as she openly demonstrated her need. "So soft. So soft and hot and melting..." He widened the space between her legs with his hands. "Put your legs around me, sweetheart," he groaned, and when she did so he let himself sink down along the length of her until he was pushing at the core of her.

"Jarrett, oh my God, Jarrett..."

He surged slowly into her, overcoming the tight tension that seemed to grip her at the last moment, just as it had the first time. She was so tight and warm and sexy. And he loved the feel of her legs wrapped around his hips. She was perfect, and he told her so as he began to move slowly within her.

"So sweet, so loving... Honey, you're all I want. Perfect."

Her arms went around his neck and she clung to him with shivering need, accepting the pace he set for their sensual journey. Through timeless moments of spiraling wonder and passion he guided her, glorying in the way she responded beneath him. She was his. His to arouse and satisfy. His to tantalize and release. His to care for and protect.

And she needed him. Tonight she had admitted it in one way. The rest would follow. That knowledge sent another rush of hot pleasure through his veins, and Jarrett knew he could not last much longer. The woman had a dazzling effect on his senses. But he had to make certain she was satisfied first. It was his duty and his pleasure as her lover. And the thrill of satisfying her was overpowering.

Inserting his fingers between their bodies, he found her exquisitely sensitive bud of desire. He touched her with care, and she responded explosively.

"Hannah, sweet Hannah," he breathed as she convulsed delightfully beneath him. He drove deeply into her. A tiny, choked cry was accompanied by the feel of her little teeth on his shoulder. The small pain sent him over the edge. His own cry of completion was a near shout of satisfaction and he buried the sound in the curve of her throat.

A long time later Jarrett stirred lazily to look down into the face of the woman he had just claimed and realized she had fallen asleep. He smiled to himself, arranging her carefully in the curve of his arm. Everything was going to be fine now. She would move in with him this week, and soon he would know what it was like to be the focus of her warmth and love.

Hannah needed him.

Seven

Hannah awoke the next morning with an overwhelming sensation of having just met her fate.

Blinking uncertainly in the morning light that cascaded into the room, she struggled upright in bed and gazed, appalled, at the sleeping man beside her. Jarrett sprawled in her bed as if he owned it, his magnificently nude body a dark, masculine counterpoint to the leafy, feminine setting. His somber brown hair was tousled and the lines of his face seemed less severe.

Urgently Hannah shoved aside the comforter. He must have pulled it over both of them sometime during the night. Good Lord! Had she gone crazy? What in the world had she been thinking of to let herself be so thoroughly seduced again by this man?

But when she had opened the door to him it had been as though her original fantasy had once more sprung to life. Only this time the fantasy had been augmented by real life memories of passion and desire and love.

For when she had seen him standing in her doorway last night, Hannah had known that what she felt for Jarrett Blade was love. Inexplicable, ungovernable, overwhelming love.

The restlessness she had been feeling since her return home, the lingering memories, the aching longing were all put to rest when she opened the door.

But nothing had changed, she told herself wildly as she let Erasmus outside for his morning run and checked on Siegfried, whose cage she had neglected to cover the previous evening. Nothing had changed. Jarrett still thought in terms of control and desire. He wanted her, but he didn't have the vaguest idea of how to love her.

"What a mess!" Hannah sighed at her reflection in the bathroom mirror. "Why did it have to be this man?"

She felt trapped and cornered, caught in a dilemma for which there didn't appear to be any easy answers. It wasn't fair that the one man capable of turning her ordered, serene existence upside down was altogether wrong for her. Jarrett Blade had a shadowy past and a rather foggy present, and he knew nothing about love except that he thought it might be nice to have her love him.

"I don't understand it, Siegfried," she announced to the parakeet as she began making breakfast with a vengeance. The bird sat contentedly in his cage, responding to her conversation with a running patter of bird talk that consisted of his normal chirps interspersed with the human vocabulary he had picked up. "I just don't understand the mess or the man. What am I going to do? I'm not sure I can get rid of him and I'm not sure I want to anyway."

After cracking the shells with an almost violent snap, Hannah briskly beat the scrambled eggs. Her brows drew together in a dark frown as she yanked whole grain bread out of its plastic wrapper and shoved it rather brutally into the toaster.

"Handsome Siegfried. Handsome Siegfried," the bird announced, surveying his preened image in the cage mirror.

"I know you're handsome, Siegfried. That doesn't solve my problem."

"Love you. Love you. Love you."

"That's just it. He doesn't love me. He...he seems to want me, but he doesn't love me. He wants me to love him, Siegfried. A one-way street."

"Fantasy man. Fantasy man. Fantasy man."

"Where the hell did you learn that?" Hannah complained. Then she realized he must have picked it up from her since she had returned from Hawaii. "Look, do me a favor and don't say that in front of him, okay?"

"What shouldn't you say in front of me, Siegfried?" Jarrett's deep, lazy drawl brought Hannah's head up with a snap, and she turned to see him standing in the doorway of her sunny kitchen. His hair was intriguingly damp from the shower and his shirt was open a couple of buttons, revealing the beginnings of the crisp mat of hair she remembered so well. Below the khaki slacks he wore, his feet were bare, making him look far too comfortably at home in her kitchen.

"Never mind, he's just chattering," Hannah interrupted hastily, aware that her senses had leaped in response at the mere sight of him. What had this man done to her?

Jarrett nodded at Siegfried and then came over to the stove to drop a familiar, possessive little kiss on the nape of Hannah's neck. "Smells good. I had a feeling you'd be a good cook. Where's Erasmus?"

"He's still running around outside," Hannah mumbled, bending industriously over the eggs. What now? Should she bring up the subject of last night? Should she initiate a confrontation? Order him out of her house? Oh, Lord. She didn't know what to do. She only knew that a part of her fiercely resisted the idea of sending Jarrett away. "There's coffee on the counter over there," she heard herself say.

"Great. I could use some." Jarrett poured himself a full mug from the automatic brewing pot and began to sip it, leaning back against the counter. He watched her as she deftly stirred the eggs into the pan. "How soon can you be ready to go?"

"Go? Go where?" She floundered a bit and almost dropped the spatula she was using to stir the eggs. Steadfastly she kept her eyes focused on the frying pan, ignoring the burning heat of his gaze.

"Home," he said gently.

"I am home."

"To my home, Hannah. Honey, don't be deliberately obtuse," he added softly.

She lifted her head to glare at him. "Maybe you're the one who's being obtuse, Jarrett. Do you realize I don't even know where you live?"

He blinked like a great cat and then grinned. "That's right, you don't, do you. Things got a little hectic in Hawaii and we never had time to talk properly. I live in northern California. Along the coast. A little town just south of the Oregon border. You'll like it.''

Hannah drew a deep breath, unnerved by the satisfied self-assurance of the man. ''Jarrett, I want to make something very clear...''

The sound of the doorbell interrupted her brave words. Frowning, she went to answer it and found Charlotte Pomeroy on the front step. She was surrounded by her three kids.

''Hi, Hannah. Sorry to bother you so early in the morning. I'm on my way to drop the kids off at day care and school, and I wanted to stop by and see if you'd gone ahead and reapplied for your old job. I talked to Edith down in Personnel yesterday and she said— Oh! I didn't realize you had company.''

''Where's Erasmus?'' the oldest of the Pomeroy children demanded, looking around for the dog, who was already bounding into the front yard to greet the new arrivals. ''Come on, 'Rasmus. Let's go!'' Scott and Corrie raced off with the dog. Jimmy, the youngest, looked up pleadingly.

''Can I see Siegfried?''

Charlotte hushed him. ''Darling, you know you're not allowed to touch Siegfried.''

''Just wanna see him!'' Jimmy protested righteously.

''Come on in, Jimmy. Siegfried's in his cage. Charlotte, will you have some coffee? This is Jarrett Blade.''

''How do you do, Mr. Blade,'' Charlotte murmured, obviously fascinated by the sight of the tall man standing just behind Hannah in the doorway. ''Where did you come from? I had no idea Hannah was seeing anyone special these days...'' She let the sentence trail off questioningly as she darted a slanting glance at Hannah.

''Call me Jarrett. Hannah and I met in Hawaii.'' As if he had been entertaining other people in Hannah's kitchen for years, he poured Charlotte a cup of coffee and sat down at the table with her. ''Hannah, I think the eggs are burning.''

''Oh, Lord! The eggs!'' Flustered, Hannah quickly began to dish out breakfast, one eye on little Jimmy as he stood staring at Siegfried.

''Go right ahead and eat, you two. I won't stay long, I promise.'' Charlotte grinned. ''I'm Charlotte Pomeroy, Jarrett. I used to work with Hannah.''

"Really? I seem to be meeting a lot of Hannah's former co-workers lately."

"Who else have you met?" Charlotte demanded, surprised.

Hannah carried the plates over to the table. "Scoville came by last night," she muttered. "Jarrett arrived just after he did."

"Oh, my. That must have been interesting," Charlotte drawled.

"It was rather awkward, actually," Hannah began. She was interrupted by Jarrett.

"I think Scoville and I came to an understanding. He won't be bothering Hannah again." Calmly Jarrett attacked his eggs.

"I'd love to have seen the confrontation." Charlotte giggled. "Did Hannah tell you all about him? How he caused her to lose her job?"

"Yes. She won't have to worry about him again."

Charlotte nodded. "Because he was forced to resign himself."

"I wouldn't know about that." Jarrett shrugged, reaching for a slice of toast. "The reason Hannah won't have to worry about him is that she's coming to live with me in California."

"Hannah! Are you really?" Charlotte was suddenly all wide-eyed attention.

"Now just a minute," Hannah started and then her attention was caught by little Jimmy, who was attempting to crawl up on a plant stand to get closer to Siegfried. "Jimmy, get down from there," she admonished severely.

"Just wanna get closer," Jimmy complained, reluctantly climbing back down.

"Go 'way, kid. Go 'way, kid. Go 'way, kid." Siegfried glared down at the boy. Jimmy retreated with a sigh.

"When are you moving, Hannah?" Charlotte demanded.

It was Jarrett who answered; Hannah was too busy trying to marshal her confused responses. "I think we'll fly down today or tomorrow, depending on how long it takes Hannah to get ready. Of course, with all these pets it might be better to rent a car and drive," he said musingly.

"And don't forget the plants," Charlotte said with a wicked grin. "You can't separate Hannah from either her pets or her plants. I'm so glad she's finally settling down with a nice man. You have no idea how I'd worried about her living here with this zoo and no real family.

She needs a real home with a man and some babies, don't you think? She's very good with kids. Loves 'em.''

''Charlotte!'' Hannah's protest was little more than a squeak of outrage. It went unnoticed.

Jarrett was alrady nodding complacently as he rose to help himself to more coffee. ''My sentiments exactly. Hannah's a born mother. I'm going to give her precisely what she needs. I'm going to let her create a home for both of us. A real home.''

''Oh, Hannah, this is so exciting! Jimmy, you heard Aunt Hannah. Get down from that plant stand before it topples over. Siegfried doesn't like you to get too close. Now, Hannah, what can I do to help? You'll need someone on this end taking care of the plants you have to leave behind. You can't possibly get them all in a car. Will you be selling the furniture? I'd love to have that little inlaid plant stand Jimmy's trying to demolish.''

''Look, Charlotte, you don't understand. I'm not planning on going anywhere!''

''But Jarrett just said...''

''Don't pay any attention to him!'' Hannah rasped, rising to her feet to confront the two adults in her kitchen.

A sudden pounding on the kitchen door announced the arrival of Erasmus and the other two children. All three bounded happily into the kitchen when Jarrett promptly opened the door.

''Hannah and I have a few things still to discuss,'' Jarrett explained easily as the kids and dog sailed past him, heading for the living room. He seemed pleasantly oblivious to the growing chaos around him.

''So I see. Well, let me tell you I'm solidly on your side,'' Charlotte announced. ''Hannah needs someone like you.''

''Yes, I know.'' Jarrett smiled, his gunmetal eyes on Hannah's harried expression. ''She needs someone to take care of her.''

Charlotte laughed as Hannah sputtered. ''It's not that Hannah can't defend herself physically, of course. I mean, did she ever tell you exactly what happened between her and Doug Scoville?''

Jarrett's eyes narrowed fractionally. ''I know he tried to get her into bed.''

''He pestered her constantly until one night he actually followed her home and more or less assaulted her. The man simply couldn't believe she wasn't madly attracted to him. Hannah took care of him easily enough with her judo, but then his wife arrived on the scene and..."

"Her judo!" Jarrett interrupted in confusion. "What judo?"

"She's quite good at it," Charlotte explained in surprise. "Flattened poor Scoville right there on the living room rug. Corrie, you and Scott put down that turtle."

"I didn't know she knew judo," Jarrett said distantly, studying Hannah.

"I'd love to have seen the event. Unfortunately, it was Scoville's wife who saw it. She chose to put all the blame on Hannah. Accused Hannah of trying to seduce Scoville. Ridiculous. At any rate, she created such a fuss that Scoville asked for Hannah's resignation. Rather than work under impossible circumstances, Hannah resigned. But now she's practically got her old job in the bag. Scoville's out of the picture and Personnel wants to rehire Hannah. Corrie, I said put down that turtle!"

"Please put Herbie back," Hannah said weakly, turning to see the two children hovering over the turtle's bowl. The whole place was in chaos. She couldn't seem to think straight. Jarrett was watching her with a curious expression in his eyes. Charlotte was chattering happily about Hannah's going off to California and the three children were scurrying around noisily. Erasmus was trotting happily around the table looking for handouts and Siegfried had set up a chattering counterpoint to all the commotion around him.

"Hannah has a chance at her old job?" Jarrett asked quietly.

"Oh, yes. She'll have no trouble at all getting it back if she wants it. But I guess she won't need it now, will she?"

"No," Jarrett stated with abrupt decision. "She won't need it. She needs other things now."

"Well, I'd better get these little turkeys out of here before they do any lasting damage," Charlotte said cheerfully, finishing her coffee and quickly getting to her feet. "Come on, kids. Back in the car."

"Ah, do we have to go? Can't we stay and play here?"

"Hannah is very busy today," Charlotte informed them severely. "In the car! Hannah, I'll call you later, all right? We can talk better on the phone. Jarrett, it was lovely to meet you. Take care and drive carefully. It's going to be a long trip with all those animals and plants in the car! I don't envy you.''

Like a small whirlwind, Charlotte left the cozy little house with her family in tow. Hannah and Jarrett sat facing each other across the kitchen table as the sound of the car disappeared down the street. Slowly quiet and order returned to everything except Hannah's heart. She looked into Jarrett's unreadable eyes and desperately strove to take control of the situation.

''Jarrett, we have got to talk. This idiotic mess has gone far enough.''

''You didn't tell me you knew judo. You didn't tell me you'd flattened Scoville.''

''What's that got to do with anything?''

He looked as if he were going to say something and then changed his mind. ''Nothing. It changes nothing. Hannah, you're coming to California with me.''

''Dammit, will you listen to me? You can't just order me around like this, Jarrett! Don't you understand? I have a life of my own, and I'm not at all sure I want to abandon it for a...a...'' The words failed her, but Siegfried happily supplied them.

''Fantasy man. Fantasy man. Fantasy man.''

''I'm not a fantasy, Hannah,'' Jarrett said calmly. ''Last night was no fantasy. I can make you want me again and again.'' He leaned forward intently. ''You need me, honey. Last night in bed you admitted it.''

''That's just sex!''

''It's a start!''

''It's not enough!''

''You love me. Admit it!'' he ordered roughly.

''I'm not admitting anything!'' she blazed.

''You did last night.''

''Dammit, Jarrett, I will not allow you to railroad me into an arrangement based purely on sex!''

''It's not based purely on sex. There's a hell of a lot more involved than that,'' he bit out savagely.

''Is that so? Then prove it!'' she challenged recklessly without pausing to think.

"How?" he countered at once, startling her. His eyes were almost silver as he regarded her across the short distance of the table.

She ought to slow down and think about what she was saying, Hannah realized. But there was no stopping the impulsive words that sprang to her lips. She had been driven too far. "If you're not just interested in a short affair based strictly on sex, then let's hear you invite me down to California for an affair without any sex!"

"What?" Jarrett surged to his feet, filling her kitchen with menace and sudden, vast, masculine annoyance. "What the devil are you talking about?"

"You heard me," she managed bravely. "If you're offering something more than a sexual affair, you can damn well prove it. Do you want friendship? Companionship? A home? What do you want, Jarrett? If it's not just sex you're after, tell me what it is you do want."

"Dammit, I'm not looking for a platonic affair!" he raged, gripping the back of the chair in which he had been sitting. "And neither are you! You like what we have together in bed, whether or not you'll admit it! You don't want to give it up any more than I do!"

"I can give it up. Can you? Or is that really all you want from me?"

"You little witch! Do you honestly think I'd chase all over the Northwest after you just for the sake of a roll in the sack?" he shot back brutally.

"I don't know," she cried. "I honestly don't know what you'd do for sex. Because I don't know you very well at all, do I, Jarrett Blade? That's my whole point, damn you! I don't know you! Yet you're asking me to give up everything to come and have an affair with you. Who the hell do you think you are?"

"I'm the man who's going to take care of you!" he gritted.

"But I don't need you to take care of me! I've got a good job waiting for me. I can handle men like Scoville with my judo. I have enough common sense not to let people use me, in spite of what you think. I've been existing very nicely for twenty-nine years and I can go on just as pleasantly. No matter how good you are in bed, you're not going to lure me to California with sex!"

"You're not making any sense!" he raged. "You're saying you'll come to California for a non-sexual affair even though you like what we have in bed. But when I offer you sex, you say you won't come with me? You're crazy, woman!"

"Which only goes to show how little you know about me!"

He shot her a furious glance as he strode to the kitchen doorway. "I know a hell of a lot more about you than you seem to realize, little hellcat." He paused in the doorway, confronting her with the full impact of his intimidating presence. "I know you're going to regret this little scene the minute I walk out that door. When I'm back in California and you're up here alone except for this zoo, you're going to think a lot about what you've thrown away. You're a passionate woman, Hannah Prescott. I don't think you realized just *how* passionate until you met me, did you?"

"Jarrett!"

"You're behaving like an emotional little fool, and I'm going to teach you a lesson. I'm going back to California this morning and I'm going to let you simmer for a while. I'm going to let you think about it for a time and then I'll call you up and see if you've changed your mind. I'm betting you will change your mind, Hannah. I'm betting I know you a whole lot better than you know yourself."

"Jarrett, wait!"

He was already in the bedroom, pulling on his shoes. She arrived at the door in time to see him finish tying the laces. "Wait for what, Hannah? More of your crazy ideas?"

"Jarrett, if you would just listen to me..."

"I have been listening. And all I've been hearing is nonsense." He straightened and came toward her. She backed nervously down the hall in front of him. He reached into his hip pocket for the car keys. "An affair without any sex. Talk about nonsense! You can't hold out five minutes when I decide to seduce you. Admit that much, at least, Hannah. Don't be a complete hypocrite!"

"I...I know I can't," she whispered sadly as he backed her down the hall and into the living room. "That's why you'd have to give me your word you wouldn't attempt to seduce me. You'd have to promise to keep your end of the bargain. Jarrett... Oh!"

The exclamation came out as he suddenly walked her right back against the wall and caged her with his arms. Hannah swallowed nervously as she found herself looking up into Jarrett's glowering face.

"Going to try your judo on me?" he challenged coolly. "I'll warn you right now that I've had a lot of karate training. Shall we see who can flatten whom?"

"Jarrett, please, you're being unreasonable," she got out through dry lips.

"I'm being unreasonable?" he echoed in astonishment. "I'm behaving with an amazing amount of restraint under the circumstances! I ought to turn you over my knee and then take you to bed. But I think you need a more effective lesson than that. You need a little time to realize what you're throwing away."

"I'm only asking for a little time to find out if we really have something meaningful together," Hannah pleaded, knowing that the whole situation was disintegrating and there was nothing she could do about it. Tears already threatened to close her throat, but she would not give in to them. Not yet. There would be plenty of time after Jarrett Blade had left.

"I'll give you that time," he snarled. "You can spend it alone, though. I think you'll be able to come to a much quicker conclusion that way." He straightened suddenly and stalked to the door, flinging it open. "If you change your mind before I get around to calling you, here's my number." He yanked his thin wallet out of his pocket and extracted a small white card. He tossed it down on the nearest plant stand.

Before Hannah could peel herself away from the wall, he was gone, the door slammed shut behind him. Erasmus stood at attention, ears cocked, listening as Jarrett drove off. Herbie poked his head out of his shell, where he had taken refuge.

But it was Siegfried who made the most intelligent statement concerning the situation.

"Fantasy man. Fantasy man. Fantasy man," he chanted in a subdued tone.

Eight

Dammit, she didn't need him. Not the way he had thought. He had been so certain...

Bitterly Jarrett returned the rental car at the airport and started the trek from one airline counter to the next, trying to find a flight back to California. It didn't take long. He was soon on his way. But as he settled back into the seat, waving aside the scrambled eggs being offered on the breakfast flight, he began to question his usually sound judgment.

How had he mismanaged things so badly? It wasn't like him. He generally had everything neatly under control in his life. But he'd never dealt with a woman like Hannah Prescott. Dammit! He'd been so determined to handle her correctly this time around. No more mistakes.

But he'd sure made a huge error assuming that she needed him. The truth was that she really seemed to get along fine on her own. Judo. His mouth curved downward in dismay. Who would have guessed that a soft little woman like Hannah knew enough judo to throw Scoville on his back? And it sounded as if she had her old job back if she wanted it. Her home was cozy and comfortable. It didn't seem to need a man in it at all.

The only place he seemed to fit was in her bed, and she didn't even

want that! A platonic affair, she said! Of all the stupid, idiotic, point-
less exercises in frustration!

Jarrett accepted coffee from the hostess and studied the seat-back in
front of him. An affair without any sex. Why the hell would she want
that? Sex seemed to be about all she needed from him. It didn't make
any sense.

Face it, Blade, he gritted silently, it's not that you couldn't make
yourself abide by her terms for a while, although it would be tough.
It's that you're afraid to abide by them.

Now he was getting to the truth of the matter, he realized with
disgust. He was afraid to grant Hannah's crazy request because he
would be denying himself the one hold he did have on her.

Why was it so important that he maintain that claim?

Maybe *he* was the one who needed *her*.

That thought sent a cold chill down his back. Grimly Jarrett requested another cup of hot coffee. If it wasn't for the fact that it was
only nine-thirty in the morning, he'd have asked for something a lot
stronger.

It took more willpower than Hannah could possibly have guessed
to pull herself back together after the scene the morning Jarrett left. It
was harder this time than it had been when she had left him in Hawaii—harder because she had acknowledged her love for him.

For an entire week following his abrupt departure she made herself
go through the motions of day-to-day routine. She saw her friends,
watered her plants, chatted with her animals. And she tried her
damnedest not to give in to the tears or the pain.

What good was a relationship with the man of her dreams if it wasn't
founded on something far more solid than a sexual liaison? Over and
over again she asked herself that question, and always she seemed to
be left hanging without a reassuring answer.

Charlotte phoned toward the end of the week, not for the first time,
demanding to know why she was still in town.

"You're crazy not to go to him, you know that, don't you? You're
not going to get a better offer, my girl. Take him up on it!" her friend
urged.

"Thanks! I'm really not doing all that badly on my own, you know," Hannah retorted caustically.

"Hah! Just remember what I said about starting your family soon. Harry and I already had Corrie and Scott by the time I was your age."

"Charlotte, I don't want to discuss this."

"I hear from Personnel that they've made you an offer. Going to take it instead of heading for California?"

"Probably. They increased my salary considerably. I'd be a fool not to take it." Hannah sighed.

"I would have said the same thing last week. But now I know you've got a better offer."

"An affair? With a man I hardly know? A man who keeps insisting I need him and that I love him but who doesn't need or love me? That's a better offer?"

"Calm down. You're getting excited."

"You're damn right I'm getting excited! I'm about at my wit's end! The only man I've been really attracted to in years wants only an affair, and my best friend is encouraging me to go through with it!"

"Hannah, do you want to spend the rest of your life talking to a turtle and a parakeet and a dog?"

"Why not? At least I know where I stand with them. They need me!"

"And you don't think your fantasy man does?" Charlotte shot back.

"No, frankly, I don't. If he does, he isn't capable of admitting it. Besides, I want more than that, Charlotte. I want to be loved. Really loved," Hannah whispered morosely. "I want it all."

"Sometimes a woman has to take what she can get," Charlotte lectured cryptically.

"You're a fine one to talk. Three beautiful children, a good job, and a loving, supportive husband. Don't tell me I've got to take less than that."

"All right, Hannah. I'll back off. But promise me you'll think about it, okay? I liked Jarrett Blade. There was something about him that made me think he'd be good for you."

"You figured that out from meeting him one morning over breakfast?"

Hannah hung up the phone a few minutes later with a feeling of being greatly put upon. She looked at Erasmus, who was dozing at her feet. "I don't even know if his offer is still open," she whispered sadly. "He never called as he said he would, Erasmus."

She reached into Herbie's bowl and plucked him out just as the phone rang again. Hannah was still holding Herbie at eye level, about to tell him what a fine-looking turtle he was when she said hello rather absently into the receiver.

"Hannah?"

The sound of Jarrett's voice nearly made her drop Herbie. "Jarrett!" Carefully she set down Herbie, then she lowered herself rather shakily into the nearest chair. "Jarrett?"

This was it, Hannah thought. He was going to make his magnanimous offer again after letting her suffer for a week. Of all the arrogant nerve! Of all the chauvinistic, outrageous, masculine nerve! What in the world was she going to do?

"Hannah, I'm calling to see if you'll come to California," Jarrett said quietly, without any emotion at all that Hannah could detect. "I'll accept your terms."

It was a good thing she had put down Herbie, Hannah realized vaguely. She surely would have dropped him by this time. "My terms?" she managed weakly.

"We'll try it your way for a while." There was a lengthy pause during which Hannah tried to corral her racing thoughts. And then Jarrett asked coolly, "Hannah? Will you come?"

She answered before she could stop to think. "I'll come, Jarrett. I'll be there in a couple of days."

There was a beat of silence on the other end of the line. "I'll fly up and drive down with you," Jarrett finally announced gruffly.

"No, no that won't be necessary, Jarrett. I'd prefer to drive down by myself. It's only an overnight trip. I'll...I'll see you day after tomorrow."

God, they were discussing this as if it were a casual holiday trip. What on earth did she think she was doing? But it was done. Jarrett had actually told her to come on her own terms. Hannah said goodbye after another long pause during which neither of them seemed to be able to say anything intelligent. And then she threw herself back into the chair and regarded her pets.

"We're going to California, pals. Don't ask me why. I'm not sure myself. But we're going."

But the next morning, as she got behind the wheel of her little compact, Hannah knew exactly why she was going to California with Herbie and Erasmus and Siegfried and Yolanda and Ludmilla. She was going because she was letting herself dare to hope.

The hope was that Jarrett Blade had discovered he needed her for some other reason than to warm his bed.

Somewhere after crossing the Oregon border it did occur to her to wonder whether or not he'd lied in order to get her to California. But Hannah only took her foot off the pedal for a few seconds at the thought.

"He wouldn't lie to me," she told her passengers. Erasmus, who was sitting in the front seat beside her, whimpered in agreement. There was an even more dangerous possibility, Hannah admitted silently, and that was that she might be lying to herself. Jarrett Blade seemed to be a law unto himself. He appeared to make his own rules as he went along, and if she deluded herself into thinking he was capable of needing more from a woman than just sex, she would have only herself to blame when she got hurt in the end.

Even as the mountainous scenery of Interstate 5 through Oregon unfolded outside the car's windows, however, Hannah knew she no longer had a choice. She was committed.

Hannah and her passengers spent the night near Medford, Oregon, and the next morning they made their way over to the coast and Highway 101. From there they wound their way down the picturesque California coastline until Hannah found the small town Jarrett had named on the phone.

The place would have made a charming watercolor scene, she mused as she guided the little car through the center of town. It had been a major fishing village once, and boats of all kinds still thronged the harbor. Some were still working craft, but many were clearly pleasure boats. Did Jarrett sail? Hannah sighed. Just one more thing she didn't know about the man.

Through the weatherbeaten town and out along the cliffs on the far side, she carefully followed Jarrett's terse directions. The house, when she finally found it, was not quite what she'd expected. Or then again, perhaps it was. It did, after all, fit Jarrett very well.

Isolated, weathered, and strong-looking, it, too, would have made an interesting watercolor. It seemed rather large for a man who lived alone, Hannah thought as she brought the car to a halt in the curving drive and studied the place for a moment before climbing out. It was two stories high, and she wondered what he did with all the extra space. The only really inviting aspect was the huge porch that wrapped the old place. Now, in summer, it would be a very comfortable area to sit and watch the sea at sundown. Jarrett really ought to put a nice porch swing on that veranda, she said to herself. And a garden out back might be nice too....

Hannah threw open the car door and got out, reaching for Herbie's bowl as she did so. Erasmus bounded out behind her and instantly began exploring the new terrain. Hannah was opening the backseat door and reaching inside for Siegfried's cage when she heard Jarrett's voice.

''Hannah!''

She whirled, cage in one hand and Herbie in the other, and suddenly she felt horribly nervous. Jarrett stood on the porch, devouring the sight of her as if he couldn't quite understand what she was doing there. His hard face was carved in intent, harsh lines and the gunmetal eyes were shadowed and smoky. He was dressed in a pair of khaki slacks, as usual, and the sleeves on his khaki shirt were rolled up to reveal his sinewy arms. The breeze off the ocean caught and ruffled his hair as he stood, hands braced on the porch railing, and regarded her.

Hannah bit her lip and wondered what the hell she was doing there. Dressed in a casual white shirt and sandals, and jeans that hugged her rounded figure, she felt awkward and uncertain. Even the prim, coiled braids on her head didn't supply the regal arrogance she wanted to use in self-defense.

For a long moment they simply stared at each other. Only Erasmus seemed at ease. He skittered around Jarrett, barking loudly. The spell between the two humans was broken when Jarrett finally reached down to pat the dog on the head.

"Hello, Hannah. I was getting worried," Jarrett began slowly as he came down the steps.

What was he thinking? Hannah swallowed and then rushed into conversation in an effort to cover her nervousness. Clutching Herbie's bowl and Siegfried's cage, she started forward.

"Actually, I was getting a little worried myself. The only motel I could find last night had a huge 'No Pets' sign up, and I had to smuggle Erasmus and Herbie and Siegfried inside when no one was looking. Then this morning when I let Erasmus out for a few minutes a maid spotted us and I thought we were done for. I had visions of having to leave Oregon on the lam or, worse, having to phone you for bail bond money for these three. Fortunately we managed to escape. I think the maid had second thoughts about turning us all in. Where shall I put Herbie?"

She breezed into the house, aware that Jarrett was right behind her, and stopped short. Before she could speak, however, Jarrett said softly, "I wasn't worried so much that you might be in jail as I was that you'd changed your mind altogether about coming, Hannah," he said gently.

Hannah ignored the statement, surveying the room in which she found herself with startled horror. "Good grief! It looks like a museum!"

Glass cases seemed to line every wall. Countless pots, statues, carvings, masks, and textiles were displayed behind the glass. At the far end a wall full of intimidating tomes completed the scene. In between there was a formal grouping of dark, heavy furniture.

"You can put Herbie down on that end table," Jarrett said abruptly, taking the turtle's bowl from her hand. "And maybe Siegfried could go over there." He indicated the top of a glass case. "Hannah? Are you all right? What's the matter?"

"Nothing. Nothing at all. it's just that I don't see how you can live with all these museum pieces around you." Hannah shook herself and then obediently carried Siegfried over to the glass counter.

"Most of these things have never seen the inside of a museum," Jarrett growled, watching her with a frown. "This is a private collection. Very private."

"Oh." Hannah stared around her. It figured. Her fantasy man lived in a private museum filled with pre-Columbian artifacts. She must be crazy to think she could change a man who preferred the company of the dead past to the living present. For a few seconds she was almost overcome with doubt. Then Siegfried interrupted her grim thoughts.

"New home. New home. New home," he announced happily, bouncing back and forth along his perch.

Hannah grimaced and set him down over a carving of a leering god. "He, uh, picked that up from me on the trip down," she explained in a mumble.

Jarrett came forward suddenly, taking her shoulders in a firm grip and turning her to face him. "Hannah, is that how you think of this place? As a new home?"

"Well, uh, yes, I suppose I do." She wiped her damp palms on her jeans and lifted her chin proudly. "Of course, it's going to need a great deal of work to turn this old museum of yours into a home, but I'll see what can be done. In the meantime, which is my room?" She looked him directly in the eye as she asked that question.

Jarrett hesitated. "You've very sure this is the way you want it?"

"I'm sure."

"For how long, Hannah?"

"Until I change my mind," she retorted firmly. "Which room, Jarrett?"

He held her for a moment longer and then released her. "Second door at the top of the stairs. I, uh, put some fresh sheets on the bed this morning."

Hannah blinked, touched. "Why, thank you. I'll just get my suitcases from the car..."

"I'll get them for you."

"Actually, if you really want to do me a favor"—she grinned suddenly—"you can bring in Ludmilla and Yolanda. I couldn't bear to leave them behind with the others. They're like family, you see. But they weigh a ton each, and I'd much rather carry the suitcases."

"I'll get the plants."

A polite, uncertain wariness hovered between Hannah and Jarrett for the rest of the day. Only the animals seemed quite content. Jarrett was treating her almost as a guest, Hannah realized. He showed her around the rambling old house, took her for a walk on the beach, and stood watching from the doorway when she unpacked her suitcases.

Dinner was a studied, exquisitely polite affair. Hannah cooked it, directing Jarrett to make the salad and pour the wine. "This is good stuff," she approved, sampling the excellent California vintage she was drinking. "Do you have a wine cellar stashed somewhere among all this old junk?" The wine had helped remove some of her nervousness.

Jarrett paused in the act of forking his asparagus. "I have a small cellar down in the basement."

"Well, that's something at least," Hannah mumbled.

"I don't exactly consider these things 'junk,'" he went on carefully.

"Yes, well, as we discovered in Hawaii, junk is in the eye of the beholder, isn't it?" Hannah retorted. She polished off the last of her wine and held out her glass for more. She had the feeling she was going to need it. The task that lay ahead of her was daunting in the extreme.

After dinner he gallantly showed her into the living room and poured her a glass of brandy. Then her gaze fell on the wall of books at the far end of the room. "Are all those books about pre-Columbian art?" she asked.

"Most of them, yes."

"How unfortunate. I didn't bring anything with me to read. I was rather hoping you might have a few racy thrillers lying around somewhere. Who would have guessed there were so many books about these old bits of pottery? Where did you get them all, Jarrett?"

His mouth curved wryly. "One or two of them I wrote," he said softly.

Hannah snapped her head around to stare at him as he sat down beside her on the sofa. "You wrote them? Good heavens. I think I'm impressed."

"Coming from you, that's a compliment." He sipped his brandy and watched her over the rim of the glass.

"Is that how you make a living? Writing books about all these artifacts?" She waved a hand at the contents of the glass cases. "I've just realized I have no clear idea of your work, Jarrett." Actually, she'd realized that much earlier, but she hadn't known quite how to bring up the subject.

"Among other things. I also do occasional appraisals."

"For whom?" She frowned.

"I act as a consultant for museums and, very rarely, Customs."

"No kidding? What else do you do? I mean, is there enough money in that to enable you to indulge your, uh, hobby?"

"Collecting pre-Columbian art is not exactly my hobby," Jarrett said gently.

"No, it's your passion, isn't it?" she sighed. "Well, what else do you do besides write books about it and consult?"

"Occasionally I take on certain jobs," he said slowly.

"What sort of jobs?" she demanded.

"Jobs like the one that took me to Hawaii."

Hannah chewed on her lower lip. "I see. You help people recover lost or stolen pre-Columbian art?"

"Sometimes."

'And there's enough money in all that to keep you in old bits and pieces of junk?" She grinned.

"I get by," he drawled. "Of course, now that I have a few extra mouths to feed, I might have to do a bit more consulting. Or a little dealing. That's something else I do. I act as a broker for private collectors."

Hannah seized on the one point that mattered to her. "About these extra mouths..."

"You don't have to worry, honey. I told you I was not a poor man. I'm not outrageously wealthy by any means, but I can take care of you and the zoo." Jarrett absently reached down to his feet to fondle Erasmus's ears. The dog stretched out blissfully.

"Jarrett," Hannah began determinedly, "I don't want you to think that we're all going to move in here and mooch off you. As soon as we find out whether or not this...this relationship of ours is going to work out, I'll get a job."

"No." He sipped his brandy.

Hannah's brows came together in a firm line. "Of course I will. I've worked ever since I got out of college. I don't intend to stop now. Besides, as you pointed out, there are a lot of mouths to feed here. You shouldn't have to be responsible for the ton of dog food Erasmus eats!"

"I can afford you and Herbie and Erasmus and the bird. There's no need for you to work."

Hannah drew in her breath and let it out slowly. "Be reasonable, Jarrett. We don't have any idea how well our *association* is going to work out. Sooner or later you'll probably get tired of me or I'll knock over one of your precious pots and you'll strangle me. One way or another this relationship could be terminated abruptly. Frankly, I don't want to find myself stranded without a job. And it's difficult to get back into the work force once you've been out of it for a while. I'd rather keep working."

"We can discuss it later."

"What on earth is the problem? I knew you were domineering and chauvinistic, but somehow I didn't think you were going to be this primitive!" she stormed.

His mouth hardened. "Can't you just trust me? I can take care of you."

"You're missing the point! Women these days work. You can't have spent your entire life buried in a pre-Columbian grave!"

"We'll discuss it some other time," he told her tightly.

Hannah groaned and swallowed the remainder of her brandy. "This is hopeless, isn't it? I don't know what I'm doing here. I should be back in Seattle getting ready to restart my old job."

"It's too late for that, Hannah. You're here." Jarrett's dark voice was like a slab of granite. Inflexible, unmoving, as certain as time. "And now that you are here, how long do you intend to keep up this game you're making us play?"

Hannah stiffened. "It's not a game, Jarrett."

"Are you afraid of me?" he pressed more gently. "Afraid of what I can make you feel?" His eyes were suddenly warm now, smoky and molten. Hopeful?

"Of course not!"

"Then why deny us both what we want?" Jarrett put down his brandy glass and stroked her cheek with his finger.

"Jarrett, you promised..."

"I'm not going to make love to you. I only want to know how long you're going to make me wait?" he murmured. "A day or two? A week?"

"I can't put a time limit on it!" she gasped.

"You expect me to wait indefinitely?"

"Jarrett, you agreed to this," she protested weakly, aware that if he decided to seduce her tonight she would be helpless to resist. "I trusted you."

He dropped his hand and sank back into the corner of the couch, some of the warmth leaving his eyes. "Is that how you plan to keep me in line? By reminding me that you had my word on this crazy arrangement?"

"If that's what it takes."

"Hannah, I won't wait forever. You do understand that?"

"I don't see why not," she rallied bravely. "You're accustomed to dealing in terms of centuries. Just look at all these old things. You're obviously quite capable of waiting for what you want. I'll bet you waited years before you acquired some of the choicer bits and pieces of this collection."

"I won't wait years for you, honey. I'm not at all sure I'll even wait a few weeks. A few days is probably more likely. I won't let you keep me dangling."

"Then why in hell did you invite me to come down here in the first place?" she blazed furiously. "I thought we had an agreement. We're supposed to be getting to know each other."

"Two weeks. At the end of two weeks we settle this issue."

"Says who?" she gritted.

"I say so," he countered mildly. "I want a woman, Hannah. Not a houseguest."

She narrowed her eyes and said nothing, but he must have sensed exactly what she was thinking.

"Going to run, Hannah? You tried that once before, remember? I'll find you again, just as I did last time."

"Threats, Jarrett?" she scoffed tiredly. "Is that the only way you know how to handle a woman? With threats?"

He blinked and frowned, and she was startled to realize that what she'd said had apparently made some kind of impact. He surged to his feet and stalked across the room to pour himself another shot of brandy. "Why don't you tell me the best way to handle a modern woman? A woman who doesn't really need a man."

She stared at him, perplexed. "I don't understand, Jarrett."

He leaned back against the wall and studied the brandy in his glass. "It's a simple enough question. And I freely admit I may not be the world's best at handling the female of the species. After all, I managed to blow my first marriage."

"I see." Hannah didn't, but she couldn't think of anything else to say.

"She was a modern woman. A beautiful, intelligent woman with a good career as the director of a museum. I met her when I first got into the art market. Elaine had everything. She didn't need men; she just used them. Used them to climb her way up to the directorship of a fine museum. Used them to obtain large foundation grants. Used them to escort her to the best parties and the best places. Used them to start her own private collection."

Hannah held her breath. "And in what ways did she use you, Jarrett?"

His mouth twisted. "All of the above. I introduced her to important and influential collectors. I helped her get that directorship. I escorted her when she needed escorting and I helped her obtain some very fine pieces for her own collection. We were married for about a year and then she met a far more important collector. One who had the backing of a huge, privately endowed foundation. One who moved in the best possible circles. She even used me to get the introduction to him. And then she filed for a divorce."

"Oh, Jarrett," Hannah whispered.

"I didn't threaten her, Hannah. I didn't lay down the law. I played the role of the modern, supportive husband. I helped her in every way I could. I agreed to hold off having children. I agreed to her extended, out-of-town business trips. Eventually I agreed to a divorce. No-fault variety."

"And now you're afraid of making the same mistakes in handling me that you made in handling your ex-wife, is that it? But it's not a question of *handling* people, Jarrett. It's a question of different kinds of personalities. You can't make comparisons between me and your ex-wife. We're two different women!"

He looked up from the golden brandy, and to her surprise he was smiling faintly. "That's what I decided in Hawaii. I thought you were different. That you needed a man. Specifically, that you needed me. Now I'm not so sure. But one thing is still certain, God help me. I still want you. Regardless of what kind of woman you are or whether I learn to handle you properly, I want you.'' He downed the last of his brandy and set the glass on a nearby table. ''So you're only getting two weeks of this crazy, sex-free affair. It's all I can stand. After that, if you're still here in my house we'll do things my way. Good night, Hannah.''

He walked past her as she watched helplessly, then paused on the bottom step. ''By the way. I have a rather unique security system set on the display cases. I turn it on at night. Don't ever try to get into the cases without making sure I've switched it off. Understand?'' He climbed the stairs without waiting for an answer. A moment later a door closed behind him.

''Fantasy man. Fantasy man. Fantasy man.''

''Shut up, Siegfried.'' Hannah roused herself from the sofa, found the birdcage cover, and silenced the parakeet by putting him to bed for the night. Beside her, Erasmus yawned. ''I suppose it's time I let you out, isn't it?'' Hannah noted.

She opened the door, and the dog trotted happily outside. Then she shut it behind him. It was nippy out there. Morosely she regarded the glass cases around her. ''What am I doing here?'' she asked herself again. She walked gingerly to the end of the room and surveyed the heavy volumes in the bookcase. ''Not a thriller in the bunch. How dull.''

But at the end of one shelf she found two with the name ''J. Blade'' on their spines. Overcome by curiosity, she pulled one of them down and flipped open the heavily bound cover. It appeared to be a discussion of certain aspects of Peruvian pre-Columbian art.

Maybe what she needed was a better understanding of the man she had fallen in love with, Hannah decided. And maybe there were some keys to be found in his writing. She lowered herself back onto the sofa and turned to the introductory chapter.

Twenty minutes later she roused herself from a discussion of the Chavín culture to let Erasmus inside. He settled down on the rug, and Hannah returned to the book.

Jarrett wrote very well, she was forced to acknowledge. In spite of her lack of interest in the topic, she found herself becoming fascinated with the tiny glimpses afforded into an ancient culture by its artifacts. Obviously, for Jarrett those glimpses were enough to inspire a lasting passion. The photographs of the sometimes charming, sometimes elegant, and sometimes grotesque art were beautifully arranged to complement the text. Slowly the sketchy story of great cultures unfolded.

It was after midnight when she turned a page to find a chapter on erotic pre-Columbian art. For a moment she was disconcerted by the unabashedly sexual aspect of the objects in the photographs and even more unnerved by Jarrett's accompanying text. She was certainly no prude, but somehow one expected a bit more prudery from such an ancient culture. On the other hand, Hannah decided with a grin, this aspect of art certainly underlined the consistency of human nature no matter what the era!

Jarrett's text seemed to acknowledge the fundamentally human quality of the artifacts. It treated the subject with both humor and respect. Hannah found herself admitting that there were more elemental human ties between a long-dead culture and the present than she would once have believed.

Reluctantly she closed the book halfway through and got to her feet with a wide yawn. The house seemed very quiet now. Erasmus and Siegfried and Herbie were all asleep. Yolanda and Ludmilla nodded in a corner near the window. No sounds had come from Jarrett's room for hours. It was time to go to bed.

Walking to the bookcase, Hannah replaced the volume she had been reading and turned to glance idly into the glass case nearby. Perhaps if she tried she might find something interesting in Jarrett's collection now that she had begun studying his book. She would be careful not to open the case.

But the first item that caught her eye wasn't in the glass case; it was sitting on top. It was the beautifully shaped shell she had found on the beach and given to Jarrett the night they baby-sat for little Danny.

Hannah's first reaction was one of disbelief. Slowly she picked it up and examined it. Jarrett had saved it. He'd actually carried the worthless little shell all the way home from Hawaii and found a place of honor for it near his priceless collection of ancient art. She could hardly believe it.

"Oh, Jarrett," she whispered, "maybe it's not so hopeless after all. Maybe you and I can find a way to make this relationship work. You must have felt something for me to make you save the shell. Something more than desire."

It was such a small thing on which to base so much hope.

Carefully Hannah set down the shell. Then she caught a familiar gleam of gold out of the corner of her eye. Instantly she froze.

She didn't want to acknowledge what she was seeing. Hannah stared at the statue under the glass and tried desperately to tell herself that the goddess she was looking at couldn't possibly be the same one that had caused her so much trouble in Hawaii.

But it was, and she knew it. The golden fertility goddess crouched now in Jarrett Blade's private collection. It had obviously never been returned to its rightful owner.

Jarrett had lied.

Nine

During the week that followed her arrival in Jarrett's home, Hannah felt as though she were walking a tight-rope. At least three times each day she vowed she would confront him on the subject of the golden fertility goddess, and each time she lost her nerve.

She wasn't exactly certain why she lost her nerve. It had something to do with not wanting to have her worst suspicions confirmed, Hannah decided. If she pretended she'd never seen the goddess, she could go on pretending that Jarrett had been honest about what he intended to do with the statue. Maybe there was a perfectly legitimate explanation.

Maybe.

In the meantime she threw herself into creating a comfortable home out of the stuffy museum in which Jarrett lived. He watched the process with a kind of fascinated wariness. Occasionally he put his foot down.

"No, we are not moving that case full of textiles over by the window," he announced when she made known her intention to do so.

"But the colors in the cloth will be much more interesting in sunlight than over here in this dark corner with that funny lamp shining on them. We need some color over there, anyway."

"If you want color, put Siegfried over there. Not my textiles. The

sunlight will fade them. Why the hell do you think I have them illuminated with that special lamp in the first place?''

"Oh. Well, how about that case of cute little pots? They'd look very
nice over there standing under Yolanda and Ludmilla. In fact, we could
plant some ferns in them. They'd made ideal planters!''

"Planters! My Nazca pots? Are you out of your mind? If you dare
put one single fern in any of those pots, I'll stuff you into one!''

"Really, Jarrett, you don't have to get so emotional about them,''
Hannah declared huffily as she wielded a feather duster along a book-
shelf. "I'm just trying to brighten the place up a bit.''

There was a pause behind her as she stood on tiptoe to dust the top
of one of his books. Then Jarrett stepped up behind her and encircled
her waist with both of his strong hands. "Believe me, Hannah, you
brighten this place up all by yourself,'' he told her roughly, dropping
a quick kiss on the nape of her neck.

If she tried she could see the goddess out of the corner of her eye.
Hannah steadfastly refused to glance at it. Instead she let herself enjoy
the feel of Jarrett's hands on her waist. The duster froze in her hand.

"I...I've been reading one of the books you wrote,'' she confided
in a tone she hoped was casual.

He nuzzled the curve of her shoulder. "Really? Did you find the
section on erotic art?''

"Jarrett!'' She flushed vividly, flustered.

"Want to see some prime examples? I've got some excellent pieces
in that case over there by Herbie's bowl.''

"Jarrett Blade!'' And then Hannah's sense of humor got the better
of her. "I suppose it does beat the old line about viewing your etch-
ings,'' she giggled. "But I do wonder what it's doing to poor Herbie
to have to be in such close proximity to that sort of thing.''

"I don't think too much bothers Herbie.'' Jarrett released her.
"What's for lunch?''

"Egg sandwiches. I thought we could take them down to the beach
and have a picnic.''

"Sounds great. I'll dig out some wine.''

In spite of Jarrett's nervous complaints and cautions, Hannah managed to rearrange his home to her satisfaction. She made him drive
her to the local nursery so that she could purchase several more house-

plants to keep Yolanda and Ludmilla company. She shifted the glass cases around so that they appeared more eclectically arranged, not lined up museum-style. A few ferns draped over the top of the glass helped soften the formal look of the cases she discovered. Herbie and Siegfried and Erasmus also added comforting, cozy touches to the place. Hannah made certain that evening meals were accompanied by wine and candlelight and plenty of conversation, even though the discussions generally tended to be about pre-Columbian art. She replaced a couple of dark old paintings that Jarrett declared no interest in at all with mirrors strategically arranged to expand the ocean view and lighten the living room.

All in all, she and the animals had settled in very nicely by the end of the week. When he wasn't following her around, keeping an eye on her, Jarrett worked in his den outlining a new volume on Nazca pottery. Occasionally she heard him making phone calls during which he discussed pre-Columbian art and not much else. At least there were no phone calls to women, Hannah consoled herself.

But there were problems, too. For one thing there was the two-week deadline hanging over her head. Oh, she could leave easily enough before the two weeks were up, Hannah supposed, but she wasn't at all certain she'd have the willpower to do so when the time came. It was unfair of Jarrett to impose the deadline.

And there were the problems associated with the little golden goddess. Every time Hannah passed the case which contained the statue she gritted her teeth. Not only did the fertility goddess raise questions about Jarrett's business activities, she raised some rather personal questions as well. Each time Hannah passed the case that held the goddess, she found herself counting days. And every day now was another day too many.

"Damn you, if I'm pregnant I'm going to melt you down and turn you into a necklace," she hissed at the goddess toward the end of the week. The complication of pregnancy was all she needed, she told herself. There were so many things to be straightened out between herself and Jarrett. She'd always wanted a family, but she hadn't planned to start one in quite this fashion!

But the one factor that made her most anxious was the question of how Jarrett really felt toward her.

She thought she knew what he wanted from her now. He didn't appear to mind what she was doing to his house. He ate her food with relish. He seemed to enjoy the walks on the beach and he was genuinely fond of Herbie, Siegfried, and Erasmus. He was even polite to Yolanda and Ludmilla. Yes, Hannah told herself, he seemed to want the comfortable, cozy home she was trying to create.

And he wanted her in his bed.

There was no doubt now in her mind that Jarrett Blade had been a lonely, self-contained man for most of his life. He wanted affection, even love, although the only way he knew how to ask for it was in a high-handed, brusquely arrogant style.

But he was also deeply wary of making a woman his equal, his partner in a relationship. Jarrett had to have the security of being needed. He wanted to know that she depended on him. It was the only way he could feel certain of her.

Yes, she was beginning to understand what he wanted. But Hannah wasn't at all certain of what he had to offer in return.

At the end of the first week Hannah took special pains with dinner.

"Our first anniversary?" Jarrett joked as he surveyed the grilled salmon with lemon butter and the hot spinach salad.

Hannah felt a little goaded by the remark. "Why not? There may never be another."

He looked up, the humor fading from his eyes. "You mean you might not be here at the end of next week?"

She couldn't quite face the directness of the question. "If I am it will be your turn to cook the anniversary dinner," she mumbled, reaching for her chilled Chardonnay wine.

"It will be my pleasure since I'll know I'll be having you for dessert," he drawled.

"You're deliberately trying to bait me," she accused.

He shrugged. "Perhaps. Maybe I don't like this period of uncertainty any better than you do."

"I'm getting by just fine!"

"Well, I'm not. I lie in bed at night and think of how you would look lying in my arms. I dream of undressing you and carrying you naked up the stairs to my bedroom. I wake up needing a cold shower in the middle of the night. I spend countless hours planning ways to seduce you when the two weeks are over.''

''I had no idea sex occupied so much of a man's thinking!'' Hannah tossed back spiritedly. ''It's amazing the male of the species has so much time for earning a living or making war or playing golf!''

''We're a versatile lot.''

''So are women,'' she shot back smoothly. ''Which is why modern women don't take kindly to being confined to the bedroom and the kitchen. It's why they want and need a few more opportunities and choices in life.''

''Are we going to argue on our first anniversary?'' Jarrett murmured.

Hannah sighed. ''I give up. You really won't discuss it, will you?''

''Anything else but the changing role of the family,'' he quipped, giving her one of his rarest, most charming smiles. ''I have a question for you, though, on a related subject.''

She eyed him suspiciously. ''Yes?''

''Why haven't you ever married? There must be plenty of men around who would be more than happy to give you the kind of marriage you want.''

''What kind of marriage do you think I want, Jarrett?'' she countered earnestly.

He hesitated. ''You've implied you want a modern arrangement. Lots of independence. No strong economic ties. No dependence on a man. A partnership with sex.''

''That's not quite what I want,'' she told him carefully. ''I want love, too.''

He shrugged and cut into the perfect salmon fillet. ''Love, too,'' he agreed casually. ''So why haven't you gotten what you wanted?''

Hannah felt a sense of helplessness. He didn't understand. ''I thought I was going to get it once,'' she tried to say lightly. ''I was in love with a man who offered me all of the things I wanted. Or so I believed at the time.''

Jarrett watched her closely. ''What happened?''

''He used me to get something he wanted more than he wanted me.''

''What was that?''

"A look at some classified company documents I was in charge of indexing and filing."

Jarrett stared at her. "You're kidding!" He looked dumbfounded.

"Nope. We indexers handle all the critical files and papers in a company. We have access to everything." She could smile about it now. "Don't look at me like that. At least he didn't leave me for another woman!"

"What did he leave you for?"

"Another job after he got fired," she admitted wryly. "I never saw him again."

"Did he get what he wanted from you?" Jarrett demanded coolly.

"No. He wasn't a very good company spy, I'm afraid. I realized before it was too late exactly what he was after. When I told him I couldn't possibly give him the papers, he tried to get them himself and got caught by his supervisor."

"And after him?" Jarrett asked.

"No one else has offered me quite what I want," she confessed gently. "There have been other men who have asked me to marry them, but somehow it's never felt quite right. Something's always been missing."

"What's been missing?"

"You're certainly full of questions tonight," she chided.

He waved the interruption aside. "What's been missing, Hannah?"

"I'm not sure, to tell you the truth. Sometimes the package contains all the ingredients but the resulting offer leaves me cold. I can't explain it. I just know something's always been missing."

"Are you sure you really know what you want?' Jarrett asked softly.

She stared at him in astonishment, about to answer with a definite "yes." And then Hannah realized she was stumbling over the single word. "Perhaps not," she admitted. "At least, perhaps not in the past. But I do now."

She wanted Jarrett Blade. In whatever capacity she could have him. Hannah knew that now with boundless certainty.

Jarrett saw the certainty in her eyes and felt chilled. Everything had been so much simpler when he'd been sure she needed him to look after her. But the soft, gentle woman he'd encountered in Hawaii had an underlying strength that made it clear she could survive quite well without him. His frustration grew as he considered the fact that the only hold he seemed to have on her was a physical one—and she'd made him swear not to use it.

"Is something wrong, Jarrett?" Hannah frowned in concern from the opposite side of the table. "Is the fish bad?"

"The fish is perfect."

"You look a little strange."

"I'm contemplating the fact that most couples celebrating their first week's anniversary generally go to bed together after dinner," he growled.

"Oh." She suddenly became very busy serving him a second help-ing of spinach salad. "Well, we're not most couples, are we? Some more sourdough bread, Jarrett?"

"Some more wine, I think," he drawled, reaching for the bottle.

The evening deteriorated after that. Hannah became increasingly nervous as Jarrett polished off the bottle of wine. By the time he'd eaten her chocolate mousse, she was positively agitated.

He helped her clear the dishes and then insisted they top off the dinner with a brandy in front of the fire. Hannah agreed, but he could see the hesitancy in her. It annoyed him, so he poured himself a double when he poured the brandies.

He was on his second double and conversation appeared to have stopped altogether when he finally demanded an explanation.

"Why are you looking like a scared rabbit, Hannah?"

She lowered her lashes and gazed into the fire. "Probably because you're starting to look like a drunk wolf."

"I am not drunk," he stated categorically. Was he? she wondered.

"If you say so. Look, Jarrett, it's rather late. I think I'll go to bed. We can do the dishes in the morning." She got to her feet and moved away from the sofa.

"We're supposed to be getting to know each other," he complained. "How can we do that if you're always running off?"

"I am not always running off. We can talk in the morning, if you like."

He eyed her intently from beneath hooded lashes. She was standing uncertainly at the far end of the sofa like a small, wild creature that doesn't know whether to freeze or run. Jarrett deliberately leaned back into his corner of the sofa, one leg resting on the cushions, the other foot on the floor.

"Don't rush off, honey," he murmured. "Don't be afraid of me."

Her eyes flashed resentfully. "I am not afraid of you, Jarrett. If I were, I wouldn't have come here to stay with you. I wouldn't have trusted your word of honor when you agreed to my terms."

"Did I give my word?" he inquired vaguely, honestly trying to recall the conversation.

"You certainly did!"

"I see. But I also put a limit on this idiotic situation, didn't I?"

"Two weeks. This is only the end of the first. Jarrett, I'm going upstairs to bed."

"That sounds lovely. You run along and I'll see to the fire. Then I'll go on upstairs myself." He smiled blandly. Hannah did not appear to find the expression reassuring. She frowned and edged toward the staircase.

"Jarrett?"

"Umm?" He glanced at the fire, idly checking the state of the glowing coals. They were dying down safely. He would just pull the screen closed and that would be that.

"Jarrett, what are you going to do?"

"I told you. Take care of the fire and then go upstairs to bed." Deliberately he smiled again.

"Stop that!" she suddenly snapped, her hand on the newel post.

"Stop what?"

"Stop undressing me with your eyes. Dammit, Jarrett, you've had too much to drink."

"Would you rather I undressed you with my hands?" he asked whimsically.

"No!"

"Don't tell fibs, honey. You know I could make you happy tonight. Why wait another week? What are you going to know about me a week from now that you don't know tonight?" He sat up slowly so as not to startle her into full flight up the staircase. Industriously he grabbed a poker and played a bit with the coals in the fire.

"Jarrett, you need to go to bed and sleep it off. You're drunk."

"You sound disapproving." He slanted her a sidelong glance, studying the way she was now clutching the newel post. "And you look disapproving," he added with a flickering smile. "You can look so damned sweet and regal at the same time. How do you manage that? Maybe it's the way you wear your hair in that crown. I think I prefer your hair down. When it's flowing around your shoulders you don't look so aloof and disapproving. You look like a woman waiting for her man."

Hannah climbed two of the steps, her eyes never leaving his face. Jarrett knew a sense of fierce anticipation. The chase was on. Her flight was still disguised as a casual attempt to climb the stairs, but they both knew she was running now. Slowly he set down the poker and got to his feet. The room spun briefly around him, and he found that annoying. Automatically his hand went out to steady himself on the arm of the sofa.

Hannah climbed another step, her eyes very wide and questioning in the shadowy light. "Jarrett, no..."

"Jarrett, yes," he drawled softly, risking a step away from the support of the sofa. Sheer, driving male need seemed to be doing a fair job of keeping him on his feet and headed in the right direction. The whole world narrowed down to the distance between himself and Hannah.

"Jarrett, don't you dare," she whispered, putting another stair tread between them as he stalked cautiously to the foot of the steps. She was about halfway up now, and the expression in her eyes was also about halfway. Halfway between anger and pure fear.

Talk to her, Jarrett told himself wisely, talk to her while you close in. It will distract her. "Hannah, don't be afraid of me."

She licked her lips. "You told me once a little fear wouldn't hurt," she reminded him accusingly.

He shook his head. "That first time I made love to you? So I did. Did you know what I meant at the time? I only wanted you to realize that what we had between us was nothing casual. I wanted you to think about the full implications of what we were doing. I wanted you to look into my eyes and know you might get pregnant. I wanted you to cling to me and know at the same time that I wouldn't let you run to safety when it was all over. I wanted you *aware* of me, Hannah.

On every level. There's nothing like a bit of fear to make a woman aware of a man. Especially a woman like you.''

"You really are drunk," she whispered, inching up another stair although he hadn't yet started his ascent. "How many glasses of wine did you have?''

"Not enough. The double brandies helped a bit, however. And then there was that whiskey on the rocks I fixed before dinner. Actually''— he broke off reflectively—"it's getting a little difficult to remember exactly.''

"An excellent reason for calling a halt to this seduction scene,'' she shot back. "What's the point of trying to pounce on me if you won't be able to remember what happened in the morning?''

He grinned at her, making no attempt to modify what must surely have been a wicked, wholly male expression of sensual anticipation. "As soon as I wake up with you in my arms, I'm sure everything will come back to me.'' He put one foot on the bottom stair and saw still greater tension stiffen her soft, curving body. "There's no point waiting another week, Hannah, and we both know it. I want you. And when I have you in my arms I can make you want me. I can make you *need* me. Are you going to run, or are you going to accept the inevitable gracefully?''

"Damn you, Jarrett Blade! I'm not going to let you touch me! You gave me your word!''

Hannah broke and ran, fleeing up the staircase like a startled doe before the hunter. Jarrett watched the pleasant shape of her derriere as she darted around the post at the top of the stairs and then, smiling with grim intent, he started after her.

There was no point in running, and in all honesty Jarrett had to admit he probably would have fallen flat on his face if he'd tried. This sort of thing took care when a man was not entirely sober. So he stalked up the stairs with slow, steady deliberation, knowing his quarry couldn't escape.

At the top of the stairs he paused for a moment to let the walls stop whirling and then he started in the direction of Hannah's bedroom. *His* bedroom, Jarrett corrected himself coolly. He owned this house, didn't he?

Her door was closed, naturally. Probably locked, too. But that didn't make any difference. The locks in this house were simple, ineffective mechanisms, except for the ones he had installed on the outside windows and doors. The ones on inside doors were meant only to remind people of privacy requirements. As the owner of the house, he didn't need to pay any attention, Jarrett assured himself. He raised a hand and twisted the knob. It didn't give.

"Open the door, Hannah," he ordered softly.

"Go away, Jarrett!"

"We both know I'm not going to go away. Open the door, honey, or I'll break the lock."

There was no response from Hannah, but his ears caught the unmistakable sound of a heavy piece of furniture being pushed or pulled across the floor. Was she trying to move the dresser in front of the door? Dammit, that would be a rather effective barrier! He'd have to act quickly, before she could shove the dresser into place.

Standing back, he gathered his senses and his energy with a supreme effort of will and slashed out with his foot in a swift, savage kick that burst the lock and shoved open the door.

For an instant he simply stood, bracing himself against the doorjamb with one hand. Trying to practice karate when drunk was a tricky business. Now the room was really spinning.

"Damn!" he snarled under his breath, fighting to regain his equilibrium. Then he saw Hannah standing with her back to the window on the other side of the room. He shook his head and took a step forward. "Like a little goddess," he muttered, forced to admire her disdainful, royal pose. "Are you going to use your judo, sweetheart? You didn't that first night in Hawaii. I wonder why."

"Leave me alone, Jarrett," she commanded haughtily.

"Can't leave you alone. That's the whole problem." He closed the distance between them. "Only place I can be sure of you is in bed, so that's where we're going. Are you going to fight me?"

"Yes," she bit out savagely.

"Won't do any good," he advised her complacently. "Whenever I touch you, you melt."

"Not tonight, Jarrett."

"Why not tonight?" He reached a point only a foot or so away from her and stood looking down at his captive. Almost experimentally he put out a hand and touched the coronet of her hair. She flinched, but she didn't move.

"You gave me your word, Jarrett," she reminded him, her aqua eyes suddenly very cool and steady.

"I was a fool."

"It doesn't make any difference. You promised me two weeks. I came to you because you gave me your word that you wouldn't try to push me into bed."

His jaw tightened as he resisted the argument. Dammit, he didn't have to listen to that sort of thing tonight. This was his house, his woman, and he could do as he pleased. Besides, there was no other way to hold Hannah, was there? His fingers dug luxuriously into her hair, tugging free the braids.

"Hannah..."

"Go away, Jarrett. I'm going to sleep alone tonight."

His fist closed around one braid and he angrily pulled her face close to his own. He watched her, feeling as if he were on fire and wondering why the force of the blaze didn't singe her. "I could take you so easily tonight, Hannah."

She licked her dry lower lip. "You won't. You promised."

"There's no one here to enforce that stupid promise!"

"You're here," she pointed out very levelly.

"Christ, Hannah, I'd be a fool not to take you to bed. Don't you understand?" Why was he trying to explain it to her? Talk about idiocy. It must be the liquor in him.

"Go to your own room, Jarrett. I'll still be here in the morning."

"No, you won't. You'll run again, won't you? Just like you did that time in Hawaii. I can't let you run again."

"Why should I run tomorrow?" she asked with gentle logic. "I've already been here a week, and I'm planning to stay for at least another week."

He shut his eyes and then opened them to stare down at her in bemused fury. "You'll run because in the morning you'll tell yourself you can't trust me," he finally explained heavily. "And you'll be right."

She said nothing, looking up at him with an unreadable expression in her eyes. What the devil was she thinking? he wondered. That she already knew she couldn't trust him because of his behavior this evening? A helpless rage threatened to overwhelm him, and then, exercising every ounce of strength he possessed, he released her and stepped back.

"Go to bed, Hannah," he snarled. "Go to bed and plot your safe return to your safe, serene, cozy little cottage in Seattle where your good job and your good friends are all waiting. Go to bed and plan your return to your pleasant lifestyle. Find some man who is happy to have a roommate relationship with you. One who will go halves on everything. A real *partner*. And when it's all over the two of you can get a no-fault divorce! Just like a couple of partners breaking up a small business arrangement!"

Turning so quickly that he had to catch himself on the edge of the bed, Jarrett headed for the door. There was silence behind him, but he didn't dare look back as he managed to make the hall and then the stairs.

An inner anger unlike anything he had ever known seized him as he stalked back downstairs to the living room. What a fool he was. He'd blown everything tonight. A damned fool!

Savagely he grabbed the brandy bottle, not even bothering with the nearby glass. He wasn't feeling civilized enough for a glass tonight. Throwing himself down on the sofa, he took a long swallow of the fiery liquor.

A fool. She'd leave in the morning, of course, just as he'd predicted. Why in hell had he let his growing fear get the better of him tonight? But that was exactly what had happened. His fear that he wouldn't be able to hold her had actually driven her away!

Jarrett lifted the brandy bottle to his lips again.

It was the sound of Erasmus barking his familar warning that roused Hannah from a restless sleep the next morning. It took several moments for the noise to register, and by the time it did she realized it had already stopped. Jarrett must have answered the door.

It occurred to her that in the week she had been staying at his house they hadn't had any visitors. Jarrett Blade was not the sociable type. Voices drifted up from the floor below as she tugged on her jeans and a wide-sleeved shirt with narrow cuffs. There was something familiar about those voices....

Hastily Hannah bound her hair up into the usual braided coronet and slid her feet into sandals. Then she opened the door and listened intently.

The voices in the room below belonged to John and Alice Clydemore. Hannah went very still with shock.

"Well, well, Blade," John Clydemore was saying almost jovially, "so there she is. Safe and sound in your fine collection. An excellent addition to it, if I might say so."

"Get to the point, Clydemore. Why are you here?" Jarrett's voice sounded weary and dulled, as if he were fighting with chronic pain. No doubt a severe headache brought on by last night's drinking, Hannah thought.

She moved silently to the edge of the landing and glanced down. John and Alice Clydemore were standing very much at ease in Jarrett's living room. Alice was gazing appreciatively at the collection of Nazca pots and John was studying the golden goddess as she crouched in the glass case. Jarrett, arms folded across his bare chest and wearing only his dark khaki slacks, propped up a wall and watched his visitors with a cold expression. He looked vicious. And he looked as if he really did have a headache.

"Come now, Jarrett, dear," Alice chuckled richly, "as soon as we found out the goddess hadn't gone back to Señor Valesquez's collection, we knew exactly what had happened to her. Couldn't resist her, could you? Of course not. Who could? Don't blame you in the least. But you're also a wily dealer, my friend, and what John and I have to offer is the deal of a lifetime. We have a buyer."

"Tell your buyer to go to hell."

"Tell Dominic Arlington to go to hell?" John Clydemore drawled. "I think not."

"Arlington!" The muffled explosion of his words was accompanied by a low groan. Hannah saw Jarrett's hand go briefly to his head. Then, as if regretting the visible sign of weakness, he set his jaw and re-crossed his arms.

"That's right. Arlington. He'll pay a fortune, Blade," John said coolly. "No questions asked. He wants her. Badly."

"She's not for sale." Jarrett's voice was much lower this time, and Hannah had to strain to hear it.

"Everything is for sale in this business. You know that," Alice murmured. "The three of us can set our price. Arlington will meet it. He's already made that very clear."

"And that's why you're here? To form a partnership with me?" Jarrett moved, and Hannah realized he was walking into the kitchen. "What about what happened in Hawaii? No hard feelings?"

"Business is business," John explained equably. "If you're fixing coffee, I'll have some too."

Coffee! Hannah stared down at the three people as they trooped into the kitchen. Jarrett was going to fix coffee while they all calmly discussed the illegal sale of the goddess? She caught her breath and then started downstairs, the carpeted treads making no sound under her sandals. Just what did Jarrett think he was doing? He had other things to consider now. He was no longer free to make questionable deals in pre-Columbian antiquities!

Head high, eyes gleaming with her determination, Hannah swung around the corner of the kitchen doorway and found John and Alice seated at the table. With a careful precision which told of his aching head, Jarrett was measuring coffee into the drip pot.

"Well, if it isn't little Hannah Prescott." Alice Clydemore smiled graciously. "I was just about to ask Jarrett whatever had become of you. I gather he found you amusing enough for a short affair, hmm?"

"Shut up, Alice," Jarrett interrupted flatly, staring at Hannah. "Hannah, I think you'd better go back upstairs."

"Upstairs! Not on your life!" she gritted.

Jarrett drew a long, patient breath. "This doesn't concern you."

"Like hell it doesn't! What do you think you're doing, Jarrett Blade?"

"Your friend Blade is about to become a very wealthy man, my dear." John settled comfortably back in his chair and regarded her with his amused, patrician gaze.

"By selling that stupid goddess? Not a chance. That goddess belongs to Jorge Valesquez and it's going back to him very soon. *Isn't it, Jarrett?*" she asked, whirling on him in challenge.

He blinked at her like a large, still-sleepy cat. "It is?"

"It most certainly is," she declared. "Mr. and Mrs. Clydemore, you might as well get up and leave right now. Jarrett will not be participating in any more shady deals. That goddess is going back where she belongs, and Jarrett will continue to earn his living by writing books and doing appraisals and brokering *legitimate* deals. Is that very clear?"

"Oh, it's clear enough," Alice said politely. "But I'm afraid it's not entirely accurate. You know nothing about these things, Hannah. Jarrett's right. Go back upstairs and wait for him in bed. That's your role in his life, isn't it? There's more money involved here than you can possibly imagine. Stay out of it."

"Hannah!" Jarrett's voice sliced like a whip across the kitchen. "Go upstairs."

"Not on your life! You're not going to treat me like a naive little idiot who just happened to stumble into the wrong scene and get in everyone's way. *You are speaking to the mother of your child.*"

The cup in Jarrett's fingers slipped from his grasp and fell to the floor. He didn't appear to notice. He was staring at Hannah in utter astonishment.

"What did you say?" he said a little thickly.

"I'm pregnant," she told him boldly. "That means that you now have a family, Jarrett Blade. This family of yours requires a man who will be both father and husband. It requires a man who knows the meaning of responsibility. You are responsible now for me and for your baby. We need a stable home and a man we can depend on. Responsible fathers do not conduct shady business deals," she concluded sweetly.

"Oh, for God's sake, Jarrett, get rid of her, will you?" John Clydemore sounded impatient and bored at the same time.

"He can't get rid of me. I belong to him and I need him. He has no time now to get involved with people like you. You two are the ones who will have to leave. The sooner the better. Jarrett and I have plans to make for our family."

"Blade, I'm warning you. Hannah is becoming something of a nuisance. I'm sure she's fine in bed, but she obviously doesn't have much of a head for business. Get rid of her." John Clydemore glowered at Hannah.

Hannah ignored him and walked serenely across the room to stand looking up at Jarrett, who was watching her with an intensity that might have been frightening under other circumstances. Delicately she put her hand on his arm and smiled.

"You don't get involved in these sorts of deals anymore, do you, darling? The goddess will be going back to her rightful owner, won't she?"

"You sound very certain of that," he rasped.

"Of course I am," Hannah said gently. "I trust you implicitly. And you've told me that you're not in this end of the business these days. Even if you were, it would be time to leave the unscrupulous side of things behind."

He swallowed heavily, gunmetal-gray eyes gleaming with a fire that warmed her. "Because I have a family to take care of now?"

She nodded. "Precisely. This sort of deal would set a bad example for the children, wouldn't it? Not to mention how nervous it would make their mother. I'm a little old-fashioned in some ways, Jarrett, my love. I expect my husband to make his living in a reasonably honest fashion."

"Your husband?" he breathed.

"And in return for everything he will do for me, I am willing to love, honor, and, within reason, obey." She smiled tenderly, her eyes shining with a hint of laughter and a great deal of love. "I'm not saying I'll do what you say one hundred percent of the time, but I am saying I respect you and trust you enough to put myself and our baby in your keeping. You are the man of the family, darling. I need you," she concluded simply.

Jarrett groaned huskily and pulled her into his arms. "Hannah..."

"Well, I must say this is all very touching, if a little cloying at this hour of the morning," John Clydemore announced in a new, harder tone of voice, "but I'm afriad Alice and I don't have time for the drama."

Hannah glanced at him and then, startled by the gun in his hand, she stepped back a pace from Jarrett's hold. Beside her, Jarrett turned.

"What the hell do you think you're doing, Clydemore?" Jarrett asked far too softly.

"John and I came for the goddess," Alice explained coolly. "We intend to get her one way or another. The sensible thing is to deal. But if you won't deal, then I'm afraid we will have to take more direct measures. Hannah, go and fetch the goddess out of the case.''

"Fetch her yourself," Jarrett snapped, his hand going out to take hold of Hannah's shoulder before she could move.

"Credit us with some intelligence, Blade," John Clydemore said easily. "Everyone knows you take care of your collection. Gossip has it that a person could lose a hand sticking it into one of those cases without your express permission."

"Don't be ridiculous," Jarrett retorted wearily. "All you have to do is open the case and lift out the goddess. Those cases aren't booby-trapped."

"Then you won't object if Hannah does the fetching and carrying, will you? After all, no harm will come to her, will it?"

"Just take the thing and go," Jarrett said, his hand still on Hannah's shoulder. She could feel his fingers digging into her flesh with abnormal strength. Worriedly she slid a sideways glance up at him.

John Clydemore waved the gun meaningfully. "Hannah, get the goddess or I'll take one of his legs out from under him."

"Hannah, wait!" Jarrett spoke urgently as she instantly slipped away from his grasp.

She halted, turning to glance back at him uneasily. "Yes, Jarrett?"

He ran a hand through his tousled brown hair, and his mouth crooked wryly. "Make sure the switch on the side of the bookcase is flipped to the off position."

Hannah nodded uncertainly. "The off position."

"Make sure, Hannah," he stated evenly.

"Yes, Jarrett." Quickly she turned back, heading for the case that contained the goddess. She passed it first, located the small switch on the bookcase, a switch she had never noticed before, and quickly switched it to the off position. Then she went back for the goddess. Through the kitchen doorway she could see Alice Clydemore keeping an eye on her while her husband held the gun on Jarrett.

"You've been nothing but trouble, lady," Hannah muttered to the round, golden deity as she lifted it out of the case with both hands. "You should have stayed buried back in Peru. On the other hand, I suppose I never would have met Jarrett if it hadn't been for you. Come on. Those two in there deserve you.''

Clutching the gold statue, Hannah carried it back to the kitchen and paused in the doorway.

''Ah, excellent. Hand her over, Hannah.'' Much pleased, Alice Clydemore stepped forward to collect the statue.

It was now or never, Hannah told herself resolutely. ''Here you go, Clydemore,'' she called out to the man with the gun. ''Catch!'' Without pause she hurled the heavy goddess straight at John Clydemore, relying on the instincts of a connoisseur, the same kind of instincts that had made Jarrett reach out to catch the statue the night she had thrown it at his head.

A man who was so wrapped up in his passion for artifacts of the long-dead past didn't do the logical thing like step aside when a golden statue came hurtling toward him. He dropped everything to catch it. Instinctively.

Alice Clydemore screamed as her husband fumbled with the gun in his frantic effort to catch the statue.

''Damn you!'' he hissed. The gun went flying at the same time that the golden goddess struck his grasping hand. But what sent the gun arcing toward the kitchen wall was the impact made by Jarrett's bare foot when it struck Clydemore's arm with a terrifying crack.

There was a cry of pain and rage from Clydemore as he dropped to his knees, holding his arm protectively against his chest. Alice Clydemore turned on the source of the disaster, leaping for Hannah with outstretched, clawing fingers.

Hannah barely had time to find her balance. An instant later the infuriated woman was upon her. Hannah caught her behind the elbow, pivoted on her foot, and used the woman's savage momentum against her. A split-second later Alice fell full length upon the kitchen floor and lay there groaning.

''Hannah, are you all right?''

Hannah glanced up from her victim to see Jarrett with the gun in his hand. He looked a bit too familiar with the weapon, she decided. Then she saw the goddess lying on the floor under the kitchen table.

''I'm fine. I hope that stupid statue is still in one piece.''

''Forget it,'' Jarrett ordered irritably. ''Get away from Mrs. Clydemore. Come over here and call the sheriff's department. The number's on the inside of the phone book. Are you sure you're all right? You didn't hurt yourself? The baby..."

"I'm sure the baby will take after his father and be a hardy little soul." Hannah smiled as she stepped across the room to pick up the phone. "Probably be born knowing the rudiments of karate."

Jarrett smiled very slowly. "Or judo."

"Or judo," she agreed, dialing the number on the inside of the directory.

It was several hours later before Hannah and Jarrett found themselves alone once more in the house. The sheriff had come and gone mumbling something about a straightforward case against the Clydemores. John and Alice, looking far less patrician than when they had arrived, had been led off in handcuffs. Siegfried, Erasmus, and Herbie had all finally calmed down.

"Not that Herbie ever did appear particularly alarmed," Hannah exclaimed as she sat on the sofa and eyed the turtle fondly.

"Handsome Siegfried. Handsome Siegfried. Handsome Siegfried."

"Yes, I know, Siegfried, you're very handsome," Hannah soothed.

Jarrett ignored the pets and sank down beside Hannah, folding her close. His eyes were deep pools of hunger that had nothing at all to do with simple desire. It went far beyond that.

"Are you sure, Hannah?"

She smiled up at him, relaxing in his arms. "About the baby? I'm sure. It's what comes of hanging out around fertility goddesses, I imagine. We shall have to be very careful in the future."

"That particular fertility goddess won't be around here much longer," Jarrett told her steadily. "She's going back to Jorge Valesquez."

"I know."

"You do?" He eyed her searchingly.

"Oh, yes. I know. You've said she was going back to her rightful owner, and I trust you completely."

Jarrett appeared to have trouble finding the right words. Then his mouth softened in a rare smile. "Thank you, sweetheart. I won't let you down. The real truth is that she was going back to Valesquez all along. After I brought the statue back from Hawaii he told me to keep it in my collection until he paid his next visit to the States. He's due sometime next month. He'll be our houseguest.''

"That's nice.''

"You really believe me?''

"Of course I do. I wouldn't marry a man I didn't trust.'' Hannah realized even as she spoke the words that they were nothing less than the truth. She trusted Jarrett Blade and she always had.

"Last night,'' he began awkwardly, his eyes darkening. "Last night I thought I'd ruined everything.''

"You got a little drunk and a little impatient.'' Hannah grinned. "I shall have to see to it that you don't have cause to do either again in the future.''

"You're going to marry me?''

"Didn't I just stand in the kitchen and propose not three hours ago?''

"Definitely.''

"Are you willing to have me for a wife?''

"Hannah, I'm going to marry you as soon as it's legally possible,'' he assured her gravely. "I'm not taking any more chances. I'm going to take care of you and the baby. I'll make you happy.''

"Yes, Jarrett,'' she agreed equably, trailing her fingers through the hair on the nape of his neck. "I have every confidence in you as a husband and as a father.''

He frowned. "About your decision to work...''

"We can discuss it later. Much later.''

"No, I want to tell you now that it's all right with me, if that's what you want.''

"You're not afraid of a working wife?'' she teased gently.

"I'm not afraid in our case. With you, your husband and your children will always come first, won't they?''

"Always. When you've waited as long as I have to obtain a family, you have your priorities firmly in perspective.''

He nodded. "I know. I've waited even longer. You and our children will always be my first priority. Do you believe me?''

"Yes.''

"I love you, Hannah.''

"I know." She smiled wistfully.

"How do you know?" he demanded, brushing her mouth lightly with his own.

"I knew when the goddess was lying flat on her back under the kitchen table where I had thrown her and you ignored her completely to find out if I was all right," Hannah explained complacently.

Jarrett looked momentarily startled; then he grinned. "To tell you the truth, I honestly didn't give her a thought at the time. All I could think about was you."

"True love."

"Must be." His grin faded into a far more intent expression. "Yes, it definitely is. Hannah, I haven't wanted to admit that what I felt for you was love, although I should have known it when I found myself agreeing to your stupid plan to get to know one another in a sex-free affair. I was scared to death I wouldn't be able to hold you without the sex. And after I blew everything last night..."

"I still would have been here for our second anniversary next week," she assured him laughingly. "But to tell you the truth, I decided last night to put everything onto a more normal footing today."

"Normal footing? Does that mean you were going to start a real affair with me?"

"I'm afraid so." She sighed. "You see, I realized last night that there really wasn't anything more I had to learn about you. I knew I loved you. That was all that mattered."

"What about all the things you wanted me to learn? That stuff about a partnership between us and the modern approach to marriage and the changing role of women in society?" He looked worried again, and Hannah lifted her fingers to smooth the lines in his face.

"Jarrett, darling, I think we're going to have to face the fact that you are a little old-fashioned in some ways." She smiled demurely. "Some might even say primitive. But that's all right, because I appear to have a bit of the primitive in me, too. I suspect that's what's been missing from my previous associations with the male of the species. I need a man who understands the fundamental things in life. Understands and respects them. A lot of modern men don't."

His mouth curved in wry amusement. "You're saying I'm not a modern sort of male?"

"Are you?"

"No. No, I guess not. I've always felt a bit out of it, to tell you the truth. As if I didn't quite fit into the twentieth century somehow."

"And now?"

"Now," he drawled, lowering his mouth to within an inch of hers, "everything seems just right. I've found my missing goddess. The one who needs me and loves me as much as I need and love her. It wouldn't matter what century we found ourselves in. The relationship between you and me will always be a little on the primitive side. Hannah?"

"Hmm?"

"Why didn't you ever use your judo against me?"

"I couldn't seem to think properly whenever you got that close," she admitted with a rueful grin. "At first you were a fantasy come to life, and a dangerous one at that. I couldn't figure out how to deal with it. Then I realized I was falling in love with you. I could hardly use judo against you when all I wanted was to be in your arms."

Jarrett's mouth curved in satisfaction. He brushed her lips tantalizingly with his own. "Remember the quilt I bought in Hawaii?"

"Yes."

"It's waiting for us upstairs on my bed."

"Yes."

Safe once more in the glass case, the golden goddess of fertility watched with wise, ancient eyes as two members of the modern generation climbed the stairs to rediscover some very old truths about the relationship between men and women.

*   *   *   *   *

CAUTIOUS LOVER

One

It hadn't been the most romantic proposal of marriage a woman had ever received. If Elly Trent wasn't so passionately in love with Jess Winter, she knew she would have told him exactly what he could do with his suggestion of marriage. Here on the Oregon coast there were several points where he could take himself and his offer for a long walk off a short cliff. In the depths of her initial disappointment, Elly would have been happy to show him the way.

But she had recovered quickly and done the only logical thing under the circumstances. She'd asked for time to think it over. She had stalled him now for a week and Jess wasn't an easy man to stall. He always seemed to be operating on some internal master plan, a schedule that he adhered to strictly. When you found yourself on his schedule, as Elly had, you soon learned you were expected to fall into place on time and on-line.

There were other reasons for not fighting the schedule. Lately Elly had become more and more aware of a curious reluctance on her part to push Jess too hard. There was something about him that warned her he was not a man to be prodded in any direction other than the one he himself chose to go. A part of her feared what would happen if she tried it. She couldn't bear the thought of losing him.

The offer of marriage had come last weekend. On Sunday evening, as usual, Jess had returned to Portland, where he spent his time as a very expensive, very high-powered and occasionally very ruthless executive consultant. Elly had never actually witnessed the ruthless side of him, but she didn't doubt for a moment that side existed. She knew from experience that a man didn't become as successful in the corporate world as Jess had been if he wasn't capable of doing a little bloodletting.

He'd reappeared this afternoon, just as he always did on Friday afternoons, pacing into her shop, The Natural Choice, with that strong, controlled stride that said so much about his basic nature. He was on time, of course. Jess was always on time.

Elly had looked up from behind the cash register, where she'd been ringing up a pound of whole-wheat flour together with two dozen granola bars and known that she wasn't going to be able to stall anything for another week. He was a reasonably patient, unflappable, coolly mannered man, but he was also calmly persistent. One look into his fog-gray eyes had been enough to tell Elly that the issue between them would be settled one way or another this weekend. She didn't need a second look to know that Jess fully expected the matter to be resolved the way he wanted it.

Now she stood in her kitchen, her mind whirling with uncertainty about the bold plans she had hatched during the long week. Elly opened the oven door and peered at the simmering lentil casserole inside. She had closed her shop an hour earlier and then invited Jess home for dinner. The invitation itself was fairly routine. She'd cooked dinner for him often enough on weekends during the past two months.

But tonight was not going to be routine. She'd made her decision. All she needed now was the courage to implement the test. She leaned over to probe the surface of the casserole.

"*Ouch! Dammit....*" Muttering disgustedly, Elly turned on the cold-water faucet and stuck her finger beneath the spray.

"What happened?" Jess wandered into the spacious old kitchen cradling a glass of Scotch in one hand. He stood frowning in the doorway, his free hand braced easily against the wooden frame.

"Nothing. Burned my finger, that's all. The casserole's hot."

"I'll bet." He smiled briefly. "Are you okay? Want me to drag out the first-aid kit?"

Elly shook her head, turning off the water. "No, I'm fine. Really." She picked up the loaf of dark, whole-grain bread that was sitting on the counter and reached for a knife. Behind her she could feel him studying her quick, tense movements.

"Be careful with that knife, Elly. I just sharpened it last week. You're used to working with dull blades."

"I know. Thursday I cut myself on the paring knife. I didn't realize you'd sharpened that one, too."

"I had to sharpen it," he told her reproachfully. "You'd been using it to dig around in the dirt again."

"I'd just used it to trim a few leaves off my ivy plants." She defended herself with a placating smile, hoping Jess wouldn't go into the subject too deeply.

He gave her an indulgent look. "Like hell. That blade had been dulled almost past redemption. You'd used it for more than whacking off a couple of leaves."

Elly coughed to clear her throat. "Yes, well, it's very useful around the plants."

"And you've got a house full of plants." Jess reached out to finger the leaves of the huge, bushy fern hung nearby. "You should use proper gardening tools, though, Elly. Not your good kitchen knives. You never know when you're going to need a good, sharp knife."

"Yes, I know." She concentrated on the bread. With any luck the bread knife would do its job properly and not betray the fact that she had used it last Friday to cut away a cardboard container that held a new plant she had purchased.

"Everything go all right at the shop this week?" Ice clinked as Jess raised the glass of Scotch to his mouth.

"Fine, just fine." She piled the thick slices of bread on a plate. "What about you? Going to be able to wind up your consulting job on schedule?"

"Yes."

Elly put down her knife and picked up the glass of Pinot Noir she'd been sipping. "Yes," she repeated thoughtfully. "Of course. Why not? You always get things done on schedule, don't you?"

Jess tilted his head slightly to one side, considering the woman in front of him. His gaze wandered over the neat coronet of braided chestnut-colored hair, took in the warm, tawny-gold eyes and the brilliant persimmon-colored sweater Elly was wearing over a pair of snug, faded jeans. The sweater was loose, not revealing the gentle swell of small, high-tipped breasts. The jeans, on the other hand, clearly outlined the flare of curving thighs. She was slightly flushed from the heat of the stove, and she looked very good to him. He wondered at the faint edge in her voice.

"Why are you nervous tonight, honey?" Jess came forward to lean against the kitchen counter. He lifted the same hand in which he held the glass of Scotch and touched her jaw with one blunt-tipped finger. "Why so sharp? You're usually so easy and restful to come back to on the weekends, but this afternoon you've been as tense as a drawn bow. Are you sure you're not having trouble at the shop?"

The glass of Scotch was so close to her face that Elly could feel the coolness coming from it. She looked up at Jess and smiled tremulously. "We're not all as calm and collected as you are, Jess."

He smiled abruptly, the expression momentarily easing the harsh, grim planes of his face. Elly's first impression of Jess Winter was that he fit in perfectly with the rugged landscape that characterized the local coastline. Nothing she had learned about him in the past two months had changed her initial reaction. There was little conventional attractiveness about the man, but for her there was a compelling element of strength and vitality beneath the quiet exterior. It was there, she was sure, both mentally and physically. The physical part showed in the solid, lean lines of his body.

Jess Winter, she knew, was thirty-seven years old. He had spent those years making himself successful, and Elly suspected that he'd made it on his own terms. There was too much raw power and passion lying just beneath the surface of the man to allow him to take the easy way out of any situation in which he might find himself. She just wished some of that passion she sensed in him could be channeled in her direction.

Until now her relationship with Jess Winter had been the epitome of a polite, friendly, all-too-casual courtship. He came to her on the weekends seeking peace and quiet, not excitement and passion. If Elly's instincts hadn't warned her that there was a vein of fire to be tapped in this man she would have given up in frustration several weeks ago. As it was she might have to face the fact that she simply wasn't the woman who could bring out the passionate side of his nature.

In certain very specific ways, she reflected grimly, Jess Winter lived up to his name. At least with her. She had wondered from time to time if there had been other women in his life who had been fortunate enough to know the full depths of this man. She didn't want to speculate too long on the subject. It was depressing.

"You're nervous because you're about to accept an offer of marriage," Jess said with characteristic insight. Amusement lit his eyes. "That's it, isn't it? You know that sometime this weekend you're going to have to stop dwelling on the matter and simply say yes. The funny part is I didn't expect the whole thing to set you on edge like this."

"Well, it certainly doesn't seem to have set you on edge," Elly muttered tartly.

Jess shrugged. "Why should it? We both know we're doing the right thing."

"Do we?"

"Elly, we're perfect for each other and you know it. You're just what I need. Just what I want."

Elly busied herself putting the bread into the oven to warm. It was easier than meeting his eyes. "Are you sure, Jess? Are you really sure you know what you're doing?"

"Is that what's worrying you? That I don't know my own mind? After the past eight weeks you should know me better than that."

Elly sighed as she closed the oven door. "You're right. I should know you better than that. You always seem to be aware of exactly what you're doing and why. The way you arrived in town two months ago and immediately began negotiating for that old Victorian monstrosity on the bluff overlooking the sea, the way you're deliberately winding down your career as a consultant so that you can move here and set up an inn, *everything* you do. It's all neat and tidy and certain." She shook her head and reached for her glass of wine again. "You seem to have all the little loose ends of your life neatly tied off."

"I've been working on it," he reminded her softly.

Elly took a long sip of the wine. "I realize that."

"Getting things in order, tying off loose ends, knowing what I want and how to get it, those are my strong suits, Elly. That's the way I operate. I didn't think it bothered you."

Instantly she heard herself rush in to reassure him. "It doesn't bother me! I admire you for the way you're taking the risk of starting a whole new career. I admire the way you get things done. You've got so many plans and ideas, and I just know you'll be successful running your inn, but I'm—" She broke off in frustration, unable to put her real fears into words.

"You're what, Elly?"

"I guess I'm just not sure why you want to marry me," she concluded lamely. "I know this sounds trite, but frankly, I wouldn't have thought I was your type."

"Ah, I see."

"Well, I'm glad somebody does!"

Jess grinned. "What kind of woman do you think would be my type?"

Elly stared stonily across the kitchen, concentrating on the row of African violet plants she had sitting on the windowsill. "Someone a little flashier than me; no, a *lot* flashier than me. Someone with a high-powered career in the city, perhaps. A fashion model, a lawyer or a corporate executive, maybe. Someone who knows clothes and the right people. Someone with style and wit and flair."

"You're describing exactly the kind of woman I don't want." Amusement underlay his words. "Besides, what would I do out here on the coast with a high-powered lady executive who was into clothes and Porsches and high-tech furniture? That kind of creature needs a city environment. She'd give me nothing but trouble here. Too much trouble."

"And you think I won't?" Elly dared.

Jess laughed and reached out playfully to grab a handful of her neatly bound braids. He gave her a light shake that rumpled her hair but didn't dislodge the coronet. "The only trouble you're likely to give me is starving me to death. When do we eat?"

"You're avoiding the question."

"No, I'm not. There isn't any question to be avoided." He leaned down and brushed a kiss across the tip of her nose. "I keep telling you, we're perfect for each other. We're—" he searched for the word "—comfortable together. Similar interests, similar tastes, similar goals. As soon as I complete my move from Portland, we're going to share similar life-styles. We both like this little town with its Victorian monstrosities. Just look at this place you call home!"

Elly ignored the reference to the old, weather-beaten two-story house she had bought two years ago. She wouldn't let herself be sidetracked. "Has it occurred to you that I may not see myself in the role of comfortable companion?"

Some of the affectionate humor faded in Jess as he eyed her challenging expression. "Are you sure nothing is wrong, Elly?"

"Of course I'm sure."

"You're not acting normally."

"You mean I'm not proving very comfortable this evening?"

"Easy, honey," he said soothingly. "As long as you're just tense because you're on the verge of getting married, I won't worry about it."

"What would you worry about?"

He lifted one shoulder casually. "If there was something more serious bothering you, I'd be concerned."

"Really? What would you do about it?" She couldn't seem to stop herself from deliberately pressing the issue. It was ridiculous. There was nothing to be gained from this approach. Besides, this wasn't the way she had planned to have the evening develop.

He looked at her oddly. "I'd do whatever had to be done," he said simply.

Elly closed her eyes in brief frustration. This was getting her nowhere. "Forget it, Jess. I don't know why I'm spitting at you. It's just that I've been thinking about you all week, knowing you'd expect an answer this weekend. I've been getting more and more anxious for no real reason." She tried a fragile grin. "After all, what can you expect under the circumstances? Women my age aren't accustomed to receiving offers of marriage every day of the week."

"Thirty is fairly advanced, all right. You should be grateful I've come along to rescue you from a life of boring spinsterhood." There was wicked laughter in his eyes.

"Is that how you see yourself? As my rescuer?"

"To tell you the truth," Jess said mildly, "I think the opposite is the case. You're rescuing me."

That caught her interest. "From what?"

"More than you will ever know," he said lightly, dismissing the subject with a casual wave of a hand. "Isn't that casserole ready yet?"

Elly decided she could take a hint when she got hit over the head with it. "I think so. Why don't you take the bottle of wine over to the table?" She turned back to the stove, occupying herself with ladle and bowls.

He teased her about saving her from spinsterhood, but the unnerving truth was that Jess Winter had made no real effort to introduce any degree of passion into the relationship. Some salvation, she thought wryly. The light kiss with which he had dusted her nose a few minutes ago was typical of the caresses Elly had received from him in the past two months. She thought about it bleakly as she ladled the rich lentil concoction into earthenware bowls and heaped grated romano cheese on top of it.

There had been casual hugs, pleasantly warm but almost cautious embraces, a great deal of hand-holding and one or two kisses that Elly thought contained the seeds of passion. Frustratingly, those seeds had not been allowed to grow. It seemed to her that as soon as Jess sensed any threat to his self-control he pulled back. It was not only odd in this day and age to have a man approach an essentially sensual relationship so carefully, it was downright disturbing. After all, Elly told herself worriedly, it wasn't as if they were teenagers who were sneaking around behind the barn. In fact, teenagers, under the circumstances, probably would have had more fun. And womanly instinct told her that Jess Winter definitely was interested in women. So why hadn't he pushed her into bed by now? He certainly wouldn't have had to push very hard. The thought that he might not be attracted to her was terrifying. It also made no sense. Why would he want to marry her if he wasn't attracted to her?

Her only hope had been the occasional glimpses of fire she thought she had detected on the few times when Jess had permitted a goodnight embrace to stray beyond the bounds he usually imposed. She thought she had sensed something more in him on those infrequent occasions, something that meant he was capable of responding to her deeply. Those hints of passion, combined with her instinctive reading of his character, were all she had to go on tonight. If she couldn't find a way to test the sensual side of his nature, Elly knew she would be forced to decline Jess Winter's offer of marriage. It would be too big a risk.

She might be thirty, but she hadn't reached the point of desperation and probably never would. She wasn't ready to commit herself to marriage simply to avoid spinsterhood. As a matter of fact, there was a lot to be said for living independently. She had grown quite fond of her freedom and her own company. Only love would coax her into marriage—fully reciprocated love. Elly had made that decision this morning.

"How long will you be staying this time?" she asked as she carried the bowls over to the round wooden table by the window. She returned to the oven to collect the rest of the meal.

Jess shook his head in mock wonder. "You're always so calm and serene about that particular question. A lot of women would have given me a great deal of static over the matter of my coming and going so frequently. But not you." He reached for a hot bowl. "You always smile and kiss me goodbye when I leave and invariably you're waiting right where I left you when I return."

"I had no idea I was so convenient." Elly sat down and concentrated on tasting her casserole.

"Ah, but you are convenient, Elly. Undemanding, good-natured, genuine, reliable, tolerant and you can cook. What more could a man ask?"

She sighed, her mouth curving wryly. "You're teasing me."

"You're asking for it." Jess's eyes gleamed. "But to tell you the truth, all those perfect female qualities I just listed aren't so far from reality. You do possess them."

"And you're a man who appreciates them?"

"You better believe it."

The depressing thing was, he clearly meant it. The rather daunting list of dull virtues was exactly what Jess did seem to admire in her.

After two months Elly believed him. The thought nearly panicked her.

"What if I turned out to be not quite so, uh, comfortable?" she dared softly.

Jess grinned. "It's really starting to get to you, isn't it?"

"What?"

"Bridal jitters."

"I'm not a bride yet," she pointed out coolly.

He leaned across the table and flicked the end of her short nose. It was a gesture of casual affection, just as all his other gestures were. "You're going to make a charming bride. Now stop worrying about it and pass me the salad."

Without a word Elly obeyed. The time had come, she thought. It was now or never. She had to start focusing the evening toward her ultimate goal or the opportunity would be lost. Deliberately she summoned up a sweet smile. "You can't blame me for being nervous. I've never been married before."

"You'll get the hang of it fast enough. All you have to do is keep living your life the way you normally live it. The only difference is that I'll be around to share it with you."

"Sounds simple."

"It will be. Want some more salad?" He dished out a large portion for her without bothering to wait for her response.

"No, thank you."

"Too late. It's already on your plate. That dressing's terrific, by the way. Invent it yourself?"

"Um-hmm."

"You know, I think that after we're married I'll move in here with you while we wait for the renovation work on the inn," he went on casually. "When it's finished we can live there."

"Jess—"

"I'm almost finished winding things up in Portland. I figure another couple of weeks and I'll be through entirely. If we plan the wedding for the end of the month everything should dovetail nicely. All right with you?"

"Jess, I think we ought to discuss this."

"There's nothing major to discuss. I'll handle all the details. Just decide how many of your local laid-back artsy-craftsy friends you want to invite to the wedding. We can have the reception right here, I think. Should be enough room.''

Elly gave up trying to deflect him from his casual planning of her life. Instead she tried to make the appropriate responses even though she was growing increasingly tense. She'd never set out deliberately to seduce a man before, and the prospect was intimidating. It would have been much simpler if she'd been certain of the reception she was likely to receive. But with Jess Winter there was no predicting the outcome.

''Leave the dishes,'' she said quickly as they finished the meal. Jess had started to clear the table the way he usually did. Elly smiled tremulously as she got to her feet. ''We can do them later.''

He nodded. ''Okay. Whatever you like.''

She cleared her throat, aware of the quickening of adrenaline in her body. ''I thought it might be nice to build a fire and have a glass of brandy in front of it. How does that sound?'' She was already leading the way into the living room, allowing him little option but to follow.

''Sounds fine.''

Jess walked over to the old stone hearth and went down on one knee in front of it. He reached for the kindling Elly had piled in the brass wood basket.

''There is some newspaper in that sack,'' Elly said as she tried unobtrusively to turn off some of the lights. ''You can use it to start the fire.''

''Newspaper and something else.'' He peered into the sack. ''What's this? Mail?'' He pulled out an envelope addressed to her and held it up inquiringly.

''That's okay. Just a letter from my cousin. I've already read it. I toss most of my papers into that sack so I'll always have something with which to start a fire.''

Jess nodded, striking a match and setting the flame to the edge of the envelope. When the paper caught fire he used it to light the kindling. ''How much family do you have besides this cousin?''

''The usual assortment, I guess. I don't have any brothers or sisters, though. My parents are retired and live back East. They're on an extended cruise at the moment. The rest of my relatives live in California. That includes Dave's parents.''

"Dave?''

"The cousin who wrote me that letter,'' Elly explained as she gazed thoughtfully around the darkened room. Jess hadn't seemed to notice that she was trying to produce a romantic glow.''

"He lives in California?''

"No, he's in college in Seattle.''

She didn't particularly want to discuss Dave just then. She had other things on her mind. She eyed Jess as he concentrated on his fire. The glow of the flames was beginning to cast a warm tone over the atmosphere of the room, just as she had hoped. In the firelight she could see hints of the silver in Jess's dark hair. There was a casual, thoroughly masculine grace about him as he knelt in front of the flames. She responded to it the way she always did, wanting to touch him. Elly dug her nails into her palms in agony over the suspense and tension. Then she drew a deep breath and forced herself to relax.

"How was the drive from Portland?'' she asked blandly as she walked over to an oak end table and poured two brandies.

"No problem. The fog's coming in tonight, though. I'm glad I got here before dark.'' Jess got to his feet and accepted the snifter from her with a smile.

"Sit down.'' Elly graciously indicated the depths of the huge, overstuffed sofa. When he'd obligingly seated himself she sank down beside him, curling her legs under and leaning into him to feel his warmth. Jess's arm slipped automatically around her shoulders, and he took a thoughtful sip of brandy. She could feel him relaxing.

"Honey, you don't know how good this is,'' he murmured. "All week I look forward to getting back here and unwinding with you.''

"I'm glad.''

"So tell me what you've been doing this past week,'' Jess invited lazily.

"Not much. Just the usual.'' Elly tried to nestle closer. It seemed to her that Jess's arm tightened fractionally but not much. He seemed content to sit like this for the rest of the evening. "We lead a very quiet life around here during the winter, Jess." She took a breath. "Are you sure it's not going to be too quiet for you?"

"I know what I'm doing, Elly. I usually do."

She inclined her head, staring into the flames. "I believe you. I just wish I knew what I was doing."

"Stop worrying and leave everything to me." He lifted his hand to toy with her braids.

Elly waited hopefully, but his touch was clearly just another absent caress, not the prelude to taking down her hair. She sighed inwardly, knowing that if she didn't take the initiative, they would sit here all evening like this. Deliberately Elly put her fingertips on Jess's thigh. Jess didn't seem to notice. Elly took another swallow of brandy to fortify herself.

"You were right about the fog," she said, a little startled that the words sounded so husky in her throat. "It's very heavy tonight."

"Umm." Jess leaned his head back against the cushions, his eyes closing in obvious contentment.

"It makes things cozy, don't you think?" Good grief. If he fell asleep on her she would know for certain there was no hope of any passion in the forthcoming marriage. Nervously Elly began drawing tiny patterns on Jess's thigh. Through the fabric of his well tailored slacks she could feel the heat of his body.

"Cozy? I hadn't thought of it that way, but I suppose it does. During the winter months we'll have to promote the inn as a quiet, cozy retreat. A place far away from the hustle of the city."

"Romantic," Elly suggested tentatively. "You could promote it as a romantic hideaway on a windswept coast. Doesn't that sound appropriate?"

"Maybe I should let you handle the advertising," he said with a trace of humor.

"Maybe you should." She took a deep breath, her fingers tightening around her glass. Then she let her hand slide down along the inside of his leg. Simultaneously she turned her face into his chest. It was obvious she was going to have to be more aggressive. "You smell good."

"Not likely. I haven't showered since this morning." Jess still sounded incredibly unconcerned.

He stirred faintly, though, just enough to let Elly know that he wasn't completely unaware of her physically. Encouraged, she put her glass down on the table at the end of the sofa, leaning intimately across Jess as she did so. When she finished the small task, she took advantage of her position to increase the closeness between them. She put her hand on the first button of his shirt.

"No, really, you do smell good," she insisted, resting her cheek on his shoulder as she fiddled with the button. "Warm and sexy."

"I had no idea what a lack of a shower could do for a man," Jess said dryly. He shifted a little. She couldn't tell if he was trying to put more distance between them or if he was just restless. "Easy honey. I don't want to spill this good brandy."

"There's plenty more where that came from." She succeeded in undoing the button at last. Her fingers strayed inside the opening of his white shirt. Elly caught her breath as she felt the crisp, curly hair. Impulsively she turned her head and put her lips to the base of his throat.

"Elly, honey—"

"I've missed you this week, Jess." She kissed him again, this time on his jaw. Her fingers slipped around his neck.

"I missed you, too," he whispered.

Elly thought she heard him sigh softly into her hair. Emboldened, she leaned more heavily into him, letting him feel the shape of her soft, unconfined breasts on his hard chest. His fingers tightened on her shoulder, and now she was sure he was no longer quite so relaxed. She could feel his body tightening as she snuggled against him.

"I've done a lot of thinking this week, Jess."

"Have you?" His hand lifted to her hair again, and this time he removed a couple of pins.

"There are some things we've never talked about," she ventured, closing her eyes as she felt her hair coming free.

"And you've been worrying about them?"

"Yes."

"Elly, honey, there's no need to worry. We've got all the time in the world. There's no rush. Everything's on schedule."

"I know that, but—" She broke off, unable to put her fears into words. Instead she clung to him, abruptly digging her fingertips into his shoulders. A little desperately she found his mouth with her own, praying for a response.

At first there was only the polite, warm, agreeable reaction of a man who knows what's expected of him under the circumstances and is willing to oblige.

But Elly had had enough of his polite, obliging kisses during the past two months. Tonight she needed to know that his feelings for her went deeper. She had to find out just what he felt for her. Her whole future depended on the answer. Inching her way appealingly into Jess's lap, she curled against him and opened her mouth invitingly beneath his. Her desire was naked now, leaving her totally vulnerable.

Elly felt the hesitation in Jess and could have wept. Then, just as she was convinced that he felt nothing for her—at least nothing he would admit to—Jess slowly began to respond.

The very fact that he seemed to be fighting his own response flooded Elly with hope. She moaned softly against his mouth, a wordless plea that was also an unwitting, very feminine form of seduction. Then she caught his hand in one of her own. Trembling, she guided his fingers under the edge of her sweater.

Jess sucked in his breath. Beneath her thigh Elly was now unmistakably aware of his growing arousal. Shivering with nervous relief and an even more nervous exhilaration, she urged his hand higher.

"Please, Jess. Please touch me. I—I need you. I want you to need me." The words were breathless pleas against Jess's throat as Elly trembled in his arms.

Jess groaned. "Elly, honey, I didn't plan it to be like this."

"But, Jess, this is the way it's supposed to be," she whispered desperately. "Make love to me, Jess. Please make love to me. I'm begging you."

"Oh, God, Elly. I don't—I didn't want—You don't know what you're asking."

But his hand closed over her breasts with a sensual possessiveness Elly had never known in him before. The last of her doubts faded as she felt the undeniable impact of the first deeply sexual contact she'd ever had with Jess Winter. He did want her. The fire she had sensed in him really did exist.

Elly almost sobbed in relief, and then she felt the room shift on its axis as Jess lowered her onto the sofa cushions. A moment later he came down on top of her. The firelight clearly revealed the masculine hunger that was at last beginning to etch his face.

Two

It was going to be all right, Jess thought as the need in him flared into heavy and demanding life. There had been nothing to worry about after all. And to think he'd been deliberately putting off this end of things. What a fool. *It was going to be all right.*

No, it was going to be better than all right. He realized that as Elly began to cling to him with increasing passion. She was so soft and hot, her tawny-gold eyes full of a totally honest plea. She wanted him. The desire in her was not a false spell she wove to ensnare him. It was genuine, completely genuine. It made her so sweetly vulnerable.

Beneath him Jess could feel the gentle swell of Elly's breasts. The need to see and touch her small, excitingly hard nipples came over him in a rush. With an awkward urgency that astonished him, he pulled the persimmon sweater up over her head, letting the garment drop to the floor. He inhaled fiercely as the fire's glow spilled over her bare breasts.

"Ah, Elly, my sweet Elly. You're so lovely."

She shivered as he carefully brushed his thumb across one thrusting peak. Her reaction to his touch heightened Jess's excitement as nothing else could have. He lifted his head and saw that her eyes were half-closed against the exquisite need building up in her. Along the length of his leg her jeaned thigh tightened, her knee flexing slightly.

It was a fantastic sensation, Jess thought, half-dazed. To think he had planned to keep sex on more or less casual terms, an easy, comfortable basis that would satisfy each of them physically but not demand too much emotionally. He knew it was possible to enjoy a physical relationship on that level because he'd had more than one such association since Marina had left. But, God help him, he would have missed so much if he'd succeeded in doing that with Elly.

It wasn't until tonight, when she had begged him to make love to her, that Jess had finally acknowledged that the sexual relationship with Elly wasn't going to be casual. Her own need and passion were pulling him into the heart of a whirlwind. There was no aphrodisiac on earth that could compare to being wanted the way Elly seemed to want him tonight.

Elly didn't know which was stronger, the dizzy sensation of relief and exultation or the flaring physical excitement. In the end it didn't matter. She was aware she had fallen in love with Jess Winter, but she'd had no real notion of the depths of the physical side of the matter. It was glorious, the most incredible sensation she'd ever known.

She felt the hard readiness of Jess's body through the fabric of her jeans. He had his shirt off now and the strong, sleek slopes of his shoulders were golden in the firelight. He crushed her deeply into the sofa cushions, his fingers lancing through her hair. The last of the pins came free, and Jess muttered something dark and sensuous. He nipped passionately at the line of her throat.

"Your hair has fire in it," he told her wonderingly. Catching a long tendril of the chestnut-colored stuff he curled the end around one nipple. The teasing caress elicited another soft sound from Elly. Jess seemed enthralled with her reaction.

"Jess, I've been so worried," Elly confided huskily as she tightened her arms around his neck. "I was afraid you didn't want me."

"That's the last thing you have to worry about now." He found her mouth with his own, kissing her with drugging desire.

Elly sighed and gave herself up to the passionate excitement that swirled around her. Loving Jess was going to be all she could have hoped. She was certain of that now.

And then, without any warning, Elly's fiery world of love and passion froze into a solid sheet of ice. Lost in the shimmering moment, it took several timeless seconds before she realized that Jess had gone utterly still above her.

"*Marina!*" The name was a thick, muffled sound seemingly wrenched from his throat. "Damn it to hell. *Marina!*"

"What is it? Jess? What's wrong?" Dazed by the sudden turn of events, Elly opened her eyes to see the savagely drawn features of the man who had only a moment before been making love to her. Jess was staring past her toward the living-room window. She swallowed and started to ask another question, but before she could get the confused words out of her mouth, he was pulling himself free of her.

"Jess!" Panicked by the change in him, Elly struggled to a sitting position. She felt suddenly cold and vulnerable without her sweater. Instinctively she crossed her arms over her breasts.

But Jess wasn't paying any attention to her. He was already halfway across the room, racing toward the undraped window. Reaching it, he unlatched the frame and shoved open the glass. The muscles of his back tightened with the swift movement. The chill fog that had been hovering outside seemed to slide eagerly into the cozy room.

"Jess, where are you going?" Horrified, Elly sprang to her feet as Jess swung first one leg and then the other over the windowsill. A moment later he disappeared into the night. She stood staring after him, the back of her hand held to her mouth in a timeless gesture of fear and incomprehension.

Time ticked past. Through the open window the cold night air continued to pour hungrily into the room, devouring the warmth it found there. The fire in front of the hearth tried to beat back at the attacking chill, but it was already beginning to flicker beneath the onslaught.

Elly shook off the mesmerizing effects of her anxiety and started toward the window. Vaguely she realized it ought to be closed before any more cold air came into the room. As she took a step forward, her toe snagged on her sweater. Hastily she bent down and retrieved it, shrugging into it quickly.

The window got stuck, as it nearly always did, and Elly was obliged to exert her full strength to get it closed and latched. With the deed accomplished she sagged against the sill and stared out into the darkness. Nothing was visible through the fog.

Unable to think of anything more productive to do, Elly continued to stare out the window. Her chaotic thoughts gradually settled back into place, and at last she began to think clearly again.

What had Jess seen that had sent him into the night? Prowlers? But you rarely called a prowler by name.

Marina. It was a name, Elly realized. A woman's name. She shivered, but this time the involuntary reaction wasn't caused by sensual tension.

Elly was still standing at the window when the door behind her opened. Eyes widening with fear, she whirled to find Jess on the threshold. His naked chest was damp, whether from exertion or the fog, she couldn't tell. Across the room his wintry eyes met hers, and Elly knew she was looking at a man who had metamorphosed from lover to stranger. Her hand curled into a small, tense fist at her side. She tried to speak, failed and began again.

"What happened, Jess? For God's sake, tell me what happened! Did you see someone outside the window?"

He broke the eye contact, turning to shut the door and lock it with deliberate care. When he turned back, Elly could see a coldness in his gaze that matched the night. Her fear rose another notch. Something in her expression must have gotten through to him. Jess frowned and started forward. He stopped when she instinctively backed up a pace.

"It's all right, Elly. I'm sorry I scared you."

"What did you see?"

He ran the back of his hand across his eyes in a weary gesture. "A face. I thought I saw someone standing on the other side of the window. But when I got outside I couldn't find a thing." His hand dropped from his face. "Not surprising. Godzilla could be hiding out there in that pea soup, and I wouldn't be able to see him."

"If you saw a prowler I should call Charlie." Elly reached for the phone.

"Charlie? Oh, yeah. The local deputy sheriff. Forget it, Elly. You can't see two feet in front of yourself tonight. By the time Charlie made it here through the fog, whoever was out there will be long gone. Hell, whoever it was is long gone now." Jess paced over to an armchair and dropped into it with a deep sigh. He stared broodingly into the flames.

Behind him Elly let the phone drop back into the cradle. She stayed very still, watching the stranger who had invaded her living room. Whoever he was, he wasn't the same man she had come to know during the past two months. The realization was frightening. A part of her urged flight. But another side of her demanded explanations.

"Jess, who did you think it was outside the window?"

He didn't move. There was along silence before he answered. "A woman."

Elly drew a deep, steadying breath. "You called her name."

"Did I?"

"You called her Marina."

He didn't respond to that. His whole attention was fixed on the fire. Slowly Elly moved closer to his chair. Her hands were shaking.

"Jess?"

"I'm sorry, Elly."

She shook her head bewilderedly. "Who is Marina?"

It was a while before he answered her, and when he did Elly got the feeling Jess was trying to convince himself as much as her. "I didn't see Marina outside that window. Just someone who looked like her."

Elly licked her lower lip. She felt as if she were walking on very thin ice. Beneath the fragile surface, endless cold waited to swallow her whole. "What does Marina look like?"

Jess rested his chin on his fist, propping his elbow on the upholstered arm of the chair. "A witch," he finally said very succinctly. "A blond-haired, green-eyed witch."

Elly closed her eyes. "I see."

"No, you don't. You can't possibly."

Her lashes lifted, and she stared again at his hard firelit profile. She asked the next question because she had no alternative. The need to know the truth was greater than the fear and hopelessness it might bring. "Who was Marina, Jess?"

He hesitated a moment longer and then said very softly, "My ex-wife."

Elly had a hard time getting her next breath. When she finally got it, her voice sounded faint, even to her own ears. "I didn't realize you had been married."

"I'm thirty-seven years old, Elly. Most men have experimented at least once with marriage by the time they reach my age."

She sank down onto the couch, clasping her hands tightly in her lap. "Yes, I suppose they have. I just hadn't thought about it, I guess. It hadn't crossed my mind. You never mentioned—"

"It's not something I talk about."

"Obviously!" A profound silence followed that remark and then Elly asked tentatively, "Children?"

"Hell, no. I wouldn't have kept quiet about children, Elly."

"Just ex-wives?" A thread of anger was beginning to weave its way into her emotions.

"There was no need to mention Marina."

"Why not?"

"Because she's dead, Elly."

Elly closed her eyes in sudden anguish. "Oh, my God. And when you started to make love to me, *really* make love to me, you saw a vision of her at the window."

The words had the unexpected effect of snapping Jess out of his brooding state. Elly was completely unprepared for the way he surged out of the chair and swept across the room in three angry strides. His face was lined with controlled fury. Halting in front of her, Jess reached down to grasp her shoulders fiercely. His gray eyes seemed to pierce her with lances of ice.

"No," he bit out savagely, "I did not see a vision of her when I started to make love to you. I saw someone outside that window."

"Someone who looked just like her?" Elly said in a tight voice.

"Someone who looked a lot like her. But I sure as hell didn't see a vision. For crying out loud, Elly, what the hell do you think is going on?"

"You tell me. I can't seem to think straight. All I know is that one minute you're making love to me as if…as if you mean it finally, and the next you're seeing your ex-wife at the window. What do you expect me to think?"

"I expect you to be rational about it," Jess grated, hauling her to her feet in front of him. "There was someone outside that window who bore a resemblance to a woman I married and divorced a few years ago. That's all. In the morning I'll take a look around and see if I can find any signs of the prowler. Frankly, though, it's not likely.''

"No," she admitted politely, letting him put any construction on her agreement that he might wish. Lifting her chin, she made an effort to evade his hands. "Well," she tried to say in a conversational tone, "it's getting late, isn't it? And it's going to be a slow drive back to your motel in this fog. You'd probably better get started. Give me a call in the morning. I'll be at the shop, as usual.''

"Elly—"

"Did I mention that Bill Franklin was asking about you this week?" she continued as she went over to the hall closet and began pulling out Jess's worn leather jacket. "He said he's got the estimates on the plumbing work ready for you. You might want to look him up tomorrow. I gather his schedule is fairly open, though. Shouldn't be too much trouble figuring out when he can do the job....''

"Elly!" Jess came forward and yanked the jacket out of her hands, replacing it in the closet. "Stop chattering at me like that. I'm not driving anywhere in this damn fog. I couldn't see my way out to the car, let alone see the white line on the road.''

Despairingly, Elly realized he was right. It had been her own agitation that had made her try to push him out of her home. The truth was she was trapped with him, perhaps until morning. Earlier the prospect had seemed an inviting one. Now it held only uncertainty and a nameless fear.

She had to get hold of herself. Taking a deep breath, Elly stalked across the room and picked up the brandy glass she had set down on the table beside the sofa. The fiery liquid trickling down her throat was a welcome and distinctly reviving sensation.

"I could use another drink, myself." Jess's voice was a low growl as he crossed the room and poured himself more brandy. He stood with his feet planted wide apart, one hand on his hips and downed a healthy swallow.

Elly eyed him covertly, thinking he looked very pagan. She wished he would put on his shirt. Belatedly she reached down and picked it up, handing it to him. "Here. You're probably cold from running around outside without any clothes on.''

Surprisingly her grumbling comment brought a twist of humor to his mouth. "I wasn't exactly naked." Nevertheless, he put on the shirt, not bothering to button it. He swirled the brandy in his glass for a couple of reflective moments, and then he looked up, meeting Elly's wary gaze. "Sit down, honey. I can see I've got some explaining to do."

She looked away. "You've made it clear it's none of my business."

"Yeah, well, knowing it's none of your business doesn't seem to have satisfied you. So sit down, Elly. I'll give you the whole, sordid tale."

"I don't know if I want to hear—"

"Sit down, damn it!"

Elly's mouth tightened resentfully, but she surrendered to the inevitable and took a seat. Jess sighed and walked over to stand in front of the fireplace. Bracing himself against the mantle with one fist, he took another swallow of brandy and began talking in a low, curiously detached tone of voice. Elly had never heard him sound so distant.

"I met Marina Carrington a few years ago. I was thirty-two at the time and had the world in the palm of my hand. I had proven to myself that I was going to be a success in business, and I knew that I was going to be a hell of a lot more successful before I reached forty. I hadn't figured out at that point that I didn't really want to be on the fast track for the rest of my life. That realization came much later. At the time I looked around and thought it all looked pretty damned good. The sky seemed to be the limit. But something was missing."

Elly slanted him a derisive glance. "The love of a good woman?"

Jess shook his head. "Nothing that simple."

"Simple!"

He ignored the outburst. "When Marina swept into my life I knew right away what I'd been missing. Excitement. In capital letters. It's very seductive at first, maybe even addictive."

"Excitement?"

"That shot of adrenaline only a creature like Marina can give you. It's sexual and it's very exhilarating. A man never knows what's going to happen next, but he knows it's going to be wild. He feels as if he's standing with one foot on the planet and one about to step off into outer space. When I was thirty-three it was pretty heady stuff. Completely outside my normal realm of experience. You've got to understand, Elly. I had gotten where I was by a lot of hard work, ambition and self-control. Marina came along and turned everything upside down.''

Elly looked down at her clasped hands. "I see."

Jess glanced at her, frowning. "I'm trying to explain something, Elly. Something that's hard to put into words. Marina was the kind of woman who, when she walked into a room, immediately had the attention of everyone there. She generated some kind of elemental excitement.''

"Lots of feminine charisma, I gather," Elly said evenly.

Jess nodded. "Charisma is probably the word for it. Whatever it is, it seemed to run in the Carrington family."

"It did?"

"Marina had a twin brother. Women react to him the way men react to Marina. Same blond hair and green eyes, the same sense of being bigger than life, not quite real somehow. And both Marina and Damon knew how to exploit their assets. They manipulated everyone around them, and they did it so easily that most people never even realized what had hit them until it was too late.''

"A witch and a warlock," Elly whispered, staring into the flames.

Jess glanced at her again, rather sharply. "That's exactly how I came to think of them," he admitted.

"Go on," Elly said with a sense of doom.

"Well, Marina exploded into my life one evening when I was introduced to her at a party. She was very beautiful, very chic and very successful in her own right. She held an executive position in a corporation. I found out later she hadn't climbed up through the ranks purely on merit. Marina used her body to get what she wanted. I knew the minute I looked at her that I wanted her. She knew it, too. And Damon... Damon was always there in the background, watching and laughing, dancing his own circles around women while Marina enthralled the men." Jess broke off, gray eyes filled with dangerous memories. "At any rate, I took her home that night. I couldn't believe my luck when she let me stay until morning. I had set out to seduce her, but looking back on it, I know it was she who seduced me. Like everyone else around her, I let myself be manipulated. In the beginning I was happy enough to participate in my own downfall. Being seen with her was an ego trip for any man. And I enjoyed the trip for a while.''

''It sounds like you were getting what you wanted out of the arrangement,'' Elly said bleakly. ''That's not exactly manipulation.''

''You don't understand. No one could understand unless they met Marina or Damon. Never mind. That night was the beginning of an affair that kept me strung out for weeks. At times I thought I was going crazy. She knew how to tease and torment and then satisfy a man. And she knew the secret of repeating the cycle over and over again. She would make me wildly jealous, and then she would laugh at me until I lost control. The battles always ended in bed. She was…very skilled in bed. I thought that if I could put a ring on her finger I could possess her completely.''

Elly wrinkled her nose and sighed. ''Did you?''

''Of course not. Things only got worse. Now she was my wife, and in addition to tormenting me with jealousy, she began going through my money at an incredible rate. Such a rate, in fact, that I finally began to get suspicious.''

''Of what?''

''That she was giving the money to another man. It turned out she was. She was giving it to her brother. Damon was plunging into one crazy business scheme after another, using my money as capital. Before I knew it, I found myself bailing him out time after time. As long as he was 'family' I felt obliged to go to his rescue. The two of them were systematically fleecing me. I could hardly believe it, at first. Me, the guy who had been so fast on his feet in the corporate world, who could outmaneuver the best business brains around and who was a natural on the corporate battleground, was getting ripped off by a couple of slick hustlers who never even went to business school!''

''I gather that when you finally realized how much money was involved you came to your senses?'' Elly knew the sarcasm simmered in her voice, but she made no real effort to quench it. She was feeling too much pain to worry about good manners.

Jess's expression darkened. He took another long swallow of brandy. ''It wasn't just the money. By the time I discovered what was happening on that front I had also begun to realize that I was growing sick of Marina's brand of thrills. The excitement she could generate began to wear thin. And I was disgusted with myself for letting her put me through the wringer. I was getting plain tired of the aftereffects of her bizarre life-style. Marina, herself, finally realized I wasn't reacting to the old cycle of blazing jealousy followed by blazing sex. When I cut off the endless supply of cash, she opted to head for greener pastures. As it happened, I was already filing for divorce.''

"Sounds like the parting of the ways was a mutual decision. How modern.''

The line of Jess's jaw seemed to tighten but he didn't respond to her sarcasm. "She left my life the way she had entered it: On the arm of another man. I was incredibly relieved to see her go. I was just as relieved to be rid of her twin. In a strange way, I guess I owe them both something, though.''

Elly looked up, eyes widening with further anguish. "What do you owe them?''

Jess's mouth twisted wryly. "It was during the aftermath, when my life was finally settling back down to normal, that I began to look around and ask just what kind of future I was building for myself. Then I asked myself if it was what I really wanted. I finally took stock of myself and my surroundings and began to restructure my thinking. I took a good hard look at every element of my life and began implementing changes. It was then that I started thinking of easing my way out of the business world and making the transition to another kind of environment.''

"That was when you decided that what you were really cut out to do was run a quaint little inn on the coast?''

"That's when the idea began to crystallize, yes. But I also made a lot of other fundamental decisions. I knew I no longer needed or wanted the kind of destructive excitement a man gets from a woman like Marina. Once was enough. I would never allow myself to be manipulated like that again. And, above all, I knew I'd never let myself get so close again to being out of control either physically or emotionally.''

"You decided you wanted a placid, serene, controlled sort of existence, is that it?'' Elly asked tightly, staring hard at his profile. "An uncomplicated life-style that didn't offer too much annoying excitement.''

Jess's eyes narrowed faintly. "Something like that."

"And when you met me you decided I'd be just the kind of placid, serene, unexciting sort of wife to fit into that life-style," Elly concluded.

"Elly, you're twisting my words. You don't understand what I'm trying to say."

"Don't I?" she said, her voice flaring. "I know that for two months you haven't shown much interest in making love to the woman you said you wanted to marry. I know that when I decide to take the chance of finding out if you're ever going to want to make love, the first thing that happens is you start seeing Marina's ghost. You did say she was dead, didn't you?"

"Elly, listen to me, you don't know what you're talking about."

"When did she die?"

Jess made an impatient movement, coming away from the mantle toward her. "I heard she was killed in a boating accident a couple of years ago. Elly, that's not important now. I want you to listen to me. I wasn't seeing ghosts tonight." He sat down beside her on the sofa and tried to pull her into his arms. "I saw someone who looked a little like her. That's all."

"You called to her," Elly reminded him bleakly. She evaded his arms and got to her feet. "You called her name."

"Hell, I was startled. It's always startling to see a face out of the fog peering in through the window. Especially one that looks familiar. Elly, you're making too much out of this. It's not like you to get so upset. I want you to calm down and forget about what happened."

"That's not likely, is it? And how do you know it's not like me to get this upset? Even we serene, placid, unexciting types occasionally have our moments. We may not cause quite the sensation you're accustomed to getting, but we're not totally predictable and comfortable, either."

"Elly, you're losing your temper."

"Damn right." She shoved her trembling fingers into the back pockets of her jeans and stood facing him. Challenge and defiance were written in her stance. "I hate to tell you this, but, while losing my temper is rare, it's not exactly the first time it's happened. Believe it or not, I do have a temper."

"I'm beginning to believe it." Slowly Jess got to his feet, his eyes softening as he studied her rigid stance. "But I'm afraid you're not going to be able to terrorize me with it."

"Why not? Because you've been terrorized by much more exciting displays of temper? You're immune to my more mundane explosions?"

Jess reached out and tugged her gently but forcefully against him, his arms locking around her with undeniable strength. Helpless, Elly stood stiffly, aware of her captor's lips in her tangled hair.

"You aren't going to be able to drive me away from you with a show of temper, honey. I know you too well. Believe me, after my experience with the Carringtons, I became an excellent judge of human nature, my own as well as others. I know you're exactly the kind of woman I want and need. When you've calmed down you'll realize that I'll be a good husband for you."

"If you really think I'd marry you after what happened tonight...!"

Very gently Jess shut off the flow of hot words by putting his fingers against her mouth. He shook his head warningly. "Don't say things you'll only regret in the morning. Trust me, honey. I know what I'm doing, and I know what's best for both of us. We're going to have a good marriage."

"Even if it is a little on the dull side?"

His patience gave a little under the taunting. Jess removed his fingers from her mouth and kissed her, a quick, hard, possessive caress that was unlike any other she'd ever had from him. It was definitely not of the more familiar, more casual variety she had become so well acquainted with during the past two months.

"I don't think we're going to have to worry about boring each other, do you?" he asked with suspicious blandness as he watched the color flood her cheeks. Then he relented, pushing her face gently down onto his shoulder. "Stop worrying, Elly. Everything's going to be fine. You know you want to marry me. You know that you're going to say yes."

"No, I do not know that. And you can give up any idea that I'm going to be pushed into making a decision this weekend. I want more time, Jess. A lot more time. I have a great deal more to consider now. It seems there's a lot I don't know about you."

"That's not true, Elly. You know the real me."

She lifted her head, her eyes overly bright from the effects of unshed tears. "Do I? What happens if you get a sudden craving for the old style of excitement? What if you start seeing Marina's ghost in our bedroom? I'm not sure I can cope with that, Jess."

His face hardened. "Stop it, Elly. You're being ridiculous."

She moved away from him, and he let her go. "You may be right. It's been a traumatic night. Unlike you, I'm not accustomed to so much excitement. I think I'll go to bed."

"Elly—"

"You can have the sofa. There are some sheets and blankets in the hall closet. Help yourself." Without waiting for him to respond, she turned and headed toward the staircase. Her foot was on the first tread when he caught up with her.

"Elly, you're upset and you're overreacting. You need reassurance."

"No kidding." She didn't look at him.

He hesitated and then said deliberately. "I don't think you should spend the night alone."

Her eyes swung to his. Then, half in shock and half in sudden fury, she said, "Are you by any chance offering to reassure me in bed?"

"Why not? After all, what's really changed, Elly? Earlier this evening you made it clear you needed exactly that kind of reassurance. You were begging me for it, in fact. I'm willing to give it to you. By morning you'll know that everything's going to be all right."

Elly was beginning to seethe. "Your generosity overwhelms me. As I said, I just don't think I can handle all this excitement. Good night, Jess. Let me know if you see any more familiar prowlers."

She flung herself up the stairs and into her bedroom. There she closed and locked the door behind her. Then, trembling so violently she was afraid she'd lose her balance, she collapsed onto the bed.

Three

It was the ringing of the telephone that brought Elly out of a fitful sleep the next morning. She struggled awake, vaguely aware that she had forgotten to unplug the instrument downstairs and bring it up to her bedroom before going to bed. Now it was screeching demandingly from the living room and would probably continue to do so until she got downstairs. Then it would undoubtedly stop ringing just as she reached for it.

To her disgusted surprise it ceased clamoring ahead of schedule. She had barely gotten her robe out of the closet when the ringing stopped. Belatedly she realized that Jess must have answered it. She opened her door in time to hear him firmly tell the caller that she was still asleep.

"It's all right, Jess," she said from the top of the stairs. "I'll take it." Hastily fastening her comfortable, warm red flannel robe, she traipsed barefooted down the stairs. Even her robe suited the image Jess had of her, she thought unhappily. Not particularly sexy or exciting, but reliable and comfortable. The mass of tangled chestnut hair hanging around her shoulders probably went with the image, too. She should have taken the time to put on her fluffy bunny slippers. That would have really completed the look.

Jess stood holding the phone, his expression intent as she came down the stairs. He was already dressed, and she wondered just how late it was. Or perhaps he was simply in a hurry to get out of her house. A glance out the window showed that the fog had cleared. Elly let her eyes slide away from his as she took the receiver from him.

"Hello?" When the caller identified herself, the small element of interest Elly had managed to summon up disappeared from her voice. "Oh, it's you, Aunt Clara."

"Elly, dear, I'm calling to tell you that the family has made its decision." Her aunt's aloof, rather arrogant tones held all the certainty in the world.

"I see." Elly slanted a quick glance at Jess, who was listening unabashedly. "And what is the decision?" As if she couldn't guess. She had known from the beginning how the rest of the family intended to vote. She had also known the kind of pressure she would be under once the decision had been made. "And what did you decide, Aunt Clara?"

"We have decided to sell Trentco Switches. I just wanted to let you know so that you would be prepared to vote at the meeting. I think it is essential that we present a united front. You know Harrigan will fight us."

Good for Harrigan, Elly thought. But she kept her voice carefully polite as she said, "Thank you for telling me your decision, Aunt Clara. I will certainly take it into consideration."

"Come now, Elly, you know there's no need to consider the matter." Aunt Clara's tone was suddenly sharp. "We have let you know what we intend to do, and it will be best for all concerned if you refrain from causing trouble. You have absolutely no knowledge of this sort of thing. What could you possibly know about buyouts and merger offers? Oh, maybe once upon a time you could have dealt with these matters, but not any longer. The business world has passed you by, and you should have sense enough to know it. Living out there with that bunch of ex-hippies, the way you do, it's a wonder you're not on food stamps and welfare. I feel so sorry for your parents. I can't imagine what they must think these days. And if it had been your mother calling this morning she would have been shocked to the core."

Elly bristled. "Why would my mother have been shocked, Aunt Clara?"

"Don't play games with me, Elly. You know perfectly well I'm talking about the fact that a strange man answered your phone this morning. I have to assume that's a regular occurrence these days. Only to be expected considering the sort of life-style you're leading. If I were you, I would at least instruct your male friends not to answer the telephone at seven forty-five in the morning. It gives a very bad impression. But, of course, I suppose that's your business."

Elly's fingers tightened around the receiver. "Yes, Aunt Clara. Considering the fact that I'm thirty years old and self-supporting, I'd say it definitely is my business. Now, if you don't mind, I haven't even had coffee yet, and I'm due to open the store in an hour. I appreciate you informing me of your decision. As I said, I will take it under advisement. Goodbye, Aunt Clara."

She hung up the phone before her aunt had finished sputtering in her ear. "This is not starting out to be one of my more scintillating days. Did you know you give a very bad impression on the phone, Jess?"

"I'll have to work on my telephone manners." He spoke offhandedly as he watched her face. "That rather rude woman is your aunt?"

"Unfortunately." Elly stalked toward the kitchen. "Any coffee?"

"Not yet, I just came in from outside. Haven't had time to make it." He followed her to the kitchen door, his eyes never leaving her as she busied herself with the coffee pot.

"What were you doing outside? Are you a jogging freak or something?" Elly asked irritably as she ran water into the pot. The way he was watching her made her more aware than ever of her rumpled, unexciting appearance. None of the fantasies she had ever had about her first morning with Jess Winter had gone quite like this.

"No. I just wanted to have a look around to see if I could find any trace of last night's visitor."

Elly's head came up quickly. "And did you?"

"Afraid not. It rained around four in the morning. Whatever evidence there might have been was long gone by the time I got outside. Don't look at me like that, Elly," he added too mildly. "There really *was* someone out there."

"I'm not going to argue the point. Lord knows I've got enough of an argument on my hands as it is."

"Something to do with your Aunt Clara?" Jess dropped casually into a seat by the window.

"Aunt Clara and most of my other relatives except my parents who are, thank goodness, out of the country."

"What's the problem?"

Elly sighed. "It's a long story. I'm sure you've got better things to do."

"Nope. Not a thing. Tell me the story, Elly."

"Look, Jess, I have to be at work in an hour. I don't have time for a long chat. Do you mind?" She hovered grimly over the coffee machine, waiting impatiently for it to brew.

"You can talk and make breakfast at the same time."

"Good grief. You're as bad as Aunt Clara. Why is everyone in my life so damned arrogant?"

"I don't think of myself as being arrogant. I think of it as being assertive."

She caught the thread of amusement in the words and glanced up sharply. Jess smiled benignly.

"Maybe I should take notes on assertiveness. It certainly seems to work for the rest of you," Elly grumbled. She poured coffee and began rummaging around in a cupboard for some granola cereal.

"Oh? Is it going to work for your aunt, then? Going to give her whatever it is she wants?"

"Not if I can help it. If she thinks I'm going to sell off the family inheritance, she's out of her mind," Elly said, flashing a determined look.

"What puts you in the position of even being able to sell off a family inheritance?"

Elly groaned. "You never give up, do you? You just keep pushing and prodding until you have an answer." She carried the canister of cereal and a carton of milk over to the table and they both sat down.

"I told you: assertiveness."

It was Elly who gave up. "I'll give you a short summary of the situation. My father's brother, Uncle Toby, founded a company called Trentco. When he died he left a sizable block of shares to me—controlling interest, in fact. Not that I wanted them, mind you, but because good old Uncle Toby knew his own relatives. He had a pretty fai hunch they'd sell off the company if they got the chance. Having put his life's blood into the firm, my uncle wanted to see it kept intact for the next generation of Trents. He had hopes someone like me or possibly my cousin Dave, or even one of the younger kids, might take charge of the firm someday. Now the rest of the family has decided they want to sell Trentco. We've had a good offer, and they've all had delusions of instant wealth.''

"So the rest of the family is putting pressure on you to vote the controlling block of shares in favor of the sale?''

"No wonder you were so good in business. You're so fast on your feet.''

Jess grinned. "You are grouchy in the mornings, aren't you? What does Trentco make?''

"Widgits.''

He arched one heavy eyebrow. "Widgits?''

"You know, little things like switches and wiring and stuff.''

"Oh. Widgits.''

"Yes. And I'm not going to vote to sell the company because my cousin Dave has shown a serious interest in it. He wants to keep it. He's studying business, and he seems to have an aptitude for that. In a few more years he'll be able to handle it. He has every right to his inheritance. And I've got a couple of little nieces whose mother needs the steady income, although she doesn't always think far enough ahead to realize it. She's too interested in the prospect of quick money.''

"So to protect the inheritance all you have to do is hold firm against Aunt Clara and the crowd?''

"Who all think I'm the typical product of an overly liberal education: An impractical, nonconforming, left-wing dropout of uncertain morals—except that after this morning, Aunt Clara is no longer uncertain about my morals.''

"Because I answered the phone?''

"Yeah.''

"You should have told her that you were going to marry me.''

"But I don't know that I am going to marry you,'' Elly retorted very carefully.

"Sure you are.'' He leaned across the table and covered her hand.

"Nothing has changed. All you have to do is admit that to yourself. Then everything can return to normal."

"It's because things weren't exactly normal between us that I started getting nervous in the first place!"

"Hence the big seduction scene last night?"

She flushed, concentrating on her granola. "I'm sure it must have been quite tame as seduction scenes go—I mean, considering what you're accustomed to in that line."

Jess didn't move, but the change in him was immediate and unmistakable. Elly shifted uneasily, knowing she had gone too far. Involuntarily she looked up to find him staring at her with the depths of winter in his eyes.

"Believe it or not, your style of seduction was a totally new experience for me. I've never had a woman ask me so sweetly or so honestly to make love to her. I'm used to games in that line, Elly. Not the real thing. I find I like the real thing very much. I'd like another chance."

Elly lurched to her feet and dropped her dishes into the sink. "I've got to get ready for work, Jess. It's getting late, and you know I have to open the shop at nine. Excuse me while I get dressed. Perhaps I'll, uh, see you later or something," she ended lamely as she hurried toward the door.

"You know damn well you're going to see me later, Elly," he said behind her, but she was already halfway to the stairs.

Some of the old anger and frustration came back as Jess watched Elly vanish. He owed this mess to Marina. Was the woman going to haunt him in one way or another for the rest of his life? Coldly, Jess dampened the threatening waves of fury. Marina was gone. He would not allow her to interfere in his new relationship with Elly.

Elly was a gentle, reasonable woman. She would calm down and return to her normal, even-tempered self. She just needed a little time. She wouldn't, she *couldn't* continue to hold the past against him.

But Jess knew deep down that matters would have been different this morning if Elly's sweet seduction scene last night had been allowed to continue to its conclusion. Everything would have been so much simpler today. Elly would have had the reassurance she needed that she was wanted and he... Jess paused, contemplating fully just what it was he had let slip away. He would have had a kind of warmth and closeness he'd never known. And he would have had one more bond between himself and Elly.

Jess swore softly and got to his feet to continue clearing the table. He had been a fool to waste so much time. He should have been making love to Elly for nearly two months. It seemed an act of malicious fate that, when at last matters in that department were finally going to get sorted out, something interfered.

Not something. Someone. Someone who looked a hell of a lot like Marina Carrington. Jess paused by the sink, thinking that last thought through. The only person he knew who looked a lot like Marina was her twin, Damon.

By the middle of the afternoon Elly had finally begun to come to terms with her reaction to the news of Jess's past. She had spent most of the day rationalizing, lecturing, analyzing and assessing. Jess had had the sensitivity to stay away from the shop. She assumed he was busy talking to the local contractors and craftsmen he would need to start the renovation work on the charming Victorian fantasy he intended to turn into a quiet, luxury inn. Uncertain as to what he would do at the end of the day, Elly busied herself stocking shelves and waiting on customers and tried not to think about the evening ahead.

The Natural Choice was one of those small-town community stores that become a meeting place for people who live nearby. In addition to buying the flours, grains, tofu and other assorted grocery products Elly stocked, local people dropped in to chat, catch up on news or just hang out. Everyone knew everybody else and shared information freely. It would have been impossible for the proprietor of such a shop to keep a romance quiet, and Elly had made no effort to do so. Everyone in the community knew of Jess Winter and his plans for the old mansion. They also knew Elly had been dating him steadily for two months. So Elly was prepared for casual inquiries even though she could cheerfully have done without them today.

"How's your friend, Elly? Thought I saw him over at Wilson's this morning?" Sarah Mitchell hoisted a gurgling eighteen-month-old baby onto her hip and reached into her handcrafted leather purse for her wallet. Everything about Sarah was handcrafted—from the long, paisley cotton skirt she had designed herself, to the fringed leather vest she wore over a denim shirt. Her hair reached to her waist and fell in a long heavy braid down her back. The baby, who went by the name of Compass Rose and who wasn't yet old enough to mind the unusual appelation, was dressed in a handknitted jumpsuit.

"I think he said something about wanting Wilson to do some woodwork in the hall," Elly murmured, packing rye flour, whole wheat pasta and tofu into a paper sack. She didn't particularly want to discuss Jess today, but she knew the questions were unavoidable. In the two months he had been coming and going between Portland and the coast, Jess had managed to make himself a familiar and welcome presence in town.

"Is he still going to want the stained-glass work?" Sarah asked a little uncertainly.

Elly suddenly realized what was making her customer anxious. She smiled reassuringly. "Don't worry, Sarah. He won't change his mind about the stained-glass order he mentioned to you. Once he makes a commitment like that he follows through."

Sarah nodded, looking relieved. "Good. The truth is, I could use the work."

"No check this month?" Elly asked commiseratingly.

The other woman shook her head. "No, and I think I'd better get used to the fact that there aren't going to be any more checks. Mark is long gone, Elly. He's not coming back. I've accepted that now, but it means I can't treat the stained glass as a hobby any longer. I've got to start making it pay. Or else I've got to find another kind of job."

"Jess will pay well for the beautiful work you do, Sarah. Don't worry," Elly said gently. Then, unobtrusively, she added several more ounces of whole-wheat pasta to the order. What the heck. Pasta was relatively cheap and the whole wheat was nutritious for little Compass Rose. Elly figured she wouldn't miss the profit on the few ounces of pasta. Sarah Mitchell could certainly use the extra food. Elly thought bleakly about the kind of man who would get a woman pregnant and then leave to "find himself." Jess Winter would never do that. Never in a million years.

"Your Jess is a good man, Elly."

"Yes." The kind of man who would follow through on his commitment to buy stained glass from an artist who was having trouble making ends meet. The kind of man who would not get a woman pregnant and then abandon her. Yes, Elly thought, Jess was a good man. His fundamental integrity was one of the things that had made her fall in love with him. She just wished he was in love with her the way she was with him—wildly, passionately, head-over-heels in love.

"Well, tell him I'm available whenever he's ready to have me start designing. I'll—" Sarah broke off as the bell over the door chimed cheerfully. "I'll…good heavens," she went on in a low tone. "Where did he come from?"

"Who? Jess? Is he here?" Suddenly tense, Elly turned to glance at whoever had opened the door and found herself blinking in astonishment at the newcomer. Sarah was still staring herself. And no wonder, Elly thought in a rush of amusement. It wasn't every day a man like this walked into The Natural Choice. "Looks like something from a calendar of 'hunks,'" she murmured.

The man who stood in the doorway nodded easily, apparently taking the feminine stares as his due. He strode forward with a nonchalance that told its own tale. This man was accustomed to being the center of attention. He was, without a doubt, the handsomest male Elly had ever seen. Tall, lean, with curly blond hair and perfectly chiseled features, he had a casual, sexy, inviting smile and a promise of excitement in his green eyes.

Green eyes, Elly thought suddenly. But there was no time to dwell on the bizarre notion that had just struck her. The man had reached the counter and with unerring instinct was already making the one move calculated to put everyone at ease. He was focusing the full force of his attention, something a few women Elly had met would have killed for, on Compass Rose.

"Hey, beautiful," he murmured to the wide-eyed toddler. "Where have you been all my life?"

"Her name is Compass Rose," Sarah explained hastily, bemused by the attention the handsome man was paying to her child.

"Compass Rose," the stranger repeated in a soft drawl. "Something tells me she's going to lead a lot of men astray during the next few years." He lifted a finger and chucked the baby under her chin.

Compass Rose's eyes got even wider and then, without warning, she started wailing. Turning her face into her mother's denim shirt, she clung fiercely, her high-pitched cry filling the shop.

"What in the world?" Startled, Sarah cradled the child closer. She cast an apologetic look at the newcomer. "I'm sorry. She's usually very good with strangers. I don't know what could have gotten into her. I guess I better get her out of here. Thanks, Elly. I'll see you later this week. You won't forget to remind Jess that I'm ready any time he is, will you?"

"I won't forget," Elly mouthed above the wails of Compass Rose. Sarah fled from the shop, cuddling the baby.

"Well," the stranger said philosophically as the door closed on the child's cries, "I guess I'm not that good with the younger set." He leaned on the counter and smiled at Sarah. "But I'm hell on wheels with older women."

Elly blinked owlishly and wondered why she felt the irrational desire to do the same as Compass Rose had done and start screaming. "Perhaps you'd like to meet my Aunt Clara," she said instead. "She's in her sixties so I guess she'd qualify as an older woman."

Green eyes flashed wickedly. "I had in mind something midrange."

Elly summoned up a polite, shopkeeper's smile. "Did you? Well, I'm sure you'll find it. Let me know if you need any assistance while shopping. There are some handbaskets over by the bread counter and one old shopping cart that I keep for emergencies. I'm afraid this isn't exactly a supermarket."

"I'm only looking for one particular item." He didn't move from the counter.

"Just as well, I'll be closing soon, anyway. What was it you wanted?"

"I came here to meet someone."

"I'm afraid I don't—"

"Nothing to be concerned about," the stranger said easily. "I've got lots of time. Some things are better if they aren't rushed." Then he reached out, the same way he had to Compass Rose and caught Elly lightly under her chin.

She was so startled by the audacity of the man that it took Elly a few seconds to realize what he was doing. Then, before she could react to the overfamiliar touch, the shop bell chimed again as the door opened. Without even looking in that direction Elly knew who stood on the threshold.

Far too gently, Jess closed the door behind himself and stood taking in the sight of Elly's uncertain, wary expression as the other man's hand dropped from her chin. Then, as if there was no particular importance about the matter, he glanced at the blond-haired, green-eyed newcomer.

Elly's pulse was racing as if she'd found herself in a fight-or-flight situation rather than safely behind the counter of her shop. She watched Jess walk calmly down the aisle to where she stood behind the waist-high barrier. The room seemed to be filled with strange tension. A part of her urged flight, but another element warned that there was no safe place to run. Then Jess was flattening his palms on the polished counter, leaning across it to kiss her with seeming casualness.

Elly didn't resist, but she knew her lips must have been as cold as his. This was not a kiss of warmth or even casual affection. This was a public announcement for the benefit of the green-eyed man who stood watching in amusement. Coolly, Jess straightened and turned to confront the other man.

"Well, Carrington, I would have been happy to live the rest of my life without ever seeing you again. But I guess that was too much to hope for. What the hell brings you here?"

Damon Carrington smiled, and Elly cringed inwardly.

"Is that any way to greet family?" Damon asked mildly.

"You're not family. Not anymore." Jess leaned against the counter, his pose deceptively cool. "I'm not overflowing with patience this afternoon. What do you want?"

"What makes you so sure I'm after something?"

"It's your nature."

Damon considered that. "Maybe you're right."

"So what is it this time?"

"Going to give me what I want without a fight, Winter? That's not like you. I expected to have to work at this a little." Damon glanced at Elly's still face. "But maybe you've got other things to worry about these days, hmm? Little projects you wouldn't want jeopardized. She's not too bad, Jess. Not in Marina's league, of course, but how many women are?" He started to lift his hand again, apparently planning to recapture Elly's chin. Green eyes examined her with calculating interest.

Jess didn't move. "Touch her and I'll kill you, Carrington."

The threat hovered in the air, as real as the man who had made it. Damon's eyes narrowed in amusement, but he dropped his hand. "Well, well. This is serious, isn't it?"

"I think it's time for you to leave, Carrington. Elly is going to close the shop, aren't you, Elly?" He pinned her with his glance. The command radiated from him in waves.

Elly didn't even make a pretense of resisting. She wanted out of that tension-fraught room more than anyone could have imagined. "Yes," she said firmly, "I am." Quickly she began readying the cash register.

"No need to run, Winter. I can find you easily enough. It's a small town, isn't it? A little too small for you, I would have said."

"Small towns have their advantages. It's easy to keep track of unwanted strangers. You might keep that in mind."

Damon shook his head sadly. "You surprise me, Winter. I would have expected you to keep going in the fast lane. All the way to the top, wherever that is. People used to say the sky was the limit where you were concerned. Now look at you, getting ready to run an inn in a sleepy little village on the coast. Picked just the right kind of woman to go with your new life-style, didn't you? She looks sweet, Winter. Maybe a little too sweet for you. After all, you're accustomed to something with a little more tang, aren't you? I never—Hey! Damn you, what the hell do you think…?"

"Jess!" Elly whirled around, stunned to see Jess come away from the counter in a smooth, coiled movement.

He had Damon flattened against the wall before Elly fully realized what had happened. Raw menace etched Jess's face, and his eyes were like ice as he leaned forward. His voice was a harsh whisper.

"Get out of here, Carrington. Don't let me see you again. Is that very clear? I swear as God is my witness I won't be able to guarantee your safety if I ever see you again. If you come near Elly I can promise you that I'll make you pay."

Damon hissed, "Pay? You're the one who's going to pay, Winter. You owe me!"

"For what?"

"For what you did to Marina!"

"I didn't do a damn thing to her except divorce her. And as I recall she was already tired of me anyway. Are you crazy, Carrington?"

"She's dead!"

"I didn't kill her and you damn well know it," Jess growled.

"She'd be alive today if it hadn't been for you."

"What the hell are you talking about?"

"You cut her off without a penny," Damon said accusingly.

"So? She'd socked away plenty while she was married to me. Not exactly my fault if she didn't invest it! You *are* crazy."

"She wouldn't have had to sleep with that old bastard if it hadn't been for the way you left her high and dry."

"I get it," Jess said wearily. "If she hadn't been sleeping with him for his money she wouldn't have been on his yacht when it capsized. Therefore, it's all my fault. Is that your logic? You're out of your mind, Carrington." He released his victim. "Get away from me. I don't want to see you anywhere near Elly again. *Get out of here!*"

Damon moved warily away from the wall, straightening his rumpled black shirt. "You owe me, Winter."

Jess ignored him, reaching for Elly's arm as she came around the counter. "Are you ready?"

"Yes," she whispered, shaken by the violence. "Yes, I'm ready."

The chime sounded as the door closed abruptly behind Damon Carrington. Elly jumped a little at the noise. "Excitement," she said almost inaudibly.

"What?" Jess was turning off the lights with swift, chopping motions of his hand.

"You said the Carringtons brought excitement into one's life. I don't think I'm into excitement, Jess. Not if that's any sample of it."

Jess halted at the door, turning to look down at her. His eyes were fierce. "And you're not going to get 'into' it. You're not going to get anywhere near it, do you understand? I don't want you in the same room with Damon Carrington. Elly, I've seen Carrington in action. The man's a warlock where women are concerned. He casts spells on them."

"Not on all women," she denied.

"You don't know what I'm talking about."

"Little Compass Rose hated him on sight." *And it didn't take me much longer to hate him,* Elly added silently. She had begun to hate and fear Damon Carrington the moment she realized he was a threat to Jess.

"Compass Rose? Oh, you mean Sarah Mitchell's kid. I'm not talking about his effect on children. But I've seen him manipulate women, and they're like putty in his hands. Stay out of his way. Do you understand me, Elly?"

"I understand." She couldn't think of anything else to say. Her instinct was to give him the agreement he demanded and then change the subject. Once again she found herself hesitating to push Jess.

Out on the street there was no sign of Carrington. Elly was grateful. "Sarah said to tell you that she could do the stained-glass designs whenever you were ready. The sooner the better, Jess."

It was obvious Jess still had other things on his mind. He frowned down at Elly. "Why sooner? I've got that work scheduled a couple of months downstream."

"There's been no word from Mark. No money either."

Jess nodded abruptly. "I get it. The bastard's skipped, huh? Okay, I'll talk to her tomorrow. I'll give her an advance on the job. That should hold her for a while."

"Thank you, Jess." A good man, Elly thought.

"Elly?"

"Yes?"

"I meant what I said a minute ago. Stay away from Carrington. He's poison."

It occurred to Elly that she had never seen Jess Winter so passionate about anything before, except for those brief moments last night when he had finally begun to make love to her. "It's obvious the Carringtons, brother and sister, had a fairly traumatic effect on you, Jess."

"It's trauma I can do without repeating. Remember how you once told me that you loved to live near the ocean, that you like looking at it, watching the changing weather on it, walking alongside it, but that you never ever went swimming in it?"

"I remember." It was the truth. She never swam in the sea.

"Well, treat Damon Carrington the same way."

"Look, but don't touch?"

"I don't even want you looking at him."

She smiled tremulously and not without a touch of hope. "Are you telling me that you might be capable of feeling a little jealousy over me?"

The ill-advised remark stopped him in his tracks. "Lady, you don't know what you're talking about. You haven't got the least idea of what jealousy does to people, so don't try to tease me. I want your word of honor that you'll steer clear of Carrington."

"Oh, Jess, I never meant…"

"Your word, Elly," he repeated roughly, his fingers sinking almost painfully into her shoulders.

She looked up at him with gentle assurance. "Jess, you don't have to worry about Carrington putting a spell on me. I feel toward him very much the way Compass Rose does."

He watched her for a moment and then seemed to come to some inner conclusion. "Good. Keep it that way."

She would, Elly thought with a sense of resignation, because she loved Jess too much ever to let herself be used against him, even if it was only his pride that was at stake. But she couldn't help wishing that more than his pride and self-respect were involved.

A part of her wished Jess loved her so passionately that he might truly be vulnerable to the fear of losing her to another man. As it was, she was very much aware that his reactions to Carrington stemmed from the unpleasantness of the past and from an angry pride that refused to let a woman lead him through hell again.

Four

On Monday morning Elly gave in to the impulse to take a walk on the beach before opening The Natural Choice. She'd taken Sunday off as usual, but the day had not been a particularly relaxing one. This morning she was tense and restless.

Jess had left for Portland the previous evening. At least he'd stopped pressuring her for an answer to his proposal, Elly thought unhappily. He finally seemed to sense that she needed more time to come to terms with the situation. She had known instinctively that he hadn't wanted to give her that additional time, and in a way it surprised her. Until now Jess had acted as if there was no rush about anything in life. He had been content to let matters take their course. But, then, that was probably because until now Jess had set the course himself. The schedule might have seemed loose, Elly decided, but it had been in place. Subtly, calmly, quietly, Jess Winter had been in control of events all along.

Until the past had intruded.

There had been no sign of Damon Carrington since Saturday afternoon. No one in town seemed to have seen him and that apparently reassured Jess. Elly had a hunch that if there had been any indication that Carrington was still around, Jess would have found an excuse not to return to Portland. It would have been an expensive excuse because

these last few weeks in the city were important from a business stand-
point. Jess was winding up a lucrative consulting assignment and fi-
nalizing his financial arrangements for the forthcoming change in his
life-style. It would have constituted another unwelcome change in his
plans.

The tide was out this morning, and Elly took pleasure in exploring
the nooks and crannies that were underwater at other times. The beach
here was a rocky one, with a number of fascinating tidepools, encrusted formations and miniature worlds tucked away in the rocks. The
small cove was dominated by a huge boulder that crouched aloofly in
the center. When the tide was in, there was no way to reach it. Foaming
water surged around it, acting like a moat around a castle. But this
morning it stood undefended, prepared to yield its secrets to anyone
who was willing to cross the damp, packed sand.

Elly had explored the rock castle before, but it never ceased to
interest her. Starfish clung to its base, small fish swam in pools of
trapped water and a variety of crustaceans scampered over the surface
in an endless quest for food.

The sea was an alien world to Elly, one she found enthralling but
also one she feared on some levels. It was all very well to study its
creatures while they were exposed and vulnerable. The thought of
meeting them in their natural environment while the tide was in struck
a primitive chord of genuine fear. And it wasn't just the life forms of
the sea she feared. The power of the surging waves was equally disturbing. Elly could swim, but she never swam in the sea. She hadn't
since that one terrifying afternoon on a southern California beach.

But this morning she poked around the huge boulder in the quiet
cove with her usual interest, her mind occupied with the problem of
Jess Winter.

She had been belatedly astonished by her initial reaction to the threat
of Damon Carrington. Her instincts had been to defend Jess, but that
was ridiculous. If anyone could take care of himself, it was Jess Winter. Perhaps a woman always felt that way about the man she loved.

"Ah, Jess," she muttered, turning away from the exposed boulder
to start back toward the house, "do you think you'll ever let yourself
really fall in love again?" And if he did, was she the kind of woman
he would choose?

Comfortable, even-tempered, sweet. Elly ran through the irritating list of adjectives Jess so often applied to her, and she wanted to scream. The list hardly allowed for passion and love. But, then, Jess didn't want to allow for either of those potentially dangerous emotions in his life.

Elly thought of those brief moments Friday night when at last she had stirred real desire in him. It was foolish to cling to such thoughts and try to build on them. After all, it was perfectly possible for a man to have his sexual appetite aroused without having any real love aroused with it.

In any event, the whole project had foundered because of a face at the window. Not for the first time, Elly wondered if it had been Damon Carrington peering into her living room that night. In the dark and the fog would Jess have briefly mistaken Damon for his twin?

Reluctantly Elly climbed the cliff path. At the top she turned one last time to gaze out at the everchanging sea. The chilled early morning breeze whipped at her braids, loosing strands of hair that blew into her eyes. Perhaps it was those tendrils that were causing the threat of tears.

The phone rang that evening just as Elly was sitting down to a quiet meal in the kitchen. The possibility that it might be Aunt Clara almost kept her from answering. The probability that it might be Jess made Elly stretch out her hand.

"Oh, Jess, I'm glad it's you."

"Who were you expecting?" There was an unfamiliar edge to the question.

"I was afraid it might be Aunt Clara."

Jess seemed to relax on the other end of the line. "Has she been pestering you?"

"No, but she will as the time of the stockholders' meeting gets closer," Elly predicted. "Aunt Clara is very persistent, especially where money is concerned."

"I've been thinking about that situation, Elly." Jess suddenly sounded all business. "Why don't I look into it for you? If Aunt Clara and the family knew you had some, er…"

"High-priced firepower to back me, she might stop bothering me?"

Elly concluded with a quick grin. "Jess, I couldn't afford even half your usual fee."

"For you I'll work cheap."

"How cheap?"

He paused and then said blandly, "An answer to my proposal would be sufficient. A *yes* answer, that is."

Elly's brief humor faded. "Jess, please don't push."

"Honey, there's no reason to hesitate and you know it." He seemed to want to pursue the argument but instead changed the subject. "Carrington hasn't shown up has he?"

"No."

"Good. I want you to let me know immediately if he does. Understand, Elly?"

"I understand." Elly wondered how Jess could suddenly sound so cold and forbidding. Only a few seconds ago he had been trying to coax her into agreeing to marry him.

"Eating dinner?"

"How did you guess?"

"Just a hunch, based on the fact that I'm about to eat mine. What are you having?"

"Leftover lentil casserole and a glass of that Washington State cabernet wine I had tucked away in the cupboard."

"Sounds good. Better than the frozen dinner I just put into the oven. I'll be down early on Friday, Elly."

Elly's hand clenched in unexpected nervousness. "Fine."

"I think you should be able to have your answer ready by then, don't you?" The question was cool and pointed.

"I—I don't know, Jess."

"I think you do, honey. Stop dragging it out. You know this is what you want. Goodnight, Elly."

"Goodnight, Jess." Unhappily she replaced the receiver. He had cut off the conversation so quickly tonight. Usually Jess talked for half an hour when he called.

The phone rang almost immediately. Elly reached for it without thinking, and this time it was Aunt Clara. With a stifled groan, Elly forced herself to listen politely while her aunt went through a harangue about the financial reasons for selling Trentco. There was no attempt at a discussion; it was purely a lecture.

Elly was exhausted by the time she hung up and for the first time she wondered if things might not be easier if she let Jess represent her. Dealing with family was always an emotionally taxing situation, especially when the relatives in question were Trents. Maybe a disinterested third party could exert a calming, persuasive influence.

The drawback to involving Jess in the thorny family situation was that it meant involving him more deeply in her life at a time when Elly was wondering if it wouldn't be best to end the relationship.

It was Sarah Mitchell who reminded her the next day of the potluck gathering scheduled for Wednesday evening.

"Good Lord, I almost forgot," Elly exclaimed. "I'm supposed to take my world-famous lentil casserole."

"I didn't know you had a famous lentil casserole. Last time you brought a salad, didn't you?"

"Believe me, this sucker is going to be famous after Wednesday evening. I've been working on it for months. I think I've got it tuned to perfection. Jess seems to like it, at any rate. What are you bringing, Sarah?"

"Thanks to the advance I got from Jess I think I can manage my usual whole wheat pasta salad. By the way, I've already started designing some glass for the entryway of his inn. I went out to the place this morning and did some studies. I'm really looking forward to doing the work."

Sarah's enthusiasm was heartwarming. Little Compass Rose jabbered contentedly while the adults talked, and Elly privately concluded that both the child and her mother were probably going to be better off without the unreliable influence of Mark Casey in their lives.

That realization made Elly think of Jess. Whatever qualms she had about marrying him weren't based on any fears of his unreliability. Jess was the kind of man you could count on when the chips were down. Elly knew that with a deep-seated instinct.

The potluck on Wednesday was a casual meeting of neighbors and friends that Elly fully expected to enjoy. A month ago a similar party had been held at the house of a local artisan who lived fairly close to

Elly. Tonight, however, a different couple had opened their home, and this time Elly had been obliged to drive several miles to the farmsite. Ann Palmer and her husband, Jim, had recently moved to Oregon from California and were intent on pursuing a back-to-the-land life-style. It remained to be seen whether they would be successful in making the farm produce, but in the meantime they were thoroughly enjoying their new life.

"Elly! There you are. I was wondering where you were." Ann Palmer approached to take the lentil casserole as her guest walked in the door. "Next month we all expect Jess to accompany you to these gala social bashes. He'll have completed his move by then, won't he?"

"If all goes according to schedule," Elly agreed diplomatically. "And where Jess is concerned, nearly everything does go according to schedule." She glanced around the room full of casually dressed craftsmen, artists, small-time farmers and boutique proprietors and wondered whether Jess knew what he would be getting into socially. Probably. He always seemed to know what he was doing.

Half an hour later Elly was in the middle of an intense discussion concerning the merits of growing one's own sprouts when the roomful of people underwent that strange phenomena of going quiet all at once. Instinctively Elly glanced toward the door, and quite suddenly she knew what Jess had meant when he had tried to explain the Carringtons' impact on a crowd.

Damon Carrington stood in the doorway, smiling in secret amusement as everyone glanced at the tall figure. He was dressed all in black and a lock of blond hair curled rakishly over one brow. His green eyes moved over the curious faces with no sign of self-consciousness, just a hint of condescension. He was not alone. At his side was Sarah Mitchell, looking happier than Elly had seen her since Mark had left.

Elly watched her friend in dismay, but she knew immediately there would be no point trying to warn her about Damon. The Carrington charm was clearly at work and highly effective. Little Compass Rose had apparently been left with a sitter for the evening. Elly wondered if the child had been wailing when her mother left with the strange man.

The hum of activity started up again, and Elly excused herself to get some more salad from the long table that had been set up against one wall. As far as she was concerned, her pleasure in the friendly evening had just evaporated. Damon Carrington was still around and that, she knew in her bones, meant trouble.

"Hi, Elly. You met Damon the other day, remember?" Sarah's voice was bubbling with enthusiasm. "I ran into him yesterday again when I went out to Jess's inn to make some more sketches. Wasn't that a coincidence? Damon is very fond of Victorian architecture, aren't you Damon?"

"Fascinated." Damon's brilliant green eyes swept over Elly. She wanted to cringe from that gaze, and found she had to make an effort to act nonchalantly. "I understand you have a very interesting place yourself, Elly."

"Nothing spectacular," she assured him quickly. "Just an old, updated beach cottage, actually."

"I'd like to see it sometime," he murmured.

"I'm afraid I really don't..."

Before Elly could finish her horrified excuse, Sarah was interrupting cheerfully. "I told Damon he would probably be bored to tears tonight, but he insisted on coming along. Said he wanted to see what life was like in a small beach town."

"I imagine it's a real change for you, Damon," Elly said coolly.

"I'm highly adaptable."

"I'll just bet you are," Elly murmured. She sipped her hot spiced cider and tried to think of a way to escape from the small confrontation.

"Damon says he'd like to take me and Compass Rose to the beach tomorrow. Wouldn't that be nice?" Sarah reached around Elly to help herself to a small sandwich.

"It's too cold for swimming," Damon said, accepting the sandwich from Sarah with a charming smile, "but I thought Compass Rose might enjoy playing on the beach."

"It's always too cold for swimming as far as Elly is concerned," Sarah said with a laugh. "She hates the water, don't you Elly? She's afraid of sharks and things. Has a real phobia about swimming in the sea."

"I didn't realize there were sharks in these waters," Damon said, eyeing Elly with interest.

"The truth is," Elly said blandly, "most of the sharks are on land. Which is lucky, I guess. So much easier to spot them that way." She didn't wait to see if Damon had gotten the point. Instead she slipped away from the potluck table with a smile. "Now, if you'll excuse me I want to talk to Ruth and Liz about that quilt they're doing for me. I'll see you later, Sarah."

"Right," Sarah smiled and turned back to bask in the attention of the handsomest male at the gathering.

From a discrete distance Elly watched her friend during the rest of the evening, knowing there was really nothing she could do to interfere. Damon had set out to make a conquest. It was easy to see, Elly decided, just what a captivating effect Damon Carrington had on women. Every female in the room was aware of him. When they spoke to him they bubbled with enthusiasm; their eyes were a little brighter, the conversation a little more intense. There was a feeling of excitement in the air. Elly could imagine what the impact on the males would be if a female version of Damon had walked into the room. She began to see what Marina Carrington must have been like in action. It was frightening.

By ten o'clock the good-natured crowd began to break up. Sarah left with Damon, her eyes still too excited as far as Elly was concerned. She worried for her friend, but she didn't know what to do. Sarah had been so unhappy for so many months it seemed cruel to step in and try to blight the one spark that had come into her life. You couldn't make other people's decisions for them, Elly told herself as she helped Ann Palmer clean up the old farmhouse parlor.

"Drive carefully, Elly. The fog is starting to get heavy out there. Take it easy going home." Ann smiled as Elly collected the empty casserole dish.

"Don't worry, I'll be careful. It was a lovely evening, Ann."

"That Carrington man certainly livened things up, didn't he? He's almost too good looking somehow. Like something out of a magazine ad."

Elly nodded, glad that at least one other woman in the room had realized that fact. "I agree with you. It's as if he's not quite real. Or quite human."

"I'll stick with my Jim, I think," Ann confided lightly. "One thing you can say for Jim; he's human!" She grinned at her bearded husband, who was scooping up paper plates. Jim growled a laughing response as Ann turned back to Elly. "You'll do fine with your Jess. By the way, that casserole was fantastic. What's the secret?"

"Wine, molasses and ground chili peppers. Took a while to get the proportions down right."

"How many times have you experimented with it on Jess?"

Elly winced, remembering how frequently Jess had found himself eating a different version of lentil casserole during the past two months. "I hate to think about it. He never complained, though."

"He wouldn't. He values homecooking too much. The last time I saw him at the store he told me he couldn't wait to get it full-time."

"Then he should hire a cook!"

Ann Palmer's expression softened. "Elly, believe me, there's nothing wrong in having a man like your cooking. That old cliché about the way to a man's heart being through his stomach didn't get to be a cliché by being untrue, you know. Clichés get to be clichés just because they do contain an element of truth. He's a good man, your Jess."

Elly smiled politely and hastened out to her car. *If only he really were my Jess,* she thought. *Completely, unequivocally, wholeheartedly mine.* Damned if she was going to let herself be married for her cooking and other convenient skills!

The interior of the car was cold, and the engine resisted starting. When she finally got it going, Elly sat in the darkness for a few minutes, letting the heater warm up. Then, with the headlights dim to minimize the glare off the fog, she started down the narrow country road.

It was slow going, and Elly told herself to relax and take her time. The fog ebbed and swirled around the car, but she could still make out the edges of the road as well as several yards of pavement in front of her. She would be safe enough if she didn't rush.

The lights of the Palmer's farmhouse disappeared after a short distance, and then there was only the reflected glare of the car's headlights. Elly turned on the radio for company. The road had no other traffic.

She was singing along to one of her favorite country and western songs when the car's engine sputtered and died. Elly let the vehicle drift to the side of the road. Stifling a small anxiety attack, she shut off both the heater and the radio and tried to restart the engine. It became clear very quickly that the task was hopeless. She seemed to be out of gas.

The next thing that became clear was that the only way to get home was to walk. Elly took a long time reaching that decision. The prospect was not a pleasant one. Briefly she considered hiking back toward the Palmers' and then decided that she was about equidistant from her home and that of her friends. She might as well head home.

One of these days, Elly promised herself as she climbed reluctantly out of the car and buttoned her parka, she was going to remember to carry a flashlight in the glove compartment. Things like this probably never happened to Jess. But if they did he'd have been better prepared to handle them.

"One of the advantages of not being married," Elly lectured herself bracingly as she started down the forbidding road. "You won't have to listen to any men yell at you when you get home a little late tonight." You had to look on the bright side.

Jess almost pounced on the phone when it rang that evening in his Portland apartment. He'd been trying to get hold of Elly since six o'clock and had been increasingly frustrated over her failure to answer the phone. She was almost always home when he called. He realized he'd begun to take the fact for granted. In what he knew Elly would refer to as typical male fashion, frustration had turned into irritation, which was rapidly metamorphosing into outright anger.

What Elly wouldn't have guessed, and Jess knew he didn't want to admit, was that the anger was being fed by a fear he dared not put into words. By the time he picked up the receiver, however, his voice was dark and rough with the combination of emotions.

"Mr. Winter, this is Mary at your service."

His answering service. Elly never used that number unless she couldn't reach him at home. He'd been home all evening. Jess closed his eyes briefly as the strange anger in him threatened to increase.

"Go ahead, Mary," he said to the faceless woman he'd never met but who faithfully answered his work number and relayed messages.

"You just had a call from a man who refused to leave his name. He said you'd know who it was." Mary's tone said she strongly disapproved of callers who wouldn't leave proper information.

Jess's fingers locked on the receiver. "Read it to me."

"He said to tell you it was going to be an interesting night on the coast and that he'll have her home by morning."

Jess stared blankly at the white vase full of some sort of tall, artificial grass fronds that stood against the far wall of his living room. He'd never liked the vase or the dull-colored grass, but it had been too much trouble to get rid of it. After all, he'd told himself on countless occasions, he'd be moving soon. He'd be living with Elly, who always kept plenty of fresh flowers and live plants in her home.

"Mr. Winter? Did you get that, sir?"

"Yes, Mary. I got it. Thank you." Very carefully Jess replaced the phone. He had to move carefully or he knew he might fracture the tough plastic between his fingers.

Carrington. The secret fear he hadn't wanted to acknowledge had become real with a vengeance.

The hell of it was, he thought as the fury and fear battled within him, he didn't even know where to start looking. Carrington could have taken Elly anywhere. Women went with him so easily, like moths to a flame.

Jess stood in the middle of his sophisticated off-white living room and thought of his sweet, gentle Elly under Carrington's spell. Quite suddenly, Jess realized he would go out of his mind if he spent the night here in Portland.

He had to go to the coast. He had to be waiting at Elly's home in the morning when Carrington brought her back. He had to see it with his own eyes; had to see Elly mussed and rumpled from a night in Carrington's arms. Then he would tear Damon Carrington apart.

Elly heard the faint sound of a car's engine before she had gone more than a couple hundred feet along the road. She glanced over her shoulder and caught the glare of headlights moving slowly through the swirling fog. Relief swept through her as she turned and started back. Chances were she would know the other driver and he or she would be happy to give her a lift home. It was a wonderful thing living in a small community where you knew your neighbors, Elly thought happily.

She was never quite certain what vague instinct made her decide to identify the vehicle before she darted out into the road to hail it. Perhaps it was the knowledge that not everyone on this road might be familiar or perhaps it was the general eeriness of the swirling fog. A woman had to take a few precautions, she reminded herself, even out here in the boondocks. Jess was always lecturing her along those lines. But, then, he tended to harp on things like that a lot.

Still, she would just make sure that her potential rescuer was someone she knew.

The fog concealed her easily enough as Elly scrambled down into the ditch beside the road and up the other side. There she stood behind the cover of roadside brush and a small clump of trees and watched as the oncoming headlights slowed and then stopped beside her car. She squinted, trying to make out the color of the other vehicle. It wasn't Jim Palmer's beat up red pickup, that was for certain. From what she could see of the car beyond the glaring lights, it looked sleek and sporty. A Porsche, perhaps.

No one she knew drove a Porsche.

Then the sportscar's door opened and a man climbed out of the front seat. Elly identified him even before the headlights illuminated Damon Carrington's blond head as he walked around the front of his car. She froze in the shelter of the brush the way a small animal freezes in the presence of its natural enemy.

Elly was suddenly very grateful she hadn't brought along a flashlight. Carrington might have seen the small beam moving along the road as he'd approached her car.

He walked to the front door of her little compact and peered into the window. A moment later he reached for the handle and yanked it open.

"Elly?"

Her name was chillingly audible in the still night. Elly crouched lower behind the brush, huddling and praying he wouldn't decide to search the nearby terrain.

"Elly? It's me, Damon Carrington. Looks like you had car trouble. I can give you a lift home. Where are you?"

He was just calling to her on the hunch she might still be in the vicinity, Elly thought as she reassured herself. He couldn't know for certain. In another moment he would have to assume that she had abandoned her car much earlier and was already quite a way down the road.

"Elly?" Some of the pleasant, helpfulness of his tone was fading, to be replaced by impatience. Damon walked a few paces down the road in front of the cars, peering into the fog. He didn't glance toward the side or up into the brush beyond the ditch. He was assuming she had continued walking straight down the road.

A logical assumption, Elly admitted to herself. It was exactly what she had done.

"Elly!"

After that last call, Damon apparently decided he was wasting his time. He swung around and headed back toward his car.

Elly watched in relief as he slid inside the Porsche and switched on the engine. The car moved slowly, partly because of the fog, of course, but also because he was probably watching for her, Elly decided. A moment later the sleek car slipped into the fog and disappeared.

She was getting paranoid and it was all Jess Winter's fault.

Shaking her head, Elly straightened from behind the brush and leaped nimbly down into the roadside ditch. Then she darted up the other side and resumed her cold, lonely walk.

It was idiotic to have hidden herself from Carrington like that. She should have been glad of the ride he was offering. Even now she could have been luxuriating in the warmth of the Porsche's front seat. Instead she was stuck with a long walk home. Ridiculous.

But Elly knew in her heart that if she had to make the choice again, she would do the same thing. Jess had warned her to stay away from Damon Carrington because he was wary of the younger man's effect on women. Elly had no fear of Carrington in that sense. She felt absolutely no attraction to the man. But she did fear Carrington's effect on the man she loved. She'd rather walk home in the fog than take a free ride from the man Jess hated.

Not that Jess was ever likely to find out about tonight's odd events, Elly thought as she finally came in sight of the welcoming light from her front porch. It was best he never did. He would put his own construction on things. Then he might go out and do something quite violent. Elly shuddered.

Wearily she tramped the last couple of hundred yards. The fog had lifted a little, but the air had grown colder. A chilled wind was starting up from the sea. The jeans she was wearing provided little protection for her legs, and they were beginning to feel quite numb as she approached her house.

Elly bent her head against the biting breeze, and thus failed to see the other car in her driveway until she almost bumped into it.

For an instant, panic gripped her as she raised her head to see the sleek lines of a pale-white vehicle. In the next instant she realized it wasn't a Porsche. It was Jess's Jaguar sedan.

Cold, damp and weary, Elly paused beside the car, staring down at it. She couldn't figure out what it was doing in her driveway in the middle of the week. Jess had said nothing about driving over to the coast before Friday. With a sigh she continued toward the porch, climbing the old wooden steps as if they were small mountains.

The door opened before she could dig her key out of her leather shoulder bag, and Elly found herself staring up into Jess Winter's taut, savage face. In the harsh light of the porch fixture, his eyes were the color of the fog that had shrouded the road behind her. The tension in him was lethal.

"Elly."

She blinked, alarmed by the harshness of her name on his lips. She drew a deep breath and stepped forward, pushing past him into her warm, inviting hall. "Well, of course it's Elly. I live here, remember? What in the world are you doing here on a Wednesday, Jess? You always do things on schedule and you're not scheduled to be here until Friday. My God, it's cold out there. My legs are absolutely numb. I need a hot shower and a cup of hot chocolate. You wouldn't believe what happened to me tonight. I ran out of gas. And don't give me any lectures on the subject because I could have sworn I had plenty of fuel. I just filled the tank on Monday at Pete's service station and I've hardly driven twenty or thirty miles since..."

"Elly!"

She swung around. "What is it, Jess?"

"Are you all right?"

"I'm fine. Just a little cold. Why shouldn't I be all right? It was a long walk but other than that..."

Jess stepped forward, his hands coming up to clamp around her shoulders. Oddly she could feel the tension in him and it frightened her. Elly realized she'd never seen Jess in quite this mood.

"I had a message from Carrington," he began grimly.

"Carrington!" She stared at him in shocked disbelief. "Why on earth would he contact you?"

"To tell me you were spending the night with him, and that he would bring you home in the morning."

Images of Damon Carrington prowling through the fog, searching for her, rose up in Elly's mind and took on new, menacing significance. "I was at the Palmers' tonight, Jess. You remember I told you about the potluck? I ran out of gas on the way home and had to walk."

"I can see that." His eyes moved over her, taking in the fog-dampened hair and parka, the mud-splattered shoes and the breeze-whipped color of her cheeks. Suddenly he pulled her fiercely into his arms. "Hell, Elly. I can *see* that."

Elly thought he would crush the breath out of her body. The driving urgency in him was totally new to her. She wasn't certain how to handle it.

"I would have killed him, Elly. I would have strangled him with my bare hands if he had brought you home in the morning."

"Then started in on me?" Elly tried to lift her head so that she could look up into his face, but Jess continued to crush her against his hard body.

"Elly..."

"Jess," she whispered, wrapping her arms around his neck, "how could you think I would go with him?"

"You don't know him, Elly."

"I know one thing for certain about him: He's not the man I want. Furthermore, I resent your thinking that I'm some empty-headed female who's an easy victim for any good-looking man who happens to come along. I'm an adult human being, Jess, and I'm quite capable of picking and choosing my acquaintances on the basis of something besides their physical appearance!''

"Calm down, Elly.''

"I will not calm down! Why should I? I've had a miserable walk home, and I arrive to find some brute on my doorstep who thinks I'm totally unable to run my own life. Your faith in me is hardly flattering, Jess. In fact, I get the distinct impression you don't have much trust in me at all. Hardly a good way to begin a marriage. The more I think about it, the more I'm convinced we're not going to make it together, after all. I want someone who has some respect for my integrity and my brains. Furthermore—''

"Elly, hush.''

"Why should I hush? In addition to integrity and brains, I've also got a mouth.''

"You can say that again!''

Before Elly could protest further, Jess stopped her tirade with the most fundamental approach of all. He covered her mouth with his own, and this time his kiss wasn't the casual sort she had come to expect from him. His hands were already moving in her hair, even as his tongue surged possessively between her teeth.

This time, Elly knew, Jess intended to set his seal on her. He was going to take her to bed.

For the first time since she had begun to acknowledge her love for him, Elly was afraid of what would happen if she let him make love to her.

Five

The fear and uncertainty were real, but neither could prevail against the desperate need for reassurance Elly read in Jess's eyes. It was odd, she thought fleetingly as he gathered her into his arms, for the past two months she had been the one seeking reassurance, eventually trying for it on a physical basis. Tonight Jess hungered for it.

But there was a sharp, inescapable difference in the underlying motives. Elly had sought assurance of his love, some indication of a passion and need that matched her own. Tonight Jess was seeking only assurance of her commitment to him. She would be a fool if she forgot that fundamental distinction. But reason and caution faded next to her overwhelming desire to give Jess what he seemed to need.

"Elly," he muttered against her mouth, "I should have done this a long time ago. I should have realized that with a woman like you this is a way to be sure. I handled it all wrong. I see that now."

"Handled what wrong? Jess, I don't—" But his tongue probed boldly into her mouth once more, and Elly moaned softly beneath the sensual onslaught.

His strong hands slid down her back, blunt fingers kneading her muscles with undisguised pleasure. When he reached her waist Jess lifted her, pulling her up into the urgent hardness of his lower body.

At least there was no doubt that he wanted her, Elly thought dazedly.

She clung to that knowledge as fiercely as she clung to him. If she could make him want her badly enough, perhaps he would let himself love her.

"Sweetheart, you're still cold. I'm going to take you upstairs and warm you." Jess cradled her in his arms as he started toward the stairs.

Elly felt the strength in him and relaxed into it. She nestled her head against his shoulder as he carried her up the stairs and down the hall to her bedroom. There in the shadows he set her on her feet while he reached down to yank the comforter out of the way. When he turned back to her she smiled tremulously

"You're very sweet, Elly Trent. Very soft. And I think the time has come for me to take what you're offering." He let his fingertip trail inside the collar of her shirt, following the opening until he came to the first button. Then, quite deliberately, Jess began unfastening the buttons. As he worked his way down to the hem of the shirt, he let his knuckles glide teasingly over her skin.

By the time the shirt hung open, Elly was trembling. She whispered his name a little brokenly and caught his hand. Lifting it to her lips, she kissed his palm with a gentle passion that made him catch his breath.

"When I think of the two months I've wasted!" Jess shook his head once, wonderingly and his mouth curved in brief, wry amusement. "Never again, honey. After tonight you're going to be in my bed every night I can arrange it. And after we're married that will be full-time."

"I'm glad you want me," Elly said simply, her eyes luminous in the shadows. "So glad." She stepped out of her shoes.

He pushed the shirt to one side, uncovering a breast. "The important thing is that you want me. Tonight you're going to show me just how much, aren't you?"

He lifted his gaze to meet hers, and for a blazing moment Elly read the intent in him. "Jess, this isn't a contest. There's nothing to prove."

"Yes, there is." He stroked her nipple, watching it harden beneath his touch. "Yes, there is." The satisfaction was plain on his face. When she shivered slightly, he became impatient and pushed the shirt off completely. Then he captured her wrist and guided her hand to the buttons of his own garment. "Help me undress, Elly."

Obediently she began easing him out of his shirt. It was a difficult task because her fingers were a little shaky. Jess seemed to enjoy her awkwardness. He watched her slow progress with a curiously intent expression.

"Now," he murmured as the shirt fell to his feet, "put your arms around my neck and hold me. I want to feel you, honey."

Slowly Elly did as he instructed, stifling a small gasp when her breasts brushed against the crisp curly hair of his chest.

"Harder," Jess ordered softly, his lips in her hair.

"Oh, Jess." Elly turned her face into his bare shoulder, shuddering as she pressed closer. Her nipples felt hard and almost unbearably sensitized. The feel of his rough skin against them bordered on the painful. "It hurts," she breathed.

"Does it?"

"Almost."

He laughed softly. "Almost isn't the same thing as actually hurting. If it ever really hurts, tell me. I'll stop. The last thing I ever want to do, Elly, is cause you pain."

She curled her arms more trustingly around his neck, and the next thing Elly was aware of was Jess's fingers moving between their bodies. He searched for and found the snap of her jeans. Then he was pushing the denims down over her hips, letting them drop to her feet. She felt his hands on her buttocks, clenching and unclenching tenderly. Only her striped cotton briefs shielded her now.

"Jess, I'm going crazy." She pressed more closely against him and heard his growled response.

"That's just the way I want you. Let yourself go, Elly. Show me how much you want me."

She snuggled closer, dropping her hands to his waist so that she could finish undressing him. But she fumbled so with the zipper that Jess finally stepped back to do the job himself.

"Get into bed, honey. You're still too cold."

She crawled between the sheets, pulling the comforter up to cover her breasts and watched as Jeff stepped out of the rest of his clothes. In the shadowed light, his body looked lean and smoothly muscled and when he turned to face her the hard evidence of his desire was so blatant Elly's glance instinctively moved away from the sight. Determinedly she kept her gaze on his face as he pulled aside the comforter and slid into bed.

"Why the shyness, Elly? We're going to be married soon. You want me. I want you. It's all very simple. It would have been even simpler if I'd come to my senses earlier." Jess put his hand on her flat stomach and let his fingers trail beneath the elastic edge of her briefs. "Lift up, honey and let me take these off."

"Jess, I'm sorry you were worried about me tonight."

"I know you're sorry. I could see it in your eyes. You have such beautiful eyes, sweetheart. My God, I want you. I've been walking your living-room floor until I thought I would go out of my mind. Now you're here and you're safe. I don't think I've ever been more grateful for anything in my life than I was to see you come through that door tonight. If Carrington had brought you back with him in the morning, I—"

"Hush," Elly whispered. "It didn't happen that way. I would never let it happen that way."

Elly's briefs came off in his hands, and he dropped them casually beside the bed. Then Jess let his palm glide up the length of her leg until he reached her thigh.

"Open up, sweetheart. Let me touch you. I want to feel you get hot and damp for me." He bent his head and slightly caught her nipple between his lips.

"Jess!" The exquisite sensation made her arch her head back over his arm, and without any conscious thought her legs parted for him. Elly speared her fingers into the darkness of his hair, gripping with sudden urgency as he probed her softness.

"I can't believe I denied myself this for two months. You're on fire, aren't you, Elly?"

"You're tormenting me," she protested, sinking her nails into his shoulders as he continued to stroke her. "And I think you're doing it deliberately."

Jess raised his head to look down into her eyes. "Maybe I am," he admitted quietly. "I like seeing you all soft and helpless. I like seeing how much you want me."

Through the gathering storm of her arousal, Elly caught the hidden meaning behind his words. "Because it makes you feel in control?

Jess, please, I don't want our lovemaking to be a...a matter of control."

"What do you want it to be?" He seemed unconcerned as he leaned down again to feather her throat with kisses.

"It should be a giving thing," she tried to say, but her words were almost lost in her throat as he did something incredibly erotic between her legs. "Jess, please...!"

"I agree, sweetheart. I want you to give yourself to me. No argument. Ah, sweet Elly, you're delicious, do you know that? If only you could see yourself right now. You're losing yourself in my arms. You're going out of control."

He was right. Elly decided there was no point trying to fight her reaction to him. The passion he aroused in her was unique, unlike anything she had ever experienced. She loved him. What more did a woman need to strip her of self-control? With a soft moan, Elly gave herself up to the swirling excitement of Jess's lovemaking. She slid her hands eagerly over his body, exploring the lean, muscled contours until she came into contact with the rock hard shaft of his manhood. Jess's eyes momentarily narrowed until they were almost closed.

"Oh, God, Elly, yes. I want you. I can't remember ever wanting a woman like this."

She sensed that the admission was almost unconscious on his part. Jess, too, was slipping out of control, and the realization set fire to Elly's own excitement. She put her lips to his chest, nipping him delicately with her sharp little teeth.

"This isn't painful; it's *almost* painful, right?" she dared as he sucked in his breath.

"Thinking of crossing the line?"

"I wouldn't dream of it."

Jess regarded her with burning eyes. "I know. I think I've known all along. You're gentle, Elly. Probably too gentle for your own good. But it doesn't matter now. I'll take care of you."

"Jess?"

"Hush, darling." He eased her over onto her back and lowered himself slowly along the length of her. "I'm going to take you now. I'm going to watch you melt in my arms. You said this should be a giving thing. So give, Elly. All of yourself. I'll take good care of the gift.''

She was too far gone along the sensual road to struggle with the message in his words. Elly closed her eyes and wrapped her arms around Jess's neck. She could feel his hard, blunt shaft waiting between her thighs, and when he used his hand to push her legs farther apart she didn't resist. Then he surged against her, and she cried out as he buried himself deep into her body. Jess paused, his body throbbing.

"Painful or almost?" he grated, holding himself very still above her.

"Just almost. Oh, Jess, I've never felt this way before."

"You've led a sheltered life." But she could hear the satisfaction in him. "I can see that." She opened her eyes as he began to move within her. "I'm glad."

His face was a taut mask of barely controlled masculine urgency. He held her so tightly Elly couldn't tell which of them was exuding the fine perspiration that slicked their skin. She felt Jess's hands under her hips, lifting her, guiding her as he increased the pace of the lovemaking.

The strange tension in Elly began to tighten and condense. She was unaware of the way her legs wrapped around Jess's waist as she closed her eyes again. The powerful driving rhythm was dominating her senses, and she could only respond to its demands. She was alive with the knowledge that the man who held her so fiercely was the man she loved, and when the shimmering climax shook her, Elly could no longer avoid saying the words.

"Jess, oh, Jess, I love you, love you, love you..."

Jess lifted his head to watch her face as she surrendered to the force of their mutual passion. He realized that the words were the finishing touch. They made it all perfect. She was his in a way no other woman had ever been. No one else had ever given herself so sweetly and completely. She loved him. She *loved* him.

Then he couldn't think at all as his own satisfaction washed over him. The release seemed endless and infinite, and at the conclusion he sprawled heavily on Elly's softness. For a long moment he lay still, luxuriating in the feel of her and then, reluctantly, he rolled to one side. When he gathered her against him, she opened her eyes and met his gaze. He stared down at her, drinking in the sight of her tawny-gold eyes. Then he smiled slightly and picked up a trailing braid that had come free of the coronet she normally wore. He toyed with it as he leaned down to brush her lips with his own.

"No doubt about it. I was a fool to wait this long."

"Why did you wait, Jess?" The tawny eyes were unexpectedly serious.

He shrugged, no longer interested in his own motivations. He couldn't begin to explain that a part of him had been wary of the kind of passion he sensed he would find with Elly. Now that he'd found it and discovered there was absolutely nothing threatening about it, that it was, in fact, fantastic, Jess saw no reason to go into the subject. "As you've often noticed, I tend to do things on schedule."

"And you haven't had time until tonight to fit me into your schedule?"

"Hey," he said chuckling, "I thought you'd appreciate not being rushed. Don't I get any points for gentlemanly behavior?"

"It made me nervous." She dropped her eyes to study his chest.

"Because you were beginning to be afraid I didn't want you at all. Then when you decided to take things into your own hands last weekend I blew it by seeing that prowler at the window. That was probably Carrington, the bastard. One of these days I'm going to have to do something about him before his mischief gets dangerous."

"You haven't answered my question," Elly persisted.

Jess sighed. "You mean about why I was such a gentleman for two months?"

"Yes."

"It was because I wanted to be sure of you in other ways, first. You're sweet and sensible and intelligent. I wanted you to see that we could make a good marriage together, that we were right for each other. I didn't want to be accused of using sex to push you into anything you didn't really want." It sounded reasonable to his own ears.

"Because someone once used sex to push you into a marriage you later regretted?"

"That's not going to be a problem with us, though, is it, Elly? You love me. You want to marry me. You've loved me and you've wanted to marry me all along.''

"Yes."

He tipped up her chin, enjoying the honesty in her eyes. "I should have known. I should have guessed how deeply you felt. If I had, I wouldn't have waited two months to make love to you."

"Now you know how I feel," she began carefully.

"Umm." He felt the satisfaction welling up in him, and knew it probably showed in his eyes. Jess didn't try to hide it. There was no need.

"I'd like to know how you feel, Jess." Elly studied him intently.

"Damned good." He stretched and yawned.

"That's not what I meant."

Something in her persistent tone finally got through to him. He blinked lazily. "What do you mean?"

She swallowed, seeking the right words. "I want to know if you love me," Elly whispered starkly.

Jess experienced the first flicker of uneasiness. She looked so serious and concerned. Tenderly he played with her braid. "Elly, honey, I'm going to marry you. I'll take care of you. I think you trust me, and you know that I want you. I know for certain that you want me. Isn't that enough for you?"

"I don't know. Is falling in love with me anywhere in sight on that schedule of yours? Or is this all I'm going to get?"

The uneasiness began to change into anger. "What, exactly, do you want from me, Elly?"

"I want you to tell me that you love me," she said with stubborn pride. "That you're giving yourself to me as completely as I'm prepared to give myself to you. That you're passionately, irrevocably, inescapably, deliriously in love with me!"

"Why?"

"Why!" She freed herself to sit up against the pillows. "Why? Because that's the way this whole thing is supposed to work. That's what getting married is all about. I love you. I'd like some assurance that you love me."

He eyed her for a long moment, taking in the sight of her emotions so openly displayed in her face. "Last weekend you said you wanted the assurance that I could feel genuine passion for you. I've given you that assurance and now you want more. How much more, Elly?''

She flinched as if he had struck her. ''That's not fair, Jess. I'm only asking that the man who claims he wants to marry me also does me the honor of telling me he loves me. But you're not going to do that, are you?'' She edged toward the side of the bed, her eyes blazing. All the warmth of the passionate aftermath of their lovemaking had changed to feminine resentment.

''Elly, come back here. Where the hell do you think you're going?'' Alarmed and irritated, Jess sat up.

''You're afraid to let yourself love me, aren't you?'' she challenged, stumbling to her feet beside the bed. She dragged the comforter with her. ''After that disaster with Marina Carrington, you're not about to risk loving another woman.''

''You don't know what the hell you're talking about! I felt a lot of things for Marina, but not love.'' Jess exploded off the bed, catching Elly by the wrist because she would have darted toward the bathroom. ''Now calm down and stop throwing a temper tantrum or so help me I'll...''

''You'll what? Beat me?'' She glared at him.

Jess relaxed, his mouth curving slightly. ''No, honey, I won't beat you. I'll take you back to bed and make love to you all over again. This time I'll try to do the job right so that you don't come out of it spitting like a scalded cat.''

She was beyond caution now. ''Maybe you can't do the job right. The only right way to make love to me, Jess Winter, is to *be* in love with me.''

''Damn you, Elly!'' Unexpectedly Jess lost his own temper. Gray eyes darkened with masculine intent. Clamping her around the waist, he lifted her so that she was eye to eye with him. Hastily she braced herself with her palms on his shoulders. Her gaze was gold with the fire of her feelings. ''You little witch, I'll teach you to provoke me. I'm going to lay you back and make love to you until you admit I not only give you what you need in bed, but that you won't ever want it from anyone else! Do you hear me, woman?''

Elly heard. She heard all too clearly. She paled at the words. *Witch.* She'd heard him call her a witch, and with that all the fight went out of her. She was not another Marina, not another witch who would deliberately bait and torment him. The fear that she had acted in a way that reminded him of the other woman swept through her. Impulsively Elly threw her arms around his neck, sinking into him, pleading with him silently to forget the outburst.

"I hear you, Jess. You don't have to prove it." She smiled tentatively into his shoulder. "But if you're intent on doing so, I won't argue."

"Elly?"

"I love you, Jess."

His hands softened on her. "I know, honey, I know." He set her gently on the bed and came down beside her, gathering her closely. "I'll take care of you and your love, Elly Trent. I swear it."

He didn't call her a witch again. As she lay in bed a long while later, Elly reminded herself that Jess hadn't called Marina's name or seen her face while he was making love. If the other woman still haunted him, at least he hadn't brought her out into the open tonight. As she snuggled down into the comforting heat of his body and closed her eyes, Elly told herself that there was no way Jess could have made love with such passionate intensity if he'd been thinking of another woman.

She thought briefly of explaining exactly what had happened on the lonely, foggy road that night but decided there was nothing to be gained except a violent confrontation. The last thing she wanted to do was involve Jess in another such scene. She had no doubt that he would put the worst possible interpretation on the situation if she were to tell him how Damon Carrington had conveniently happened along shortly after her car had run out of gas. He might have been right, she admitted sleepily. Combined with the evidence of the mischief-making message Damon had apparently sent to Jess, that business out on the road was a little too much of a coincidence.

Had Carrington really thought that he could casually pick her up, take her somewhere for the night and seduce her? Had he actually thought she would allow him to do it? The man must have an ego the size of a football field. Well, she had proven she could take care of herself where Carrington was concerned. There was no point bringing in the heavy guns and risking genuine violence. Elly went cold at the thought. It seemed much smarter to keep Jess and Damon separated.

Just as it had the last time Jess had spent the night, the phone rang early the next morning. Elly blinked herself awake even as Jess shoved back the covers.

"Damn," he said. I'll get it. We're going to have to start leaving your phone unplugged at night." He paced toward the door, not bothering to collect any clothes en route. Arrogantly unconcerned with his own nakedness, he stalked out into the hall, heading for the stairs.

Elly watched him leave, bemused by the novelty of waking up with a man in her bed. She really had led a quiet life until Jess came along, she thought, yawning. All things considered it had remained fairly quiet for a couple of months after he had come along, too! Things had definitely changed last night.

She could hear his voice faintly as he responded to the caller. Elly was content to stretch grandly and take her time about heading for a shower, until she realized that Jess's muffled tones were sounding cold and impatient.

Frowning, Elly sat up and pushed back the comforter, trying to listen. When she heard the name *Trentco,* she was jolted into full wakefulness. Hastily she scrambled out of bed, grabbed her robe and started for the stairs. She was in time to catch the last of Jess's conversation with her Aunt Clara. He was speaking crisply, with more than a faint trace of aloof arrogance.

"That won't be necessary, Mrs. Gaines. I've got all the resources I need at my disposal. Advising people in situations such as this is my business and I'm good at it." There was a pause while Clara Gaines apparently tried to argue. "Don't bother. Elly will have me to consult. I'll be handling the matter for her, and I'll make sure she reaches the right decision. For the record, as her consultant in this deal, I'd like to point out that I don't want her hounded anymore. In other words, no more seven A.M. phone calls. We high-priced financial wizards get irritated by early-morning calls."

"Jess!" Elly stood clutching the lapels of her robe, trying to get his attention. "Jess, get off the phone. Let me talk to her. This isn't your concern."

But Jess ignored her as he responded to Aunt Clara's next remark. "I wouldn't worry too much about her offbeat life-style, Mrs. Gaines. It doesn't impact her ability to vote her shares in Trentco, and that's the only aspect of it you have to concern yourself with, isn't it? I'll look forward to meeting you next Monday at the stockholders' meeting. What's that? Of course, I'll be attending as Elly's adviser. Should be interesting. Good-bye, Mrs. Gaines."

He threw the phone carelessly back down into its cradle and turned to eye Elly with an indulgently lifted brow. "What's the matter, honey? You look as if one of those sharks you're always worrying about just swam ashore."

"Jess, you shouldn't have interfered. You have no right to involve yourself. What was all that nonsense about your being my consultant? This is very messy, very complicated family business and I really don't think you should just, well, invite yourself into it."

"I realize it involves your family, Elly," he said placatingly, "but it also involves you, and it involves business finance. Both are areas in which I'm an expert. That gives me the right to act as your consultant."

"Expert! You're not an expert on me, for heaven's sake!" She gestured wildly, lost control of the robe and had to make a quick grab for it, which effectively ruined the impact of the gesture. "You think one night in bed somehow gives you the right to make my business decisions for me? Well, you're wrong. I've been dealing with this family for a long time, and I can handle the situation on my own. I don't need any high-priced financial consultant taking over for me. Stay out of this, Jess. If I want your advice, I'll ask for it."

He studied her for a long moment, taking in the ruffled chaos of her hair, the comfortable old robe and the militant gleam in her eyes.

"Elly, don't be ridiculous. Why should you walk into that meeting alone on Monday? It's going to be you against the rest of them, and they're going to be furious if you don't vote the way they want you to vote. Why face it all by yourself when you've got me?"

"It won't be just me. Harrigan's on my side," she reminded him huffily.

"Oh, yes, Harrigan. The CEO. That reminds me, I want to give him a call this afternoon." Absently Jess glanced around the room until he spotted a pencil and a notepad. Bending down, he jotted himself a quick message and dropped the pencil.

"Jess, please, listen to me." Elly decided to stop arguing and try the reasonable approach. "Harrigan and I will be fine. Aunt Clara and the gang aren't going to chew me up, you know. There's absolutely nothing they can do if I decide to vote against them."

"They can put a hell of a lot of pressure on you, make you feel guilty, make you distrust your own judgment. Believe me, Elly, I've seen people in this kind of situation. Even the normally mild-tempered ones can turn into cobras if they see profits slipping through their fingers."

The reasonable approach gave way to pleading. "Please, Jess, don't get involved. Can't you understand? I don't want you involved!"

He stepped forward and drew her into his arms. "I understand what you're saying. What I can't figure out is why you're saying it. I'm your lover, and soon I'm going to be your husband. Why are you trying to keep me out of family business?"

Elly tried desperately to find the words to explain her fears, but in the end she couldn't bring herself to say them aloud. Maybe Jess didn't see what was happening, but she certainly did and it terrified her.

She could see him letting himself being dragged into an unpleasant, potentially nasty family-business situation just as he had been when he'd married Marina Carrington. True, the circumstances were different, but the essense of the situation was the same. It hinged on money. Jess had already been burned on the subject of family and money. She vividly remembered what he'd told her about having to bail Damon Carrington out of one financial disaster after another.

Jess didn't even realize how awkward things could get. If *Trentco* wasn't sold, Aunt Clara and the rest would probably insist that Elly's "financial consultant" offer a great deal of free financial advice to the firm. From their point of view, he would have been responsible for keeping them from realizing a quick, sure profit. He would therefore be expected to compensate by ensuring a long-term profit.

If he chose not to cooperate, there would be endless recriminations, badgering and pleas. If he did cooperate, there would be demands, phone calls, arguments and petty complaints. And there were certain members of the Trent family who were not above asking for a loan.

Shades of Damon Carrington. The unpleasantness would never go away because families never go away. Elly knew that for a fact. She had moved as far from her relations as possible, and she still couldn't escape from them.

Last night, when she had provoked Jess, he had called her a witch, the same term he used so disparagingly for his dead ex-wife. If she allowed him to get involved in her family financial problems, how long would it be before he would resent the ceaseless demands? How long before he would realize she was causing him as much trouble as the Carringtons had once caused him?

Elly realized with a sense of nervous dread that she was fighting for Jess's love. She wanted nothing to remind him of the past. If she was to have any chance at all of getting him to take the risk of loving her, she would have to shield him from certain elements in her world.

Above all, she must not say or do the things that would make him think of her as another witch, and she must not allow him to be pulled into another nasty, vicious family-business situation.

"Jess," she said with grave dignity, "this doesn't concern you. Please don't worry about it or about me. I'll be fine." She turned on her heel and climbed the stairs to her bedroom.

Six

Maybe he'd come down too heavily on her this morning when he'd warned Elly again about steering clear of Carrington. Jess's eyes narrowed as he guided the Jaguar toward Portland and thought of Elly's uncertain mood.

No, he'd given her the lecture just before leaving, and she'd been in an odd temper long before that.

Perhaps she was upset by the unexpected manner in which their relationship had been altered overnight. They were lovers now. Jess tasted the words with a sense of deep satisfaction. About time. He should never have waited this long. There had been nothing to be wary of, after all. He still felt totally in control of the affair. More so, to be perfectly honest, than he had before making love to her.

He had Elly's sweetly passionate nature to thank for his sense of sureness about her. She gave herself so completely, so trustingly, all softness and heat and feminine need. Jess's hands tightened abruptly on the wheel as the images flowed again through his mind. Wryly amused at his own reaction to the memories, he forced himself to relax and go back to the main problem.

Elly was trying to resist some element of their relationship, and he couldn't figure out why. It wasn't the sexual side of things. He'd proven that to himself last night. The truth was she hadn't resisted that aspect from the beginning. She would have come to him any time. All he would have had to do was beckon and she would have flown into his arms. He should have started beckoning two months ago. Ah well, live and learn. That angle was settled now, anyway. It wasn't the source of the problem, he felt sure.

So why was she so nervous around him this morning? Why the temper over the way he'd handled the call from Clara Gaines? When he'd told Elly he'd not only be advising her on the Trentco matter, but that he'd accompany her to California, she'd really become withdrawn.

It was that strange withdrawal that annoyed him. It was as if Elly were trying to keep him out of a part of her life. He didn't like it, and what irritated him most was that he didn't understand it. Why fight him in that area when she welcomed him so passionately in others? Jess frowned, automatically bringing the Jag smoothly out of a tight curve, and asked himself what the hell was going on. Whatever it was, he intended to get to the bottom of it soon.

In the meantime he had work to do. Aunt Clara promised to be a real dragon, and the rest of the family probably followed her lead. He'd get in touch with Harrigan, the CEO, as soon as he got back to Portland. There was another task waiting for him this afternoon, too. He wanted to call the very exclusive, very reliable firm of investigators he had hired on Monday.

Elly made one last, weak attempt to stay the inevitable that night when Jess called to tell her the results of his conversation with Matt Harrigan.

"You were right when you said he seemed to know what he's doing, Elly. He's going to use Trentco as a basis for building his reputation as the kind of executive officer who can rescue struggling firms. That's a good incentive. He's more than happy to work on a bonus plan, which means he won't make big money unless he's succssful. Seems to have a solid knowledge of Trentco's problems and assets, and last but least, he isn't intimidated by Aunt Clara and the crowd."

Elly listened to the summing up of Matt Harrigan's strong points. A part of her was deeply relieved to know her intuition had been correct. "I'm glad you think he's a good person to have at the helm.

Since you're confident of his abilities, you must see there's really no need to go down to California with me. I can handle the meeting.''

"Forget it, Elly. I don't want you facing that crowd alone and that's final. Now, I've arranged our flight out of Portland for Saturday afternoon. You can have Sarah Mitchell take over the store for you. You've used her before to cover the place, as I recall. You were going to have her open for you on Monday, anyway. I'm sure she'll be glad of the extra day's work. I'll expect you here in Portland sometime before noon. Don't be late. The plane leaves at one-thirty and I don't want any last-minute snafus.''

Elly winced at the stream of directives. There was clearly no stopping Jess. Irritably, she leaned back against the sofa and crossed her jeaned legs on the footstool. She glared at the opposite wall, listening to the list of instructions.

A collection of ivy plants occupied an old wooden bench that was positioned against the wall. The vines cascaded in rich abundance all the way to the floor. From where she was sitting, Elly could see the handle of the paring knife she had again borrowed from the kitchen to use for gardening work. If Jess could have seen it sitting there he would have had a few pithy things to say. *"How many times have I told you, you never know when you're going to need a sharp knife?"* It was probably distinctly juvenile to take this much satisfaction out of having defied him in one small department.

When Jess finally halted to ask if she had it all down, she answered him a little too smoothly. "Yes, sir. I've got it all written in indelible ink on the back of my hand. Be in Portland by noon. Don't be late. Get Sarah to cover the store. Does it occur to you Jess that I managed to survive for thirty years without you to schedule me?''

There was a pause from the other end of the line. Elly had the distinct impression Jess was deciding just how to deal with her unexpected flippancy. She'd probably regret it, herself, later. But right now she was feeling frustrated and a little angry.

"Something wrong with my schedule?'' Jess finally asked calmly.

"You know there's nothing wrong with it. It's just the principle of the thing, I guess.''

"Elly, why are you so reluctant to let me help you with the Trentco problem?''

She tried to think of a reasonable answer and finally decided to hint at the truth. Taking a deep breath, Elly said quietly, "Has it occurred to you that if you get involved in Trentco at this stage there might be a lot of pressure from Aunt Clara and the gang later? They can be a very demanding bunch, Jess. Very difficult."

Is that what's worrying you? Forget it. Aunt Clara and the crowd are bunny rabbits compared to some of the stockholders I've dealt with in the past. Which reminds me. I called your aunt and told her we would be taking her and the others out to dinner Saturday evening."

Elly jerked upright. "You did what?"

"You heard me."

"Jess, that's positively the last thing I feel like doing! You had no right. What's the point, anyway? For heaven's sake, this is my family problem, not yours."

I decided it would be a courtesy to gather them together and explain your position and why you were going to vote not to sell. I'll lay out the facts and figures for them."

"Harrigan and I have already beaten them over the head with facts and figures!"

"That's the whole point," Jess said patiently. "Coming from me, maybe it will make more of an impression."

Visions of Saturday evening degenerating into a screaming match boggled Elly's mind for a fraught moment or two. Frantically, she tried to think of counter arguments, but Jess was already pursuing another line of thought.

"Do you relaize," he was saying with a touch of anticipation, "that this will be the first time you and I have actually gone away together for a weekend? I've spent the past two months driving over to the coast, but you haven't had a chance to grab a small vacation. We'll have a good time, honey."

"Jess, this is hardly a minivacation!"

"We'll make it one. I've already made the reservation." He named one of the big hotels near Union Square in downtown San Francisco. "I know a couple of great places for dinner and maybe some dancing. Do you dance, Elly?" he added interestedly. "That's something else we haven't done together."

"But, Jess..."

"Don't worry about not having the right clothes. San Francisco's very stylish, of course, but no one's going to notice if you don't look as if you just stepped out of *Vogue*."

"Thanks." Elly could hardly breathe through her fury.

"I'm really looking forward to this, honey," Jess concluded.

"Good night, Jess."

Elly hung up the phone before her temper exploded. Surging to her feet, she paced the comfortable living room until she had managed to work off some of the seething resentment. By the tenth or fifteenth trip across the floor, her sense of humor finally began to assert itself. Also her sense of reason.

She had to remember that Jess had never seen her in anything but jeans and the exceedingly casual clothes work in a small coastal town. As he had just pointed out, they hadn't gone anywhere more sophisticated together. He hadn't intended to be condescending on the phone. He'd been trying to reassure her.

Sweet man.

Sweet man, hell. It would be a pleasure to shake him up a little. Jess Winter was entirely too sure of his own judgments.

Reaching for the phone again, Elly dialed Sarah Mitchell's number. When her friend answered after a couple of rings, Elly burst into speech.

"Sarah, do you want to handle the shop for me on Friday and Saturday as well as Monday?"

"Well, sure, Elly. That's no problem. What's up? Going out of town early?"

"Yes, as a matter of fact. I wanted a chance to do some shopping in Portland before I go to San Francisco."

"Okay. I'll take care of The Natural Choice. You won't get any argument from me. I can use the money; you know that."

"Great. Oh, Sarah?" Elly remembered something. "How did the outing go?"

"You mean with Damon Carrington? Don't ask."

"It didn't work out?" Elly thought of Compass Rose's violent reaction to the man.

"It wasn't that bad, I guess. We went to the section of beach near your place. You know that cove with the big rock sitting in the middle of it?''

"Sure.''

"Well, the tide was in, so we couldn't get near the rock to check out the tidepools. The breeze was cold. And Compass Rose had a fit. All in all, not a memorable outing. Haven't seen Damon since.''

"Oh. I'm sorry, Sarah.''

"It's probably just as well. If you want to know the truth, there was something about him that reminded me a little too much of Mark.''

"How's that?''

"You know, all surface glitter and no depth.''

"I think that was Ann Palmer's reaction, too,'' Elly said thoughtfully. "Maybe we country women are a little more astute when it comes to judging men than city boys like to think we are. I know one city male who's going to find out that he's got a few things to learn about a particular country woman.''

"Jess?''

"How did you guess?''

Sarah laughed. "A hunch. He's going with you to San Francisco?''

"I can't seem to stop him. The thing is, he's never seen me out of a pair of jeans.'' Unless you counted the times he'd seen her naked, Elly amended silently, her cheeks warming.

"He doesn't know you once lived in San Francisco? That you worked there?''

"Somehow the subject has never arisen.''

That was the truth, Elly realized as she hung up the phone. Jess had only seen her in her small-town setting. He'd assumed she'd always lived on the coast and hadn't seemed interested in hearing too much about her past. Since Elly no longer had any real interest in her own past, that arrangement had suited her fine. Besides, she had sensed that Jess had liked her the way she was. She fit his inner concept of the kind of wife he wanted. There had been no point in telling him that she'd once lived quite a different life-style. She had been cautious about jeopardizing his image of her.

But his comment regarding her feeling underdressed in San Francisco was really too much. If Jess Winter was going to find out just what Aunt Clara and the family were like this weekend, he might as well learn that there was another side to Elly Trent, as well.

Elly stayed by herself in a Portland hotel on Friday evening. She wanted time to assess the purchases she had made that day and play with makeup. She hadn't delved into blushers and eye shadow for quite a while. The tiny Italian shoes were going to hurt her feet, but she vowed to ignore the pain. She would be back into moccasins on Tuesday. Recreating the elegant chignon she used to wear when she worked in San Francisco took a little practice, but eventually she was satisfied with the results. The peach silk blouse, narrow white wool skirt and soft peach jacket were nothing short of perfect. She hardly recognized herself.

On Saturday morning Elly put the whole look together, examined herself in front of a mirror and declared herself satisfied. She looked very "Big City." She drove to the address Jess had given her with a sense of grim anticipation. Whatever else happened this weekend he was going to learn that he didn't know everything there was to know about Elly Trent.

It wasn't until she stood in the hallway of Jess's expensive apartment building that Elly had a few second thoughts. Hesitantly, she raised her hand and then, telling herself it was too late to change her mind, she knocked. The door was opened almost immediately, and Jess stood staring down at her. He was dressed to express quiet corporate power, from his gray vested suit to his subdued silk tie. She found herself staring back. Neither one of them commented on the other's attire.

"Am I on time?" Elly asked sweetly, glancing around the sophisticated living room.

"Yes." He shut the door and stood wih his hands behind him on the knob. Jess watched her survey the room. "You're on time."

"I didn't want to interfere with your schedule." She swung around, smiling brilliantly.

"I rarely let anyone interfere with my schedule. Let me grab my flight bag and I'll b ready to go." He walked past her, heading for the bedroom.

Elly experienced a moment of trepidation as she heard the coolness in his voice. This wasn't quite what she had expected. On the other hand, she hadn't been certain exactly how he would react to the "other" Elly Trent.

He hadn't even kissed her hello.

"Where's your suitcase?" he asked as he returned.

"Downstairs in my car."

He nodded. "We'll put your car in my slot in the garage. We can take the Jag to the airport." With calm efficiency he went around turning out lights, picked up a file folder lying on an end table and then he held the door for Elly.

Slightly bemused by his attitude, Elly stepped meekly out into the hall. Wasn't he going to say anything at all about the way she looked? She waited for some comment all the way to the airport.

"I don't know if I ever mentioned it or not, but I used to work in San Francisco," she said later when they were strapped into their seats aboard the southbound jet.

Jess glanced up from the papers he had removed from the folder. "Did you?" He didn't seem particularly interested.

"I had a job with a large corporation. I was working my way up through management when I decided that wasn't what I wanted to do for the rest of my life." God help her; she was starting to babble. Why was she telling him all this? He hadn't asked. She had wanted him to ask.

"I had no idea." He went back to the file he was studying.

"Well, I didn't just spring into existence at the age of thirty behind my cash register."

"Apparently not."

Elly gave up. Subsiding into a thoughtful silence, she accepted a glass of juice from the flight attendant and contemplated the seat in front of her. Damn it, she could be aloof and cool, too. That attitude went with her clothes and hairstyle, didn't it?

It wasn't until she walked into the hotel room that afternoon and took in the significance of the double bed that Elly began to have a few doubts about her own ability to maintain the arrogant, feminine facade. Of course Jess would expect her to stay in the same room with him. After Wednesday night he had no reason to think otherwise. If she admitted the truth to herself, she couldn't deny that was the way she wanted things, too. But she felt strangely unsettled. The only solution she could discover was to retreat further and further into her sophisticated, cool image.

"When's your meeting with Harrigan?" She stood in front of the mirror, tucking wayward tendrils of hair back into a chignon. She watched Jess as he crossed the room to pick up the phone.

"In an hour. I'm going to call him now and let him know I'll be on time."

"You mean that *we'll* be on time." Elly turned to confront him, frowning faintly. "I'm going to this meeting, too, Jess."

"There's no need for you to be there."

His casual dismissal of her role in the proceedings almost took her breath away. "May I remind you, Jess Winter, that I am the major stockholder of Trentco? If I may be blunt about it, Harrigan works for me. And as long as you're playing financial consultant, you damn well work for me, too! I'm going to attend that meeting between the two of you. Do I make myself clear?"

He glanced at her as he dialed Harrigan's number. One brow rose consideringly. "Very close, *boss*. You must have been hell to work for back in the days when you were climbing up through the management ranks."

Elly felt as if he'd slapped her. She watched, shocked, as he spoke to Matt Harrigan. *Hell to work for.* Was that how he saw her in her new clothes and elegant hairstyle? Sh had wanted to appear sophisticated and dynamic. But perhaps she was coming across as cold and hard-edged. He had described his ex-wife that way. Belatedly Elly recalled that when Jess had met Marina she had been an executive in a large corporation.

Perhaps she was beginning to remind him of Marina Carrington.

Quite suddenly, Elly saw her attempt to impress Jess in a whole new light. What if everything she had done today had only served to make him think of Marina? Elly could have wept in sheer frustration. She began to feel trapped by the image she had created. On top of that she didn't know how to breach the barrier that seemed to be between herself and Jess today. She thought of the rather daring, off-the-shoulder black silk dress she had bought to wear that evening and shuddered. She was very much afraid it would make her look like a very expensively attired witch.

Resentment picked her nerves, making her feel restless and defiant. She had a right to dress the way she wanted. If she were to marry Jess she would continue to dress this way on the occasions when they traveled. Damn it, she couldn't go through her whole life terrified of saying or doing something that reminded him of Marina. She was an individual in her own right with all the corresponding rights and privileges.

"Four-thirty will be fine. We'll meet you downstairs in the lobby." Jess paused, flicking a glance at Elly's warning expression. "Yes, Elly's coming along, too. Says she wants to be there. Pointed out that all things considered, she's the boss."

Elly could hear the faint sound of Harrigan's laughter on the other end of the line. He said something that made Jess grin reluctantly before he replaced the phone. He stood with his hands on his hips, feet slightly apart and regarded Elly thoughtfully.

"Harrigan says you're the one who hired him."

Elly lifted her chin, daring him to criticize. "He seemed like the right man for the job. I had to make a decision when my uncle died, Jess. The family was at each other's throats, bickering constantly about the fate of the company. No one was doing anything constructive for Trentco. I, ah, came down to San Francisco and made what I guess you'd call an executive decision. I put Harrigan in charge and went back home."

"How did you know him in the first place?"

"He'd been working for my uncle. I knew Uncle Toby trusted him and had been more or less grooming him to take over the responsibility of running Trentco."

"You authorized one hell of an incentive package for Harrigan, apparently. Good salary, bonuses, a lot of decision-making power."

Elly couldn't tell if Jess was criticizing her or not. "It seemed like the right thing to do at the time. I have faith in Harrigan, and I'd like to give him a chance to revive Trentco. There are a lot of people's jobs at stake, Jess. People who worked for my uncle for years and who were fiercely loyal. A lot of them would go if the company were bought out. It seems wrong to sell off a company that's been in the family for so many years. I know my aunt and a lot of the others are only thinking of the immediate profit, but there's another generation coming along. Kids like my cousin Dave. In a sense, Trentco is part of their heritage. Someday one of them may want to take a crack at running it.''

"It comes down to the fact that you don't want to sell.''

"Exactly.'' She wondered if he were going to advise her otherwise. "My uncle left me the controlling portion of shares because, even though he knew I didn't particularly want to run the firm, I'd keep it safe for the next generation. It's a responsibility I can't just walk away from, Jess.''

"I know.''

She relaxed a little. "I'm glad you understand.''

"Let's go meet Harrigan.''

Matthew Harrigan was in his early thirties, an intelligent, aggressive man who could also be quite charming when he chose. He was dark-eyed, attractive and recently married. Elly was a little disappointed that his wife hadn't accompanied him. She said as much as she introduced him to Jess.

Harrigan chuckled. "Diane said she preferred to stay clear of the screaming match. I guess she thought your aunt and uncle and some of the others were going to be here.''

"The screaming match comes later,'' Elly said. "Jess has invited them all to dinner.''

Harrigan regarded the older man with blatant admiration. "Brave man.''

"Are they that bad?'' Jess led the way into the quiet atmosphere of the hotel lounge and seated Elly.

Harrigan eyed him thoughtfully. "I think you'll be able to handle them. Elly does it the easy way by putting a lot of distance between herself and them.'' He smiled at Elly. "A policy her Uncle Toby would have understood even if he would have been disappointed.''

Jess's eyes narrowed. "Disappointed?''

"Didn't you know? Toby Trent had always hoped Elly would assume control of Trentco. He claimed she was the only one in the family who had a head for business. Elly very gently tried to tell him she didn't think she wanted the job, but Toby was as stubborn as everyone else in the family. He figured if he left the shares to her she wouldn't have any choice.''

Cool curiosity dawned in Jess's eyes as he glanced at Elly, who was concentrating on the glass of Napa Valley chardonnay she'd ordered. ''But Elly went ahead with her own plans?''

Harrigan grinned, either unaware or choosing to ignore the tension at the table. ''Elly had already made her decision. Toby figured the move to the coast was merely a passing fancy that she would outgrow. He figured she'd return after his death.''

''But she didn't.''

She came back long enough to put me in charge, an act for which the rest of the family isn't prepared to forgive her.'' Harrigan's eyes lit up as he broke into laughter.

''Perhaps,'' Jess said coolly, ''they'll change their minds this evening.''

Elly winced at his unruffled confidence. Jess simply didn't know what he was going to be facing.

But Elly did have an idea of what she was going to be up against, and in the end she dressed to meet the challenge. There was no point reverting to her casual seaside look. The damage had probably already been done, as far as Jess was concerned. She might as well finish off the evening the way she had started the day. Feeling as if she were writing her own unhappy ending, she disappeared into the hotel bathroom shortly before dinner to dress.

When she had bought the coolly elegant yet undeniably sensuous silk, she had imagined overwhelming Jess with the impact. Now she slipped into it feeling as if she were dressing for battle. She knew she had become quieter and quieter during the afternoon. So had Jess. The result had been an almost complete cessation of communication. Elly didn't want to think about what would happen when they eventually returned to the room that evening. How did you go to bed with someone with who you weren't on speaking terms?

Jess took one look at the distant, serenely aloof vision that appeared from the bathroom and nodded once. His eyes gave no indication of what he was thinking, but Elly shivered as she saw the ice in them. She began to panic about what would happen later.

"Ready?" he asked, making a final adjsutment to his tie in the mirror.   "Yes." At his lack of response to her elegant armor, Elly retreated even further behind it. Her sole goal in life focused on a grim determination just to get through the evening.

Jess's expression darkened, but he said nothing. He merely reached for his keys and opened the door for her.

The ring of stubborn, hostile Trent faces waiting downstairs in the lobby of the hotel was enough to make Elly feel even grimmer than she already did. As she always did on those rare occasions when she was pushed into a corner from which there was no escape, she fought back with a kind of grim determination. She was a Trent, to, and there were times when she could be just as stubborn as the rest. This time the war was waged with cool hauteur and almost savagely polite manners. Challengingly she made introductions.

Aunt Clara stepped forward first, a battleship moving into combat. She examined Jess with a critical eye. She was dressed in the customary knit suit that sheathed her elderly figure. Her gray hair was pinned into a severe bun, and her eyes sparkled with the prospect of battle.

"I do hope you will listen to reason, Mr. Winter, since Elly obviously will not."

"I always listen to reason," Jess murmured and then proceeded to dispense his most charming smile. "Especially when it's all in the family."

To Elly's surprise, Aunt Clara blinked under the impact of the smile and then stepped back to introduce her husband and the remainder of the small landing party. She had brought only the most formidable members of the clan with her tonight, Elly observed as she went through the ritual of introductions. In order, she greeted Clara's husband, Uncle Frank, who always backed his wife's judgments; Aunt Alice and Uncle Jim, who had their eyes on a yacht that they hoped to buy with the profits from Trentco's sale; and cousin Cathy, who had no interest in business and even less in thinking of the future. She had just been through a divorce and was bent on retructuring her social life. Cathy was a likable woman, but she tended to live very much in the present. Her two young children were part of the reason why Elly wanted the family to hold on to the company. If it were sold tomorrow, Cathy would have the profits spent by next Thursday. There was no malice in Cathy, but it simply wouldn't occur to her to sock the money away for the children's education.

"How did you get involved in all this?" Frank Gaines inquired aggressively of Jess as the crowd was seated in a corner of the hotel's dining room.

"Isn't it obvious? I'm about to become part of the family. It's only natural Elly would ask for some advice."

Elly's eyes widened at the blatant lie. She had never asked him for advice. In fact she'd been doing her utmost to keep Jess out of this.

Aunt Clara was already pouncing. "Part of the family? What's that supposed to mean? Just because you're living with her on a casual basis doesn't mean you're *family!*"

"Elly and I will be married next month." Placidly, Jess opened his menu while everyone else at the table absorbed the news.

It was Cathy who recovered first and turned to Elly in amazement. "You're marrying him? He doesn't look at all like the sort of man I thought you'd end up with. I thought you were dating various and assorted bearded dropouts."

"The wedding," Elly tried to say firmly, "hasn't been actually scheduled yet."

Jess glanced up from the menu. "The wedding," he said just as firmly, "is very much on schedule."

Elly didn't know how to respond so she took refuge once more behind her barricade of silk and makeup.

From that position, she watched Jess clamly take control of the evening. He listened until Aunt Clara ran out of breath and arguments, and then he put forth his own rationale for not selling Trentco. To Elly's astonishment, everyone paid attention.

Not only did they pay attention, but as the dessert arrived there was even a gathering sense of agreement around the table. Jess's assurance and obvious expertise were proving persuasive. He never once lost his temper and he was extraordinarily patient. But he had an instinct for using the right approach on each individual at the table.

"Cathy. Elly tells me you have to young children. I realize you probably think that taking the immediate profit and putting it in the bank for the kids' education is the safest move, but in the long run there will be more economic security in this if Trentco is revived."

"Well, I..." Cathy stammered, unable to explain that she really hasn't been thinking that far ahead.

"I know you're a good mother and want to do what's best for the children," Jess went on easily. "Believe me, this is your best option.

"Now about that boat you're thinking of buying, Jim. I think we can arrange some kind of loan against your stock. Something just between you and me. Believe me, after looking at the Trentco financial picture, I have no objection to your using your shares as collateral. Wouldn't mind owning some in the least. That way you'll have the best of both worlds.

"Clara, we're talking family tradition here. I seriously doubt that you'd want to sell off the Trent family heritage. You're the kind of woman who values the important things in life, the meaningful things. It's people of your generation who have to protect family heritages, don't you agree? I want you to take another look at this."

It went like that for some time, with Jess managing to find just the right button to push with each member of the family. By the time everyone rose to leave, Elly was mesmerized by the adept way Jess had handled the entire evening. Monday's vote had become a mere formality. The family was now in agreement. Aunt Clara paused in the lobby to pat Elly's hand.

"You're a lucky young woman, my dear. You've always had such an unruly streak of independence in you that we couldn't help but worry on occasion. Now I think you're in good hands. Good night, Elly." She beamed at Jess, who was standing beside Elly. "See you both on Monday."

Uncle Jim pumped Jess's hand. "Did you mean what you said about the loan?"

"I always mean what I say," Jess assured him.

"Great! That's wonderful. I'll get in touch with you later." He grinned at Elly. "Elly doesn't understand how badly I've wanted a seagoing boat. She hates the sea, you know. Or, at least, she hates swimming in it. It's scared her ever since that time when she was a teenager. She was at the beach with my boy, Dave, who was just a little tyke, then. He got out too far and got himself into trouble. Elly swam out to get him. Brave kid. The water was rough, and some fool watching on shore thought he saw a shark. You can imagine the panic.

But Elly here just kept swimming, dragging little Dave back with her. Gave us all one hell of a scare. Elly's stayed out of the sea ever since.''

"Elly can be very determined about some things," Jess murmured with a sidelong glance at her. "Good night, Jim. I'm glad to have met you."

The other man nodded pleasantly and turned to join the others.

Elly stood very still in the center of the plush lobby, unaware of the well-dressed people coming and going around her. She stared after the last of the family.

"Very impressive, Jess," she said at last.

"I told you they weren't going to be all that tough, Elly." He took her arm and guided her toward the elevators.

"But it won't be the end of it, Jess," she said desperately. "Don't you understand? Aunt Clara will start calling on you constantly for advice. And what was all that about a loan to Uncle Jim? And Cathy's going to expect you to take a lasting interest in her two kids now. Jess, don't you see? You're getting yourself involved in a very messy family situation!"

"I can handle it." He seemed totally unconcerned. In the hall outside their room he paused to get out his key. "They're all easy to figure out. You're the tough one, Elly." He opened the door.

She glanced up at him warily as she walked inside.

"What do you mean, I'm the tough one?"

He shut the door and turned to study her. "I think you know." His eyes moved over the cool, expensive facade she had created for herself. He folded his arms and leaned back against the door.

The sensation of being pushed into a corner intensified. Elly stared at him, torn between uncertainty, resentment and fear. Instead of coming out of the corner fighting this time, she frantically began to explain.

"It was all because you implied I wouldn't have the right clothes for the city. I was upset because you kept insisting on getting involved with this messy business. I decided to show you that I wasn't just a...a hick who had only jeans in her closet. Jess, it's very complicated to explain, but I guess I wanted you to see there was another side to me. I never thought...never realized..."

Jess came purposefully away from the door. "Any more surprises in store?"

She shook her head forlornly. "No."

"Good. I think I've had about enough today. I'm ready for the real Elly." He came to a halt in front of her and threaded his hands through her carefully contrived chignon. Quite deliberately he pulled her chestnut hair free and watched in satisfaction as it tumbled around her shoulders.

"You're not angry?" she asked hesitantly.

"Still love me?" he countered.

She threw herself into his arms, wrapping him fiercely around the waist. "Of course I still love you."

"Then I'm not angry." His voice darkened with the first stirrings of desire as his hands went to the thin zipper at the back of her gown.

Seven

A long time later Jess quietly contemplated the hotel room ceiling and the sense of relaxation that pervaded his body. He was cradling Elly in one arm. She seemed to be asleep and that pleased him somehow. She looked so trusting, so *right*—a woman who had just surrendered to her lover and who now bore the subtle evidence of his claim on every inch of her body. Jess's claim. When she was lying like this, limp and still damp from his lovemaking, he felt so much more certain of her.

Lately it seemed as if he'd been engaged in some sort of unnamed warfare, the rules of which were being set by Elly. She was both his opponent and the prize of victory. For the past two months everything had been proceeding on schedule. The shift in his life-style was going according to plan. Elly had seemed to fit into that plan so perfectly that Jess couldn't believe she didn't see it for herself.

But there was no doubt about the fact that things had been going wrong ever since Carrington had pulled that Peeping Tom stunt. Damn the man. He had always been a source of malicious mischief. Jess had been so sure the guy was out of his life for good. Why the hell did he have to choose now to reappear? This time, Jess vowed, he would have to do something permanent about Carrington. That threat on Wednesday evening was the last straw. There were ways of dealing with men such as Carrington. Jess decided he would find one. The man was a born con artist. He couldn't have lived this long without having broken a few laws involving fraud or misrepresentation. Perhaps the research that the investigation firm was doing would turn up enough to throw the fear of jail into him. If that didn't work Jess had no qualms now about taking more drastic steps.

Carrington had come near Elly. Any closer and, as far as Jess was concerned, the other man had written his own sentence. No one would really miss Damon Carrington.

But some damage had been done, there was no doubt about it. Elly had begun questioning the relationship and all the plans Jess had spent so much time making. She had begun withdrawing, as if she were trying to put an emotional distance between herself and him. She had tried to keep him out of the private side of her life. And this morning, when she'd arrived on his doorstep looking so coolly formal and aloof, he'd known just how far things had gone.

It was a battle, all right. He'd had to force his way into her family business. She should have welcomed his advice and expertise. She should have wanted to share the problems with him. Instead, he'd been obliged to push past her defenses and assume the role of her consultant.

It wasn't, Jess decided objectively, that he had any real doubts about winning the war. The little barricades Elly tried to maintain were fundamentally undermined by the fact that she loved him. Still, it annoyed him that he had to fight in the first place. She should have accepted the situation for what it was. Jess was considering that when she stirred in his arms.

"Jess?"

"Hmm?" He tightened his arm around her and rolled onto his side to look down into her face. The shadows of the room concealed the color of her eyes, but he thought he could detect some of the warmth of the gold in them.

"I wasn't sure if you were awake," she murmured.

"I don't dare go to sleep while you're lying on my arm. It would be numb by morning."

"Oh! I'm sorry, I didn't realize." She started to struggle but he gently pushed her back.

"Don't worry about it. I'll let you know when the circulation problem gets critical.'' He dipped his head and kissed away a trace of dampness between her breasts. The scent of her filled his mind and his body. It was a warm, earthy, utterly feminine fragrance, and he realized vaguely that he was incredibly attracted by it. It was uniquely Elly and he would know it anywhere. The human male was a very primitive animal in many respects. ''You smell so good.''

''Very gallant. The truth is I probably smell the way I do after I've spent a day stocking shelves and hauling out old produce.'' She touched his shoulder experimentally, drawing a small pattern on his skin.

Jess turned his head to kiss her wrist. ''You smell sexy and very female. I like it.''

''Beast.''

''I was just thinking the same thing.'' He met her eyes again, the small smile that had been edging his mouth disappearing. ''Elly?''

''Umm?''

''I want you to tell me you're finished playing stubborn little games as far as your family business problems are concerned.'' He felt her stiffen slightly under the weight of his sprawled body, but he made no move to ease away from her. Damn it, Jess thought, he wanted her to know she couldn't keep trying to dodge him on this issue.

''I'm not playing games, Jess.''

''You've been trying to keep me at arm's length ever since Carrington showed up at your window the night you set out to seduce me. You wanted time. You didn't want me getting involved, you said. You started backing away, started acting warily. Don't pretend otherwise, Elly. Everything was going fine up until that point. You knew we were going to get married, and you weren't questioning it or anything else.''

She stared up at him. ''That's not quite true, Jess. I was having a few qualms. And after you thought you saw your ex-wife at the window, I had a lot more!''

''After seeing Carrington you must realize I wasn't having visions that night!''

She nodded uneasily. ''I realize that. You've told me they were twins, and I suppose a brief glimpse of his face at the window would be enough to startle you into thinking you'd seen her face.''

''Since there's a logical explanation for what I admit wasn't exactly the most diplomatic thing I've ever done, why the continued wariness? Why try to keep me at bay?''

She braced her hands against his chest as if trying to keep him from holding her closer. The action irritated him. Deliberately, Jess leaned more heavily along the length of her.

''I told you, Jess, I'd been a little uncertain about our relationship before that night. Afterward, I started doing some serious thinking.''

''You mean you started getting nervous,'' he corrected bluntly.

''Well, yes, I did.''

''Even though you know damn well you're in love with me.'' Her lashes lowered, veiling her gaze. She didn't respond to the statement, but Jess sensed the stubborn resistance in her and was determined to break it. He leaned forward and brushed his mouth lightly over hers. ''Say it, Elly,'' he murmured. ''Tell me again that you love me.''

She surrendered on a small sigh. ''I love you, Jess. But that doesn't mean I'm going to marry you.''

''You will,'' he said. ''I guarantee it.''

''I have to be sure, Jess,'' she whispered pleadingly.

''Of what? That I want you? You've got proof of that by now, and I'll be happy to supply more. Sure of the fact that I'll look out for your best interests? I've shown you I'll do that, too, even though I have to get past your roadblocks in order to accomplish that goal. Sure that we're compatible? We've spent enough time together for you to know that by now, too. Elly, for over two months you've known where we were headed. What's more, you've come along very willingly until recently. There's no need to get stubborn and defensive now. You're in love with me, and you're going to marry me. That's final.''

''It is not final,'' she said, her temper flaring. ''I'd like to be sure of a few other things, too!''

''Such as?'' He caught her wrists and pinned them to the pillow beside her head.

''For starters, I'd like to be sure I won't have to spend the rest of my life walking on eggs, worrying about saying or doing something that reminds you of your past.''

He was startled. ''Reminds me of my past? What in hell are you talking about?''

Her eyes turned mutinous. ''I saw your face when you opened the door this morning. You took one look at me and went cold. You've been acting that way all day. It was because I reminded you of Marina, wasn't it? That was probably the way she used to dress. All you've ever seen me in is jeans. Then you found out I used to work in the business world the way she did. I haven't spent my whole life in a small town on the coast. I used to be very 'Big City,' too. Just like she was.''

He glared at her for a minute and then groaned as he realized what was going through her head. "Listen to me, Elly Trent, you couldn't remind me of Marina Carrington if you tried. The difference between the two of you is like night and day.''

"Then why were you so…so distant all day?''

"Because I thought you had deliberately used the clothes and the hairstyle and the makeup as another way of keeping me at arm's length,'' he said growled. "It was as if you were trying to wear a sign that said Don't Touch. If you want the truth, it made me angry. It sure as hell didn't remind me of Marina. What made you think you could hide the real Elly beneath the stylish clothes and the big-city manner? Or that I'd ever mistake you for someone else?''

Looking up at him, Elly suddenly realized he was telling the truth. No man could look that impatient and that thoroughly annoyed unless he was genuinely irked at her misunderstanding. She began to feel a little foolish. "Well, it was a logical assumption for me to make. It was the only reason I could think of for your actions today.''

"It was not a logical assumption. It was a damn stupid assumption. Now that we've disposed of that notion, let's talk about something else. Why have you been trying to keep me out of your family business problems? You've been digging in your sweet heels every step of the way. I'd like a good reason.''

She gazed up at him mutely for an instant. Then Elly said carefully, 'I've told you, Jess. I didn't want you getting involved.''

"That's not good enough. I want to know why.''

Elly lost her own patience. "Because I was afraid that would remind you of the past, too. You'd told me about all the family financial problems you'd had with the Carringtons. I was terrified you'd start equating my family business problems with them. I was afraid you'd see us all as leeches.''

His gray eyes gleamed with sudden fierceness. "Of all the dumb, idiotic, crazy ideas. Elly, that's nonsense. There's nothing remotely similar about the two situations. There couldn't be. Don't you understand that? You're you. Nothing connected with you could be in any way the same as it was with the Carringtons. Believe me, it's inconceivable."

"Jess, are you sure?" She searched his face, seeking confirmation.

"Of course I'm sure. Damn sure! And I think you know it. You're just using this as a smoke screen, aren't you? An excuse to take your time making up your mind about whether or not to marry me."

"That's not true!"

"Good," he said forcefully, "because it's not going to work. I've put up with your shadow dancing long enough, Elly. You and I are getting married. Next month, just as I told your relatives. I'm not giving you any more rope, lady, or you'll manage to get both of us snarled in it."

"Please, Jess, be reasonable. We can't just rush into marriage because you've established a timetable for it. You've got to see that there are too many things we don't yet know about each other. We need time."

"What don't we know about each other?" he challenged.

"Well, take my past, for instance. You didn't know anything about it before today. You never even asked about it."

"It wasn't exactly a crucial topic as far as I was concerned."

"Because the way I am, my life-style on the coast seemed to fit so perfectly into all your plans and requirements," she shot back. "That's all you saw and that's all you cared about."

For a moment frustrated anger burned in his eyes, and his hands tightened on her wrists. Elly wished she didn't feel so terribly vulnerable.

"It wasn't all I cared about, but it seemed to be all that was important at the time. It's still all that's important. But if it makes you feel any better, tell me about your past. What made you decide to leave San Francisco and the business world?"

"This is hardly the time to go into that," she protested.

"Seems like the perfect time to me. The fact that I haven't asked until now appears to be another roadblock you're throwing out. So, okay, I'm asking.''

"I don't get the feeling you're really interested.''

Jess smiled faintly. He used the pad of his thumb on the inside of her wrist. "You're wrong there, Elly. Everything about you interests me. The subject of your past is now on the table and open for discussion. Talk.''

"All right, I'll keep it short and simple so as not to bore you. I realized three years ago that big-city business and big-city living wasn't something I wanted on a full-time basis. When I began to understand that, I began to change my life. At the time it was easy enough. My family was upset, but basically there wasn't anything they could do. I decided I wasn't obliged to live my life to suit them. Unfortunately, Uncle Toby made up his mind I wasn't going to be allowed to escape so easily. He always said I was the only adult member of the clan who had a head for business and a sense of responsibility.''

"So he left controlling interest in Trentco to you. You're in charge until the next generation comes along. In a sense the company still ties you to your old life.''

"You've got it.''

"That's all there is to it? No tragic love affairs? No failed marriage? No flickering fires of passion that never had a chance to run their course?''

"No! Damn it, stop teasing me, Jess. I was running toward something, not away from it. It was an intellectual decision as well as an emotional one.''

"Elly, my sweet, this may come as a shock to you, but your lurid past isn't exactly a big surprise.''

"It isn't?''

"Honey, I've seen your wine collection, your tape collection and your book collection. I've seen the skill with which you run your business and the way you keep accounts. I've seen the way you use gourmet cooking techniques to make things like sprouts and lentils into fine cuisine. If I'd worried about it, it wouldn't have been hard to guess that you spent a few years somewhere else besides a tiny town on the coast.''

"Oh."

"You made a decision, the same kind of decision I made," he concluded blandly.

She looked at him suspiciously. "What's that supposed to mean?"

His expression softened. The element of indulgent amusement that she was accustomed to seeing in his eyes was back. "Just that you and I have one more thing in common now. We both chose to leave the world of big business for another kind of life-style. Does that give you a little more reassurance? Because that's what you're looking for, isn't it?"

"Perhaps." A flicker of resentment went through her. She wouldn't need all this reassurance, she realized, if she just knew that Jess loved her. "Can you blame me for being uncertain, Jess?"

"Yes," he said unhesitatingly. "You've had time enough to get to know me. You shouldn't still be questioning my actions or my motives. Furthermore, you ought to have a little more faith in my ability to think for myself. I can tell the difference between the past and the present, and I sure as hell know the difference between you and Marina Carrington."

Elly nodded, feeling chastened. "I believe you."

"Fine. Then believe me when I tell you we're going to be married next month, and there's not a thing you can do about it except show up on time."

"I don't think you even realize just how arrogant you are."

"I realize it, all right. But I'm running out of patience."

"You mean your schedule is starting to slip, and you don't like to have your plans upset," she told him bluntly. "I, on the other hand, don't take too well to being programmed. One of the reasons I decided to leave corporate life is that I don't like being on someone else's schedule. It's too much like being on a menu. There's a fair-sized chance of being chewed up and swallowed."

Jess considered her for a long moment. "Are you by any chance afraid of me, Elly, honey?"

"No, I am not!"

"Still love me?" His fingertips on her wrists began to move in wider circles. His gray eyes were taunting. He knew the answer.

Flustered, Elly sighed in exasperation. She felt trapped. "Yes, I still love you, but that doesn't mean I'm going to marry you next month!"

He lowered his head and lingeringly kissed her throat. "You're the only woman who has ever told me she loved me and meant it. Do you have any idea of how much that means to me? I'd walk through hell for your kind of love. Pacifying a few relatives for you is nothing."

"Oh, Jess..." She felt herself weakening almost at once. She was so very vulnerable to him, Elly thought in despair.

"We both know you're going to marry me, sweetheart." His mouth glided gently over the tip of her breast, and Elly shivered faintly. "I want your love. I want all the softness in you as well as the fire. I need to know you belong to me."

"And in return, Jess?" Her fingers trembled as her palm flattened on his shoulder. "What will you give me in return?"

"Everything that counts. Everything I have to give a woman."

"I want to be loved, Jess. Do you think you'll ever be able to give me that?"

He went still, lifting his head to meet her pleading gaze. "Elly," he said slowly, "I don't know. I'm not sure I ever really knew what it meant to love in the first place. I said I'll give you all I have to give. That's as much as I can promise."

"You seem willing enough to take my love."

He framed her face with his hands and smiled down at her. "That's because your love is so beautifully easy to recognize for what it is. It's very clear, very soft, very real. I know you love me. My own feelings are too complex for me to sort out right now. But they're real, too. Elly, I want you so badly I can taste it. Maybe that's love. Do you want me to use the words?"

She put her fingertips against his mouth. "No, not unless you know what you're talking about. Not unless you mean them. I think you're the one who's afraid, Jess."

"Afraid of what?" His eyes lost some of their indulgent warmth.

"Of surrendering to love. It's easy enough to let someone love you. After all, there's no risk involved. But it's far more reckless to be the one who loves. I think you've become a cautious man over the years. Perhaps Marina Carrington made you that way. Or perhaps you were always that way. It doesn't really matter now. What does matter is that you feel safer when your life is very firmly under control and on schedule. Having me love you fits in very nicely with your plans. But loving me in return would entail some unknowns, wouldn't it? You'd have to take a few risks. You'd have to make yourself vulnerable. I'm sure you find it much safer to stay on top of the situation emotionally. This way you think you have it all.''

''I think,'' Jess said coolly, ''that's about enough of the amateur psychoanalysis. I like it better when you're making love to me, not discussing it.''

''You'll have to excuse me,'' she snapped. ''Maybe all this sex is rotting my brain.''

''The problem,'' Jess informed her as he slipped boldly into the cradle of her thighs, ''is that you haven't had nearly enough yet to set your thinking straight. But I'll be happy to work on the problem.''

''Jess, this is no way to settle an argument! We should talk this out.... Ah, *Jess*.'' His name was a husky sound of capitulation. He was there between her thighs, probing the soft folds of her feminity, testing for a renewed response. In spite of herself, Elly knew her body was already giving him what he demanded.

She could feel herself growing moist and sensitized, knew Jess was taking blatant satisfaction in the reaction he was provoking. He nestled his head beside her on the pillow and began whispering heavy, dark, infinitely arousing words of passion and promise. All the while he teased her with his body. The slow entrance was followed by a tantalizing withdrawal. Over and over again Jess played on the pattern until Elly thought she would go out of her mind.

Finally, in gathering desperation, she pushed at him. He fell back obediently, and she slithered astride his hips. Closing her eyes she lowered herself, taking her fill at last. She moaned in soft pleasure as she took him inside her. When Elly lifted her lashes, she found Jess laughing up at her with his eyes, the triumphant male.

''You are a beast,'' she told him and ran her fingers upward through the curly hair of his chest. Slowly, she leaned forward until her breasts were pressed against him.

''So are you, sweetheart. A very sweet lady beast who's been running free a little too long. But I know how to tame you.''

"Think so?" She felt good up here on top of him, Elly decided. She felt in command for once.

"Watch this," he ordered, his voice thick with promise. "I'll have you eating out of the palm of my hand in no time."

Slowly, he began to move inside her. His hands went to her hips, holding her in place while he established the cadence he wanted. Elly shuddered and gripped his shoulders, seeking to quicken the pace. She felt the tension began to coil inside her and became more assertive as she sought its release. This kind of excitement was still new to her. It was associated with only one man, and she knew in her heart it would always be that way.

"Jess, you're deliberately tormenting me."

"It's nice work if you can get it. And I've got it."

Her nails sank warningly into his shoulders when he refused to pick up the pace beneath her. Jess ignored the small punishment. The slow entrance and withdrawal pattern continued, and even though she was on top of him Elly found herself helpless to alter it. The frustratingly slow rhythm seemed to be setting fire to all her senses. She tried to wriggle a bit and found herself anchored by Jess's large, strong hands.

"Tell me you love me, Elly."

"What will you give me if I do?"

"What you're looking for."

"Promise?" she breathed.

"My word of honor."

Voice aching with passion and love, Elly whispered, "I love you, Jess."

"Don't ever stop telling me, Elly."

His fingers slipped around her thighs to cup her buttocks, and he began to move with fierce power. Elly cried out softly as the sensation in her lower body became unbearable. The inevitable release sent spasms of excitement through her, leaving her shivering and voiceless for a long moment.

Jess felt the pulsating response and was drawn by it into his own shuddering satisfaction. He gripped Elly with all his strength, driving up into her until both of them gave way beneath the overwhelming onslaught.

"I love you, Jess."

The words were mere threads of sound as Elly collapsed in a damp, sensual sprawl.

"Elly, my sweet, sexy, lovely Elly..." Jess held her close, making no effort to separate their still-fused bodies. This time he went right to sleep without spending any time contemplating the ceiling or the future.

On Tuesday evening Elly wandered through her house watering plants and dusting various surfaces with a preoccupied air. Jess had phoned a few minutes earlier to make certain she had arrived safely from Portland. He had sounded satisfied with himself in more ways than one, and she knew he thought he had everything, including her, under control.

"We're back on schedule," she told the African violets in the kitchen window. "On time and on line. Trentco has been saved for the next generation, some semblance of family ties has been restored, and yours truly has been brought to heel. Leave it to an expert to get things back in order. I suppose I should be grateful he's not charging his usual fees."

She could hardly complain about the way Jess had handled the family situation, Elly told herself. The man had done exactly what he'd said he would do. He'd convinced everyone, including Aunt Clara, that he knew what he was doing, and they had all obediently voted not to sell Trentco. Matt Harrigan was delighted and promised immediate signs of increased profits. Order had been brought out of chaos and discord.

Elly had been forced to realize that she had been fretting over nothing. Jess hadn't associated her short-lived stylishness with his ex-wife. He'd simply been annoyed because he had assumed Elly was trying to maintain a certain distance. Nor had he been even slightly ruffled by the effort it took to deal with her squabbling relatives. Apparently after dealing with the Carringtons, the Trents seemed quite tame to him. Again she had worried for no good reason.

Elly wandered into the living room and stood glaring thoughtfully at the collection of ivy plants. She'd done a lot of worrying lately. In fact, it amounted to more than worrying, and it was all connected to Jess Winter. She'd accused him of being afraid to love, but when she viewed the matter objectively, she could see that she was the one who had spent so much time being afraid lately.

She'd been afraid of pushing him, afraid of provoking a violent confrontation between Jess and Damon Carrington, afraid of reminding Jess of his ex-wife, afraid that her own family troubles might be equated with the problems he'd had with the Carringtons.

Good grief, Elly thought as she tipped the watering can over the ivy plant, *I'm the one who's been running scared.* She had let her love of Jess make her a nervous wreck.

Alarmed by the sudden direction of her reasoning, Elly continued through the house with the watering can. By the time she arrived back in the living room she was deep in thought. Absently, she gazed at herself in the mirror that hung over the fireplace. Her intently frowning image gazed back at her.

She was formulating a lecture, one she intended to administer to herself, when another face materialized in the mirror. Through the open drapes of the window behind her a woman was watching her—a stunningly beautiful woman with long blond hair.

Elly knew before she whirled around that even though she couldn't see the woman's eyes clearly, they would be a vivid green.

"Marina!"

Eight

Shock held Elly immobilized for several endless seconds after the woman's face had disappeared. If that was the mysterious prowler Jess had seen the night she had tried to seduce him, it was no wonder he had muttered his ex-wife's name. Elly went cold as she stood staring at the window. Damon in a wig? A woman made up to resemble Marina Carrington? And for God's sake, *why*? Whoever it was had been laughing at her.

It was that fact that finally gave Elly the impetus to lurch away from the front of the mirror. Without pausing to think, she hurled herself across the room and yanked open the front door.

She found herself staring into Damon Carrington's amused face. He was standing on her front porch, and he was holding a small, snub-nosed gun. The cold smile looked exactly like the one worn by the woman in the window, but with an indefinable difference.

"Hello, Elly. I was just about to knock. Something shake you up? You look nervous."

Instinctively, Elly flung herself backward into the safety of the house, intending to slam the door. But it was too late. Damon already had his foot over the threshold, and he lifted the gun in his hand with casual menace.

"Sorry, I'm afraid I can't let you run and hide. I need you tonight,

Elly love. I've got plans for you. Keep in mind that I will use the gun if necessary. I'd prefer to keep you in reasonably good condition, but I can adapt to changing circumstances if there's no alternative. Translated, that means don't oblige me to put a bullet in your leg.''

Elly's eyes jerked from the gun to Damon's face. Her voice felt dry and raspy. ''That was you at the window?''

''In a way.''

''What's that supposed to mean?'' Elly demanded, using anger to hold back some of her fear. It wasn't Damon who answered.

''He means that the woman in the window was me.'' Blond hair cascading around her shoulders, Marina Carrington walked through Elly's front door.

There was no mistaking her. Elly knew her at once. She was a feminized version of Damon, right down to the amusement that flickered in her green eyes. She was wearing a black silk shirt and black slacks that presented a striking foil for the silvery blond hair. A pair of boots fashioned of obviously expensive leather completed the outfit. The clothes reminded Elly of a twentieth century version of a traditional witch's black cape and pointed shoes.

''All you lack is the hat,'' Elly muttered, hugging herself in an unconsciously defensive gesture.

''What hat?'' Marina closed the door and examined Elly from head to toe. She didn't appear to be overly impressed.

''You know. Something with a broad brim and a point.''

Marina tilted her head to one side, considering the comment and then she laughed. ''Ah, a witch's hat. I see Jess has been discussing me with you.''

''The subject came up after he saw you playing voyeur at my window.''

''Shook him up a bit, did it? I'm not surprised. Always reassuring to know one hasn't been forgotten completely.'' Marina's eyes narrowed coolly. ''But I don't suppose that's likely as long as he's amusing himself with boring women. His mind is bound to recall the good old days from time to time. Remember that the next time he decides to take you to bed. I gave him something a woman such as you will never be able to provide.''

''A pain in the ass?''

Marina's fine teeth came together in a small snap. "You were right, Damon. She is a little bitch."

"Jess thinks you're dead," Elly said flatly, deciding the only thing she could do was keep talking.

"So does the insurance company," Damon said pleasantly. "They paid off very handsomely for the unfortunate loss of life at sea. We've been doing quite well on the income for the past three years. But now, sad to say, the money is running out."

Elly caught her breath, knowing what was coming. "Well, if you're thinking of supplementing your income by tapping my bank account, you're out of your mind. What I have saved wouldn't begin to keep you two in the style to which I'm sure you've become accustomed!"

Damon grinned. "It's not your money we're after, Elly. I think you know it."

Marina's grin mimicked her brother's and her eyes gleamed like those of a cat. "How much do you think Jess would pay to get you back safe and sound, Elly Trent? He seems to be quite fond of you. From what we hear he even plans to marry you."

Elly's fingers dug into her arms but she managed to keep her voice reasonably steady. "I don't see Jess paying ransom money."

"Then you don't know him very well," Marina informed her with vast assurance. "The man's got a streak of responsibility in him a yard wide. If he feels he got you into this mess, he'll do whatever he has to do to get you out."

Elly swallowed, aware that Marina was right in her assessment of Jess Winter. He was a man of integrity. He wouldn't send Elly to the wolves. But how would he react when he realized Marina was still alive?

"I can see why the two of you weren't compatible," Elly murmured, treating Marina to the same cool, analytical stare. "You obviously don't suffer from an excess of integrity."

"The man proved to be a little dull in some ways." Marina threw herself down into an arm chair. "But it was fun putting him through hoops for a while. Certainly did wonders for the family finances, didn't it, Damon?"

"Uh-huh." Damon motioned with the gun and Elly backed up a couple of steps.

"But unfortunately Jess had his limits. When I came up against them I knew the game was over." Marina eyed Elly again. "I wouldn't have expected him to settle for someone like you, however."

"Maybe you don't know him as well as you think you do."

Marina shook her head, a sardonic expression on her classically boned face. "You may be right. There were times when I wondered what he was really thinking, what made him tick. That generally doesn't happen. I can usually read a man's mind. Just as my brother always seems to know what a woman is thinking."

Elly swung her gaze to Damon, who was lounging near the telephone, the gun idly pointed in her direction. He was digging a slip of paper out of his pocket.

"Did you guess what I was thinking the other night when you sabotaged my car and then conveniently happened along that lonely road to 'rescue' me?" Elly dared.

Carrington's eyes slitted. "How did you know I was there? You'd already left by the time I arrived."

"I watched you from the bushes. I waited until you had given up and driven off before I walked home."

Damon's brows rose in mocking admiration. "Smarter than the average female. Well, at least I had the pleasure of throwing a scare into Winter. I'll bet he went crazy when he got my message."

"Did you do it just for spite?"

He shrugged. "Yeah. Seemed like fun. It would have been a convenient way of nabbing you. But no harm done. Everything's working out just fine, isn't it, Marina?"

"Beautifully," his sister agreed. "Are you ready to make the call?"

"Almost. This whole thing has to be properly timed. Tides, you know," he added helpfully as he glanced at Elly.

Elly's mouth went dry. Her tongue felt like sandpaper. "Tides? What about the tides?"

"You, my dear, are going to spend the night in a cozy little cabin a few miles from here," said Marina. "But tomorrow night you will spend it in a much more scenic location. You'll be able to watch the sun come up from a really choice vantage point." Marina languidly crossed one booted ankle over the other. "Go ahead and dial," she told Damon.

Elly stood frozen in front of the gun, watching in dull horror as Damon dialed the number on the slip of paper. It was Jess's number, she was certain of it. A moment later she was proved correct.

"We're all in luck," Damon said easily, without any preamble as Jess came on the line. "You're spending the evening at home. Elly will be delighted." There was a pause as Jess said something in response, and Damon's eyes filled with malicious amusement. "Of course she's here. I'm calling from her living room. Want to talk to her?" Without waiting for an answer he thrust the receiver toward Elly.

She took the instrument with shaking fingers. "Jess?"

"Christ, Elly, what the hell's going on?"

"The gruesome twosome has arrived on my doorstep," she managed to say, her tone as uneven as her grip on the phone.

"Twosome?"

The savage alertness in the single word told Elly all she needed to know about Jess's mood.

"Marina's not dead, Jess."

"That fits," he responded.

"With what?"

"Nothing, I'll explain later. Get rid of them, Elly. They're nothing but trouble. I want them out of your house now."

Elly glanced at the gun in Damon's fingers. "I couldn't agree with you more. Unfortunately, it's not going to be that simple. Damon has a gun, Jess. He's talking ransom."

The silence on the other end of the line seemed to reach out and chill Elly's entire living room. When Jess finally spoke he sounded unbelievably cold. "Are you all right?"

"Yes," she whispered.

"Put Carrington on the line."

Mutely, Elly handed the phone to Damon, who smiled as he spoke into the receiver. "As you can hear, she's in good health, Winter. And if everyone, especially you, follows orders, she'll stay that way. Marina and I aren't overly greedy. We just want what's coming to us. I'd say sweet little Elly here is worth about fifty thousand, wouldn't you?" He paused, listening. "No, I realize you can't lay your hands on that kind of money tonight. But you can get it first thing in the morning can't you? The banks open at ten. We'll expect the cash to be packed neatly in a briefcase. You will drive here to Elly's house and wait for a phone call tomorrow evening. We will arrange the exchange at that time. Oh, and Winter. I probably don't have to spell this out, but I will for the sake of mutual understanding. Come alone. This is a small, isolated area. We're bound to notice if you bring the cops along for company. And if you do, Elly's going to disappear for good.'' Damon slammed down the receiver before there could be any further response.

''I think,'' said Marina, ''that we'd better be on our way. Get a coat, Elly. You'll be spending the next twenty-four hours with us.''

''Where?''

''At a deserted vacation cabin several miles from here. Damon and I have been staying there for the past few days, and so far no one's even noticed our presence. As long as we stay clear of town we're safe. It should be good for one more night. Now hurry up and get that coat unless you want to spend a very cold night.''

''You don't have any heat at this cabin?'' Elly asked as she obediently started to walk toward the hall closet. En route she had to pass the cluster of ivy plants on the bench against the wall. Beneath their cascading vines was the paring knife she had been using to trim dead leaves—the knife Jess had taken such pains to sharpen.

''Oh, the cabin is warm enough. But tomorrow night you're going to spend in a fairly uncomfortable situation, I'm afraid,'' Marina said smoothly. She watched Elly open the closet door and pull out a bulky down parka. ''That should do the trick. Come on now, let's get going. Winter knows we called from your home. We don't want to give him time to mobilize the local cops, although I don't think he'll take the risk.''

Elly stood clutching the parka, watching the other two uneasily. ''But I don't understand,'' she began as she awkwardly started to struggle into the jacket. She made a production out of it, not bothering to fake her nervousness. It was quite real. ''What will you do when you have the money? Jess won't let the matter rest. You know that. You know he'll find a way to track you down....'' She deliberately swung her arm wide as if having a problem fitting it into the parka sleeve.

The edge of the garment trailed along the row of ceramic ivy plant containers, knocking two of them off the edge of the table. With a haste that seemed impulsive and automatic, Elly turned to grab at the falling pots. She saw the paring knife as she swung around. For an instant her back was toward Damon and Marina. The sharp little knife disappeared up her sleeve even as the pots hit the floor with a jarring crash.

"You clumsy fool" Marina snapped, her eyes automatically following the small disaster. "Forget the damn plants and let's get going."

Turning slowly, her expression frightened and resentful, Elly shoved her hands into the pockets of her jacket and waited. Inside the right pocket she released the small knife.

"You'd better tie her wrists now, Marina." Damon removed a length of cord from his jacket and tossed it to his sister. "We wouldn't want her getting any clumsier."

Marina shook her head disgustedly as she stepped forward to tie Elly's hands behind her back. "Jess's standards have definitely slipped lately. I can't imagine what he sees in you. Stupid little country girl."

The knife seemed to be burning a hole in Elly's pocket, but Marina made no effort to search her. Why should she? The jacket had come straight out of the closet and couldn't be expected to have anything other than a stray tissue or some pennies tucked away in the pockets. "That's funny. Jess was just saying the other day that he can't remember what he ever saw in you," Elly remarked.

Marina gave the cord a vicious little jerk, and Elly immediately regretted the impulsive dig.

"Jess knows damn well what he saw in her," Damon said. "The same thing every other man sees in her. They all follow like lemmings to the sea."

"You didn't answer my question," Elly went on. She felt a little bolder now that it was becoming obvious Marina wasn't going to discover the knife. "What are you going to do when you have your hands on the money—assuming Jess brings the cash in the first place?"

"Oh, he'll bring it." Marina was serenely confident. "And he won't act until he has you safely back. That will give Damon and me plenty of time to leave the country." She glanced at her brother. "Ready?"

"All set. You drive and I'll keep an eye on Elly. Wouldn't want her to forget the position she's in."

Elly's gaze went from one incredibly attractive, determined face to the other, weighed the malice in the two sets of green eyes and knew she would be very lucky to get a chance to use the paring knife.

Damon grabbed one bound arm and led his victim toward the front door.

In Portland, Jess very carefully placed the receiver into its cradle. He didn't want to be careful with it. What he really wanted to do was hurl the damned instrument against the nearest off-white wall. The rage inside him was simmering so close to the surface it threatened to take over completely.

But the discipline of years did battle with the fury and won. There was nothing to be accomplished by blind rage at this point. The satisfaction of destruction would have to wait until later. So the phone was very carefully replaced. But Jess realized his fingers were almost shaking with the effort it took to control himself.

The Carringtons had dared to touch Elly.

Jess sat with his hands clenched between his knees, every muscle in his body screaming for action and revenge. The fools. Damon and Marina had played with fire so many times and gotten away with it so often that they no longer knew when to fear getting burned. Jess glanced at the neatly typed reports he had been studying when the phone had rung a few minutes earlier.

The papers carried the discrete, impressive letterhead of the very expensive, very efficient agency he had hired. It had cost a fortune, plus expenses, but the agency was convinced there was a high probability that Marina Carrington had not died in the yachting accident, and that she and her brother were alive and well and living very nicely on the coast of Mexico.

They should have had the sense to stay there, Jess decided as he got to his feet. They should have had the sense to keep clear of him and anything that belonged to him. But Damon and Marina had never been blessed with an overabundance of common sense. They saw no need to play by anyone else's rules. Until now, by and large, they had gotten away with their dangerous games.

Jess walked into the bedroom and found his briefcase. It appeared to be about the right size. He thought about what he knew of Damon and Marina. Both were inclined to be reckless, emotional, a little wild. They derived some kind of high from the turmoil and excitement they created around them. They fed on the trouble they caused the way a shark feeds on the smaller fish around it. But the fact that they got their kicks from creating trouble was also their chief weakness, unless you counted the strange bond between the twins. They were two halves of a whole, functioning at times almost like a single entity. That, too, could be a weakness. Jess contemplated the thought for a while.

In a way he understood the link better now than he ever had in the past. During the time he had known Elly, a silent bond had been formed, the strength of which he had only recently begun to comprehend. With the instincts of natural predators, the Carringtons had found his main weakness. Jess would do whatever he had to in order to see Elly safe. To Damon and Marina, Elly probably appeared to be a weak point through which they could reach Jess. What they didn't realize was that she had also become a source of strength to him.

There was nothing to do now but wait. For a moment he stood quietly, picturing Elly bound and helpless in the Carringtons' hands.

Once again the savage rage simmered to the surface, almost swamping him, and once again Jess controlled it. He would get Elly free first. Then he would deal with Damon and Marina Carrington. This time he would see to it that they were finally consumed by the fire they had started.

Fire was reputed to be the one sure way of dealing with witches.

Elly was uncomfortable, stiff and disgusted. Fear had given way to other emotions as time passed. Nothing was working out the way it did in the movies. She had expected to be tossed into a closet or a bedroom and left by herself. At that point she could have begun industrious work with the paring knife. Instead she had been kept seated on a worn-out couch in the main room of the small beach cabin in full sight of the Carringtons. Even asking to use the bathroom facilities had not brought her any solitude. Marina had accompanied her, bringing the gun along.

The little knife continued to burn a hole in her jacket. The only measure of satisfaction she had was that she hadn't been told to remove the garment.

When it became apparent that Damon and Marina had decided to take turns staying awake during the night, Elly finally decided to try getting some sleep. After several restless attempts she finally succeeded.

She awoke a long time later, vaguely aware of the low murmur of the twins' voices as they sat talking near the fire. For a moment Elly didn't try to concentrate on what they were saying. For one thing, her arms ached and she had developed a headache from her awkward sleeping position. It seemed more trouble than it was worth to make the effort to shift her position. She lay still, eyes closed and wondered what Jess was doing.

She knew, just as the Carringtons appeared to know, that he would come for her. He would pay whatever price was necessary. That fact depressed Elly more than anything else that had happened. Once again he would assume his responsibilities. Once again he would endeavor to bail Elly out of trouble. She longed to make him aware of a wild, passionate love he had for her and all she succeeded in doing was finding odd little ways of drawing out his sense of responsibility and integrity—if you could call getting yourself kidnapped an odd little way of doing things. When this was all over would he finally decide she was too much trouble?

There I go again, Elly thought morosely. *I'm acting nervous and afraid of having pushed him too far.* What she had to remember was that this kidnapping, at least, was hardly her fault. Unless, she decided on a wave of uneasy guilt, it might have been prevented by telling Jess earlier that Damon Carrington was still hanging around. No use letting her thoughts drift too far in that direction. What was done was done. The low voices near the fire filtered slowly into her mind.

"We'll arrange the pickup to be here at the cabin," Damon was saying quietly. "We'll be able to see if any cars other than Winter's Jaguar come near. If they do we'll know he's been followed."

"He won't go to the cops," Marina said with amused certainty. "He'll handle this by himself."

"Just in case, one of us will stay out of sight when he arrives with the money. I'll pick up the briefcase and we'll make him think you're guarding little miss wholesome over there. He won't move on one of us as long as he thinks the other has Elly."

Marina laughed softly. "She won't be needing any guard out on that rock. I'll wait in the car for you. In the time it takes Jess to figure out where sweet little Elly is and call in the cops, we'll be on a plane out of Portland. We can be safely out of the country before anyone figures out which direction we've gone."

The word *rock* worried Elly more than anything else that had happened so far. She had been subconsciously working on the assumption that the Carringtons hadn't progressed to the point of contemplating murder. Maybe she was wrong. That realization sent the first of several cold chills down her spine.

But the real chills began much later that day when she finally realized what was in store for her. The short twilight was falling across the ocean when the Carringtons finally jostled her into the Porsche.

"I'm going to hate leaving this baby behind," Damon said, patting the leather-bound steering wheel.

"You can get another."

"The fifty thousand isn't going to go far if I start out using most of it to buy another car." Damon frowned as he turned the vehicle down a back road that led close to the beach.

"We'll get it on credit. We can make the fifty thousand look like five hundred thousand to a potential creditor. Look how long we made that insurance money last," Marina reminded him. She was the one holding the gun now. She kept it loosely aligned with Elly's midsection. "When the fifty thousand is gone we'll think of something else."

"We always do," Damon agreed with a strange smile.

"It keeps life interesting." Marina smiled at Elly. "You should be grateful to us. This is probably the most excitement you've ever had. Enjoy it."

"I can live without your brand of excitement."

Marina laughed. "That's what Jess eventually decided, too. Wonder what he's thinking now that he's having to cope with it again."

Elly looked away, not bothering to answer. Her mind was filled now with the path Damon was taking to the sea. It would be totally dark soon, but she knew where they were. They were nearing the cove that was less than a mile from her home—the cove that contained the castle rock. Elly remembered what had been said earlier about leaving her on the rock. Then she frantically tried to recall the tide schedule. A new kind of fear began building in her.

"This should be it," Damon announced, parking the Porsche at the edge of the bluff. "Let's get moving. I don't want to stay out here in the open any longer than necessary."

"It's getting dark," Marina pointed out. "No one can see us."

"Still, I don't like it." He reached for Elly, pulling her out of the car so abruptly that she stumbled and fell to her knees. "Get up, bitch." He glanced at his twin. "Got the rest of that rope?"

"I've got it."

"Give it to me. I'll take care of this." He yanked Elly across the wet sand, pushing her toward the castle rock. "I hear you don't like salt water, Elly, love. In fact, I gather you have a real fear of swimming in the sea. In another couple of hours that's the only way you'll be able to get off that rock. That's assuming you found some way to untie yourself first, which isn't very likely, is it? Besides, I got a good look at this place the other day when I brought Sarah and her brat down here. When the tide is in, even a good swimmer would have trouble with those waves. Even after we tell him where you are, Winter probably won't be able to get you off until morning."

Elly flinched as she stared straight ahead. The sea was already beginning to foam around the base of the rock. It licked eagerly at her feet as Damon forced her toward the encrusted fortress. In another hour the waves would be crashing roughly and the water would be waist deep in the imaginary moat that protected the castle. In two hours it would be over her head and pounding the cove violently. Only the tip of the rock would remain above the water. If it stormed, even that position would be untenable.

"This is hardly necessary, Damon," she tried to argue calmly. "Why not leave me tied up on shore? I'm not going anywhere with both hands and feet tied."

"Just an added precaution. I don't want any surprises. Marina and I have this planned down to the minute, and I don't want anything happening to alter our plans. And," he added with an evil grin, "it appeals to my sense of humor."

"Leaving me stranded here? You've got a very distorted sense of humor."

"I know. But it helps keep life amusing. Move, Elly." He forced her into the ankle-deep water, chuckling when she instinctively recoiled. He motioned for her to start climbing to the top of the rocky castle.

Elly tried not to think about the crunching sound her feet made as she slithered and slipped on the shells of the small creatures clinging to the sides of their private fortress. When she had to grip the rocky surface in order to keep her balance, her hand came in contact with something that moved hurriedly out of the way, and she almost screamed.

"Hurry up, Elly. I haven't got all night."

She wanted to plead with her captor and knew it would be useless. He would only derive more pleasure out of what he was doing to her. Grimly, Elly tried to push her imagination to the furthest corners of her mind while she finished the awkward scramble. In a few more minutes she wouldn't be able to see much at all, and then what would she do when the small things skittered and darted in and around the rocky pile they called home?

Ten minutes later Elly sat alone, imprisoned queen of the castle, and watched the lights of the Porsche disappear. Below her the sea began to surge more and more impatiently around the base of the fortress.

Elly decided she could certainly understand why the Carringtons' brand of excitement had begun to pall on Jess.

Nine

It was when she began fumbling for the paring knife that Elly realized there were other aspects of her situation that didn't fit the movie stereotype. It was damned hard to work her bound hands around to the pocket on the side of her jacket—especially when the sound of the sea and the silence of her fellow inmates kept distracting her.

She was sitting on a reasonably level surface of the rock, a position that would have been visible if someone had happened by on the bluff above the beach. And if it had been daylight.

Her fingers seemed to have grown rather numb, although Marina hadn't tied her wrists tight enough to cut off circulation. Perhaps it was the cold evening air that was causing the lack of feeling.

Something moved around her toes, probably a small crab. Elly jerked her bound feet away and felt her ankle scrape across a rough-edged shell. It was impossible in the dim light to tell if she had cut herself, but Elly was very much afraid she had. The thought panicked her for an instant. Would blood draw more of the rock's denizens?

She mustn't think about that. She had to focus every ounce of concentration on getting free. Soon the rendezvous between Damon and Jess would take place, and if there was to be any hope of resolving this mess she had to get off the rock. Damned if she would let Jess shell out fifty thousand dollars for her. And damned if she would let the Carringtons get away with using her to get at their old enemy.

The paring knife came into her fingers at last. It seemed slippery as she drew it carefully from her pocket, and her initial fear was that she would drop it and never find it again in the darkness.

Cautiously, she grasped the knife's handle and tried to angle the blade toward the cords that bound her wrists. She made contact easily enough, but there was no magical parting of the strands. Instead she seemed to be sawing away uselessly. The knife had been dulled by her insistence on using it on her plants. Jess had been right. You never knew when you were going to need a sharp knife.

Chagrined, Elly closed her eyes in frustration and wondered how she would make excuses the next time she saw Jess. Contemplation of that gave her the energy to continue sawing on the cords. Surely there was some cutting edge left on the blade. Jess had spent time and care sharpening it. With a growing sense of desperation, she continued working away at the cords and finally something began to give.

She was making some progress, Elly realized. The knowledge gave her the courage to continue.

The process took far longer than she would have expected. By the time Elly's wrists were freed and she started in on the ankle ties, she was chilled and tired. Her muscles ached from the constant pressure of trying to cut through the bonds, and her jeans were damp from the restless spray of the incoming waves. The knowledge that the spray was already leaping as high as her perch told Elly just how deep the water around her was becoming. Frantically, she renewed her efforts and cried out in shock and rage a moment later when the frail knife finally snapped.

"Damn it to hell!" Tossing aside the useless handle, Elly leaned down to wrench at the remaining cords. Perhaps they had already been nearly severed, or perhaps her fear and anger made her stronger than she knew. In any event, she was finally free a few moments later.

She scrambled to a kneeling position, wincing as her palms found the wet, rough surface of the rock. Her legs were chilled and so were her hands. Thank God for the goosedown parka.

There was only one way down from the top of the castle and that was the same way she had climbed it. It was either that or cower up here until Jess finally found her.

The thought of Jess searching for her sent Elly over the side. Once again she closed her ears to the awful crunching sounds. When she accidentally came into contact with a scurrying crab she inhaled sharply, but she didn't lose her grip. The stupid crab could just get out of the way, she told herself resolutely. Five more minutes and she would be off his house.

The hardest part came when her feet slipped into the foaming surface of the water. She was startled at the strength of the surging tide.

"Well, at least it's headed in the right direction," she told herself aloud in hopes of arousing another drop or two of courage. "I won't be carried out to sea. I'll be washed ashore."

Being battered about on the rocks didn't sound like a heck of a good alternative, however. Elly clung to the wall of the castle and tried to remember exactly what the terrain around her looked like when it wasn't inundated with water. Slowly the picture formed in her mind. While she thought about it, she remembered to unzip her down jacket. She should try to keep it as dry as possible. She was going to need it when she got to shore. She would be chilled to the bone from the cold sea. She tied it awkwardly around her throat.

To her right there was a shoulder of rock that contained several pitted areas. They could prove treacherous footing. She inched to the left and lowered herself a little farther. She was seeking the sandy bottom at the base of the fortress. How had the water become so deep so quickly? She was losing track of time.

She found the bottom with jolting force when a playful wave ripped her free of the rock and tossed her toward shore. Elly floundered, trying to right herself and staggered violently when her foot touched bottom. The water was up to her waist. She was soaked. Her clothing and her shoes seemed to be deadweights trying to drag her under.

Once again she remembered the possibility of her ankle having been cut earlier. Primitive fears of sharks and other creatures being drawn by blood sent Elly splashing desperately for shore. The swirling water caught at her, playing with her, terrifying her, but it didn't succeed in tripping her. For a split second she almost considered climbing back up the rock.

Closing her eyes against the salty sting of the sea, she again pictured the terrain in her mind. When she risked lifting her lashes again, she knew where she was and what she had to do in order to get to shore.

Jess would be frantic worrying about her, and he would be in danger from the twins. Elly had no alternative but to get to shore—just as she'd had no alternative that day so long ago when she'd gone into the sea to rescue Dave. When there was no alternative, you did what had to be done.

The struggle to the beach seemed to last forever, and it drained so much energy that by the time she reached the damp sand Elly could hardly stand. She wavered for a moment trying to savor her victory, but she was beyond any thoughts of triumph. There was a vast sense of relief but that was it.

She was so cold. She had never been so cold. The sudden fear of hypothermia made her untie the damp jacket. Hastily, she shrugged into it. It provided the warmth the core of her body needed. Knowing there was no longer any time to waste, Elly turned in the direction of her home. She would take time later to congratulate herself on the battle with the sea.

The only goal in her life right now was to get to the beach cottage before Damon and Marina got away with using wholesome little Elly Trent against Jess. As she jogged heavily down the beach, Elly realized she didn't feel very sweet or wholesome at all tonight. She felt like committing murder.

The house was deserted when she reached it. If Jess had come there to wait for the phone call, he had already received it and left. The front door was unlocked, Elly discovered. He must have left in a hurry. Not like Jess to overlook details.

She walked into the front room and stood there dripping while she examined the scene. Jess had been there, all right. A half-empty glass stood on the table in front of the sofa. It didn't appear to contain Scotch, however. It looked more like mineral water.

Jess wouldn't have risked dulling his reactions with alcohol, Elly decided. Not when he was on his way to meet Damon Carrington. Hastily, she stripped off her jeans and wet clothing, dashing up the stairs as she did so. Grabbing for dry clothes in her closet, she put them on with the same fumbling haste. Then she was racing back down the stairs. The car keys were sitting on the table in the hall where she always left them. She had them in her hand and was out the door in seconds.

. Halfway to her destination Elly belatedly began to wonder if she shouldn't have called the local authorities. Well, it was too late now to have second thoughts. She pushed the accelerator closer to the floor. She would have to leave the car some distance from the beach cottage or the Carringtons would be warned of her approach. She knew exactly where to put the vehicle. She'd place it squarely across the road that Damon would take when he and Marina started for Portland.

Parking the car where she had intended, Elly abandoned it and started toward the cabin. With any luck the distant rumble of the sea would hide any noise she might make as she approached. It wasn't until she rounded a corner and saw the tail of the Porsche in her path that she remembered Marina was supposed to be waiting in the car. The thought brought Elly to an abrupt halt.

Changing her direction, she slipped into the trees alongside the road and stayed out of the sight of anyone sitting in the Porsche. As she went past, she thought she saw Marina's blond head in the driver's seat. Elly went on toward the cabin.

The white Jaguar was sitting in the driveway. Elly halted again, uncertain of what to do next. There were lights on inside the old house. Slowly, she approached from one side. When she reached a window she realized she was looking into the main room.

Jess was standing there, the briefcase at his feet. He looked deceptively casual, as if he were only talking business. It was Damon who looked nervous. He was holding the gun very tightly, not with the studied ease he'd used when aiming it at Elly. His evident tension told Elly all she needed to know.

Damon might be reckless and dangerous, but he was also smart enough to be scared. He'd gotten himself in fairly deep this time, and he seemed to be realizing it. So did Jess. Elly couldn't hear his muffled voice through the window, but she could hear Damon's. The younger man's words were too loud and too sharp—further evidence of his unstable emotional state.

"Don't you dare threaten me, Winter. Not if you want to see your precious little country girl again. Believe me, it will be easy enough for Marina to leave her where she is. You'll never find her in time to save her unless I tell you where we've put her. So just shut your damn mouth and open that briefcase. I want to see the money."

Jess said something quietly in response. Elly couldn't make it out, but she saw him go down slowly on one knee to open the briefcase.

Unable to think of anything else to do, Elly yelled through the window, "Hey, Carrington! If you think we're going to let you have that money, you're…" She didn't get any further.

Elly wasn't at all surprised when Damon whirled to face the window with a shocked expression. She had meant to get his attention. But she was more than a little startled to see him raise the gun with deadly purposefulness. He'd clearly panicked at the sight of her. Realizing belatedly that he was going to pull the trigger, Elly threw herself down onto the cold ground.

The gun roared and the window shattered as the bullet tore through it. Elly ducked her head instinctively, staying down. But there was no second shot. She heard Damon's violent yell from inside the cottage and then the sound of crashing furniture.

"Elly!"

She glanced up from her crouching position to see Jess leaning out the window, an expression of savage concern on his face.

"I'm all right, Jess."

He didn't wait. Instead he turned back into the room before she could move.

Alarmed at the thought of what might be happening, Elly leaped to her feet and stared at the scene in front of her. Clearly Jess had jumped Carrington in the same moment the other man had pulled the trigger. The impact of his lunge had sent Damon crashing up against the wall, stunning him. Now the two men were sprawling across the floor in a short, violent battle that was ending almost as soon as it began. Damon didn't stand a chance.

The gun had been sent flying in the first assault and Jess's sheer fury had taken care of the rest. With a ferocity that left Elly wide-eyed and voiceless, he pinned his younger opponent to the floor and started to hammer at Damon's beautifully chiseled face.

Damon's cries of pain became mere grunts and then faded altogether. Elly realized he was almost unconscious from the punishment.

She darted around the corner of the house and dashed through the front door.

"Jess! Jess, that's enough, you'll kill him!"

Her voice seemed to break the raging anger that was dominating Jess. He went still above his victim and his burning eyes swung to Elly.

"You're all right." It was a statement, not a question.

Elly nodded and finally found her voice again. "I'm okay, Jess."

"I should kill him."

"He's not worth it. Let the law have him. Besides, we've got Marina to worry about." Desperately she tried to distract him with mention of the other twin. The thought of Jess killing a man because of her was more than Elly wanted to contend with just then. There would be endless inquiries and explanations. Perhaps worse. She'd already caused her lover enough trouble. Her only goal now was to end this mess before it got any more difficult.

It was something of a joke when you thought about it, she decided. She was always trying to keep Jess from becoming embroiled in trouble on her behalf, and all she accomplished was another disaster.

"Marina! Christ, I almost forgot about her." Jess staggered to his feet, wiping a trace of blood off his mouth. "Where is she?"

"In the Porsche outside."

"He said she was guarding you."

"He lied. They stuck me on that rock in the middle of the cove."

Jess's eyes narrowed. "The tide…"

"I know. I'll tell you about it later. Right now we've got to stop Marina." Even as Elly spoke the roar of the Porsche's engine split the night.

"She's leaving! Damn that witch. I swear to God, this time I'm going to put these two away for ten years."

"Damon probably told her to get out if she heard gunfire and he didn't immediately appear. But she's not going far. I parked my car across the road."

Jess swung around, one brow lifting. "You're just full of surprises tonight, aren't you? Come on, help me with handsome over there."

"What are you going to do?"

"Use him to stop Marina."

Jess ignored the small handgun on the floor and knelt down to open his briefcase. From inside he withdrew a wicked-looking weapon of his own. It gleamed a dull blue-black in the cabin light. Elly stared at it.

"What on earth? I thought you had money in there!"

"I do. I also had this. Come on, let's get Carrington on his feet."

He reached down to haul Damon upright. Carrington was so groggy he didn't seem to realize who was bracing him or what was happening. When he was forced to move toward the door of the cabin, he groaned but he didn't argue. Elly drew his arm around her shoulder to steady him while Jess kept him on his feet.

In the darkness outside, the Porsche headlights cut a swath through the night as the car swung violently around on the narrow road. Marina had just realized the exit was blocked. She was starting back toward the cabin. As she gunned the sportscar's engine, Jess pushed Damon out into the middle of her path. The injured man staggered and fell to the ground.

Simultaneously the Porsche's tires screamed as the brakes were applied with savage force. Then the car door opened.

"Damon!" Marina ran toward her brother. "Damon!"

"Stay right where you are, Marina, or I'll put a bullet in him. Maybe one in you, too, for that matter. I'm really getting sick of Carringtons." Jess stepped out of the trees. The lights of the car fell harshly on the gun in his hand. "This time I think I'm going to do more than just hope you'll stay out of my life. This time I'm going to do something permanent to make certain you stay out of it."

"You hurt him! You hurt Damon!"

"He hurt Elly," Jess responded in a voice as cold as his surname. "He's lucky I didn't kill him and you both. Believe me, the temptation to finish this right here and now is overwhelming. Don't tempt me, Marina."

Kneeling beside her brother in the glare of the headlights, Marina looked up at Jess. Perhaps it was the harsh light or perhaps it was the equally harsh expression on her face; for whatever reason she didn't seem very beautiful just then. Elly felt almost sorry for her. Marina Carrington appeared to be finally comprehending the fact that this time she might have gone too far.

"You can't prove anything, Jess," Marina said in a last-ditch effort. "It'll be your word against ours."

"If I have trouble making the kidnapping charges stick, we'll see how well the insurance company does with its fraud charges. On your feet, Marina. We've got a lot to do."

Something moved on Marina's face as she stared at him. Her voice softened, took on a gently pleading note. "Jess... Jess, please. Listen to me. For the sake of what we once..."

"Forget it, Marina. That act hasn't worked in a long time. You wore it out with too many performances. That's your whole problem, you know, as well as your brother's. You were born thinking you could get away with anything forever. But you pushed your luck a little too far this time. You had the stupidity to threaten something I want very badly. Stupidity is the one crime for which you always have to pay in this world."

"Bastard," Marina hissed, the softness leaving instantly as she took in the unwavering set of his face.

Jess smiled faintly. "Now you've got it, Marina."

It was much later that evening when a subdued, watchful Elly sat sipping the brandy Jess had just poured. She had spoken very little to him during the past two hours. In truth there hadn't been much opportunity. The local law authorities hadn't experienced any difficulty in believing Jess's side of the tale. After all, Deputy Charlie Atkins knew Jess and Elly. In a small town the burden of proof tended to be on the outsiders, not on the locals who filed the complaints against them.

Besides, as Charlie took pains to explain to his superior, there were those Porsche tracks on the bluff above the cove, all that money in a briefcase and Elly Trent's wet clothes. Everybody knew Elly Trent wouldn't go swimming voluntarily. In point of fact nobody in his right mind went swimming in a cold sea at night. In addition, everyone in town knew Jess and Elly. Good people. They wouldn't make up a thing like this. Charlie's boss concurred.

Elly turned over in her mind the scene in the sheriff's office as she watched Jess pour his own glass of brandy. He hadn't settled down yet. There was a tension in him that wasn't dissolving, even though the Carringtons were safely in custody. When he'd finished pouring the brandy, he picked up the glass and began pacing the room in front of her. Elly curled her legs beneath her as she sat on the sofa. Her wariness increased.

"How did you know about the insurance fraud?" she finally asked. She had been trying for several minutes to think of something to break the taut silent.

Jess took a sip of his brandy. "I had a firm working on it. The report was waiting for me when I got back to the apartment yesterday."

"An investigation firm?"

"Yeah."

Elly frowned. "But how did you know? I mean, what made you hire a detective agency?"

"After Damon showed up here I decided to do a little checking. I knew he was up to something, and it made me wonder how he'd been surviving on his own for the past three years. He and Marina had always functioned as a team—a pair of wolves who hunted together. I made a few inquiries and learned he'd been out of the country until recently. That made me even more suspicious. Why stay away from the States that long? And if he really felt I'd been somehow responsible for Marina's death, why didn't he come looking for revenge before now? I kept the inquiries going." Jess shrugged, pausing by the fireplace. "One thing led to another. The investigators turned up fairly convincing evidence that Marina was still alive."

"I see."

"I got Carrington's call just as I'd finished reading the report."

It seemed to Elly there was a trace of accusation in his words. Jess swung around to face her, his thumb hooked into the waistband of the jeans he was wearing. Out of force of habit she almost began to apologize. She stopped herself just as the words trembled on her lips. "Thank you for coming to my rescue," she said instead, her voice very formal.

Jess stared at her thoughtfully. "You were doing a pretty good job of rescuing yourself. I'm proud of you, Elly. When I think of how you must have felt trapped on that damn rock with the tide coming in I could strangle both Carringtons. Was it very bad?''

"It was…'' she hesitated, seeking the appropriate word, ''manageable. The worse part actually turned out to be the cold. That's why I had to change clothes before driving to the beach house.''

Jess shook his head, looking appalled. ''How did you get free? I thought they had you tied hand and foot.''

Elly cleared her throat. ''Yes. Well, Jess, thereby hangs a very interesting tale. Remember that little paring knife you said I shouldn't use for trimming the plants and digging around in the dirt?''

He eyed her with sudden alertness. ''I remember.''

"It, uh, happened to be sitting conveniently over there under the ivy. When Marina ordered me to put on my coat I was a little clumsy and managed to knock off those pots you see on the floor. When I pretended to try to catch them I palmed the knife.'' She smiled widely. ''Brilliant, huh?''

Jess lifted his eyes heavenward in silent supplication. ''I won't ask how the knife got to be under the ivy. I'll just be grateful that it was.''

"Look on the bright side, Jess. If you hadn't sharpened it recently it probably wouldn't have cut through the cords at all.''

"I'll take comfort in that.'' He began to pace. ''I won't take any comfort in the memory of the way you jumped up on the other side of that window at the beach house, though. Damn it to hell, Elly, Carrington could have killed you. He was a stick of dynamite waiting to explode, and when you distracted him he lost control. Not to mention what you did to my frame of mind.''

Elly heard the beginning of the censuring tone again and stirred restlessly on the couch. ''Now, Jess…''

"By the way,'' he went on ruthlessly, really warming to his theme now, ''the deputy said he heard that Carrington put in an appearance at that potluck you went to last week. You never mentioned seeing him.''

Elly coughed faintly. ''I didn't see any point in saying anything. It would only have upset you and besides, I—''

"Upset me! Elly, if I'd known he was still in the neighborhood I could have taken some action. I could have protected you better. As it was, I was sitting blithely in Portland thinking there was no immediate concern. You should have told me he was still in town.''

"I was trying to avoid an embarrassing and possibly dangerous confrontation.''

"What did you get instead? An extremely dangerous confrontation.'' He swung around sharply, starting toward the far side of the room. His dark brows formed a solid line above his gray eyes. "I know the present situation is resolved, but this whole mess only goes to show that it's time I stepped up the schedule. I don't want to spend any more evenings than absolutely necessary sitting alone in Portland wondering what you're doing. My nerves won't tolerate it. We've wasted enough time. There's no reason we can't be married next week. I can wind up my last consulting job by Friday and move in here with you on Saturday. Once I'm finally living here I won't have to worry about what's going on all week.''

Elly's cautious nature began to disintegrate. "Now hold on just a minute, Jess.''

He ignored her, lost in his plans. "I can contact a moving company tomorrow. We can also apply for the license this week. I'll arrange for the ceremony on Monday. You might want to have a few friends in for a reception or something. That's fine with me. In the meantime I'll get my consulting reports out of the way.''

"Damn it, Jess, just slow down for one blessed minute!'' Elly leaped to her feet, her eyes blazing as her temper and her wariness collided in a small internal explosion. "This is my life we're discussing, not just yours, and I've got a couple of things to say about it.''

Wanting to quell her tirade, he slanted her a glance. "Calm down, Elly, I'm just making a few plans.''

"You're shuffling me around on that damned schedule of yours, and I'm not sure I want to be shuffled. Sit down, Jess Winter, I've got something to say.'' She advanced on him, her fists planted on her hips. "Go on, sit down!''

"Elly, you've been through a lot tonight. You're probably feeling tired and you're still under a strain.''

"I'm not in a mood to be soothed or consoled or patted on the head and sent to bed. Sit down, Jess.'' She was too wound up to be surprised when he did exactly as she ordered. Warily, he sank down onto the couch and took another sip of brandy. She stood facing him determinedly. "Now, let's get specific about these plans of yours. In case you hadn't noticed, my whole future is at stake here. And I have a few comments I'd like to make."

"I'm listening."

"I accused you of being afraid to let yourself love me. I decided you were running scared."

"Elly…"

She held up a hand. "But I had it all backward, Jess Winter. I'm the one who's running scared. I've been nervous and wary and…and cautious around you since day one. I was afraid of pushing you on the physical side of things, so I spent weeks agonizing over the reason you didn't ask me to go to bed with you. You always seemed to be on some sort of schedule, and I was afraid of disrupting it. After I finally worked up my nerve to try the big seduction scene and had it so rudely interrupted by Marina, I began fretting over the fact that I might say or do something to remind you of her. Then I saw you face to face with Damon, and I worried that if I didn't keep you two apart there would be violence."

"Elly, let me—"

"I'm not finished yet. When my family business problems became pressing, I panicked about you involving yourself for fear it would bring up more memories of your experiences with the Carringtons. I've been getting increasingly nervous about the fact that you can't seem to admit you love me. That, Jess, is the last straw."

Jess suddenly went still. "What are you saying, Elly?"

"That I'm through running scared—through being wary, through walking on eggs around you when it comes to sticky issues. I'm not going to let you make me nervous or afraid any longer. I'm giving you an ultimatum. I'm not going to fit conveniently into your schedule anymore, Jess. We're not getting married until you find the guts to admit you love me. And you're going to have to make me believe it."

Ten

"**Y**ou do? You know?" The room had been fraught with silence when Elly finally spoke.

"I know."

Elly stared at him. Jess's mouth crooked slightly as he glanced down into his brandy and then back up to meet her eyes. He didn't elaborate. She continued to stare at him, finally remembering to close her mouth.

"You do?" she managed weakly. She felt as if the fire that had been driving her had suddenly flamed out. "How long have you... I mean, when did you decide you loved me?"

"I think I've known since the beginning," Jess said with a strange gentleness. "You were so very right in every way. Before I realized what I was doing I was fitting you into all my plans. I couldn't schedule my future without you. But I didn't want to spell it all out to myself. You were right in that regard, too. I was running scared."

"Oh, Jess, I didn't really mean that."

"Sure you did, it's the truth. I've been coming to terms with it for quite a while, ever since you tried to stage your sweet seduction act. But I wasn't ready to talk about it in San Francisco. I was still trying to come to terms with it myself. I've spent too many years learning to be in control, Elly. I wanted to be in control of myself and of everything around me. I think I've always been inclined to be that way, but after that fiasco of a marriage with Marina I really decided to stay in command of myself and others. Never again was I going to let myself get strung out the way I did with her. I made a total fool of myself. That's a hard thing for a man to live down, Elly.''

Elly was consumed with remorse for having pushed him into the confession. She rushed forward, throwing herself onto her knees in front of him. Catching one of his big hands between hers, she looked up at him earnestly. ''I know, Jess. I thought that was the problem. I should never have provoked you into admitting it. You have every right to deal with this in your own way and in your own time. Forget I said anything, okay?''

He looked amused. ''It's too late. You've already said it. And so have I.''

''Well, we'll just pretend that you haven't.''

''The hell we will.'' His eyes were warming with a sensual laughter. He set down the brandy glass and moved his free hand to her braided hair. ''One of the things you're going to have to learn, Elly, is that if you insist on pushing a man to the wall, you have to take the consequences.''

''What consequences?''

''You said I was not only going to have to admit I loved you, but make you believe I meant it.''

''I believe you. I have to believe you, Jess. I love you so much I just knew you loved me, too. Or that you'd love me if you just gave yourself a chance. That's what I was really afraid of, you know,'' she added confidingly. ''I was terrified you'd take what I offered and resist...well, you know what I mean.''

''You'd thought I'd take everything you had to give and resist surrendering in return.''

Hurriedly Elly denied that. ''It wasn't that you didn't give me a lot in return. You did, Jess. For one thing I trust you, and that means more than I can ever say. You're an honorable man and you're generous. You even tolerated my obnoxious relatives. And you've definitely managed to reassure me that you want me. You have given me a lot.''

''But it wasn't quite enough to make you agree to marry me.'' Slowly, Jess began to work loose one of the pins that held her braids in place.

"I guess I'm a greedy woman," Elly admitted humbly.

"Mmm." He removed the next pin. "I'm glad."

"You are?"

"Definitely. Elly, my love, if you and events in general hadn't pushed me a little during the past couple of weeks, I might have taken months getting around to acknowledging my own feelings. What a waste that would have been."

She smiled gently. "Why?"

"Because I've decided I like admitting that I love you. It's a great relief, you see. I no longer have to worry about maintaining my control when it comes to you. I began realizing that after the first time I took you to bed. Everything felt good afterward. It felt right. Now I know I can just relax and surrender to the inevitable. I don't have to worry about the end results. You taught me not to fear them, sweetheart. I owe you for that. And I intend to spend the rest of my life thanking you."

"You do?"

"Beginning right now," he assured her. Under his deft touch more pins came free from her hair, and a moment later the braids tumbled down around her shoulders. "I love to take your hair down, Elly. There's something so full of promise about the whole thing." He threaded his fingers through the chestnut strands, loosening them until they cascaded over his hands. "I want you, Elly."

"I'm glad," she said simply, her eyes brimming with her love. "Because I love you so much, Jess."

His palm cupped her face as he looked down at her with an intensity that took away her breath. "In the beginning I told myself you had nothing to worry about because I would take good care of your love. I promised myself I would treasure it, protect it, keep it safe. Now I know that I want to give as much as I get."

She caught his hand and turned her lips into the warm palm. "I'll treasure your love, Jess. I'll protect it and keep it safe."

"I know. I trust you, Elly. I've never really trusted a woman before in my life. But I trust you."

She looked up at him, aware of the depth of truth in his words. She decided to take the risk of clearing up one last point. "Once you called me a witch. It was that first night we made love. Remember? We argued afterward and you called me a witch.''

"Did I?'' Jess didn't seem particularly interested. He was lifting her to her feet and standing up beside her. Strong hands settled on her shoulders. ''That worried you?''

"Because it's what you always called Marina.''

"There are two kinds of witchcraft, my sweet Elly. Haven't you read enough fairy tales to know that? Believe me, I've learned about both kinds the hard way. From Marina I learned about the dark, destructive sort. But you taught me about the other kind—the kind associated with sunlight and life and love. There's no one who's more certain of the truth than a man who's seen both the false and the real. Trust me to know the difference, honey.''

She wrapped her arms around his waist, resting her head on his shoulder. ''I trust you, Jess.''

He bent and scooped her up in his arms. ''While we're on the subject of trust,'' he began as he strode toward the stairs with her in his arms, ''this is probably a good time to mention that I don't particularly want to be protected from certain facts in the future. I want you to trust me completely, Elly.''

Elly lifted her head. ''Do I hear a lecture coming on? Something pithy about the way I neglected to mention Damon's lingering presence in the community?''

"You're very perceptive, sweetheart.'' He reached the top of the stairs and turned toward Elly's bedroom.

"I hope you're not going to get into the habit of lecturing me every time you carry me off to bed. It could spoil the mood, you know. Might give me a headache.'' She let her fingers slide persuasively up to the nape of neck.

"I have an excellent home remedy for headaches.'' He stood her on her feet and removed the burnt-orange sweater she was wearing. It came free in one easy sweep of his hands and his eyes shadowed with desire as he touched the tips of her breasts. ''Guaranteed not to fail.''

She felt herself growing warm with the beginnings of sensual tension at the husky tone of his voice. ''Unfortunately, I don't have a headache so we won't be able to experiment with your remedy.''

"Then we'll go straight to bed. I'll get back to the lecture later.''

He undressed her with an urgency that told its own story, his fingers trembling slightly as he stroked her.

Elly fumbled with his shirt until it joined the growing pile of clothing on the floor, and then she unfastened his jeans. As the last garment fell away, he pushed himself into her hands, letting her know the full weight and readiness of his need.

"Elly, my sweet, exciting Elly." He picked her up again and settled her on the bed. "Do you know what I regret most about the last couple of months?"

"What's that?" She reached for him as he came down beside her.

"I regret my own stupidity in waiting so long to take you to bed. When I think of all the nights together we missed…" His words broke off as he leaned down to kiss the swell of her breast. Then his hand tightened on her hip. "I could kick myself."

"That's what you get for being so schedule-conscious."

"Don't sound so smug. There's a lot to be said for schedules. I'm good at them. For the most part I stick to them." Suddenly he lifted his head and gave her a searching glance. "Is that going to bother you? I can't change myself completely, honey. In the last analysis, I'm afraid I tend to run my life on an organized basis."

Elly laughed softly. "I'm not worried. Lately you've shown yourself to be highly adaptable." She pulled him close, pushing her leg tantalizingly between his thighs. His low groan of arousal was her immediate reward. When she let her fingertips trail down his chest to the excitingly rough hair below his flat stomach, he groaned again.

Jess reached out and felt the shape of her hip with his hand, letting his fingers sink into her soft, resilient skin. "I'm amazingly adaptable when it comes to making love to you. Haven't you noticed? I didn't really mind the first time you threw off my schedule by trying to seduce me ahead of time. I'll be just as adaptable forty or fifty years from now. A man has to be flexible about some things."

Elly grinned, touching him intimately. "Flexible isn't exactly how I would describe you at the moment."

"I warned you. I told you that if you were going to push a man, you'd have to learn to take the consequences." He rolled over on top of her, pinning her beneath him. The brief humor faded as he felt her wrap herself around him. Gray eyes gleamed in the shadows, and the lines of his harsh face became etched with his hunger.

"I love you, Jess."

"I know," he whispered. "I've never known what it was like to be loved until I met you. I could never let you go now. Do you realize that? I love you so much, Elly. It's such an incredible relief to finally say it."

He moved then, joining his body to hers in a rush of passion that brought with it a sense of forever. Elly didn't question the feeling. She clung to it and to the man who created it. Jess was giving himself completely, just as she had given herself to him. Jess Winter always seemed to know what he was doing.

*   *   *   *   *

GREEN FIRE

One

His eyes were the color of the green stone in the ring on her hand. Rani Garroway registered that fact in the same instant she realized she'd opened the door to the wrong man. She was startled off balance and oddly shocked. Not just because she'd made a mistake in opening the door, but because of those eyes. The wind howled in the darkness beyond her doorstep, driving the rain through the tall pines and sturdy fir trees. The stranger didn't vanish with the next crackle of lightning. He continued to stand there in front of her, looking like a battle-scarred alley cat demanding shelter from the storm. His green eyes locked with hers.

"I'm sorry," Rani managed, wondering what to do next. "When I heard your knock I assumed you were someone else." Then a sense of self-protection came into play. The local mountain community, normally quiet, was filled with hunters arriving for the fall deer season. That meant a lot of strangers in the area. Armed strangers. Strangers who often mixed guns and alcohol. Her best bet was to make sure this man knew she wouldn't be alone for long. "I'm expecting someone else, you see. He'll be here any moment."

The man ignored her comment the same way he was ignoring the fact that he was drenched from the downpour. There was little shelter from the rain to be had from the porch roof. It leaked like a sieve. His gaze went briefly to the ring on her hand and then back to her tense, uncertain features.

"I'm Flint Cottrell." The voice was low, rough, unpolished; the voice of a man who didn't spend a lot of time discussing art films or vintage wine years. "I work here."

That was enough to trigger all of Rani's interior alarms. "The hell you do," she said, and slammed the door in his face. The phone. She would get to the phone and call Mike. If he didn't answer she would know he was on his way. If he did answer, she could tell him to hurry

Rani was slamming the dead bolt in place when something nudged her foot. She jerked back and then glanced down, unnerved and irritated because of it.

"Get out of the way Zipp. There's somebody out there, and he reminds me far too much of you."

The mottled brown tomcat looked up at her with streetwise eyes He had dashed into temporary hiding when the first knock had sounded on the door. It was his standard routine. Zipp didn't like strangers especially male strangers. He disappeared and sulked for a long time when people came calling on Rani. This time he hadn't stayed out of sight very long, though, Rani noted distractedly. Here he was already looking curious. This wasn't part of his normal response.

When the impatient knock sounded again on the door, the huge cat rumbled something that was presumably a question. Rani paid no attention. She turned away, hurrying across the room to where the phone stood on an old pine table. The knock came again as she was dialing Mike Slater's number. Rani's fingers shook slightly as she stood staring at the door, the receiver to her ear. The line was busy.

Rani lowered the instrument slowly into its cradle, her eyes never leaving the door. She was debating with herself about what to do next and seriously wondering whether to slip out through the kitchen, when she saw the dirty white envelope being shoved under the door.

"Read it," the man called through the wooden barrier. "I'd appreciate it if you'd hurry."

Hesitantly Rani moved toward the scruffy envelope. Zipp was already investigating it with interest. "Here, let me see that," Rani murmured, reaching down to pick up the object. She glanced at the front and saw that it was addressed to her. Tearing the envelope open, she reached inside and unfolded the single sheet of paper.

Dear Miss Garroway,
This is to introduce Flint Cottrell. He will be living in the back cottage for a few weeks while doing some yard work around the cottages for us. We were very fortunate to find someone on such short notice this year.

Chagrined, Rani skipped down to the signature at the bottom and read no further. She yanked the dead bolt and flung open the door. The man with the green eyes was still standing where she had left him, his hands shoved into the pockets of his well-worn sheepskin jacket, a stoic, patient expression on his hard face as if he had spent a lot of time waiting around in darkness and rain. The yellowed fleece collar was pulled up around his neck, framing features as weathered as the jacket. Both jacket and man appeared to be nearing forty. It looked as though both had gotten there the hard way.

"I'm terribly sorry, I didn't realize you were going to be my neighbor," Rani said quickly, standing aside. "Please come in. I'm sure you're wet clear through. That porch roof leaks very badly. I doubt that the back cottage is habitable right now. I could have gotten it ready, but no one told me you'd be arriving."

The man said nothing, stepping over the threshold with a kind of aloof arrogance that again made Rani think of her cat. He came to a halt as Zipp moved into his path.

"Don't mind him. That's Zipp. My cat," Rani added helpfully when there was no immediate response. "Short for Zipporo. He usually dashes off to sulk somewhere when visitors arrive, but he seems to find you interesting. Here, let me have your coat. You're soaked."

Flint Cottrell eyed the cat thoughtfully and then slowly began unfastening the old sheepskin jacket. Without a word he handed the garment to Rani. When she took it from him to hang in the hall closet, he ran his broad hand through his damp hair. Droplets of water glistened in the dark-brown depths and then fell to the floor at his feet as Cottrell carelessly scattered them with the movement of his large, blunt fingers.

Automatically Rani followed the descent of the water drops, sighing silently as they hit the wooden floor. Cottrell had apparently used the doormat, but his scuffed boots had still managed to track dampness into the hall. Then she reminded herself that the old hardwood floor had undoubtedly survived far worse disasters.

"Sorry to startle you," Cottrell said, not sounding particularly sorry at all. "Someone should have called. I take it you're Rani Garroway?"

"Yes," Rani agreed crisply. "And someone should definitely have called. Won't you sit down, Mr. Cottrell."

He nodded once, then stalked across the room to take the largest, most comfortable chair in front of the fire. The man apparently didn't need a second invitation. She'd better be careful about what she offered by way of refreshment. He'd probably let her go to the trouble of fixing a five-course dinner if she volunteered. Something about him gave her the impression he made a policy of taking whatever freebies came along in life on the general principle that there probably weren't going to be all that many. He sprawled easily in the chair, watching her as she came slowly toward the fire. Zipp padded toward his feet and nosed curiously around the scarred boots.

Rani glanced down at the letter she still held in her hand. She concentrated on the lines she had skipped over earlier. "You're going to be making some minor repairs on the house and getting the grounds in shape?"

"A sort of general handyman-gardener was how the job was described," Cottrell said calmly. "In return I get free lodging for a few weeks this winter."

From the look of him, the man probably couldn't afford to turn down free lodging. "This is October, Mr. Cottrell. There isn't much to do in a garden in October."

"There's always something to be done in a garden. I'll keep busy. I always earn my keep."

"I'm sure you do." Rani folded the letter very carefully. The light from the fire flickered briefly on her ring, creating a brief illusion of cold green flames trapped in stone as she stuffed the sheet of paper back into its envelope. It was a very fleeting illusion.

The letter had been signed by the people who were renting the main cottage to her. There was one other smaller cottage on the grounds and a great deal of yard that had more or less run wild the past summer from what Rani could see. She didn't know much about gardening, but she suspected the Andersons' garden did need attention. She didn't doubt Mr. Anderson's scrawling signature. "Would you care for a cup of tea, Mr. Cottrell?"

"I'd rather have a shot of whiskey if you've got it. It's cold out there."

Give him an inch, Rani thought humorously. Aloud she said, "I'll see what I can find." She got to her feet and headed toward the kitchen. Behind her Zipp continued staring up into the stranger's face and then, without any warning, leaped onto the wide, overstuffed arm of the chair. Cottrell exchanged a long look with the big cat and then leaned his damp head back against the cushion. He closed his eyes. He didn't appear weary so much as simply determined to rest when the opportunity offered. It was a quality Zipp had.

When Rani emerged from the kitchen with a small glass of golden liquid, her visitor lifted his lashes with the lazy alertness of a dozing feline.

"What's that?"

"Sherry. It's all I've got unless you'd rather have a glass of white wine? The sherry's stronger."

He didn't bother responding to the implied question. Stretching out his arm, he took the delicate glass from her and took a healthy swallow that nearly drained it. His mouth crooked with faint scorn as he tasted the sherry. "This'll do."

Rani flashed him a wry glance as she sank back down into her chair. "You don't know how relieved that makes me feel."

His mouth moved again, this time in a fleeting attempt at a smile. "I didn't mean to be rude. It's been a long drive."

"How long?"

"I left San Francisco over three hours ago. The weather's been like this the whole way. Took me half an hour just to find the Andersons' turnoff after I'd found Reed Lake."

"Perhaps you should have waited and driven up in the morning."

He tilted his head slightly, listening to the faint lecturing tone in her voice. On the arm of the chair Zipp responded in exactly the same fashion, his ears flicking once or twice. The cat knew the tone and generally made a practice of ignoring it.

"I wanted to get here this evening." Flint swallowed the rest of the sherry and closed his eyes again. "That fire feels good. Any heat in the cottage?"

"I don't know. I've never been inside. I'm sure it's got all the amenities or the Andersons wouldn't have told you to use it."

"You never know. I've had people hire me before without bothering to mention the details."

"You're a professional, uh, handyman-gardener?"

He considered that. "Yeah, I guess I am. I suppose you've already eaten dinner?"

Sensing what was coming, Rani wanted to hedge. But her innate honesty got in the way. Even if the honesty hadn't been a problem, the fragrance of the stew simmering on the stove would have been a bit difficult to explain. "No, I haven't, but I was expecting company."

Flint's teeth showed in a strange smile. "And now you've got it. I'm starved."

"You don't understand. A friend of mine is due at any moment and I—" She broke off as the telephone rang imperiously. With a strange twinge of intuition, Rani knew who it was going to be before she picked up the receiver. When Mike Slater spoke on the other end, she wasn't surprised. She knew before he said anything that something had gone wrong. Rani tried to disguise the vague uneasiness she was feeling. If Mike didn't show up this evening, she was going to be left having to deal with Flint Cottrell all on her own. For some reason the prospect wasn't enthralling.

"Hello, Mike. I've been waiting for you."

"Rani, I'm sorry as hell, but there's a tree down across my drive. I won't be able to get the car out until morning. I've been on the phone for the past half hour trying to line up someone to clear the drive, but no one's going to come out on a night like this unless it's an emergency. Mind if I take a rain check on the meal?"

"Of course not, Mike. Everything else okay?"

"Oh, sure. Still got power and the phone's working. How about you?"

Rani looked at the man seated across from her. "I'm all right. I still have power, too. It's turning into quite a storm, isn't it?"

"You can say that again. Listen, keep some candles and a flashlight handy tonight. You might need them. I'd give my eye teeth for some home-cooked stew, but I guess I'll have to wait. I was really looking forward to my first meal with you. Just my luck. Take care. I'll give you a call in the morning."

"Thanks, Mike. I'm very sorry you won't be able to make it tonight. I'll talk to you in the morning." Rani hung up without another word.

Flint watched her face. "I take it there's going to be some extra stew?"

Once again Rani didn't know whether to laugh or groan at Cottrell's blunt approach. "It would appear so, Mr. Cottrell. Would you care for some?"

"Yes." There was a pause. "Please." The "please" sounded rusty. "And call me Flint." He glanced down pointedly at the empty glass in his large hand.

Rani didn't need any more of a hint. "I'll get you some more sherry."

"I'd appreciate it."

"Will you?" Smoothly she took the glass from him and started toward the kitchen. *Or will you simply take it for granted,* she asked silently, *the way stray cats are inclined to do?*

Flint watched her walk into the kitchen, something in him approving the proud, graceful way she moved. He liked the shape of her, he realized. In the snug-fitting jeans and golden-yellow sweater she appeared nicely rounded. There was an appealing hint of lushness in the gentle fullness of her hips and breasts. He had never been attracted to the emaciated-model type.

The rest of her didn't look much like a model, either. Her features were too gentle; very feminine but not sharply defined enough to be riveting, yet they held his full attention when he looked into her face. There was a certain womanly self-confidence in her tawny eyes, but it was a sincere, earnest quality, not cold female arrogance. It was the expression of a woman who had found a place for herself in life, established the boundaries and was satisfied with it. Her hair reminded him of a mixture of dark spices, all deep browns and golds. She wore it in a loose knot on top of her head. From what little he knew of her he guessed she was nearly thirty.

The most important thing was that she had the ring. Flint took a deep breath and flexed his big calloused hands. The cat sitting on the chair arm yawned and gave him an inquiring look.

"Don't worry, there's room for both of us," Flint told him quietly. "The legend says so."

"I'm ready to serve," Rani called from the doorway. She watched Zipp jump down from the chair and pad briskly toward her. "You've already had your dinner," she reminded the cat.

"That stew probably smells as good to him as it does to me." Flint came up out of the chair with an easy movement. "Where can I wash my hands?"

Rani nodded toward the hall. "Down there on the right." She turned away to serve the simmering stew and accompanying biscuits. For better or worse she was stuck with uninvited company so she might as well be polite. As she ladled out the aromatic mixture, she started worrying about the condition of the little cottage that sat behind the main house. She was concentrating so intently that she didn't hear Flint walk into the kitchen until he spoke from less than two feet behind her.

"How long are you going to be staying here, Rani?" He took a chair as if he ate at her table every night.

"Three and a half weeks. I arrived a few days ago." She deliberately put a certain amount of repressiveness into her tone. It should have been Mike Slater sitting across from her, not a handyman-gardener who had the arrogance of a free-ranging cat.

"Vacation?"

"Yes. I had some time coming from the library where I work, so I decided I'd better take it or risk losing it." Firmly she turned the conversation around. "What about you, Flint? How long is your job here expected to last?"

"Until I finish a project I'm working on." He slathered butter on one of the biscuits and bit down hungrily. Then he spotted the pot of honey and enthusiastically spooned some onto the remaining portion of biscuit.

"I see." She didn't, of course, but it seemed the logical thing to say under the circumstances. "What made you apply for this particular position?"

He looked up, his emerald eyes trapping hers for an instant. "I didn't exactly apply. I talked my way into the job because I found out you were going to be staying here for a while."

Rani stared at him, her earlier sense of unease turning into an outright chill. Very carefully she put down her fork. "I'm afraid I don't understand."

"It's the ring." He nodded at the green stone set in old metal.

The chill became a faint shivering that she couldn't quite control. Rani's hand closed into a tight fist, and she pushed it into her lap where the ring would be out of sight. "What are you talking about? This ring is junk jewelry. Look, Mr. Cottrell, I don't know what you're up to, but you're starting to make me very nervous. If you've come here to steal my ring, you've made a long trip for nothing. There might be a few dollars in the setting, but the stone itself is practically worthless. Just nicely cut glass. Now, I think you'd better leave."

He ignored her tense command and took another biscuit. "The value of the ring to me lies in the history behind it, not in the stone. Relax, Rani. I'm not here to steal it. It wouldn't do me any good. It doesn't work that way," he added cryptically.

"You're not making any sense."

"I'm writing an article, Rani. In my spare time I do articles on legends and treasures. Objects that have interesting histories like the one behind that ring. A piece on the Clayborne ring is my current project."

"It's just a ring, not a special piece of jewelry," she said bewilderedly. "What about the handyman-gardening job?"

"I told you, it's how I'm going to finance the time to write."

"Have you written a lot of articles, Flint?"

"A few."

She felt as though she were sinking into a bottomless sea. "Have they sold?"

"Some have."

"I don't understand. How did you know about my ring?"

Flint shrugged. "It's one of the legends I've tracked on and off through the years. For some reason I've grown very curious about this particular tale. When I decided to do the article, I tried to find out what had happened to the ring. I discovered it had been left to you by your uncle.''

Rani's mouth felt dry. ''You seem to know a great deal about me. Far more than I know about you.''

''You'll learn.''

''About you? I hate to break this to you, Mr. Cottrell, but learning more about you isn't exactly high on my list of priorities.''

''You keep a list?'' He sounded genuinely interested.

''It was a figure of speech! Just how much do you know about Uncle Ambrose?''

''He was a fine craftsman.''

''That's a nice term for it. He made a living creating fake jewelry like this ring. He could make a piece of red glass look like a ruby or cut a bit of crystal so that it shone like a diamond. His work was often good enough to fool anyone but a professional. Supposedly he had an honest business creating paste. There are plenty of people who don't want to wear their genuine valuables in public and prefer to have duplicates made. But the truth of the matter is that my uncle made his real money working with jewel thieves who wanted to leave a piece of paste behind when they stole the real thing. My uncle's stuff was so good that often the switch wasn't discovered for years.''

''You seem to know a fair amount about Ambrose's career,'' Flint said mildly as he started energetically on the stew.

Rani's mouth curved wryly. ''I learned it the awkward way along with the rest of my family after Uncle Ambrose was killed in a car accident back East a couple of months ago. When his business accounts were examined after the funeral, a great deal of information came to light. Uncle Ambrose kept excellent books. Two sets of them. Several old jewel theft cases were partially cleared up, thanks to Uncle Ambrose's accounts.

''And after his death you inherited that ring.''

''Along with a whole bunch of other fake jewelry. My uncle's work is actually quite beautiful. The jewelry was forwarded to me by his lawyer, who said Ambrose wanted me to have it. I'm not sure why. It's not as if we were close. Ambrose kept his distance from the rest of the family. We never saw much of him through the years.'' Rani pulled her hand out of her lap and deliberately spread her fingers so that the kitchen light reflected off the emerald-green ring. "But it's all equally false, Flint. Believe me."

"You're an expert?"

"No. I had them appraised. Some are plain glass, beautifully cut. Others are inferior stones cut and polished so perfectly they look like the real thing. The settings look good, just as this one does. But they're not worth more than any other piece of nice costume jewelry."

Flint eyed the ring thoughtfully. "You seem to enjoy wearing that ring."

Rani waggled her fingers. "I like all the pieces. They're fun to wear. Very pretty in their own way. Big, gaudy pieces of colorful junk. I've always liked bright colors." She flushed in a burst of self-deprecating amusement and glanced down at her bright sweater. "I have rather garish tastes, you see."

"Is that right?" There was a flicker of humor in the green eyes.

"Believe me, if this thing was real, I'd have it sitting in a safe-deposit box," Rani stated firmly. "I wouldn't dare wear it."

"I've just told you that the value of the ring lies in the story behind it."

"Any legend worth its salt would be about a real emerald, not a phony one. If there ever was a genuine stone in this ring, Uncle Ambrose removed it long ago. If the police are to be believed about Uncle Ambrose's business methods, it would have been cut up and sold on the black market." Rani picked up her spoon and began attacking her bowl of stew with a grim determination. She could only hope she'd said enough to discourage Cottrell if he was here with some vague notion of stealing her ring. It would be impossible to physically kick him out of the house. The man was big. But surely he wouldn't be sitting here chatting calmly about the ring if he intended to steal it.

"Legends are strange things. Very persistent things. Aren't you even curious about the ones concerning your ring?"

"Not particularly."

"Suit yourself. Is there any more stew?"

Rani stifled a sigh. "Yes, there's more stew. Have you brought linens and dishes with you, Flint?" She got to her feet to ladle out more food. "I doubt the cottage has any. From what I've seen of the place it's been vacant quite a while."

"I'll get by. I've slept in worse places."

"I'll bet," Rani muttered as she brought the dish back to the table. "When you've finished eating, I'll show you the cottage."

He looked up at her searchingly. "You're anxious to get rid of me, aren't you?"

"I'm sorry if I appear rude, but, frankly, this evening isn't going the way I planned, at all."

"Because I'm not the man you spoke to on the phone?"

"That's certainly part of the reason," she replied too sweetly. Rani resumed her seat. "The other part is that it makes me extremely nervous to know you've followed me all this way just because of a fake ring."

Flint put down his spoon and touched her hand, his gaze intent. "Don't be nervous. I brought good references, haven't I?"

"That letter from the Andersons? I don't know if it's a good reference or not." She withdrew her fingers, instinctively retreating from his touch.

"It's legitimate." He sounded arrogantly offended, as if he weren't accustomed to having his word questioned.

"Oh, I'm not doubting the signature. But who knows how much they knew about you when they rented the cottage to you? Who knows what you told them to get the job? You admitted you talked them into thinking they needed a…a handyman-gardener."

"Suspicious little thing, aren't you?"

"Wouldn't you be if you were in my shoes?" Rani asked coolly.

To her surprise he appeared to give the matter serious consideration. "I don't know. I can't imagine what it would be like to be in your shoes. I can imagine being attracted to you, but I can't imagine being you. We're at opposite ends of a spectrum."

Rani set down her spoon, aware that her pulse was racing for no good reason. No, she immediately told herself, that wasn't true. Fear was a good reason. "I think it's time I showed you to the cottage, Flint."

He stared at her for a moment, taking in the sudden, regal tilt of her chin and the firm decision in her eyes. Then, to Rani's infinite relief, he nodded. "All right." He reached for one last biscuit, put down his napkin and got to his feet.

Rani didn't hesitate. She wanted him out of the house, and he appeared to be in a mood to go. She didn't dare waste the opportunity. "I'll get a flashlight."

"I have to get some things from the jeep." Flint swallowed the last of his biscuit and started toward the front door, pausing to pull his old sheepskin jacket out of the closet. Bareheaded, he stepped out into the rain, closing the door behind him. Zipp lifted his head to watch him go and then went back to dozing in front of the fire.

Rani scurried around, putting on a yellow trench coat and locating her red umbrella. She wanted to meet Flint outside so that he wouldn't have any further excuse for coming back into the house. When she yanked open the front door, he was already standing there, waiting for her. He had a scarred leather travel bag slung over one shoulder.

Rani felt a flash of guilt as she realized he was already wet again. "Here, get under the umbrella," she instructed briskly, opening it. Obediently he ducked beneath the shield. She had to stretch her arm high in order to cover him. It was awkward. "Do you have a key?"

"The Andersons gave me one."

"Fine. The cottage is around back. This way." Rani led him around the corner of the old mountain house, following a brick path that was missing several bricks. "Watch your step," she called above the steady drone of the rain. She promptly stepped into one of the small holes in the path, herself. "Damn!"

Flint took her arm in a grip that resembled a predator's hold on its prey. "Are you all right?"

"Yes, yes, I'm fine, thank you." Unobtrusively she attempted to free her arm. He didn't appear to notice her efforts.

"I'll make sure I take care of this path first thing," he said seriously.

Rani gritted her teeth. "Wonderful."

The cottage loomed up out of the wet darkness, uninviting and depressing. When Flint shoved his key into the lock, the door swung open to reveal a room of deepest gloom. Fortunately the light switch worked. Unfortunately it didn't do much for the general sense of neglect and disrepair. There wasn't much to the old cottage, just a main room that served as both a sitting and sleeping area, a fireplace, bath and a tiny alcove of a kitchen with a small assortment of aging appliances. Rani began to feel guilty again, even though she knew she had absolutely no reason for it. Still, she couldn't imagine anyone not being depressed about the idea of living there for a few weeks.

"You may want to change your mind about the arrangement you made with the Andersons," she said, glancing around the room.

"I doubt it." Flint dropped his leather bag onto the old linoleum floor. "I've learned to take what I can get. This place is free, remember? Can't beat a deal like that."

Irritation began to build in Rani. "You could if you had a decent job. You'd be able to afford something much better than this. Have you spent your whole life bouncing around from one makeshift job to another?"

He slanted her an unfathomable glance. "That and chasing legends."

"Oh, yes. I forgot about the legends," she retorted tightly.

"You shouldn't. Especially now that you've become part of one." Flint's tone was suddenly very soft, faintly dangerous.

"If you're talking about the ring—" she began resolutely.

"I am," he assured her.

"Then you can just forget this particular legend!"

"I can't do that. It's the basis of my next magazine article, remember? Besides," he added with a fleeting smile, "if there's any truth to the legend, I can't forget about it."

"What are you talking about?"

"Maybe if I tell you the first part of the tale, you'll understand."

"I told you, I'm not interested," she tried to say. But she was. Vitally interested. Flint seemed to sense it.

"The story goes back to the seventeen hundreds," Flint said as he closed the door behind her. "I'll spare you the details, since you say you're not interested, but the important part is that the woman who owns the ring has an affinity for cats and a woman's power over one particular man. She doesn't know who he is, but once he's drawn to her his future, as well as her own, is sealed."

"That sounds very uncomfortable."

"In each generation that the ring finds its way onto the hand of a woman who can control it, there's a man who is fated to be drawn into her power."

"Whoever said life was fair?" Rani smiled with a flippancy she didn't really feel. "Lucky for you, this ring is a fake."

"I don't know about that. I seem to be here, don't I?"

Rani stepped back, her hand on the doorknob. "Does the legend say what happens to men who chase false rings?"

Flint shook his head, watching as she opened the door and prepared to flee back to the main house. "No. But the second part of the tale explains the technique the ensnared man uses to make certain the lady is as bound to him as he is to her."

"Really?" she asked scornfully. "What's he supposed to do? Boil up a caldron full of dead bat's tongues?"

"Nothing that complicated," Flint said gently. "All he has to do is take the lady to bed. After that the lady belongs to him, body and soul."

Rani's breath seemed to catch in her throat. Her body was suddenly vibrating with the primitive need to run, even though Flint hadn't taken a step toward her. It was all she could do to summon a cool, derisive expression. "Lucky for both of us then that the ring is a fake. Good night, Flint."

"I'll see you back to the house."

"No," she said with soft arrogance, "you won't." She stepped out into the rain and slammed the door behind her.

It wasn't until she reached the kitchen door of the main house and stood shaking out the umbrella under the leaking porch roof that she realized she'd been followed. Startled, she glanced up and peered through the rain-swept darkness. Flint was standing there, not more than a few feet behind her, his hands deep in the pockets of his jacket as he watched her.

"Good night, Rani."

She couldn't think of anything to say so she hurried inside and locked her door. Leaning back against the wood, her hands on the knob, she drew several steadying breaths and then lifted her lashes to stare at the empty bowls of stew on the table. Zipp was calmly preparing to help himself to what remained in Rani's dish.

"Get off that table, Zipp!"

Unrepentant, Zipp jumped down and wandered back out into the living room. Thoroughly annoyed, Rani scooped up the dishes and carried them over to the sink. The cat and Flint had a similar philosophy of life apparently. They both took what they could get.

She was going to have to keep an eye on both of them, Rani told herself as she did the dishes. She was going to have to stay in control. The life she had created for herself was very safe, very risk-free. She had no intention of changing her pattern of living to accommodate a man who had eyes that held green fire in their depths.

Two

The first thing Rani noticed the next morning was that the storm had passed through, leaving a chilled, slightly damp but basically sunny day in its wake. The second thing she noticed was that she didn't appear to be alone in the house. The distinct clash and clang of pots and pans and a slamming refrigerator door came from the kitchen.

She could probably assume it wasn't a burglar, Rani decided as she shoved back the covers and padded over to the closet. Most burglars would have better manners. She wrapped the turquoise-and-shocking-pink bathrobe around herself, stepped into her fluffy bright pink slippers and started grimly down the hall.

At the entrance to the kitchen she came to a halt, silently studying the scene before her. Zipp was seated on the windowsill, watching with interest as Flint systematically created chaos. Cottrell was working hard at the project. A wide assortment of utensils and bowls dotted the countertop. Two frying pans had been set out on the stove. A carton of milk stood open, and the lids were off the canisters that lined one wall. Flint himself was standing in front of the open refrigerator, examining its contents as if he were plotting an assault strategy. He was dressed for attack in an olive-drab fatigue sweater and a pair of jeans. Like the jacket he had worn last night, both garments looked as if they'd been around a long while. The income of an itinerant handy-man-gardener was probably rather meager.

Rani propped one hand against the doorjamb and drummed her fingers meaningfully. "If you'll give me a minute, I'll find you an apron."

Flint didn't glance up from his serious perusal of the refrigerator's interior. "That's okay. I don't need one."

"Are you sure?" she asked dryly. "You appear to be about to cook breakfast for a battalion."

He looked around when she said that, his green eyes moving with interest over her bright robe and sleep-tousled hair. "No. Just you and me and the cat."

"Really? I'm included? To what do I owe the honor?"

"I got the refrigerator going but there isn't any food in the other cottage," he explained simply, still looking at her. "I felt like pancakes."

The intentness of his stare was beginning to ruffle her composure. Rani resisted the urge to clutch the lapels of her robe more tightly closed. She was decently covered. There was no reason to let him unnerve her. "I see. So you just decided you'd break into my kitchen and make yourself a batch?"

"I haven't had pancakes for a long time."

"That's certainly a valid explanation for all this." She waved a hand at the clutter on the countertop.

"I just felt like pancakes," he repeated stubbornly.

"Do you make a habit of invading other people's homes when you feel like helping yourself to something they have?"

Flint closed the refrigerator door and leaned against it, his arms folded across his chest. "This house and the cottage seemed to be part of the same package rental. I sort of think of it as all one territory. After all, I'm going to be working on both as well as the garden."

Rani straightened away from the wall, no longer making any pretence of controlling her irritation. Her normally well-ordered life did not allow for this sort of disturbance. "I think we should get something clear between us, Flint. You are installed in the small cottage. I am renting this house. You will enter my portion of the 'territory' only upon invitation. We are not all one big happy family vacationing under the same roof. If I remember that letter from the Andersons, you are the hired help. Nothing more. Do you understand the situation now?''

He watched her through slightly narrowed eyes. "I understand," Flint said softly. "I just felt like having pancakes.. I told you, there isn't any food in the cottage."

Rani gritted her teeth and waved one hand in a gesture of frustrated disgust. "All right! You can have your pancakes. But this is my kitchen and I will make them. You will kindly get the hell out of here until I call you for breakfast. Go pluck weeds or something."

Flint ran a hand around the back of his neck. "What I'd really like is a shower. The one in the cottage wasn't working."

Rani glared at him, appalled at the new direction of the conversation. "Not my bathroom! You're surely not suggesting that you have access to my bathroom."

"Just the shower. The rest of the plumbing in the cottage works fine."

"I don't believe this."

"Don't worry, I won't use all the hot water."

"I'm not taking my chances." She whirled and stalked back down the hall. "I'll take my shower first. You can have whatever hot water is left over. In the meantime, don't touch another thing in that kitchen."

"Yes, ma'am."

Rani groaned inwardly at the suspiciously meek tone of his voice, then gathered a pair of jeans and a crimson-and-papaya colored pullover and stepped into the bathroom. She locked the door firmly behind her. The action made her wonder how Flint had gotten into the kitchen. She could have sworn she'd locked the door the night before when she'd returned from the cottage. Then she remembered her sense of nervous awareness when she'd glanced out into the rainy darkness and realized he'd followed her. Maybe she'd been too startled to remember to lock the kitchen door. Or maybe he was good at getting into locked places.

Half an hour later she poured pancake batter into neat circles on the heated griddle and laconically wondered how on earth she'd let herself get maneuvered into making breakfast for Flint Cottrell.

"This has gone far enough, Zipp," she confided to the cat who was sunning himself in the window. "I've got to get control of the situation or the next few weeks are going to be a disaster."

Down the hall the shower finally clicked off. Flint sauntered into the kitchen a few minutes later, running a rather beat-up comb through his damp hair.

"Smells good. Hey, you've got real maple syrup, not brown sugar water."

He wore such an air of pleased expectation on his hard face as he sat down at the table that Rani almost felt guilty about the grudging way she was fixing breakfast. Almost. Her natural wariness about the bizarre situation in which she found herself was enough to prevent an outright attack of feminine guilt.

"You can pick up some supplies in Reed Lake today so that you'll be able to cook your own breakfast tomorrow morning," Rani said as she placed a stack of steaming pancakes in front of him. "Also your own dinner this evening," she added bluntly.

He nodded disinterestedly, his attention clearly on the pancakes as he carefully buttered each one and poured syrup over the top. "This is nice country. Clean and green. I noticed you could see the lake from your living room window. Can't see anything from my cottage except the trees."

"Theoretically gardeners should be more interested in the greenery than the lake."

"I guess."

"Have you done a lot of gardening, Flint?"

"When the jobs come up, I take them."

"But you've worked quite a bit as a handyman also?" Rani pressed as she seated herself.

"Yeah."

"Have you, uh, had any other professions?" She wasn't sure why she was asking the questions. A strange kind of perverse curiosity probably.

He looked up. "I've been fairly flexible. I've generally done whatever came along. I like gardening best, though."

"Your résumé must be quite long by now," Rani observed with a hint of disapproval.

"It probably would be if I ever got around to typing one. Most of the people I've worked for didn't expect to see formal résumés."

"How long have you been job-hopping like this?"

Flint shrugged. "Since I got out of school. I took a job on a freighter during my junior year in college. One thing led to another. I never looked back. Tended bar for a while in Singapore. Acted as a stringer for one of the wire services in North Africa. Worked in the oil fields in the Middle East. Did a stint as a guide for some anthropologists in Indonesia. Hired myself out as a bodyguard for an industrialist in Italy. The industrialist had a great garden. I spent a lot of time in it when I was off duty. There's always something for a man who's flexible and who doesn't mind hard work."

Rani's fork went still. "And in between you chase legends."

"I like tracking them down," he admitted.

"What do you do with them when you track them down?"

"Find out the real truth, do an article and try to sell it."

"The real truth?" Rani paused. "What sort of article are you planning to do on the Clayborne ring, Flint?"

"A factual one. I'm going to straighten out the record on it the way I've done with the other legends I've chased."

"What do you mean?"

"I prove the wild tales are generally false."

"You mean show that things such as the Bermuda Triangle aren't really mysterious or strange after all? That there's no curse on the mummy of a certain Egyptian pharaoh? That everything can be explained in a rational fashion? That sort of approach?"

He nodded, pouring more syrup on his pancakes. "You've got it."

Rani straightened in her chair, frowning across the table. "I've got news for you, Flint. You're doomed before you start. Take my word for it. I work in a public library and I know what people read. They don't want their legends debunked. You'd do better to write articles emphasizing the exotic nature of the legends, not the truth. I have a fairly good feel for what people are interested in and most of them want the wonder and the mystery left in their legends."

Flint gave her an impatient glance. "Well, I write the truth."

"Had it occurred to you they may not want to read it?" Suddenly Rani held up her hand. "Forget I said anything. Why on earth am I sitting here arguing with you about it? You're certainly entitled to write anything you please. In fact, it sounds as if you've spent most of your life doing exactly as you please. You're obviously not going to listen to someone like me.''

''Why do you say that?'' He sounded genuinely interested.

''Well, it's pretty clear you've indulged yourself to the hilt in the classic male fantasy of never being tied down. There's no reason on earth why you should start listening to someone trying to tell you to do something you don't feel like doing. What's the longest period of time you've ever stayed on any one job?''

''I don't know. A year or so maybe. No, wait, there were at least two years in Indonesia.''

''I won't ask if you've ever been married,'' Rani murmured, finishing her pancakes.

Flint's brows came together in a hard line. Beneath them his green eyes were brooding and watchful. ''There's never been the time nor the place nor the woman.''

''Bull. You mean you've never wanted to make a commitment that would require you to give up your freedom.'' She gazed at him very levelly. ''Do you want any more pancakes?''

''Wait a minute. What do you mean with that crack about commitments?''

''Most men aren't terribly good at making them and keeping them,'' she explained, as if he were a little slow in the head. ''Not long-term ones. Ask any woman.''

''I'm asking you.''

''Oh, I'm a great witness. My father came and went all during my childhood until one day when I was about fourteen he announced he couldn't handle being a husband and a father any longer. He had his own life to think of and he didn't want to waste it on a nine-to-five job in the suburbs and a dull little family. He divorced Mom and walked out for good. Went off to live his dreams, I expect. Since getting out of college I've discovered that the world is full of men who can't make commitments. At least not to a woman. Most of them would probably secretly sell their souls to live your type of life-style though. Do you want any more pancakes or not?''

''You seem to have accepted this particular weakness you've iden tified in the male of the species,'' Flint growled, ignoring her question about the pancakes.

"I have. I've just recently turned thirty. What's the sense of growing older if you don't also grow up?"

"What do you do? Go through life being wonderfully understanding and not making any demands on the men you go to bed with?" he demanded roughly.

Rani blinked owlishly, uncertain of his mood now. "Men can be quite entertaining on occasion. Some have a great sense of humor. Some are talented. Some are even quite intelligent. I enjoy their company at times. But I've learned that it's best not to let them get too close. Physically or emotionally. The thing with men is not to take them too seriously." she explained gently.

"Are you sleeping with that guy who called last night?"

She stiffened. "Mike Slater? That's really none of your business, is it?"

"I keep forgetting. I'm just the hired help, aren't I?"

"I'll try to make sure you remember in the future." Angrily Rani got to her feet and picked up her dishes. The sunlight streaming through the window glinted off the green stone in her ring as she dumped the leftover pancake batter into the garbage.

"Wait a second," Flint yelped as the batter disappeared into an empty can, "I was going to have some more."

"I gave you your chance," she reminded him with a sense of satisfaction. "You didn't answer my question when I asked if you wanted more. So you're out of luck."

"You run a tight ship," Flint complained as he grudgingly brought his own dishes over to the sink.

Rani turned to confront him, her hands braced on the sink behind her. "I'm glad you realize that. For a while there this morning I was afraid I'd have to spell it out more clearly. This is my home for the next few weeks, Flint. I run it my way. Stray cats who happen to wander in and out when it pleases them will have to accept that or stay the hell out of here."

His mouth curved faintly, and he glanced at Zipp. "Is that how you see me? A stray cat who just happened to wander over the threshold last night?"

"The analogy seemed appropriate."

"Yeah," he said thoughtfully. "It does. But I don't think you realize yet just how appropriate." He reached out to touch her ring. Rani jumped a little as his callused fingers drifted over the back of her hand. "The lady who commands the ring attracts stray cats. You're the current owner of the ring and therefore only you can wield its power. You can have as many cats under your spell as you wish, but there's only one man in your future, Rani."

She shivered a little in spite of herself, but her voice was steady. "What a pity. You mean I only get to exercise my power over one man?"

"And a few stray cats such as Zipp."

"Do I get to pick the man and the cats?"

"No. They pick you. Didn't you know that, Rani? When it comes time to settle down, free-roaming alley cats always choose their own homes. A man who's spent his whole life roaming does the same."

She swallowed at the sight of the subtle green fire in his eyes. "I thought you said that it was one particular man's fate to be summoned to the lady who wears the ring, to be in her power."

"Sometimes it's hard to tell the difference between fate and an act of will."

He seemed to move closer. Rani could still feel his fingers lightly gliding over the back of her hand. She was suddenly, vitally, intensely aware of him, and the knowledge was frightening. She felt trapped against the sink, far to conscious of the sleek power in his body and the sense of urgency she discovered in herself.

"I know all about acts of will," she managed.

"Do you?"

"I'm going to exercise one right now. Get out of my kitchen and get to work, Flint Cottrell. You were hired to pull weeds and fix broken footpaths. When you're done with that, I'll make out a list of other things that need attention around here, starting with your shower. Now move! Breakfast is over."

He stared down at her for a long moment, reading the determination in her face. For a few timeless seconds a subtle battle of wills was waged. Rani felt it in every inch of her body. She refused to back down. Instinct warned her that retreat would only be inviting som unspecified disaster. She didn't dare back down or turn the small scene into a joke. She was completely serious, and she knew Flint realized it. Without any warning, he appeared to accept the situation.

"Yes, ma'am. I'll get to work right away. Thanks for the pancakes. Like I said, it's been a long time." He turned and walked out of the kitchen. A moment later the door slammed shut behind him.

Rani realized she had forgotten to breathe for a couple of tense moments. She inhaled deeply, staring at the closed door. Then, very slowly, she swung around to draw water into the sink. The pleasantly ugly cat on the windowsill cocked one ear inquiringly.

"I think I won that round, Zipp. It was close, but I did win it. The trick will be to stay on top. Give that man an inch and I can forget all about the mile. He'll take it before I even realize what's happening."

Zipp yawned and stretched out one paw to bat playfully at the dishrag.

"I'm not sure you're on my side, Zipp."

Two hours later Flint paused to lean on his rake and watch as the somewhat staid-looking Oldsmobile nosed out of the driveway and onto the main road that circled the water. Rani's car appeared to have been purchased with an eye for safety and utility. Flint guessed she was the type who never took chances when she drove and who wouldn't dream of buying herself a hot little sports car. He was coming to the conclusion that her vividly colored clothes constituted her chief outlet for the adventurous impulses that cropped up in her mind. She was a lady who didn't take undue risks.

Rani was on her way to Reed Lake, the small town located at the north end of the large, meandering lake. She was going to do a little shopping and pick up her mail, she'd explained as she'd waved the keys at him on her way out to the car.

Flint knew she was going to do more than that. He'd heard the phone ring in the living room earlier when he'd been working at the front of the house, and his intuition told him that the man who hadn't made it to dinner the night before had probably called to set up a lunch date in town. Flint wondered if she'd tell Mike Slater about her substitute guest. There was also the possibility she might not take Flint's presence seriously enough to bother explaining his presence to another man.

Flint's fingers locked fiercely around the rake handle, and he went back to cleaning leaves out of the hedge. Quite suddenly nothing on earth was more important than having Rani Garroway take him seriously.

He hadn't missed the amused disdain in her eyes that morning when she'd casually implied he shared a commitment problem with the rest of his sex. She seemed to think his past was ample evidence to support the implication. What really bothered him now was that he hadn't viewed his wandering life as a result of an inability to settle down or make a commitment. He knew it looked that way to other people, but it hadn't felt that way to him.

Rani didn't understand, Flint told himself. She didn't know what it felt like to be driven all of your adult life by a restlessness that didn't allow any peace. She couldn't know the feelings of isolation and aloneness it brought, that sense of being completely on your own. After a while the knowledge that a man could depend on no one but himself became so much a part of him that he stopped trying to imagine any other way of living. He kept going; kept searching for something he couldn't name because he didn't seem to have any choice.

Flint knew it wasn't a sense of wanderlust that had kept him on the move since his early twenties. It was something far more insidious and potentially destructive. It had to do with an odd kind of desperation, a feeling that out *there*, somewhere, lay the answers he was seeking the end of his quest.

It was strange. For a long time he hadn't consciously thought about the unnamed demons that drove him. Years ago he'd stopped trying to analyze and fight them. He'd come to accept them as a part of himself. He'd kept searching, even though he frankly admitted he didn't really know what he sought. Chasing legends became a way of chasing an elusive truth about himself.

But last night when Rani had opened her door to him, everything had begun to change. It was as if his very isolated, very private world had shifted subtly on its axis. He'd crossed the threshold, had sat down in front of Rani's fire and had realized that things that had never been in focus for him were suddenly beginning to solidify.

That morning he'd awakened with an overpowering hunger for pancakes. The chilled autumn morning, together with the tall, sunlit pines and peaceful lake, had demanded a breakfast of hot pancakes and real maple syrup. Flint hadn't quite understood it. Usually he could take or leave a pancake breakfast the way he could take or leave anyone or anything. But that morning he'd needed it. Memories of teenage camping trips, Sunday morning breakfast as a child and the occasional times in his past when things had seemed to be going right all coalesced into a desire for pancakes. Hot, homemade pancakes fitted the morning perfectly. He'd known without asking that Rani's kitchen would contain the makings.

He hadn't realized until he was blundering around between cupboards, refrigerator and too many pots and pans that he needed more than pancakes. He needed someone there to share them. The sense of things coming slowly into focus had intensified when Rani had walked into the kitchen and made breakfast for him.

The problem was that Rani hadn't seemed to realize how right the whole situation was, or perhaps something in her was afraid of seeing the rightness of it. He'd known at once that she was careful and cautious by nature and that she didn't approve of people who weren't. She'd sat across the table, delicately lecturing and scolding and dismissing him until he'd suddenly wanted to pull her down onto the kitchen floor and make love to her until she acknowledged his right to be there.

He'd known just how he'd do it, too, even though the wild impulse had startled him. He would have kissed her until the feminine challenge in her tawny eyes was replaced with passion. Then he would have held her very close, crushing her soft breasts against his chest while he stripped away the brightly colored sweater and the snug jeans. Flint knew with sure instinct that her body would fit his perfectly. He could imagine the soft roundness of her thighs, the heat he would generate in her and the clinging, yielding way she would hold him.

He would have made love to her until she took him very, very seriously; until she admitted he had a right to make love to her.

Instead he'd let her order him out of the kitchen and send him off to work. Flint swore softly and wielded the rake with controlled force. He reminded himself grimly that if the legend of the Clayborne ring held any truth at all, the scene in the kitchen had ended the only way it could for now. After all, the lady wore the ring. Until he'd taken her to bed, he was more or less at her mercy.

When he was near Rani he had to keep reminding himself that he didn't believe in legends.

Rani ordered a hamburger with an extra-large portion of french fries and sat back as Mike Slater told his amusing tale of trying to get the fallen tree cleared out of the drive of the lakefront cottage he was renting. Beyond the café window the main street of Reed Lake was busier than usual as trucks full of deer hunters stopped at the gas station, bought beer from the general store or stopped at one of the two cafés for coffee.

Rani frowned at the sight of the rifles hanging in the back of the red Ford pickup that was parked just outside the window. Two laughing men in camouflage shirts were returning from the grocery store with six-packs of beer under their arms.

"Why the disapproving librarian look?" Mike asked good-naturedly, following her gaze.

Rani smiled wryly. "You'd think those men would have better sense than to mix rifles and beer."

Mike grinned, his pleasantly intense eyes crinkling at the corners. "Are you kidding? The main reason they're here is to have an excuse to party all night long with their good buddies. For most of them this is their yearly fling away from the wife and the kids. For two week each year they get to pretend they're macho survivalists instead of nine-to-five clock-watchers. The deer hunting just provides the excuse. If it's any consolation, you can bet most of them won't manage to kill a damn thing."

"I trust that will be some consolation to the deer. I suppose hunting is an example of the old male bonding thing. It's one way men prove their manhood to themselves."

"And have a good time while they're doing it. Don't be too hard on them, Rani. The tradition of hunting season is too old and established for you to be able to change it."

Rani was forced to laugh a little. "I know. I wouldn't think of depriving men of their yearly flings. But I'm glad you're not a hunter, Mike.''

He leaned back in the booth and smiled at her. ''If I were, would you be having lunch with me?''

She shook her head. ''I doubt it. I much prefer artists.''

''Actually, a real macho hunter with a pickup under him could probably have managed that tree in my driveway a lot more efficiently than I did.'' Mike chuckled as he continued with his story. His blue eyes were full of self-directed amusement.

Rani sat across from him and realized she was mentally comparing Mike to Flint Cottrell. But how could you compare a successful artist to an alley cat? Mike was in his mid-thirties, his features sharp and aquiline, his sandy-brown hair a little long and a bit on the shaggy side, which only seemed appropriate for his profession. He had a lean, wiry build, and there was a certain artistic intensity about him that fit the image of a painter. He wore a long-sleeved, white, open-necked shirt and a pair of faded, paint-stained jeans. He had a pair of expensive running shoes on his feet. Rani had met him the first day she'd stopped at the Reed Lake post office to pick up her general delivery mail.

As in most small towns, the post office was a cheerful meeting place for the regulars as well as visitors. It was also the center of local gossip, and Mrs. Hobson, the woman in charge of the Reed Lake post office, took her role as good-natured gossipmonger seriously. She was already waiting with avid attention to see if anything serious developed between the vacationing librarian and the wintering artist.

A casual friendship between Rani and Mike had sprung up immediately, and Rani had a hunch that if she allowed it to develop further, Mike would be more than willing. But Rani had no intention of getting too involved with an artist or a vacation romance. It wasn't the sort of thing she did. She knew where to draw the line to ensure that her safe little world stayed neat and orderly. As she bit into her overstuffed hamburger, Rani remembered Flint asking bluntly if she was sleeping with Mike. Nothing could have been farther from the truth.

''How about another try at dinner?'' Mike asked, pouring ketchup on his french fries. ''My treat this time. I haven't got the nerve to ask you to go to the trouble of fixing another meal after I failed to show up for the last one. There's that resort restaurant at the other end of town. The one that overlooks the lake. We could give it a try.''

"Sounds great. Tomorrow evening?"

He nodded. "I'll make reservations. With all these hunters in town, we might need them."

"I doubt it. This crowd doesn't look like it dresses for dinner. These guys will be sticking to taverns and cafés, not dining at a resort. I'll be ready at six. Okay?"

"I'll clean the paint off my hands in honor of the occasion," Mike assured her.

Rani parked the Oldsmobile in the driveway of her rented house an hour later, shoved open the door and reached behind the driver's seat to pick up an armful of groceries. She was bent over, struggling with the heavy bag, when she felt a large, masculine hand settle all too casually on the small of her back, just above the waistband of her jeans.

She overreacted, her instincts telling her at once whose hand it was. "What the…? Flint!" Her head came up too quickly, striking the roof of the car. "Ouch!"

"Are you all right?" There was genuine concern in his voice. "Here, I'll take that bag for you."

She backed hurriedly out of the way and collided with his sweat-streaked, bare chest. The fatigue sweater had apparently been long since discarded. When she glanced upward, she saw the rivulets of perspiration gathering at a point just beneath the line of his throat and trickling down through crisp, dark hair. He frowned at her as she ducked aside and then he leaned forward to pick up the bag. She wasn't really sure she wanted to know how he had received the wicked-looking old scar on his shoulder.

"Is your head okay?" Flint demanded as he straightened with the bag cradled easily in one arm. Zipp, as usual, had raced out to meet Rani and was now making himself a nuisance around her feet.

"It's fine, thank you. Just fine," she declared firmly. "Get out of my way, Zipp. Here, I can manage the bag, Flint."

"That's all right. I'll take it into the kitchen for you. How was lunch?"

"How did you know I had lunch? Have I got ketchup on my sweater or something?"

Flint shook his head, leading the way toward the front door. "I just figured you were probably meeting that guy for lunch. The one who didn't show last night."

"What amazing perception. As it happens, I'm meeting him for dinner tomorrow night, too." Rani shoved her key into the front door lock with undue energy. "Anything else you'd like to know about my schedule?"

"What are you doing for dinner tonight?"

"Dining alone," she informed him with a sugary smile. She knew what was coming and vowed silently not to let it happen. She had to put her foot down somewhere. The problem was that once you'd fed a stray cat it was damned tough to get rid of him. She should never have fed Flint Cottrell the night before.

Flint looked at the black four-wheel drive Jeep he'd arrived in the previous evening and then back down into Rani's wary eyes. "I don't think I'm going to get a chance to drive into town this afternoon. There's a lot of work around here. I won't be able to pick up any supplies."

"Really? How lucky for you that I took the liberty of picking up a few things for you."

A startled expression flashed through his eyes. "You did?"

"Uh-huh. Milk and cereal for your breakfast tomorrow morning and a frozen dinner you can pop into the oven this evening. I also picked up a six-pack of beer for you." At the time she'd selected the items in Reed Lake's small grocery store she'd been pleased with herself for keeping one step ahead of Flint. Now Rani found herself having to stifle a niggling sense of guilt.

"A TV dinner?" he asked reproachfully as he followed her into the kitchen. "You bought me a TV dinner?"

"Don't worry. From the sound of things you've been out of the country a lot during the past few years so you probably don't realize how they've changed. They're much better than they used to be. I got you fettuccine Alfredo."

"I don't go in for fancy gourmet stuff," he stated, setting the bag down on the kitchen counter with an air of challenge.

"Think of it as macaroni and cheese."

He swung around, suddenly filling her kitchen with dark, lean, male aggression. It was an aggression made all the more intimidating by his obvious self-control. "I'd rather have whatever you're having."

Rani swallowed and stood firm. "I'm afraid that's not possible. I'm eating alone tonight, Flint. Hadn't you better get back to work? I wouldn't want to keep you from your chores."

She had the distinct impression it was touch and go for a moment. Flint looked as if he were having difficulty deciding how far to push her. Then, just when she was very much afraid he was going to carry the challenge further, he picked up the six-pack of beer, and turned and stalked to the door.

Rani sank into a chair, relief overcoming her for a moment. The situation was getting outrageous. She was right to take a firm stand. She had to draw the line and make it stick because if she didn't Flint Cottrell would just keep pushing.

She had no intention of letting a man with Flint's unstable background push his way into her world.

Three

———

Rani didn't know what woke her shortly before midnight. She had read until nearly eleven and had been asleep for less than an hour. There was no sense of danger, merely a feeling of something being different in the room. She lay still for a few minutes, analyzing the situation with sleepy care. Then she turned slowly on her side to peer at the curtained window. The shadowed figure of a man stood outside the glass, his solid shoulders silhouetted in the watery moonlight.

When she realized there was someone in the garden, Rani's sense of danger came belatedly into play. The quick breath she sucked in caught in her throat, and her hands suddenly tingled with that prickly feeling she always got when she was startled or alarmed. For an instant she couldn't move. With a sense of horror, she recalled that the catch on the window was broken, and there was no way to lock it.

But even as she watched, her nerves chilling, the figure slipped past the window. There was a soft, rumbling meow and a small thump as Zipp uncoiled from the foot of the bed and leaped onto the sill. The cat poked his head between the thin, white cotton curtains and sat staring steadily into the darkness.

Rani suddenly knew who was abroad in the garden. What she couldn't figure out was why Flint was roaming outside at this late hour. It was cold, probably no more than thirty-five or forty degrees outside. The days had fallen into the typical pattern of autumn in the mountains: chilled nights and mornings that warmed into comfortable, short-lived afternoons.

Lost in thought, she pushed aside the comforter and padded barefoot across the old wooden floor. Zipp turned his head briefly to acknowledge her presence beside him at the window, then returned to stare fixedly out into the shadows.

"What's the matter, Zipp? Do you envy him? Want to go outside and do a little night hunting? I knew sooner or later you'd miss the old days. He reminds you of them, doesn't he?" Rani smiled wistfully at her cat. "I'm not surprised. I thought of you the minute I saw him standing on my doorstep in the pouring rain, demanding shelter and a meal. And like a fool I gave him both, just as I gave them to you. But at least you've got enough sense to come in out of the cold. Apparently Flint doesn't." She straightened away from the window and reached for her coat and a pair of shoes. "Come on, we'd better go and bring him inside before he catches a chill."

She flung the trench coat over her long-sleeved, ankle-length night gown, slipped into her leather loafers and started down the hall. Zipp bounced off the windowsill to trot at her heels. When Rani reached the kitchen and opened the back door, the cat dashed past her into the darkness, alert to the kind of excitement only night can bring a cat. Rani followed more slowly, wondering what sort of excitement the shadows brought Flint Cottrell. Memories of past hunting expeditions. She knew without giving the matter much thought that if Flint had ever gone hunting it wouldn't have been for the usual game. He wasn't one to take pleasure in killing animals. She remembered the scar on his shoulder: it was a good bet a human opponent had been the cause.

She found him around the corner of the house. He was apparently studying the broken brick walk in the pale moonlight, the collar of his sheepskin jacket pulled close around his neck. His head was bare as usual as he bent to examine the path, and his hands were thrust deep into the pockets of his jacket. Rani knew he was aware of her presence as she slowly approached, but he didn't look up.

"It's cold out here. You'd better get back inside," Flint said without looking at her.

Rani's chin lifted as she huddled into the trench coat. "Interesting enough, that's just what I was about to say to you. What in the world are you doing running around outside at midnight, Flint?"

"Thinking."

"Oh, that explains it," she assured him dryly. "Do you always do your best thinking when you're freezing?"

"I wasn't doing any decent thinking at all indoors. I decided to try a walk in the garden." His voice was edged with annoyance as he finally turned his head to look at her. "Any objections?"

"Yes, plenty of them. You're disturbing my cat, for one thing."

Flint scowled. "Zipp? What the hell's wrong with him?"

Rani half smiled. "I'm afraid seeing you abroad in the moonlight has brought back memories of his own free-wheeling past. When he saw you out here he couldn't wait to get outside himself. But I don't believe he's using the opportunity to think. He's probably hunting. Lord knows what he'll bring into the house tomorrow morning."

Flint watched her for a long moment. "If he does bring something home, he'll expect you to tell him what a terrific hunter he is."

"No doubt."

"You will, won't you, Rani?" Flint suddenly sounded quite certain. "You'll scold him at first and then you'll relent and tell him how magnificent he is."

"I don't see what all this has to do with your being out here at midnight. What were you trying to think about?" Rani took a couple of steps closer to him, attempting to read his eyes in the shadowed light. The gaze that was so unusually green in the daytime, however, was mysteriously lacking in color tonight. She couldn't begin to guess at his thoughts.

"I was trying to work on the article."

"I see. It's not going well?"

"It's not going at all," Flint growled. "I was sitting there surrounded by a ton of notes and I couldn't write page one. I've been thinking about this article for a long time. I know the facts cold. But it isn't going nearly as smoothly as it should. Not like the others I've written. Tonight I couldn't even figure out how to write the first sentence."

Rani heard the frustration in his voice and impulsively reached out to touch his jacket sleeve. "Are you a night person?"

Flint eyed her warily, and she continued, "Is that when your thinking is clear? Is that when your biological time clock is at its peak?"

Flint shrugged. "Lady, I don't know what you're talking about. All

I know is that I couldn't even make a start on that damn article to-night.''

"And now you're tense.'' Rani tugged lightly at his sleeve. "Come inside, Flint. I'll make us some hot cocoa and then we can discuss your problem.''

She wasn't surprised when he followed without protest. Any offer of food seemed to hold a definite allure for Flint. Silently he allowed her to lead him into the kitchen where he took off his jacket. Then, his gaze following Rani's every movement as she set about making hot cocoa, he sprawled on a chair with an unconscious, arrogant grace.

Leaving her trench coat on as a makeshift robe, Rani switched on the stove and measured milk into a pan. "Now, about this biological time clock, Flint.''

"What about it?''

"I was under the impression you're an early riser.''

"I am. So what?''

"Well, so am I.''

"Something in common,'' he murmured a little too blandly.

Rani disregarded his tone of voice. "Exactly. Now, we early risers generally have something else in common. We usually do our best work, regardless of what it is, in the morning. What sort of work were you doing bright and early this morning?''

"You know damn well what I was doing. I was raking leaves, haul-ing rocks and pushing a wheelbarrow.''

Rani turned to glance at him, her smile triumphant. "Precisely my point. You put most of your energy into hard physical labor today, using up your best hours on that kind of thing instead of on your article. Then you wonder why you can't seem to get it together at midnight to do your writing.'' She stirred briskly. "Want some ad-vice?''

"I'm listening.''

"Get up early and do your writing in the morning. Save the gar-dening and repair work for after lunch. You've got several weeks to get the grounds in shape and fix the odds and ends that need repairing. Use your evenings to relax and get some sleep.'' She poured the cocoa into mugs and brought them to the table.

"Is this valid scientific fact or pop psychology?''

"Trust me. It works.'' Rani sipped at the hot drink. "Tomorrow morning get out of bed bright and early, have your breakfast, pour yourself a cup of coffee and then go to work on your article. At lunchtime you can quit and start the outside work.''

Flint looked at her over the rim of his mug. "You know, you're sweet when you're giving orders."

"Nobody said you had to follow them," she retorted.

"Ah, but I do. For now at any rate. You're wearing the ring, remember? Maybe I'm the man fated to be drawn under your spell."

"The ring," she announced grandly, "is phony, remember? Besides, you don't believe in legends. You're a professional debunker of tall tales.''

"Who knows?" There was amusement in his face, even though the hard line of his mouth hadn't crooked into a smile. "The fact remains I seem to find myself doing what I'm told these days."

"Thank you. I'll treasure that compliment."

They sipped the cocoa in a surprisingly companionable silence for a while, and then Rani remembered the question she had been meaning to ask. "How did you come to know about Uncle Ambrose and this ring, Flint?"

Flint shifted slightly in his chair. Rani wasn't sure, but she thought some of the relaxation engendered by the cocoa had abruptly faded. It seemed to her there was a certain tension in him now as he studied his mug.

"Ambrose and I ran into each other a year and a half ago when the ring came into his possession."

"Uncle Ambrose bought the ring?" Rani raised an eyebrow in astonishment. "Or was it stolen by one of his confederates?"

Flint shook his head once, a short, brusque gesture that told her nothing. "What does it matter now? He and I never discussed exactly how he had acquired the thing, but there was no doubt it was a favorite object of his. At any rate, he'd come across an article I once did for a gem trade magazine. Just a short piece giving a history of the ring, not a major article like the one I'm doing now. He wanted to know more about it so he tracked me down through the publisher. As it happened, I'd just submitted another piece to that same publisher and he knew where he could get in touch with me. He gave me Ambrose's address in New York and I contacted him. I was just as interested in finding out who now owned the ring as he was in learning more about its history. Ambrose and I got along fine. He was a real character. I liked him, Rani.''

Rani smiled. "Most people did, I gather. It was one of the reasons he was so successful. A natural con man probably. I only met Ambrose a few times. I never really got to know him. He never married. My father's side of the family was always very scattered and out of touch. I was quite surprised when I discovered he'd left all that wonderful fake jewelry to me. It's really beautiful stuff. Probably his finest work.''

"What else was there besides the ring?''

"A great necklace that looks as if it came out of an Egyptian pyramid, a couple of pairs of earrings set with such beautifully cut paste that most people would mistake them for diamonds. A couple of other rings besides this one and a brooch.''

"And you had them all appraised?''

Rani nodded. "My uncle had a business acquaintance in San Francisco. His name's Charles Dewhurst and he's a gemologist. Dewhurst had occasionally referred customers who wanted a high-quality reproduction to my uncle. He knew nothing about the shady side of Ambrose's business, of course. Few people did. He was as shocked as everyone else to learn about it after my uncle was killed. But, like you, he'd been fond of Uncle Ambrose and he greatly respected his talent. Mr. Dewhurst contacted my father after he learned of my uncle's death and offered his condolences. Said that whatever else Ambrose had been, he was one of the finest craftsman in the world. When I received the jewelry, I decided to have someone who was familiar with my uncle's work take a look at the stuff.''

"And Dewhurst confirmed it was junk?''

"Very beautiful junk,'' Rani corrected with a smile. "But, nevertheless, fake. Apparently Uncle Ambrose had kept his finest pieces for himself.''

"I wonder what he did with the real stone that was originally in that ring,'' Flint mused.

"Probably recut and sold it for a tidy fortune,'' Rani grinned. "Or perhaps it now belongs to a successful jewel thief.''

Flint downed the last of his cocoa and sat cradling the mug between his large hands. "I think the setting might, at least, be original,'' he said slowly.

"Why do you say that?"

"Because the damn thing seems to be working on me." He lifted his gaze to her suddenly wary face. "Perhaps there's a little magic left in the ring, even though the stone itself has been replaced. What do you think, Rani?"

"I think," she said very carefully, "that's a strange thing for a man who doesn't believe in legends to say. I also think that it's time for both of us to get some sleep. It's almost one o'clock, Flint."

"I know." He got to his feet when she did, but he made no move to go to the door.

"Flint." She should exercise whatever small power she did possess to order him out of her kitchen. This business of feeding strays at midnight was very dangerous. The tension that was suddenly filling the room was rapidly replacing the cozy warmth. She felt it thrumming along her nerves, urging her to take a step or two forward. Steps that would bring her very close to Flint. He was a vibrant, masculine presence in her kitchen, filling the room with his particular brand of strength.

"I'm the one under the spell, Rani," he whispered huskily. "You're in control, remember? I can't take any more than you want to give."

She clutched the lapels of the trench coat. "What do you want from me, Flint?"

"A little warmth. A little gentleness. I've been restless a long time. I want some peace and comfort." He moved toward her, a soft, gliding step that closed the distance between them. "I need it. I've never needed anything this badly."

Rani felt his arms going around her, drawing her against him until her palms flattened on his shoulders. She couldn't seem to tear her own eyes from the banked, emerald fires in his. She should stay in control, she reminded herself. It was her nature to avoid risks. Now here she was suddenly on the verge of being drawn into a green vortex of excitement. She mustn't let that happen. She must stay on the edge of the storm and not let herself be whirled into its heart.

But a part of her was longing to sample a bit of the green fire. Her face lifted as Flint brought his mouth down on hers. The arms wrapped around her were heavy and strong and made her feel unexpectedly secure. Her palms moved up over his shoulders and around his neck.

The heat and the need in Flint beat at Rani in waves. She could feel it in every inch of his hard body. As his mouth moved hungrily against her, she realized just how much self-control he was calling upon, and the knowledge that he was doing so reassured her somehow. When Flint's tongue probed at the edge of her lips, seeking entrance, she opened her mouth to him.

He groaned as the kiss became hot, damp and intimate. Rani felt Flint's hands kneading the small of her back, his fingers sliding down to find the shape of her buttocks. She shivered beneath the onslaught of powerful, sensual sensations that were startlingly new to her, even though she was far from being a naive teenager. He felt the tremor that rippled through her and pulled her deeper into the heat of his thighs.

When Rani murmured his name far back in her throat, Flint shifted her so that she was cradled in one of his arms. He didn't break the fierce kiss as he used his free hand to find the belt of the trench coat. Rani felt the edges of the coat part, and before she could decide how to deal with the new level of initimacy, Flint's hand was on her breast.

"Rani, I want you. I'm beginning to think I've always wanted you."

She heard the rough urgency in his words and couldn't tell if he were pleading or stating some irrefutable fact of life. Either way it wreaked havoc with her senses. Her fingertips curled in the fine hair at the base of his neck, scoring him very gently with her nails. She could feel the strength in his shoulders, and it tantalized her. When his thumb moved across one of her nipples, coaxing it forth beneath the fabric of her nightgown, she shuddered and pressed closer.

"That's right, honey. This is the way it has to be." Flint freed her lips, continuing to talk to her in low, dark tones as he brushed his mouth across her cheek and down the line of her throat. The words were timeless, heavy with passion, thick with masculine hunger. Rani felt them sink into her, adding fuel to the fires he was building with every touch.

When the front of the nightgown opened, Rani barely felt it. But when Flint's fingers traced the shape of her breast, she nestled her head against his shoulder. She could feel the hardening lines of his body as he pulled her closer.

"Rani, look at me. Let me see your eyes," Flint ordered softly.

She lifted her head, feeling dazed and unfocused. He studied her face for a long moment and then nodded as if satisfied. He fit his hands to her throat and held her still for another kiss. Then he brought her slowly, deliberately against him so that the peaking tips of her bare breasts were pushed against his wool sweater. The sensation was exquisitely teasing. Rani sucked in her breath.

"This is only the beginning, sweetheart. Only the beginning." Flint ran his palms down her arms. His expression was full of sensual promise.

"Flint?" From out of nowhere, Rani remembered her own words about the dangers of feeding stray cats. There was danger here, in her kitchen now. As if her thoughts had summoned up the interruption, a whining meow sounded outside the kitchen door. Rani stilled and then turned her head. It was a shock to realize she was standing half-naked in Flint's arms.

"It's all right, Rani." Flint touched her hair, twining his fingers through the spice-colored thickness of it. "I'm going to take you to bed and everything will be all right."

The demanding meow sounded again outside the door. Rani stepped backward, seeking escape. Somewhat to her surprise, Flint didn't try to stop her. Hastily she retied the belt of the trench coat, aware of the flush of heat in her face.

"Rani?"

"It's Zipp. He wants to come back inside."

"Yes." Flint's eyes never moved from her strained face. "He'll always want to come back inside. Just as I will."

She shook her head, trying to clear it. "I dont quite know what to say. This probably shouldn't have happened. I...I shouldn't have allowed it to happen."

"I don't think either of us had any choice."

That struck a chord. "I don't believe in fate and I doubt that you do, either. You're the one who writes articles illustrating the falseness of old legends, remember?"

"Yes, ma'am."

"Oh, for heaven's sake. You'd better get back to your own cottage. It's very late and you're going to need sleep if you're to try the new writing schedule tomorrow." She glared at him, brow drawn together in a ferocious line.

"I hear you, lady."

"I want you up bright and early."

"Yes, ma'am."

"If you say that one more time, I won't be responsible for my actions!"

"Yes, ma—I mean, good night, Rani. I'll let the cat in on my way out." He walked toward the door, his step soundless. When he opened the door, Zipp flicked his tail upward and walked haughtily into the room. His jaws were empty. Flint looked down at the cat. "No luck, Zipp? Well, don't feel bad. I didn't have much myself."

Before Rani could say anything suitably scathing, the door closed behind Flint.

The house felt empty the next morning. Rani opened her eyes and listened intently for the sound of clanging pots and pans. She heard nothing, which was exactly what she should be hearing, she reminded herself bracingly as she headed for the shower. She certainly didn't intend to spend the rest of her vacation fixing breakfast for Flint Cottrell. She ought to be glad he'd gotten the message.

The comfortable, stylishly baggy cotton trousers that nipped in at the waist and ankles were a neutral shade of off-white. They were one of the few neutrally shaded garments in Rani's closet. She offset the effect with a brilliant camp shirt patterned in orange-and-green jungle flowers. The look was supposed to be one of relaxed sophistication. Rani peered at herself in the mirror and couldn't decide if she'd pulled off the desired style or not. She'd achieved her usual loud impact, however. She clipped her hair into a loose coil on top of her head and headed down the hall to prepare herself a peaceful breakfast.

Zipp was already in the kitchen ahead of her, sunning himself on the windowsill. He flipped an inquiring ear in her direction as she opened the refrigerator door.

"Did you have a good time running around in the middle of the night?" Rani asked as she fixed a bowl of cereal for herself. The cat didn't bother to reply. "I noticed you didn't stay out very long last night. What happened? Decide a warm bed was a better option than a cold night of hunting? Better watch it, cat. You might be getting soft and civilized."

Zipp appeared neither soft nor civilized as he stretched out his battered frame in the sunlight, but he did look decidedly content. Rani thought about that for a moment, wondering how old the cat was. He had been full grown when she'd adopted him, so she had no certain knowledge of his age. He'd just appeared out of nowhere one rainy night at her home in Santa Rosa. But he still had the strength and agility of an animal in the prime of its life, so she didn't think he was old.

"A mature cat who knew a good thing when he saw it, huh, Zipp? Is that what you were when you landed on my doorstep and demanded a meal?"

Zipp began the deep rumbling that, for him, passed for a purr. Then he rolled off the windowsill, landed on all four feet on the counter and dived for the floor. He ambled across the room and stood waiting impatiently to have the kitchen door opened for him. With a sigh, Rani obediently got to her feet and performed the service.

She watched him stalk out into the chilly sunlight. A moment later it became obvious where he was heading: straight for Flint's cottage. Rani leaned in the doorway, sipping her coffee and watching as the animal lazily made his way through the garden. A few moments later he reached the front step of the cottage. Rani didn't hear the demanding meow, but it wasn't long before Flint opened the door.

He looked across the garden as he stood waiting for the cat to enter. When he saw Rani, Flint nodded a solemn good morning and then shut the door. Cat and man disappeared.

So Flint was up and apparently working. Rani considered that, aware of a pleased sense of satisfaction. She could only hope he was accomplishing something. Smiling a little to herself, she shut her own door and started in on the few chores required in her vacation home.

An hour later there was still no sign of Flint. He wasn't in the garden, and she hadn't heard the Jeep leave. She had to assume he was still working. Curiosity began to get the better of Rani's sense of discretion. She put down the British-style mystery she had been reading and wandered out into the rapidly warming day. It came as no great surprise to find herself standing outside Flint's door a short time later. Rani stood still, listening for the clack of a typewriter. She heard nothing, and when Flint opened the door without any warning, she jumped a good half foot.

"Sorry, didn't mean to startle you," he apologized idly, studying her with grave interest. "What are you doing out here? Listening at keyholes?"

"I just came to ransom my cat."

"You'll have to wake him up, first. He's sleeping on top of my desk." Flint stood back, silently inviting her into the small cottage.

A little warily Rani stepped over the threshold. "Your desk?"

"I turned the kitchen table into one." He closed the door and nodded toward the room's single table. A small portable electric typewriter stood in the center. It was surrounded by notebooks, paper and several weighty texts.

Rani cast a quick eye over the lot, ignoring Zipp who was, indeed, sound asleep between a dictionary and a thick, leather-bound tome. "Any luck? Writing, I mean?"

Flint smiled slightly, his eyes on her curious face. "Foolhardy as it probably is, I have to admit you were right. When I sat down this morning, things came much easier. My thinking was far more organized."

Rani grinned, pleased with herself. "Well, there you are then. You're on your way to fame and fortune. I'd better not keep you from your work."

He shook his head, moving over to the stove to turn the heat on under a dented steel kettle. "I was just about to take a break. Want some coffee?"

Rani hesitated and then nodded. "All right." She wandered over to the littered table. "Where will you submit the article when you're done with it?"

He shrugged. "Probably *Legends and Fantasy*. They bought the last couple of things I did. If they don't take it, I might try *Treasure Lore*."

Rani nodded. "We get both of them at the branch library where I work. They're quite popular. Kids like them. So do adults who daydream about going treasure hunting."

"My audience awaits," he said dryly. "All I have to do is get it written. I'm beginning to think the problem with this article is that I might be becoming, uh, emotionally involved with my work."

"Since you claim you don't believe in legends, you'd better be careful about becoming too involved," Rani tried to say lightly.

Flint gave her an enigmatic look. "The catch is that if there's any truth to the legend I don't have any choice."

Rani stared unseeingly down at the sheaf of papers on the table, her senses strangely ruffled into almost painful alertness by the underlying edge in his words. "Flint, I'm not looking for a one-night or even a one-month stand."

"You're a woman who doesn't take chances."

"And you're a man who's accustomed to taking them?" she whispered.

"For as long as I can remember," he agreed.

The shrill whistle of the old kettle demanded his attention. Flint reached for two mugs and spooned instant coffee into them. There was a tense silence in the small cottage as he prepared the brew. Then he picked up the mugs and handed one to Rani.

"Going to spend your whole life looking for a sure thing?" he asked, green eyes steady.

She resented the implied criticism. "Perhaps," Rani said coolly. "What about you? Going to spend your whole life leaping from one job, one adventure, to another?"

"People change, Rani."

"When?"

"When they find what they're looking for, I guess."

"I'd have to be awfully sure," she said cautiously.

"Before you'd take a real chance on a man?"

"Yes."

"When you're dealing with human beings, there aren't any certainties."

"That's probably especially true when dealing with a man whose track record doesn't exactly provide evidence of stability," she retorted, feeling trapped.

"What about that artist you're seeing here in Reed Lake? You think he's the stable type?"

"No," she admitted. "But with him it doesn't matter."

Flint smiled gently. "With me it does?"

Rani's mouth went dry as she realized the truth of her own words. "Yes," she said bluntly. "It does."

"I can't give you any guarantees."

"I know."

"I realize my track record isn't exactly reassuring."

"You're right."

"But I'm not a boy. I've been looking for something for a long time. Something it takes a man to recognize."

"You think you've found it?"

"I think so. But the lady is going to have to take a chance, too, before either of us can be certain."

Rani moved uneasily beneath the steady regard of his green gaze. "Don't you think this is an odd discussion to be having after only knowing each other such a short period of time?"

He looked at her intently. "What's time got to do with it?"

Rani's mouth tightened with feminine resentment. "You expect me to simply hop into bed with you, don't you? Do you have any conception of just how much you're asking?"

"Sure. I'm asking you to take a chance on a man who doesn't fit your image of male perfection. But no man ever will fit it, Rani, so why should I give up and humbly depart? I want what you've got to offer and I don't think you're ever going to find someone who will appreciate it more than I will." He paused, considering his own words and then added with brutal honesty. "Even if I did think you stood a chance of finding a man who would appreciate it more, I'm not inclined to leave the field open for him. Us stray alley cats have developed a habit of looking out for ourselves first."

"How can you possibly know what you want or what I'm prepared to offer? And why in the hell would I want an alley cat of a man in the first place?" Rani blazed. "You're absolutely right, you don't fit my image of the ideal mate. No fixed address, no fixed job and no fixed future." She was working herself into a fine, righteous temper but Flint seemed oblivious.

"I don't care about the fixed address or the fixed job. I've relied on my wits long enough to know I can take care of myself. But I am in the market for a permanent woman. I'm ready for a home, Rani. A fixed future."

"But that's ridiculous!"

"Why? I told you, I'm a man, not a boy. I can recognize what I want when I find it."

"You hardly know me," she wailed indignantly.

"Before either of us can be sure, you're going to have to take a chance on me."

Rani caught her breath at the masculine command buried in the words. She was almost physically aware of his willpower reaching out to grapple with hers, and the sensation was frightening. Frantically she summoned up her self-control.

"I think," she managed with a cool poise she was far from feeling, "that you'd better get back to work. I wouldn't want to get in the way of your excellent start."

"Want to hear a few of the tales surrounding that ring you're wearing?"

"No, I do not." Rani moved imperiously to the door, setting her mug down on the tiny drainboard.

"Some other time? Say, over dinner?"

Rani paused at the door, exceedingly grateful for her previous engagement. Ruthlessly she willed herself to ignore the hopefulness in his voice. "I'm going out to dinner tonight."

"That damn artist."

"Yes." The single word was almost a hiss.

"What time will you be back?"

Her eyes widened. "I haven't the faintest idea. I might not be back until morning!"

He grinned at that, a fleeting, amused, thoroughly wicked expression that contained far too much masculine arrogance and more than a hint of real danger. "You'll be back at a decent hour."

"Or what?" she challenged recklessly.

"Or I'll come looking for you."

"Get back to your typewriter, Flint." She slammed the door but not before she heard his laconic last words.

"Yes, ma'am."

Four

Dinner had been an enjoyable occasion, but as Mike Slater parked his nondescript little Ford compact in Rani's driveway, matters started to disintegrate. Rani stared at the light shining through the curtains of her living room windows and frowned.

"I don't recall turning on the lights before I left this evening," she remarked as Mike opened the car door for her.

"Maybe you just forgot to switch them off when I picked you up tonight." Mike glanced toward the house.

"No, I would have remembered." Rani sighed as she dug her key out of her shoulder bag. "My neighbor was probably raiding my refrigerator."

Mike's brow lifted inquiringly. "I didn't know you had a neighbor."

"He's a handyman or gardener or something. The Andersons hired him to put things in shape around here. He's staying in the back cottage."

"You didn't mention him."

Rani shrugged as she pushed open the front door. "He just arrived a couple days ago. I guess I forgot to tell you about him." There was a sharp hiss of annoyance from Zipp, who took one look at the stranger standing next to Rani and promptly disappeared.

Flint's voice called out from the kitchen. "Hey, you two are back early. Want some coffee? I just made a pot.'' He sauntered to the kitchen doorway and stood leaning against the frame, a suspiciously bland smile on his hard face as he looked at Mike. He was wearing a dark long-sleeved shirt with the sleeves rolled up casually on his fore-arms. His jeans were faded and worn, and he had on a pair of low, scuffed boots. Standing there with a coffeepot in one hand, he looked very much at home, intimidatingly so. He seemed aware of it. ''You must be the artist.''

Mike blinked but rose to the occasion. He kept his voice just as politely dry as Flint's had been. ''You must be the handyman or gar-dener or something.''

Flint nodded agreeably. ''That's me. Very handy. Here I am stand-ing here with hot coffee just as you walk in the door. Where else are you going to get that kind of service?''

Rani stepped forward aggressively and took the pot from his hand. ''This sort of thing isn't on your list of job duties and you know it,'' she muttered furiously, sweeping past him into the kitchen. ''You've got your own kitchen. Kindly stay out of mine.''

''Not my fault you walked in just as I was making the coffee.''

''Really?'' She smiled dangerously as she hauled cups out of the cupboard. ''How long have you been here?''

Flint shrugged, ignoring Mike. ''I came over to find something to read earlier and decided to make the coffee.''

''Uh-huh. In other words you've been here all evening.'' Rani swung around, two coffee cups in her hands. ''Excuse me, Flint, you're in the way.'' She moved forward, silently daring him not to move out of the doorway. When he stepped aside, she hid her relief. ''Here you are, Mike. Come on into the living room and sit down. Flint was just leaving.''

''Actually,'' said Flint, ''I wouldn't mind joining you. It's been a long, quiet evening. I'm Flint Cottrell, by the way.'' He nodded at the other man.

''Mike Slater.'' Mike glanced at him and then smiled quizzically at Rani. ''Maybe I'd better be on my way.'' He left it a question.

''Don't rush off on my account.'' Flint sprawled in a chair, a mug of coffee in his hand. Zipp immediately appeared from wherever he had been sulking and hopped into Flint's lap. After a few glares in

Mike's direction, the cat finally settled down to a machine-gun purr. "You two have a nice evening?" Flint said conversationally.

"It's been lovely up until now." Rani urged her guest to a chair. Mike sat down somewhat reluctantly and accepted the cup and saucer she handed him.

"We went to the resort at the far end of the lake," Mike said politely. "Good steaks."

Rani's smile was determined. "Good band, too."

"The place was probably full of deer hunters," Flint observed, oblivious to the chill in her voice.

"Not really," Rani said. Mostly resort guests. The only signs of the hunters were the rifle shots we heard between here and the resort."

Mike nodded, frowning. "It was just at dusk. Some hunter must have been making one last try for a deer before nightfall. He was too near the road if you ask me. We could hear the shots quite clearly."

"Crazy hunters. No common sense," Rani complained. "They have no business shooting that close to civilization."

"Every hunting season someone gets hurt," Mike said. "Usually another hunter. It's a dangerous sport."

Rani grimaced. "Frankly, my sympathy is with the deer."

Flint looked at Mike. "You come up here to Reed Lake regularly?"

"I usually head for the mountains at this time of the year," Mike acknowledged politely. "Spent last winter in Tahoe and the winter before that in Lake County. I like mountains in winter."

Rani smiled, doing her best to shut Flint out of the conversation. "Are mountains in winter good for the creative juices?"

"I do some of my best work during winter."

Flint smiled blandly again. "Being an artist must be a lot like being a handyman. Not too stable a profession."

"Oh, I work on a regular basis," Mike assured him. "I show relatively often and have a fairly steady following. I haven't been a starving artist for a very long time."

"Where do you show?" Flint asked.

"Down in the Bay area and Carmel mostly. Why? Are you interested in art?"

"In a way. I'm in the process of changing careers, you see," Flint told him.

"I see." Mike tried to look politely interested.

Rani decided it was time to step in and regain control of the situation. "Well, I don't. There's not much connection between painting and career hunting."

"Sure there is," Flint said, looking offended. "They're both creative efforts, aren't they?"

"Perhaps you should be making a bit more of a creative effort," she suggested coolly as she glanced pointedly at her watch. "In fact, maybe it's time you went back to work."

Flint shook his head. "Not tonight. I've taken your advice and given up trying to write at night." His green eyes glittered between his narrowed lashes as he looked at Mike. "Rani prefers me to work during the day and keep my evenings free."

Patience exhausted, Rani set down her cup and saucer with a clatter and got to her feet. "Good night, Flint."

He looked up at her. "I haven't finished my coffee."

"Take it with you."

"What's the rush, honey? It's not that late."

Before Rani could respond, Mike was getting to his feet, mild embarrassment on his lean face. "Uh, maybe I'd better be on my way, too. It is getting kind of late. Thanks for a great evening, Rani. I'll probably see you at the post office in town tomorrow."

"There's no need to leave," Rani said grimly. "Flint was just on his way out."

Flint stretched hugely, putting down his mug. "You're right, Slater. It is late."

"Yes, well, see you tomorrow, Rani." Mike was already at the door.

Rani shot a glare at Flint and hurried forward. "I'll walk outside with you." She let the door close behind herself and Mike and wound up standing on the porch, smiling apologetically at her date for the evening. "I'm sorry about that. He's a very strange man. Just sort of moves in and makes himself at home."

"Where did he come from?" Mike looked down at her, bracing himself with one hand against the porch railing.

"Beats me. Here, there and everywhere from the sound of things. I asked him about his previous jobs and he implied he's had a lot of them. Very unstable."

"I hope that applies to his job history and not his psychologica profile."

Rani's eyes widened. She rubbed her forearms with her palms "Surely you don't think he's dangerous?"

Mike looked immediately chagrined. "No, of course not. I don' know anything about the man, do I? It's just that you made him sounc weird and he does seem to have assumed he's got a right to wande in and out of your house without permission. That's hardly the behav ior of the average handyman."

"I wouldn't know. I haven't met too many handymen." Rani trie a nervous smile. "Or gardeners either, for that matter. Actually, he' also a part-time writer of some sort. Does articles for magazines, o so he says."

"What kind of articles does he write?"

"Articles about legends."

"Legends?"

"Umm." Rani held up her hand so that the porch light gleame dully off the green stone in her ring. "Legends concerning things lik this ring, which he thinks might be very old."

Mike took a closer look at the ring. "He's interested in this rock?

"He says it's one of the reasons he's here. Oh, it's a long stor The bottom line is that this ring once belonged to my Uncle Ambros who died earlier this year. Flint knows the history of the ring, an when he decided to write his article he wanted to see what happene to it. He found out it had been left to me." She broke off at the od expression on Mike's face.

"Rani, are you telling me the man got a job here just to be near th ring?"

She swallowed uneasily. "Put like that, it does sound rather strang doesn't it? But I think it's the truth. There's nothing really menacin about his actions. He's just a…a different sort of man."

"Is the ring valuable?" Mike asked sharply.

"Oh, no," she hastened to assure him. "At least not from a jev eler's point of view. The stone is paste. I had it appraised. Beside have you ever seen a real emerald this size?"

Mike grinned. "Are you kidding? I don't shop at the kind of stor that sell emeralds that size."

"Neither do I." She waved her hand airily. "It's junk. Pretty yes, but junk nevertheless. The only value is in the legend, and that's why Flint is interested in it."

"How valuable is the legend to him?" Mike asked flatly.

"He says the ring can only be worn by a woman. He's not likely to steal it."

Mike ran a hand through his hair and shook his head. "I don't know, Rani. It's a strange setup."

"I know. But I honestly don't think it's a dangerous one."

Mike hesitated. "As long as you're sure."

"I'm sure."

Mike glanced away. "Am I, uh, stepping into his territory?"

"His territory?"

"Yeah. I don't want to get involved in a touchy situation. If you and he are, uh…"

"We most definitely are *not*." Rani's eyes narrowed. "And you are not stepping on his turf. I don't conduct my social life on that primitive a level. I date whom I wish and I am not *involved* with anyone. Clear?"

Mike nodded quickly. "Very clear. Sorry about that. I just wanted to know where you stood."

Rani forgave him immediately. He appeared thoroughly abashed. "Don't worry about it. I know how it must have looked, the way Flint was hanging around my kitchen with the coffeepot. The problem is that the cottage he's got is in very poor condition. It hasn't been used in years, and he probably hasn't even got a coffeepot." That wasn't strictly true. He had a kettle in which he could boil hot water for instant coffee, but Rani thought she wouldn't go into too much detail.

"Well, in that case, do I dare risk asking for another date?"

She laughed up at him. "You bet. I had a wonderful time tonight, Mike. Thanks very much." She started to stand on tiptoe so that he could give her a polite good-night kiss, but at that moment the door opened behind her. She closed her eyes in disgust and sighed.

"Isn't it getting a little chilly out here?" Flint asked cheerily.

Mike nodded. "A little. I'll be on my way." He trotted down the steps and got into the Ford.

Rani stood watching until the small Ford had disappeared from the

drive. Then she turned to confront Flint who was standing in the doorway with Zipp at his feet. Slowly she gathered herself, struggling to
keep her temper under control. She would not lose it, she vowed. She
would be cold and disdainful and not give into the temptation to yell
at him like a fishwife. The vow lasted all of five seconds.

"Of all the rude, insufferable, socially inept people I have ever met
in my life, you take the honors, Flint Cottrell. You should be ashamed
of yourself. You had no business being here when I got home with
Mike. And no business forcing yourself on us while we had our coffee.
Who do you think you are? Didn't you learn manners anywhere along
the line, or have you spent so much time hopping around the globe
that you neglected to learn the basics? No wonder you don't stay long
in any one place. You're probably asked to leave when you start becoming impossible." She was starting to yell. She knew she was. Savagely she bit off the last words and stormed past Flint into the living
room.

Flint slowly closed the door and turned to face her. He didn't say
anything. He seemed to be waiting. That infuriated Rani even more.
She flung herself down on the old, padded sofa and scowled. "I suppose you've got an explanation for your behaviour?"

"I was waiting for you."

She gritted her teeth. "Why?"

"You know why, Rani." He spoke softly, moving silently across
the room to collect the used coffee cups.

"No, I don't know why. I'm thirty years old. I've been handling
my social life all by myself for a long time. I don't appreciate some
heavy-handed big brother type waiting around for me when I come in
the door."

"I'm not the big brother type so you can stop worrying."

"That's the way you were acting tonight."

He shook his head, walking into the kitchen. "No."

She jumped to her feet and went after him. Halting in the kitchen
doorway, she eyed him with suppressed violence as he put the dishes
in the sink. "Then how would you describe your own behaviour?"

He kept his attention on the cups he was putting into the sink, but
his expression grew thoughtful. "Possessive might be a good description. Protective. Concerned."

Rani held her breath as he said the words. She sensed the tension in him, knew it communicated itself to her. "You have no right, Flint."

He turned his head to look at her, his green eyes unfathomable. "I also have no choice."

"What's that supposed to mean?"

"I can't let another man make love to you, Rani. Not now. I've been searching for you for too long. It would drive me crazy to know someone else was touching you now that I've found you."

She stared at him. "I think you already are a little crazy."

He didn't move. "You don't believe that."

"Mike suggested it might be a possibility," she said recklessly. "I told him about the ring and why you were working here this winter. You've got to admit, it does sound strange, Flint. And your behavior doesn't exactly make it seem less strange."

He ignored that. "What did he say about the ring?"

"He asked if it was valuable. I think he was worried you might try to steal it."

"You gave him your opinion that it was strictly paste?"

This wasn't the direction she had intended to take the conversation, Rani thought wildly. "It's not just my opinion! I had the thing appraised. I keep telling you that."

"Did you tell Slater that?"

"Yes, damn it! Will you forget about the stupid ring? It's not an issue here."

"What is the issue?" he asked interestedly.

"Your rude and objectionable behavior."

"Oh, that."

"Yes, that." Rani threw up her hands in surrender. "I've about had it for tonight, Flint. It's obvious you have no intention of listening to what I say or in apologizing. Kindly go back to your cottage and leave me in peace."

He came toward her, his big hands lifting to settle heavily on her shoulders. Flint smiled with a touch of genuine sympathy. "Poor Rani. You're used to being in command of your life, aren't you?"

"Nothing has changed. I am in command of my life. I intend to remain so. Get out of here, Flint. In case you haven't noticed, I am angry and disgusted. I would like some peace and quiet. Maybe I'm the one who's a little crazy. I must be for tolerating your behavior.''

"Rani—"

"I mean it, Flint. I want you to leave.''

He hesitated. Rani could feel the weight and strength in his hands. Such big hands. They were hard and callused from a lifetime of rough work. She didn't want to think about what those hands might feel like on her body. She would not allow herself to think about such things. She really would drive herself crazy. Rani could feel Flint's willpower pushing against her own. He wanted her to back down, wanted her to retreat and relax. She knew without having to hear the words that he wanted to stay the night. He seemed to think he had a right. It took far more of her own willpower than it should have to resist the possessive demands that flamed in his green gaze.

"Maybe not tonight, Rani, but sometime soon," Flint said quietly. "It has to be soon. I want you.''

"What you want," she got out between clenched teeth, "has nothing to do with it.''

"You'll want it, too. I swear it.''

"That sounds like a typical male ego talking.''

"How long are you going to fight me, Rani?''

"As long as necessary. Now go, Flint.''

He wanted to kiss her. She waited tensely, not certain what would happen if he did. It would be so much easier if he didn't. Rani was more afraid of her own reactions than his actions. A kiss could be such a casual, meaningless thing. It would have been casual and meaningless with Mike, for example. She was sure of that. But it was altogether different with Flint. That made the prospect seem very dangerous.

But he didn't kiss her. He stared down at her for a moment longer and then, very lightly, he brushed his fingertips across her lower lip. Rani trembled as she felt the roughness of his finger on the delicate tissue of her lips.

"I'll go, Rani. You can still send me away. But someday it won' be this easy. You know that, don't you?''

Easy, she thought wretchedly as he walked out the door. It would never be easy. But it was certainly necessary.

Zipp meowed plaintively at her feet. Rani glanced down at him as the back door closed behind Flint. "Don't look at me like that, cat. I'm in charge around here. I decide who stays and who goes."

Zipp looked unconvinced.

Rani awoke the next morning with an uneasy feeling that refused to recede. Restlessly she showered, then dressed in a pair of comfortable jeans and a black sweater that had big starbursts of yellow on the front and back. When she opened the refrigerator door to get a carton of skim milk for her cereal, the sunlight glanced sharply off the green stone in her ring. The gleam caught her eye, and she paused to look at the piece of jewelry.

It couldn't be valuable. Charles Dewhurst was a professional with years of experience. He couldn't have made a mistake about the stone in the ring. She wiggled her finger and watched the play of light on the surface of the green gem. It looked like nicely cut green glass to her. It had to be glass.

But if it were real that fact would change everything.

Rani chewed on her lower lip as she considered the ramifications of that thought. If the stone was genuine she had a problem. For one thing, she would have to stop viewing Flint Cottrell as an annoying, intriguing, unsettling male to whom she was attracted. She would have to view him as dangerous, just as Mike had suggested the night before.

It couldn't be real. Dewhurst couldn't have made a mistake.

Lost in thought, Rani closed the refrigerator door and went into the living room to stare at the phone. A phone call might reassure her, and heaven knew she could use some reassurance right now.

She didn't have Dewhurst's number, but it was easy enough to get it from information. Rani sat nervously on the edge of the sofa as the phone rang in Dewhurst's elegant little shop near Union Square in San Francisco. She could visualize him behind the counter, surrounded by the delicate tools of his trade, his balding head with its gray fringe bent over a fine ruby or a diamond necklace. Rani had only met him on the occasion when she had taken Ambrose's collection of jewelry in to be evaluated, but she had liked the short, stout Dewhurst. He had been cordial and helpful, happy to share the knowledge of her uncle's idiosyncracies. When he came on the line, Rani smiled in relief.

"Mr. Dewhurst, this is Rani Garroway. Ambrose Garroway's niece?"

"Of course, of course, Miss Garroway. How are you? Good to hear from you again. Are you enjoying your uncle's fine creations?"

"Very much. I get a kick out of wearing them, especially the green ring. You remember the ring?"

"Naturally. An excellent example of your uncle's art. Do take care of the setting, though. It's rather old, I'm afraid, and fragile. One of these days you're going to have to have the stone reset."

"Actually I'm calling about the stone, Mr. Dewhurst."

"Has it come loose already? I was sure that with care it was good for a while yet."

Rani idly touched the green stone with her finger. "It feels solid enough in the setting. That's not why I called."

"Then how can I help you, Miss Garroway?"

She hesitated and then took the plunge. "Mr. Dewhurst, there's no possibility that there's been a…mistake, is there?"

"A mistake?"

"I mean in the identification of the stone. It really is paste, isn't it?"

"Definitely." Dewhurst sounded regretful but absolutely positive. "Your uncle did a fine job on it, Miss Garroway, but it's definitely not an emerald. Ambrose wouldn't have been interested in a real emerald. He was a unique craftsman. He saw his skill as a talent for imitation and, you will excuse the term, deception. He took pride in his ability to make the false appear genuine."

"I know, it's just that lately I've had some questions from some acquaintances."

"Questions about the ring?"

"Someone suggested it might be the real thing," Rani admitted lamely, wishing she'd never called. This was getting embarrassing.

"Impossible." Dewhurst chuckled. "Not unless you've switched it with another since I last saw it. Once you've seen real emeralds, worked with them and studied them, it isn't easy to be deceived, Miss Garroway. I know this sounds melodramatic—jewelers sometimes get that way—but the fact is, a good quality, genuine emerald is like a bit of frozen green fire. It's almost hypnotic. One looks deeply into the stone and finds oneself having to make an effort to look away. Good emeralds are almost unbelievable, Miss Garroway. They take away one's breath. Believe me, I couldn't have made a mistake.''

Rani heard the conviction in his voice and smiled wryly to herself. He was right; he did sound impassioned on the subject. She held the ring up to the light again as she listened to Dewhurst. Squinting, she tried to determine if there was any possibility of there being flames of green fire locked inside the stone. She could see nothing of the sort.

It definitely looked like a beautiful cut green glass to her. Rani heaved a small inner sigh of relief. Of course it was glass. As she had told Mike the previous evening, no one saw emeralds this size outside of a classy jewelry store or a rich collector's safe-deposit box. Glass. Pretty green glass. With, perhaps, a legend attached.

"Someone mentioned to me the possibility of the ring having once been the focal point of a legend, Mr. Dewhurst. He said it was once called the Clayborne ring and that it dates back to the seventeen hundreds. Any chance the setting itself is that old?''

"As I recall, it appeared to date from the late eighteen hundreds. Possibly turn of the century. Not terribly old as these things go, but interesting, perhaps. Ambrose undoubtedly came into possession of the setting when he, uh, arranged to copy the stone that had once been in it.''

"So there might once have been a genuine emerald in this ring?''

"Quite possibly. It would make sense that if Ambrose created a replica, he would have faithfully copied the original. I don't see him having created a paste version of an emerald, for example, if the stone in the ring had once been a ruby or a sapphire. He took pains to duplicate exactly.''

"I see. But all things considered, the setting isn't more than a hundred years old?''

"If that.''

"And the stone is definitely fake.''

Dewhurst sighed. "I'm afraid so.''

"Don't sound so sorry,'' Rani laughed. "Actually, the reassurance comes as a great relief. I would hate to think I'd been blithely waving a huge emerald around as though it were junk jewelry.''

"There is no danger of that, Miss Garroway.''

"Thanks, Mr. Dewhurst. I appreciate your time."

"I'm happy to have been of service."

Rani hung up the phone, feeling vastly relieved. Zipp meowed lazily, wandering in from the kitchen to inquire about his own breakfast. He saw Rani sitting on the sofa and meowed again, putting some demand into it.

"You are a bossy sort of cat, Zipp. What did you ever do before you had me to fetch and carry for you?"

Zipp watched her as she got to her feet. He trotted quickly after Rani as she went back into the kitchen, satisifed that breakfast was back on schedule.

Rani spent the morning working on a jigsaw puzzle, finished the mystery novel she had started and then wrote notes to friends. It occurred to her that she might be getting a trifle bored on vacation. It was a strange feeling. Normally she was quite content with her own company. Perhaps she would see about renting a rowboat to take out on the lake. The idea of going out in a boat made her think of picnic lunches, and picnic lunches made her think of sharing the outing with someone.

She was trying not to picture anyone in particular sitting in the boat with her, when Flint walked past the open window. He had a shovel over one bare shoulder, and he waved as he walked through her line of vision. The sun had warmed the day to a pleasant temperature, and Flint's chest had already grown damp with perspiration. He worked hard, Rani told herself, tapping the end of her pen against the table where she sat. You had to say that much for the man. Whatever else he did, he didn't shirk the rough work his job required. The Andersons were getting their money's worth.

Rani sat staring thoughtfully out the window after Flint had passed. She had never pictured herself as the Lady Chatterley type. She didn't intend to fall for a handyman-gardener. A woman had to take enough risks with men in the world as it was. There was no point deliberately compounding those risks by getting involved with a man who had no clear-cut past and an even less well-defined future.

On the other hand, she thought, I'm only going to be here for another three weeks. That wasn't long enough to get truly involved i one was careful, was it? A real relationship took time and effort. She intended putting neither into her association with Flint Cottrell.

Involved relationship or not, three weeks is long enough to find yourself in bed with him if you aren't careful, she warned herself grimly. But if she were cautious, she might be able to walk the fine line between friendship and an affair. And a part of her wanted to be friends with Cottrell, even though he could easily annoy her. It was a matter of maintaining control of the situation, Rani decided as she got to her feet. She could do it.

"Flint?" She stepped outside into the sunlight and looked around for him. When he didn't answer, she shoved her fingers into the back pockets of her jeans and walked to the side of the cottage where the broken brick path was. Flint was on his knees in the dirt, prying loose a brick. There was a stack of old dirt-covered red bricks beside him. Rani looked down, noticing how the light disappeared into the depths of his thick, dark hair. "What are you doing?"

"What does it look like I'm doing?"

"Handymen aren't supposed to be flippant with their betters," she drawled. "You're going to have to work on the proper attitude of meek deference."

He looked up at that, green eyes narrowing against the sun. "Deference?"

"Yes, deference. Know what it means?"

"I'll look it up this evening."

"You do that. I came out here to ask you if you wanted to go boating with me tomorrow afternoon."

He rocked back on his haunches, dusting off his hands. "Does this mean I'm forgiven for playing the heavy-handed lover last night?"

"The role isn't yours to play, is it?" she retorted.

"I'd like to go boating with you," he answered, paying no attention to her comment. "What are we going to do for a boat?"

"They rent rowboats and outboards down by the lake."

His mouth curved faintly. "Can you row?"

"The reason I'm inviting you along is so that you can do that part," she answered sweetly. "You're the handyman around here."

"Yes, ma'am. I'd be pleased to row my lady's boat." He tugged at an imaginary cap and smiled ingratiatingly.

Rani groaned. "I don't think you're ever going to be any good at it."

"Deference?"

"Yes, deference. And here I was going to pack a picnic lunch and everything."

"I promise to get real good at exhibiting deference if you promise to pack a picnic lunch. I can't even remember the last time I had a picnic lunch. Ants and all?"

"I was hoping to skip the ants." She smiled down at him, and Flint grinned back.

"It's a deal."

She nodded, pleased. "I called Dewhurst this morning," Rani added on a softer note.

"Dewhurst?"

"The man who originally appraised this ring for me." She held out her hand. "He reassured me that it was definitely fake."

Flint shrugged, looking unconcerned. "It's a little large to be real, I suppose."

"He also said the setting isn't more than a hundred years old, if that. So there goes your theory of this being the ring that belongs in your legend."

"He's wrong about that." Flint went back to work on the brick path. "Ambrose was sure of the setting's history. He might have replaced the real emerald with a fake, but he wouldn't have messed with the setting."

"I don't think Mr. Dewhurst would make that kind of mistake, Flint," Rani stated firmly. "Perhaps this isn't the same ring that was originally in my uncle's collection. Have you thought of that?"

"It's the same one Ambrose showed me a year and a half ago."

"But, Flint, it's just not as old as it would have to be to fit your legend. Why do you have to be so stubborn? Can't you just accept the fact that the whole thing is a fake?"

"No."

Rani exhaled with a groan of disgust. "Stubborn, hardheaded man. Do you come from a long line of mules?"

"I doubt it. Mules are sterile, aren't they? They don't breed."

"Details," she snapped. "I'm speaking in general terms. Why are you so dead set on believing this is the ring that belongs to your legend?''

He stopped work on the path again. ''I've done a lot of research on that ring, Rani. I know that at least the setting is for real. Want to hear some of the stories that go with it?''

''I'm not sure,'' she hedged.

''They're very romantic.''

She hesitated and then nodded, ''Well, in that case, tell them to me.''

Five

"**I** think I'm going to need a beer to help me get through these stories." Flint got to his feet. "Besides, I deserve a break. Want one?"

"A break or a beer?"

"A beer," Flint confirmed dryly, starting toward the cottage "You're already on a month-long break. Do you do this every win ter?"

"Take so much time off? No. I told you I had some unused vacatio from last year and I had to take it or lose it. To tell you the truth, was just thinking this morning that I was getting a little bored. thought a nice long, relaxing rest in the mountains sounded wonderfu but as it turns out I think I should have opted for something mor exciting. Like Club Med."

Flint laughed. Rani realized it was the first time she had heard hin truly laugh. It was a full, hearty sound that came from deep in hi chest. She decided as she trotted after him that she liked it. He ough to laugh more often.

"What's the matter?" she challenged. "Don't you see me as th Club Med type?"

"I'm not sure what the Club Med type is," he hedged, opening th door of the cottage.

"I'm not sure either, but I know what the image is." Rani waited on the step while he collected the beers from the refrigerator.

"Sexy?" he asked as he came back outside. He popped the top on a cold can and handed it to her. Green eyes moved consideringly over her from head to toe. "You'd qualify on that basis, I think. You're not the centerfold type, but there's something about you that makes a man know you'd feel good in his hands. Something soft and warm and lively."

Rani nearly choked on her beer. "Lively! Lively?"

"Yeah, you know." Flint waved his hand in a vain attempt to collect the right word. "*Lively*. Exciting. Responsive. Enthusiastic. Eager."

"Oh, lord." Rani sat down on one of the folding chairs Flint had set on the lawn in front of the cottage. "Forget lively. Next time I want to know what a man thinks of me I'll hand him a thesaurus first."

"I've already got one," Flint told her. "I looked you up in it last night. That's how I came up with lively."

Rani felt the heat in her face and tried to extinguish it with another swallow of cold beer. It was definitely time to get the conversation back under control. She seemed to spend a great deal of time keeping Flint under control. "About these stories you said you were going to tell me," she prompted firmly.

He shrugged, the smooth muscles of his bare, tanned shoulders moving easily as he took the second chair and stretched out his legs. Sitting there with a beer in his hand, his jeans scruffy and stained and his hair awry, he looked exactly what he said he was: a hardworking man who was taking a temporary break. Rani stared at him from beneath her lashes wondering why her intuition was telling her that Flint Cottrell would never fit neatly into a single category. It would be easier if he did, she thought. She'd like to be able to pigeonhole him so that she could feel more in command of the relationship between them. It wasn't going to be easy. It was hard to categorize and forget a man who had spent his life chasing legends.

"The first story takes place in the seventeen hundreds. That's when the Clayborne ring first appeared. It was given to the eldest daughter of a very wealthy English lord. She was wearing it one evening when her coach was held up by a highwayman."

"How exciting."

"The truth is it was rather dangerous. The lady and her chaperon were terrified. The highwayman was in the process of stealing their valuables when another highwayman appeared. The second man sent the first one packing."

Rani smiled. "And then took milady's jewels himself?"

"Nope. The second highwayman is our hero. He nobly apologized to the lady for the poor manners of some of his brethren on the road and then he stole a kiss."

"Only a kiss?" Rani asked skeptically.

"According to the story. At any rate, the Clayborne lady was exceedingly grateful. She was allowed to proceed on her way. But the next evening she met the highwayman who had rescued her. She recognized him at once, even though he was introduced as Lord Creighton, a new neighbor."

"How did she know who he was? Hadn't he worn a mask that night?"

"She just knew, although she kept the secret to herself." Flint shrugged. "The thing was, she was furious at the deception. She had been dreaming of a romantic highwayman only to discover he was just a staid neighbor who had inherited the next-door estate. Creighton realized he was in trouble and tried desperately to redeem himself. After having kissed the lady, he was well and truly under the spell of her ring, according to the tale. He would do anything for her. He was the perfect gentleman until he realized it wasn't going to get him anywhere. Then he took desperate measures. He dressed up in his highwayman's costume again one dark night and waylaid the lady's coach. This time he took more than a kiss. He took the lady herself and kept her overnight on his estate. The next morning, of course, she had no choice but to marry him. Her family insisted."

"Compromised," Rani said sadly.

"Things were simpler in those days."

"I suppose the punch line is that they eventually lived quite happily together?"

"How did you guess?" Flint tilted the beer can for another swallow. "Milady fell passionately in love with her fake highwayman."

"What was he doing playing at being a highwayman in the first place?"

Flint grinned. "That part of the story isn't clear. From what I can learn it appears there's every likelihood Lord Creighton was a real highwayman, but that he gave up the dangerous game as soon as he realized he was in love."

"Let's hear another story."

"The next one is about Robert and Sara, and it's the best documented."

"When did they live?" Rani asked curiously.

"Early eighteen hundreds. During the Regency period in England. Sara was the daughter of an aristocratic family. She received the ring on her eighteenth birthday. According to the story, she was a very beautiful, very well-bred young lady. Her family not only had money but a title."

"Ah-hah. Making her a prize on the marriage market."

Flint's mouth curved upward briefly. "A very valuable prize. She made quite a splash when she was introduced to society, and the offers for her hand came pouring in during the course of her eighteenth year. From all accounts, Sara enjoyed her status and the situation thoroughly."

"Good for her," Rani cheered.

"She was spoiled."

"So what?" Rani sipped her beer.

"She had a fiery temper. She was quite capable of cutting a man dead at a ball if he annoyed her. She was proud and probably quite vain and much too independent to her family's way of thinking."

Rani raised her beer in salute to the distant Sara. "Attagirl, Sara."

Flint eyed her speculatively. "Why do I get the feeling you're already taking sides in this story?"

"Because I am."

"Yeah, well, Sara met her match when she was introduced to Robert."

"Who was Robert?"

"A brash young sea captain from Boston. He was in England to settle the estate of a distant relative. While he was there he met Sara and immediately fell for her. Sara apparently found him quite a novelty. An amusing change from the soft, pampered males she was accustomed to seeing in society. She turned on the charm, and presumably the ring, and Robert was soon dancing at the end of her string. Apparently she got a kick out of shocking her parents and friends by being seen with him at some of the best social functions.''

''A lady has to take her pleasures where she can,'' Rani said commiseratingly.

Flint frowned. ''Sara found Robert amusing and useful for causing all sorts of interesting commotion, but she was very much aware of her status. She had no intention of going too far and finding herself compromised.''

''There's that word again. Compromised,'' Rani repeated thoughtfully. ''An outmoded word. No longer applicable in today's society.''

''Well, it was still applicable back then. Sara knew perfectly well she might have been obliged to marry Robert if she went too far in her fun and games. So she kept things under control.''

''With the aid of the ring?''

Flint exhaled slowly. ''So the story goes. Who knows? At any rate, Sara kept Robert dancing at a discreet distance, close enough to tantalize him, but not so close that she would find herself in an untenable situation.''

''Robert tolerated this treatment?''

''Until Livermore appeared on the scene.''

Rani smiled. ''Who's Livermore?''

''A gentleman with a title as good as the one held by Sara's family. He decided Sara would make the perfect bride. Her family was ready to marry off Sara, and Lord Livermore looked like a viable candidate as a husband for their daughter. The perfect match.''

''How did Sara feel about all this?''

''Oh, she agreed with her family. It was an excellent match. Livermore was reasonably good-looking and in the right age bracket. He had good estates and lots of horses. Sara was very fond of hunting. She was quite happy with the marriage proposal and was on the verge of accepting it when the truth came to light. Lord Livermore was virtually bankrupt. He wanted Sara for her money.''

''Where was Robert while all this was going on?'' Rani asked.

''The poor guy was trying to convince Sara to forget her grand marriage plans and run off to America with him, of course. Sara found the idea laughable. She had no intention of banishing herself to the uncivilized wilds of North America, even though she was very attracted to Robert."

"A woman has to look after her own future. Robert undoubtedly appeared to be a high risk."

"Undoubtedly," Flint agreed neutrally. "Well, things got messy when Sara's family turned down Lord Livermore's marriage proposal. He arranged to kidnap Sara and hold her for a few days at his hunting lodge in Scotland."

"After which," Rani said knowledgeably, "she would have found herself thoroughly compromised and more or less obliged to marry the evil lord."

"Exactly. Enter our hero, Robert, to the rescue. He discovered Livermore's plans at the last minute and raced off to rescue Sara. He caught up with the coach, which was on its way to the border, fought a duel with Lord Livermore and rescued Sara. Robert had her safely delivered back into her family's hands before morning. Her honor was saved."

"What about Livermore?" Rani demanded.

"He spent several weeks recovering from his wounds."

"Oh. In other words, he was out of the picture. Did Sara fall madly in love with the brave Robert?"

"Not quite. Robert made the tactical mistake of telling Sara exactly what he thought of her high-handed, arrogant manners during the trip back to her family's home the night he rescued her. He was rather blunt about it and implied she was a selfish, spoiled young lady who needed a firm hand on the reins."

"Uh-oh. I'll bet Robert then went on to tell her he was just the man to bring her into line, right?"

"How did you guess?"

"I could see it coming," Rani sighed. "Stupid of Robert. There the poor woman is, probably terrified at having barely escaped being kidnapped, still in shock from having witnessed a bloody duel. She's thoroughly traumatized and then this rude upstart from America starts in on a lecture. I'm sure Robert wasn't her idea of a hero."

"Apparently not, because although her family was extremely grateful for her safe return, Sara refused to see Robert after that. But Robert, poor soul, was very much in love with her."

Rani waved that aside. "Then he shouldn't have yelled at her."

Flint's gaze narrowed. "She deserved it."

"Now who's taking sides in this story?"

Flint took a long swallow of beer before continuing. "Moving right along..."

"Yes, let's."

He shot her a quelling look. "As I said, Robert was still desperately in love. Given the fact that Sara was treating him badly and had all along, we have to assume he was under the spell of the ring."

"That's one explanation," Rani agreed blithely.

"But after the rescue, Sara pushed Robert a little too far. When she refused to see him, he decided he had to do something drastic. So he kidnapped her."

Rani was startled. "Another kidnapping? Just like the hero did in the first story? I think I see a pattern developing here."

"You're right. Robert made his way into Sara's bedroom, wrapped her up in a blanket and carried her off one night."

"Good grief! He thought that was going to make her look on him more favorably?"

"He thought," Flint stated bluntly, "that it would leave her with no other choice but to marry him."

"He deliberately compromised her! Just like the first guy did to the Clayborne lady, and the evil Lord Livermore tried to do." Rani was incensed.

"It probably seemed the simplest approach under the circumstances."

"It was despicable."

"Yeah, well, whatever, it worked. The next morning a very subdued young Sara married him under a special license. Her family had no choice but to accept the situation. Sara and Robert left for America a month later."

"Poor Sara! What happened to her?"

Flint grinned. "She raised six kids and captivated Boston society. Everyone said she was a fine example of the perfect wife. Loving, obedient and fertile. Just as the lady in the first story had been. The ladies who own the rings make excellent wives."

"And Robert?"

"Robert is said to have been a very satisfied husband. He was wildly in love with his wife and she with him for the rest of their lives."

"So Sara fell in love with him after all, hmmm?" Rani thought about that.

"Once Robert had taken her to bed, she didn't have any choice. According to the legend of the ring, she was then as ensnared as he was."

Rani frowned. "Do you think he raped her that night he kidnapped her? Was that how he subdued her?"

Flint scowled and tipped his beer can to his mouth. "No, I don't think he raped her. He seduced her."

"Hah. That's your interpretation."

"The few people who saw Sara the morning after the kidnapping said she was quieter than usual but not at all unhappy. In fact, it was said she was the image of the happy, blushing bride."

"Amazing how a legend can smooth over some of the facts." Rani remarked. "Are you going to straighten things out when you write these stories? After all, you're the one who's going to force the truth down everybody's throat, right?"

"Facts are facts. I'm not going to change the verifiable details of the tales. In the case of the story of Sara and Robert, I'll simply point out that their marriage undoubtedly came about because a temperamental young woman pushed a passionate young man a little too far. The first story involves a similar situation. Both men lost their patience and took advantage of the conventions of the times to force the ladies into marriage. There was no magic involved."

"Just passion?"

Flint smiled. "Don't you think that's sufficient explanation?"

"Do you? You seem very ambivalent about this ring, Flint. Sometimes you scoff at it and other times I get the impression you half believe in it."

He tilted his head, studying her intently in the sunlight. "Maybe you'd better hope I don't buy the legends as fact."

Rani felt chilled. Much of the companionable warmth that had enveloped her as she listened to Flint's tales evaporated. "Why is that?" she asked softly.

"Because if I decide the legend is for real, I might decide to put it to the test. I might seduce you the way those other two men seduced their ladies. If the tales about the ring are valid, you'd be helpless to resist me then, wouldn't you? You'd be bound to me.''

Rani felt caught, trapped in a glistening, silky web that made it impossible to get out of the chair and stalk off toward the house. The sunlight was suddenly too strong, causing everything around her to become too sharp and clear and full of color. The green of Flint's eyes, for example, was now far too vivid. She remembered what Charles Dewhurst had said about true emeralds. There was a fire trapped within them, green flames that mesmerized whoever looked too deeply. In that instant, Rani knew, she had looked far too deeply into living emeralds.

''Rani?''

She blinked, struggling to break free of the odd, trapped sensation she was experiencing. ''What would you do to me if I were bound to you?'' she heard herself ask.

''Make love to you often and well.'' He spoke as though he had already considered the question and had long since decided on an answer.

Rani felt strangely breathless. She must get away from him, but she still couldn't move. ''Until your next handyman or gardening job took you to another state or another country? Or until another, more interesting woman came along?''

He smiled faintly. ''You forget the ring works both ways. I'd be just as trapped as I was before I made love to you. The only difference is that after I've seduced you, you'll no longer have the privilege of being in charge. You won't be able to keep me dancing at the end of the string.''

''I don't see much evidence of your dancing now!''

''Think not? Look at how easily you handle me.''

Rani flushed. ''I hadn't noticed.''

''You tell me when and how to write, imply I'm shiftless and unstable—''

''I never said shiftless!''

''You chew me up one side and down the other just for being in your kitchen when you bring home your date—''

Rani was incensed now. ''You deserved that.''

"You only let me kiss you when you want to be kissed and you call it off when you want to stop."

Rani's mouth tightened. "It's a woman's prerogative."

"You assume I'm available when you get bored and want someone to row a boat for you," Flint continued blandly.

"That's not true. I invited you along because I thought you might enjoy the outing."

"You've made it clear that, as a lover, you think I'd be a high risk."

"Well, you would."

"And you've also made it clear you're a lady who doesn't take risks. That's not very good for my self-esteem."

"I didn't realize your self-esteem needed to be pampered," Rani snapped. She finally managed to get to her feet. "Look, if you don't want to go out on the lake, just say so. I thought you'd appreciate the break, but I guess I was wrong. Thanks for the story hour. I don't think I want to hear any more Clayborne ring stories today." In her agitation she clutched the empty beer can. There was a crunching sound, and she looked down in astonishment to see the can crumpled between her fingers.

"Don't get the idea you've turned into Wonder Woman," Flint advised with a faint grin. "Anyone can do that with an aluminum beer can."

"I'll remember that." Rani tossed the can in his direction. He plucked it easily out of the air as she turned to stride toward the back door of her cottage.

"Rani," he called after her. "What time tomorrow are we going to the lake?"

She swung around to glare at him, her hand on the doorknob. "This is not a good time to ask me. I am seriously considering withdrawing the invitation."

Flint shook his head in mild reproach. "You're playing with fire. You know that, don't you?"

Rani stepped into the house and let the door slam shut behind her. She was playing with fire, all right. Emerald-green fire. The flames were licking at her heels.

* * *

By three o'clock that afternoon, Rani was too restless to convince herself any longer that she was simply enjoying a quiet day around the house. She had to get out. Perhaps she would walk over to the lake and throw stones or something equally exhilarating. Anything to get away from the feeling of being surrounded by Flint Cottrell's presence.

Even as she came to that conclusion, he opened her front door without bothering to knock. He stood on the threshold, wiping his damp forehead with the back of his bare arm.

"I'm going to have to run into town to pick up a few things at the hardware store. Want to come along?" he asked.

"No thanks," Rani said, aware that she sounded waspish.

"Okay. Suit yourself. I'll be back in a half hour or forty-five minutes."

Rani moved over to the window to watch as Flint slid into the black Jeep and turned the key in the ignition. He was gone before she could think of a graceful way of changing her mind. Just as well, she told herself. She didn't want to give him the wrong impression. He already had enough misconceptions about their association.

She prowled restlessly around the cottage, looking for something to take the edge off her uneasiness. She walked out into the garden and examined Flint's work. He really did have a knack for this sort of thing, she admitted to herself. It was obvious he took a deep pleasure in what he did. Sitting on the back steps, chin in hand, Rani contemplated the changes Flint had already made in the chaotic yard. Bushes had been trimmed, plants pruned for winter, grass raked. An orderly atmosphere was being gently established here. It made Rani even more nervous suddenly. She got to her feet, dusted her hands and decided to take a walk to the lake.

Zipp meowed at her feet as she opened the door and urged him into the house. Rani glanced down. "No, you can't come with me. I'm going over to the lake and you might get lost."

Zipp looked distinctly scornful of the possibility. He jumped onto the windowsill to watch forlornly as Rani headed off across the road. She turned to wave once to him and then set about making a serious effort to enjoy herself. She wasn't going to let flint Cottrell influence her whole vacation with his tales of the ring or with his purely masculine interest in acquiring a convenient bed partner for the remainder of her vacation.

That was what he was after, of course. A bed partner. It was the only answer that made sense. He was the kind of man who would be gone on the next breath of wind. Furthermore, he didn't come from her world. He didn't even come from a world with which she was vaguely familiar. He was a restless wanderer, a man who chased legends for a hobby and who made his living by doing whatever came to hand. It wouldn't surprise her to learn that some of the things that had come to hand in the course of his life had been less than respectable. He hadn't gotten that scar on his shoulder while gardening.

Rani crossed the road and started into a stand of fir and pine. The needles were occasionally slippery underfoot, and she had to use some caution on the long, gentle slope down toward the water. Rani knew from a previous walk that the hike would take about fifteen or twenty minutes. Through breaks in the forest she caught glimpses of the lake shining in the bright sun. Here in the trees the light was pleasantly dappled and golden. She began to relax. Taking the walk had been a good idea. She realized that she was going to have to organize more outings for herself, however. She wasn't the type to simply sit around and relax for several weeks. It had seemed like such a good idea at the time, but the reality was proving to be full of complications.

Rani made a firm decision not to involve Flint in any of her plans. She wouldn't have him accusing her of using him as a convenient companion or a source of entertainment. She frowned to herself, annoyed at the way he'd interpreted her invitation to go boating. She would ask Mike Slater instead. It occurred to her that Flint would probably interpret that action as spiteful and juvenile. She was stuck, regardless of what she did. Maybe she'd just go out by herself.

There were several cabins along the shoreline of the lake. The woods were safe through here, even during hunting season. The area was posted, and any sane hunter would know better than to risk coming so close to a populated region. Rani paused for a while to study some pinecones that had fallen. She knew people who did remarkable things in the way of Christmas decorations with pinecones. With a sigh, she decided she wasn't one of them. She couldn't really see herself making a wreath out of them or gilding one with gold paint. She just wasn't the type.

What type was she? Rani stood still for a while under the dappled, shadowed trees and wondered about that. She had been very sure for a long time now that she knew exactly what sort of woman she was, what she wanted out of life and what kind of relationships she sought. She had been in control of herself and her environment for several years. Ever since college she'd become increasingly independent and content with the safe, careful world she had created.

Her home in Santa Rosa, one of the pleasant towns just north of San Francisco, was cozy and comfortable, every inch of it done to her personal satisfaction. She hadn't had to consult anyone else's opinion. She liked her job at the public library where she was in charge of the reference department at one of the branches. Her social life was as full as she wanted it to be, no more, no less. The men she dated were never allowed too close. They were pleasant companions or interesting dinner dates drawn from her circle of college-educated, upscale friends. The various points of reference in her universe orbited around her in neat, predictable paths, and she was always in control of those paths. The possibility that such neatness and controlled predictability had meant she'd steered clear of violent passion or outrageous risks bothered her not at all.

At least it hadn't bothered her until a man with emerald eyes had appeared on her doorstep and demanded entrance into her life. Now Rani found herself silently having to defend the way of life she had created. She shouldn't have to justify her decisions. She'd made them with intelligence and a clear knowledge of what she wanted and needed. The restlessness she was feeling today bothered her. She knew deep down it didn't stem from boredom.

She was considering the ramifications of what was happening to her when she slid on a patch of pine needles. She lost her balance, clutched wildly at a low branch and sat down with awkward heaviness, just as the fierce crack of a rifle shot echoed through the trees.

"Hey, you with the gun," she yelled blindly, staying on the ground. "There are people around here. This isn't hunting land."

There was no response. Rani was more shaken by the proximity of the shot than she wanted to admit. It was still quite far to the safety of the lakeshore and there was little in the way of civilization between here and her cottage. She decided to stay put until she was certain the hunter had realized his mistake and departed. He was probably as startled by her shout as she had been by his shot.

But even as she lay on her stomach, hugging the ground behind a wide fir, another shot split the still air. The second shot left her not only angry but scared and puzzled. Perhaps the hunter hadn't heard her yell. The sound of a rifle shot probably carried a good deal farther than a human voice. Some fool hunter had probably caught sight of her movement through his field glasses and had fired without making certain she was a deer. She ought to have worn her red sweater instead of the black one with the yellow sunburst embroidered on it. Rani decided to try another yell.

"Whoever you are with the gun, I am not a deer, understand? You're shooting on posted land." She waited for a response. There was none. It occurred to Rani that she ought to move herself from the vicinity.

Very cautiously she began inching her way back to the cottage. Not daring to raise herself too far off the ground, she crawled painfully over needles and small pebbles. There was silence for a while, and she began to hope that the stray hunter had finally realized his mistake.

She was almost at the top of the gently sloping hillside when she saw Zipp. He came trotting into view looking extremely purposeful, as if he knew exactly where he was going.

"Zipp! For Pete's sake, what are you doing here? I told you to stay at home." Rani started to sit up and reach for the cat when a third shot rang out. The hunter was following her. Rani gasped, clutched Zipp and started to yell again. She was very scared now. But before she could try another warning call, Flint's voice cracked through the gloom, low and sharp with command.

"Stay down."

Startled, Rani turned her head to see him slithering over the rise to join her. He came around the side of a fir tree with all the easy skill of a man who has more than once clung to the ground while under fire. She didn't see the blue steel pistol in his fist until he raised his hand to aim it past his shoulder.

"My God, Flint, what are you doing?"

The pistol barked furiously in the dappled silence. Zipp jumped nervously in Rani's grasp. Before the echo of the first shot had died away, Flint squeezed off another. Belatedly, Rani realized he wasn't aiming high in warning. He was shooting at the level a man would be standing. Rani saw the coldly savage expression in his face as he waited, gun in hand, for the hunter's response.

Silence descended on the woods. For a very long time Flint said nothing, his full attention on his surroundings. Beside him, Rani sat motionless. She shivered, thinking of what might have happened. But she shuddered even more when she stared at the weapon held so expertly in Flint's fist. Her eyes went mutely from the gun to his green gaze. Cold green fire. She had never seen anything so cold.

"Are you all right?" he asked quietly.

"Yes." She paused to dampen her lips. "Yes, I'm fine. Just a little shaken. How did you…?"

"I got back from town and found you gone but your car was still in the drive. I figured you'd decided to take a walk, and since the lake is the only place anyone would walk to around here, I started after you. Zipp wanted to come along. He knew exactly where you'd gone."

"But the gun," she protested weakly.

"I keep it around as a security blanket," he said dryly, getting slowly to his feet. "Come on, I think we're safe enough now. Let's get back to the house."

Rani wanted to ask him why he had brought the pistol with him when he'd followed her into the woods. She wanted to know why he'd aimed low instead of firing a warning shot in the hunter's direction. She wanted to know why Flint kept a gun as a security blanket. A hundred questions hovered on her lips.

But Rani said nothing as she held Zipp tightly under one arm and allowed Flint to take her free hand to lead her quickly back through the woods toward her cottage.

Six

"**S**tupid hunters," Rani muttered as she stepped gratefully into the security of her cottage. She plopped Zipp down on the floor and turned to face Flint. He had been surprisingly quiet on the trip back through the woods. "We should report this incident to the sheriff, not that it'll do much good. By the time anyone gets around to investigating, whoever was doing the shooting will be long gone. After those shots you fired, he must have realized he had come too close to something that wasn't a deer."

"I'll give the sheriff a call," Flint said quietly. He reached for the phone. "Why don't you go clean up?"

Rani looked down at her dusty clothing. She had pine needles stuck in her sweater and a few more in her hair. "Good idea. Tell him that those shots were awfully close. One of them broke off a piece of bark on the tree beside me. If I hadn't slipped on some needles at the right moment, I might have been hit."

Flint's face was very lean and hard, devoid of almost all expression. But Rani sensed the fierceness in him, saw it glowing in the emerald of his eyes. When she glanced up and caught his gaze, she felt an uneasy twinge. It overrode some of the relief she had been experiencing. Remembering the gun, she looked around for it. Flint had set it down on the end table that held the phone. Rani wasn't quite certain what to say about it. One of her many rules in life was not to get involved with men who were interested in firearms. Of course, she reminded herself, she was hardly *involved* with Flint Cottrell.

"You shouldn't have gone for a walk in the woods during hunting season, Rani."

"I was only going over to the lake. That's hardly open hunting land. There are cabins all around this part of the woods. Hunters aren't supposed to be anywhere near them."

"You've said yourself, they aren't always careful or law-abiding." Flint was dialing a number he'd found in the front of the small local phone book. "You should have stuck around here until I got back. I had no idea you were planning on going for a walk. We could have driven to the lake."

"Flint, this has been a very unsettling experience, to say the least. I would appreciate a little understanding here. I have never been shot at in my life. I could have been killed out there."

"Yes," he agreed, waiting for the phone to ring on the other end.

"So why are you lecturing me?" she demanded. "I need sympathy, not a lecture. For heaven's sake, I wasn't doing anything wrong or even particularly reckless. The short distance between here and the lake is posted land and should be perfectly safe."

"I'll see what I can come up with in the way of sympathy and understanding while you're taking a shower and changing your clothes. I might be a little short on both for a while. I'm still using what sympathy and understanding I've got on myself. You gave me one hell of a scare, lady." He broke off to answer the greeting on the other end.

Rani glowered at him for a moment as she listened to the succinct, factual report of the shooting incident. From the way he handled it, a person could get the impression Cottrell had handled this sort of thing before. Rani groaned and headed for the bathroom. It was irritating to have to admit it, but Flint did have a point. She knew one had to take precautions during hunting season. It just had never occurred to her that the walk from her cottage to the lake would be a dangerous one.

It was almost dusk when Rani emerged from a lengthy shower and pulled on a fresh pair of jeans and a bright orange shirt that was patterned with a thin black stripe. She fluffed up her hair, coiling it into a knot at the back of her head and then paused to examine herself in the mirror. She looked normal enough, but she wasn't feeling normal.

The restlessness she had felt earlier in the day had turned into a definite feeling of uneasiness. Perhaps the jolt she had received from having a careless hunter take potshots at her had produced a kind of shock to her system. It certainly wasn't the sort of incident one got over in a hurry.

Zipp sat on the bed behind her, watching her through half-shut eyes. Rani turned around to scratch his ears. "You were a hero today, Zipp. Did you realize that? Tracked me down through the woods like a smart hunting dog. Sorry, no offense."

Zipp's purring engine rumbled into full throttle. Rani watched him for a moment as he sprawled contentedly on the bed while she thought about her other rescuing hero. Flint hadn't quite matched up to her inner image of a hero, although she had to admit he had arrived on the scene with excellent timing. Timing was undoubtedly a major factor in that sort of thing. In all her safe, prosaic life Rani had never before gotten herself into a situation from which she needed rescuing. She wondered at her odd reaction.

Maybe it was the sight of the gun Flint had been carrying when he'd shown up out there in the woods that had upset her. Here she was complaining about all the hunters on the loose in the vicinity without even being aware that her nearest neighbor had a very ugly weapon of his own. Rani knew enough about guns to know that handguns did not come under the heading of sporting equipment. Handguns were designed with only one purpose in mind. That purpose wasn't shooting deer.

Something else was bothering her, too. There had been a quietness about Flint when he'd found her in the woods. A lethal, efficient, competent quietness that she only now acknowledged. It had seemed to come from deep within him, and it hadn't faded much when they'd reached the safety of the house. Rani stood gazing out her window into the garden, absently stroking Zipp. It was Flint's unnatural inner stillness that was causing part of her feeling of unease. Rescuing heroes were supposed to sweep you into their arms and offer comfort and soothing sympathy. Rani didn't think she was likely to get very much of that from Flint. Perhaps it was just as well. She wasn't quite sure how she would react if Flint ever took her in his arms and offered real comfort.

The clatter of glasses being taken from the kitchen cupboard jerked her attention back to the moment. Rani sighed, stopped petting Zipp and headed down the hall to the kitchen. Aware that the free stroking was over for the moment, Zipp bounded off the bed and followed.

"Want a drink?" Flint inquired calmly as Rani appeared in the doorway. "Personally, I need one." He was already pouring himself a glass of amber liquid.

"Where did you get the whiskey?" Rani asked, more for something to say than anything else. She just couldn't quite figure out how to take Flint Cottrell, she realized.

"Picked it up in town after I went to the hardware store."

"Oh. I think I'd rather have a glass of wine."

"Suit yourself." He opened the refrigerator and pulled out a bottle of Chemin Blanc that Rani had been chilling. "How are you feeling? Still shaky?"

Rani began to relax a little, coming to the conclusion that Flint was now genuinely concerned about her emotional state. "Not really. But I feel a bit strange. I guess near misses affect a lot of people that way."

"Ummm." He removed the cork efficiently and poured wine into a glass. Vaguely Rani recalled that he'd once tended bar in some far-off corner of the world.

"You, uh, been around a lot of near misses in the course of your career as a handyman-gardener, Flint?" She hadn't intended to ask such a provocative question, but as he put the cold glass of wine in her hand, Rani couldn't seem to stop herself. Something about him made her want to goad and provoke a little. She was beginning to realize she wanted some answers about this man.

"A few." He leaned back against the sink and sipped the neat whiskey. His steady green gaze rested on her face. "The sheriff said he'd send someone out to scout the area where the shots were fired but warned us not to expect anything. Whoever was hunting out there will be long gone by now."

"Especially after having taken return fire from the 'deer' he thought was going to be such an easy target. I'm sure you put a scare into whoever it was, Flint.''

"You looked more than a little scared yourself when I found you. I'm glad you had the sense to get down and stay down.''

"It came naturally after the first shot went overhead,'' she retorted.

"Yeah, I guess it would. Don't go for any more solitary hikes again, Rani.''

She slanted him a half-resentful glance. "I don't need the lectures, Flint. I've told you that. If it's any consolation, you don't have to worry. I won't be running around in the woods until after hunting season is over.''

"Poor Rani. You're not used to getting lectures, are you?''

"Nope.'' She smiled suddenly. "But I do know how to say thank you. I do owe you my thanks. I was very glad to see you coming through the trees this afternoon, Flint.'' She put down her glass and stepped toward him. He didn't move as she stood on tiptoe to brush her mouth against his.

"You always say thanks like that?''

Rani flushed slightly, moving away. She didn't understand his reaction. She'd assumed he'd appreciate the small kiss. "Sorry, I didn't mean to insult you. Would you prefer a check instead? For services rendered? I believe you told me that you'd done some bodyguarding during your career as a handyman. I'm willing to pay for professional expertise.''

"Stop it, Rani.''

"Stop what? I don't know how to handle you, Flint. You come to my rescue as though you've done that sort of thing a lot. Then you act as if it was mostly my fault that I needed rescuing in the first place. Now you criticize me for trying to express a little gratitude. What is it with you?''

He stared at her for a moment and then muttered something under his breath that she couldn't quite catch. "I told you, you gave me a scare this afternoon.''

"I gave myself one, too!''

"I know. I'm feeling a little tense.''

"Is that an explanation or an apology?'' she asked.

"Just a statement of fact.''

"Try some more whiskey," she suggested blandly. "Maybe it'll help."

He shook his head, a reluctant smile catching the edge of his mouth. "I think it's going to take more than a little whiskey. How about you?"

She slowly returned his attempt at a smile. "Speaking for myself, it's going to take at least a second glass. I'm a little tense, too."

"You want some company for dinner?"

"Don't be subtle, Flint. Why don't you come right out and ask to stay for dinner?"

He grinned and took one gliding step forward. He rested his arm on her shoulders, his glass still held in his right hand behind her head. Very slowly he lowered his mouth to kiss her, a slow, lingering, hungry kiss that penetrated all the way to her toes. When he lifted his head, there was a hint of green fire in his eyes.

"May I stay for dinner?"

"Yes," Rani agreed, aware of the huskiness in her voice. "You can stay."

For a moment they stood very still, looking at each other and then, as though satisfied with what he saw in her face, Flint nodded his head once and released her. "I make one of the world's best salad dressings."

"You do?" She watched in amusement as he opened the refrigerator again and started moving items.

"Worked for a guy once who had a French chef. I spent a fair amount of time in the kitchen. Mostly I spent the time eating. The salad dressing was the only thing I really learned how to make."

Rani didn't ask what kind of work Flint had done for the guy who had his own French chef.

The dressing was delicious. It went perfectly on the spinach-and-mushroom salad. By the time dinner was over, Rani's inner tension had dissolved. So, apparently, had Flint's. He made himself at home in the living room after dinner, sprawling in a chair with Zipp on his lap and talked lazily about the article he was trying to write. Rani sat listening, her feet curled under her and wondered about this most unusual man who had wandered into her life. She felt bemused and amused, fascinated and wary, attracted and cautious. All in all, she simply didn't know what to do with Flint Cottrell.

"I didn't tell you the last story I've documented concerning the ring," said Flint.

"Does it follow the pattern of the other two tales?"

"Yeah. Except the lady in this case was the daughter of a wealthy Texas rancher. She got kidnapped and held for ransom by outlaws."

"Was the hero one of the outlaws?"

"No. He was a cowboy with a somewhat shady past who knew how to handle a gun. The lady's father hired him to get his daughter back."

"Which he did, right? And then he proceeded to fall in love with the lady who, of course, spurned him," Rani concluded spiritedly.

"Have you heard this story?"

"No, but I told you, I'm beginning to see a pattern in these Clayborne ring stories of yours. What happened this time, Flint? Did the gunslinging cowboy lose his patience and rekidnap the lady for himself?"

"You *have* heard this story before," he accused.

"No, just a couple of very similar ones. It's a male fantasy, you know."

"What is?"

"Women falling in love with their captors."

"These women don't fall in love with just any captors. They don't fall for the bad guys. Just the good guys. Who, according to the legend, are captivated themselves."

"Because of the ring?"

"Or something." Flint smiled cryptically.

"Going to spend your whole life chasing legends, Flint?"

"I've already spent enough time chasing legends. What about you, Rani?" Flint asked suddenly. "Going to work in a library all your life?"

"What's wrong with working in a library?"

"Nothing. Going to get married?"

"Maybe. Maybe not. I don't feel any great urge to marry. Do you?"

He looked thoughtful. "I haven't until now."

"You're almost forty, aren't you?

"Don't remind me."

"If you have successfully resisted marriage this long, you'll probably manage to do it a while longer."

"It's not that I've resisted it, exactly," he said, frowning. "There just hasn't been room in my life for a single, special woman."

"Because you're always on the move? Always chasing legends?"

"That part of my life is ending, Rani."

"How many times have you told yourself that in the past?" she countered gently.

He looked startled. "Not once. This is the first time."

"Don't worry. I'm sure by the time you're finished here, you'll be anxious to move on again."

"Is that why you're so wary of me? Because you're afraid I can't make a long-term commitment? You always play it safe, don't you? You're such a sweet little coward, Rani."

"No," she protested softly. "Just cautious."

He smiled faintly and pushed Zipp off his lap. The cat stalked off to the kitchen to see what was left in his food dish. Flint watched him go and then looked at Rani. "You'll never get rid of that cat, you know. He's with you for the duration."

"He knows a good thing when he's got it."

"So do I, Rani." Flint got to his feet and reached down to tug her up beside him. "So do I."

Rani felt the jumble of emotions within her suddenly begin to swirl together in a dizzying mix. She tried to recover her sense of wariness but found herself getting excited instead. Instinctively she made another grab for self-control only to discover she was clutching desire. It was unsettling. Flint was unsettling.

"Show me you're not a coward," he whispered, wrapping her slowly, inevitably, within his arms. "Thank me again for coming to your rescue today."

"Subtlety is definitely not one of your social skills." But she was smiling up at him, her eyes full of the precarious mixture of emotion she was feeling.

"I'll skip the subtlety and try for honesty." Flint took her mouth with sudden intensity, one strong hand curving around her head to anchor her for the deep kiss.

Rani sucked in a shaky breath and felt the most dangerous of the swirling emotions rise to the surface. Flint's mouth was hard and warm and infinitely exciting. She closed her eyes and gave herself up to the passion that flared between herself and the unpredictable, mysterious man who held her. There was no doubt about the need in him, no question of his desire. Of that much she could be absolutely certain.

Rani's hands settled on Flint's shoulders where she could feel the strength in him. But there was a curious gentleness in the way he held her, a tenderness that took away any fears she might have had. When she parted her lips for him, Flint groaned and eagerly took the offering. He explored her mouth urgently, seeking to know the warmth and promise there. Only when he had drunk his fill did he break off the kiss to taste the skin of her throat.

"Flint." His name was a faint, breathless whisper on her lips as Rani nestled against his shoulder. His leg moved, his thigh pushing deliberately against her. The hardness in him took away what remained of her breath.

"You're trembling, sweetheart." He held her even more tightly, as if to stop the fine tremors that rippled through her. "Don't be afraid of me."

"I'm not," she said simply, unable to explain why she was shaking. The thrilling excitement rushing through her could not be contained. She caught his head between her palms and kissed him with soft fierceness. When she opened her eyes, she found him looking down at her, his gaze so brilliant it almost dazzled her.

"I'll take care of you, Rani. I swear it. I'll take good care of you."

"I believe you." She smiled gently. "But I'm not sure that being taken care of is quite what I need tonight."

He bent his head and delicately nipped at her earlobe. "No? What do you need?"

"Do I have to put it into words?"

"Please," he asked in a dark, husky voice. "I need to hear the words."

She sighed, leaning into him so that she could feel all of his heat and desire. The last of her caution evaporated in the flames of this new, raw emotion. "I need you."

"Ah, Rani, my sweet, Rani." Exultantly he scooped her up into his arms and strode toward the bedroom. Rani clung to him, burying her face against his shoulder, one hand toying with the button of the blue cotton work shirt he wore. With a conscious act of will, she put all thoughts of past and future out of her head.

The bed lay in darkness, and Flint didn't bother to turn on a light. He settled Rani down on the quilt with infinite care and leaned over her, his hands planted on either side of her. She lay looking up at him, her eyes slumberous, her mouth slightly parted. When she touched the side of his face with her fingertips, Flint turned his head to kiss her palm.

"Trust me, Rani."

"Trust you to do what?" She trailed her fingertips around to the nape of his neck and buried them in the thick darkness of his hair.

"Just trust me." He lowered himself beside her, one leg sprawling heavily across her own as if to pin her to the bed. Slowly he began to undo the buttons of her bright orange shirt.

Rani gasped, her fingers briefly clenching him as the material of her shirt fell aside. He murmured her name in soft wonder as he touched her breast. When she lifted herself against his hand in unconscious need, he found the catch of her bra and released it. A moment later Rani was nude to the waist.

"You feel so good, Rani. How did I ever survive without knowing how good you feel?"

She couldn't answer. The words seemed locked in her throat as the urgency in her body threatened to swamp her senses. He was the one who felt good, she thought dazedly. His rough, callused hands were gentle and tantalizing on her nipples. She was becoming aroused with a speed and intensity that was strange and new. For a woman who had always practiced great caution in her relationships with men, this fierce passion was far more dangerous than deep water or thin ice.

Her own fingers fumbled as she tried to remove his shirt. Flint let her struggle with the buttons, clearly enjoying her trembling touch, but when she had finally freed the last button, he yanked off the garment with obvious impatience. Then he came down on top of her, cushioning himself on her breasts.

"I've been wanting this so long," he breathed, his lips at the pulse in her throat. "All this time and I didn't even realize what I was missing."

"Flint... I, oh, please, Flint." She could not talk, not coherently, not at that moment. She was aching for him, and her need was obvious. He gloried in it, making it plain his only desire was to satisfy the passion he had aroused.

When his fingers slipped the fastening of her jeans and tugged them and her panties down her hips, Rani made no protest. She had no wish to halt the inevitable flow of desire that had been unleashed. She waited while he got rid of the last of his own clothing and caught her breath at the undeniable evidence of his own desire. He was rock hard, his rugged body taut with a passion still barely under control.

Flint's eyes met hers as he came back down beside her. Deliberately he stroked the silky skin of her inner thigh. "You could drive me crazy with wanting. Do you realize that? You have such power over me, sweetheart." His fingers moved wickedly on her, finding the center of her physical sensations with unerring accuracy. Rani cried out softly and heard his muttered groan of response.

In that moment she felt alive with feminine power. It gave her the courage to tease and tantalize. "Afraid of me?" She trailed her fingers over his shoulder and down his side to his hip. "Don't be. I only want to hold you and please you."

His mouth curved faintly in the shadows, and it seemed to Rani that his eyes were flaring with an excitement that should have seemed dangerous to her but was not. "You please me, honey. Never doubt that." He took her arm and wrapped it around his neck, then he slid over her, securing her beneath him.

Rani's eyes widened as she felt the first probing touch at the warm, passion-dewed entrance to her most secret place. He was hard and strong, and when he took her he would be overwhelming. Rani knew that with deep, feminine certainty. She wanted him in a way she had never wanted any other man in her life, and yet she was suddenly aware of a new kind of uncertainty. Some of the wariness returned in that moment. Flint didn't push. He held himself firmly under control, savoring the damp readiness of her as he gently stroked the skin of her shoulder with his tongue.

"You want me, honey," he told her thickly.

"Yes."

"And God knows, I want you. Don't be afraid of me. Please don't ever be afraid of me."

"It's all right, Flint. I'm not afraid." She was trembling again as she waited for him. She wasn't afraid, but there was something else going on, something of which she should be wary. It was useless to try to understand. Everything had gone much too far. What was going to happen, had to happen. There was no way now to call it off or change the course of forces that had been set in motion the moment she had opened her door to the man with the emerald eyes. Rani sighed and tightened her arms around Flint.

Sensing her very private surrender and reading the acceptance in her body, Flint chose that instant to move against her and into her. The melding was slow and thorough. He made sure of that, needing to possess her and be possessed by her on every level. Rani whispered his name far back in her throat as his body locked tightly into hers. He swallowed the soft sounds she made, filling her mouth even as he filled the soft, velvety passage between her warm thighs.

The exultation in him was a heady thing. It played with his senses, sending him zinging and ricocheting until he felt exuberantly disoriented. The world narrowed down to the depths of Rani's bed and the hot, tight depths of her body. Nothing else mattered. Nothing else held any long-term importance. This was what he had sought for so long. The restlessness that had dominated him all of his adult life would finally be calmed.

"Wrap your legs around me. Hold me, Rani. Hold me as tightly as you can."

She obeyed. Flint groaned, tightening with spiraling desire as her legs closed around his hips. She felt so right in his arms. So perfectly right. He knew she was still trying to adjust to him. Her inner tension was both physical and emotional. The last thing he wanted to do was hurt her. Desperately Flint reined in his own white-hot need. He would give her time. It had to be good for her. It must be right for her. That was the most crucial thing. Now that he was in possession, he would make sure she took satisfaction in that possession.

He felt her adjusting to him as her body accepted his. Slowly he began to move, seeking the rhythm that would please her. She responded so beautifully, so completely. He could hardly believe the

sweet evidence of her eagerness. She was suddenly very hot and clinging, making small, seductive demands that fed the flames of his own
passion. Eagerly Flint surged into her, lifting her with his own hands,
letting himself get buried in the tight, fiery depths.

Then he sensed a new kind of tension in Rani. She was clinging to
him more tightly than ever, her nails raking his shoulders in an unconscious movement that delighted him. Flint felt the tiny, delicate
tremors that started deep within her, waited until she cried out and
then, with a final deep thrust he allowed himself to find his own near-
violent satisfaction. Dimly he heard his hoarse shout of triumph and
pleasure mingling with her soft, breathless cries and then he was sinking heavily back into the depths of the quilt.

Slowly, the world that had begun to shift on its axis the night Rani
had opened the door to him settled into a new and stable position.
Everything was finally the way it was supposed to be, Flint thought
fleetingly as he cradled Rani protectively in his arms. Everything felt
right.

"Cold?" he asked as Rani's lashes lifted to reveal a languid expression in the depths of her eyes.

"A little," she admitted.

He smiled and tugged the quilt over both of them. "How's that?"

"Much better."

He waited for her to say something else, and when she didn't, he
realized he didn't quite know what to say either. It was as if what had
just happened between them was too new and dazzling to put into
words. Perhaps it was better not to try. Still, there were things that
should be said.

Flint took a breath and touched the corner of Rani's mouth. "I know
I'm not exactly what you had in mind," he began carefully.

She lay very still in his arms. "Not exactly what I had in mind for
what?"

"I know I don't quite match your inner picture of the ideal man.
But I meant what I said earlier, Rani. I'll take care of you."

"You keep saying that. It's as if you feel you have some sense of
responsibility for me."

"I do," he informed her simply.

Her brows drew together in a small frown of concern. "That's not true, Flint. You don't owe me anything because of tonight. I'm an adult woman. I know what I'm doing."

He felt a wave of amusement. "I should hope so."

"Then why the oversized sense of responsibility?"

"I thought you approved of men who have a sense of responsibility. You like nice, stable types, remember?"

"Are you trying to convince me you're really a nice, stable, responsible type under all that vagabond charm?" She smiled up at him and tugged at a lock of his hair that had fallen over his forehead.

"I didn't know you thought I had much at all in the way of charm." He wasn't sure "vagabond charm" was a compliment.

She grinned playfully. "If you didn't have your own peculiar brand of charm, I wouldn't be lying here right now, would I?"

In spite of his need to be serious, Flint found himself responding to the teasing quality that was bubbling through her. He discovered he liked it when she teased him. It was a rare sort of intimacy for him, and he found he thoroughly enjoyed it. "Are you saying you were seduced?"

"Swept off my feet." she told him.

"Now you know how Sara and the other ladies who once owned the Clayborne ring probably felt after they found themselves in bed with the man who was drawn by the ring."

"An entirely different matter," she assured him. "Those three ladies were all hopelessly compromised after the night. Their fates were sealed after they'd been seduced because of the rigid rules of their times."

Flint chuckled. "And you don't think your fate is just as sealed?"

"Times have changed," she retorted.

"Not for you they haven't."

"What are you talking about?" Rani demanded, a faint trace of wariness filtering into her expression.

Flint realized she was now hovering somewhere on the line between renewed caution and the playful mood that had swept over her in the aftermath of their sensual union. He decided he preferred the playfulness. The last thing he wanted tonight was to alarm her. There would be time enough in the future to impress upon her that she was going to share the same fate as the other women who had owned the ring.

"I was only teasing you," Flint said easily, beginning to trace a curling pattern around the tip of her breast. He smiled to himself as the nipple began to tighten in reaction. She was wonderfully responsive to him. It was as though she'd been made for him. Flint had learned long ago not to question a free gift or a stroke of good fortune. A man grabbed at opportunity when it crossed his path and held on for dear life.

Rani seemed to relax. Her smile returned, warming her eyes with sweet, sensual promise. "What are you doing?"

"Having fun."

"If you're going to play the game, you have to be a full participant."

He looked down at her. "You're still a bossy little thing, aren't you?"

"Still?"

"According to the legend, the ladies all turn sweet and willing after the big seduction."

She smiled. "You keep forgetting that your business is debunking legends, not proving them to be true." She put her arms around his neck. "Come here," she ordered throatily. "I'll show you sweet and willing."

"Yes, ma'am."

Seven

Rani awoke to the sound of the bedroom closet door being opened. For a moment she lay still, trying to assimilate both the memories of the night and the fact that it was morning. Life had changed overnight. She wasn't sure how to deal with the change.

The closet door squeaked, and there was a shuffling sound. Hangers scraped along the wooden rod. Blinking sleepily Rani turned and peered across the room. Zipp was sitting on the foot of the bed, watching intently as Flint hung three work shirts and a couple of pairs of pants beside Rani's brightly colored garments. His clothing looked somber and masculine next to her own.

"What in the world is going on?" Rani sat up, grabbing for the sheet as it fell aside. She had never gotten around to putting on her nightgown last night. Flint was fully dressed in his customary jeans and faded shirt. She felt awkward and shy in her nakedness, overly conscious of her hair falling in a tousled mass onto her shoulders. "What are you doing Flint?" Even as she stared at him he reached down to the battered leather bag at his feet and removed several pairs of socks. These he set about placing in one of the drawers of the dresser.

"I'm just getting comfortable." He arranged the socks in neat, orderly rows and then added a stack of masculine underwear.

"Comfortable! It looks more like you're moving in."

He grinned and shoved the drawer closed. "No sense running back and forth to the other cottage every morning. Of course I'm moving in. What did you expect after last night?" He was beside the bed in two long strides, bending down to kiss her fully on her astonished, upturned mouth.

"But, Flint…" The confused protest was blocked by the kiss. Rani found herself crushed firmly back against the pillows. When Flint released her mouth he looked satisfied. No, it was more than satisfied, Rani decided. There was a distinctly male kind of arrogance about him that morning and it would need watching.

"You," he told her, surveying her critically, "are a very interesting sight in the mornings." He reached down to pat her tousled head. "Nice and warm and rumpled."

"Rumpled!"

"And grumpy. What you need is a morning coffee. I'll go get it started."

"Flint, wait a minute. Where do you think you're going? We have to talk about this."

"Later," he promised from halfway down the hall.

Rani sat staring after him, totally at a loss. It was just as she had predicted the first night she had met him. Give the man an inch and he would grab a mile. One night in her bed and he was moving in on her without even asking permission. It was outrageous. It was also entirely her own fault. She had to say one thing for herself: when she finally did decide to take risks with a man she had certainly done it in a spectacular manner.

Feeling alarmingly helpless, Rani pushed back the covers and padded quickly into the bathroom. She needed a hot shower before she could deal with Flint Cottrell. She undoubtedly would need a great deal more than a hot shower, but she couldn't imagine what it would be that would do the trick. Cottrell was outside her ken, a man from another world. *And she had let him make love to her last night.* What on earth had she been thinking of to allow that to happen? More importantly, she wasn't sure what to do about the situation now.

It was the way she had awakened to find him calmly moving his things into her bedroom that really brought home the enormity of the situation, she decided as she stood under the hot spray and tried to analyze the mess in which she found herself. If Flint had politely retreated to his own cottage that morning and had made it clear he would only return when and if she wished, Rani thought she might have been able to deal with the traumatic events of the previous night. She would have retained some sense of control, some sense of safety. Instead he had simply assumed that the one-night stand was the beginning of a full-fledged vacation affair.

Rani groaned to herself in the shower. It wasn't that she had wanted a one-night stand, but neither had she intended to start an affair with a man like Flint Cottrell. She was experiencing that trapped feeling again, and she didn't know what to do about it. It was, after all, her own fault that she had found herself in bed with Flint.

She couldn't blame him and she couldn't hate him, she realized. The night before had been uniquely wonderful. She had been a thoroughly willing party in the seduction. Although she was feeling wary and ambivalent now, she knew she couldn't bring herself to regret the previous night's lovemaking.

Rani just wished she didn't feel on the defensive. That much was definitely Flint's fault. He had a lot of nerve to simply move into her bedroom after only a single night in her bed.

Gathering her determination and her willpower around her as though it were an invisible suit of armor, Rani dressed in a pair of fuchsia pants and a fuchsia-striped knit pullover. She put her hair up in its assertive little knot and headed boldly for the kitchen.

Zipp was in his usual position on the windowsill, soaking up the early morning sun. Flint was standing near the stove, eyeing the contents of a frying pan.

"You like your eggs up or over?"

Rani thought about it. "Over."

He nodded. "So do I. This is going to be easy, isn't it?"

"What's going to be easy?" She picked up the mug of coffee that was waiting for her.

"Living together."

Rani coughed as a swallow of very hot coffee went down awkwardly. "Flint, this is going a little too fast for me."

"Don't worry, I'll handle everything."

He spoke with a confident assurance that left Rani with almost nothing to say. She watched, bemused, as he deftly served up the eggs, added toast and brought the two plates over to the table. She wanted to argue or scold. She wanted to regain control of the relationship. She wanted to reassert her ownership of the kitchen if nothing else. But when she met his emerald-green gaze, Rani found herself meekly accepting the plate of eggs and toast.

"Thank you," she mumbled. It was those eyes of his that were her undoing. Perhaps she could have fought the bold way he was acting if it hadn't been for the deep hunger and the barely visible trace of uncertainty that flared briefly in the green depths of his gaze. He was acting as if he had every right in the world to take over her life, but underneath he knew he could do nothing unless she accepted him.

The fact that he was pushing his luck and knew it startled Rani. A part of her found the actions unexpectedly endearing. Another part of her found them incredibly attractive. She didn't know why she should find herself so thoroughly fascinated by a man who came nowhere near her inner image of the right kind of man for her, but Rani was forced to admit the truth. Flint was square in the middle of her small, mountain vacation world, and she could no more bring herself to kick him out than she could have evicted Zipp.

She had taken the sort of risk she had never planned to take. The deed was done, even if it did seem strangely unreal. She might as well commit herself to the excitement and the fantasy because she couldn't possibly terminate the reality.

"How are the eggs?" But Flint was asking another question as he sat down across from Rani, and both of them knew it.

Rani took a delicate bite of toast and egg. "They're very good," she whispered carefully.

"Just right?"

"Yes. Just right."

He grinned again, showing a flash of strong white teeth in an expression that some might have termed feral. Green eyes gleamed in satisfaction. "Good. I'm glad you're pleased."

Rani decided to make some attempt at directing the conversation at least. "What are your plans for the day?"

"The usual. I'll spend the morning on the article, do some work in the garden later on and then we can take the boat ride you mentioned yesterday.''

She blinked. ''Oh, yes. The rowboat trip. I'd forgotten about it.''

''You promised me a picnic,'' he reminded her.

''Did I?''

''Uh-huh.'' He glanced down at the flat black metal watch on his wrist. ''I'll probably be ready to go around one o'clock. I like tuna fish.''

''I'll keep that in mind.''

He didn't seem to notice the wry tone of her voice. Instead Flint went blithely on, talking about the weather, the section of the garden he planned to work in for a couple of hours that day and how he would continue to use the small cottage for his writing. By the time breakfast was finished, Rani felt as if she'd been caught up in a huge, gentle wave. There seemed no strong reason to fight it, so she stopped trying. When Flint got up from the table and leaned down to kiss her goodbye in a casually proprietary fashion, she obediently lifted her face for the caress.

''Don't forget the tuna fish sandwiches,'' he said as he slammed cheerfully through the kitchen door with Zipp trotting after him.

Rani sat for a long, thoughtful moment, staring at the closed door. Then, shaking her head over her own odd mood, she got up to clear the table.

''Are you ready? We'll take the Jeep down to the lake. No more hikes through the woods,'' Flint said as he came back through the kitchen door at twelve-thirty that afternoon. He had spent the last hour and a half in the garden, Rani knew, but he'd showered and changed his clothes. He glanced around until he spotted the bulging black-and-white-striped tote bag sitting on the table. ''Is that lunch?''

She smiled. ''That's it. You're in luck. I had some tuna fish.''

He nodded, obviously pleased, and picked up the tote bag. ''Then let's get going.''

''You're awfully eager to start rowing.''

''I'm eager to start eating, not rowing,'' he said. ''I can't even remember the last time I went on a picnic.'' Flint glanced down at

Zipp who was eyeing the tote bag with interest. "You're on your own, cat. We'll be back by sundown."

Zipp put on his most wistfully endearing expression, but Flint ignored him, taking Rani's arm instead and striding purposefully toward the front door.

"I thought we could stop at the post office on the way," Rani said, hurrying to keep up with Flint's long, eager stride.

"No problem."

He was in a very amiable frame of mind, Rani decided. It was probably the prospect of free home-cooked food. And possibly the prospect of more free homemade love tonight. Both of which she was providing, Rani reminded herself. She mentally shied away from the long-term ramifications of her decisions.

Mike Slater's nondescript compact was parked outside the Reed Lake Post Office when Flint wheeled the Jeep into a slot near the door. Rani glanced at the familiar vehicle and felt a small pang of anxiety.

"I'll be right back," she said quickly. It would be best if Flint stayed in the Jeep.

"That's okay. I'll come with you." He was already opening the Jeep's door.

Rani glanced again at the artist's car. "Uh, Mike's inside."

Flint lifted one heavy brow in a faint challenge. "So?"

"So I don't want any embarrassing remarks, Flint Cottrell, do I make myself clear?" It was the first time she had been anything resembling assertive all day. Flint eyed her with amused interest.

"I wouldn't think of making any embarrassing remarks. Stop worrying."

Rani shot him a warning glance and turned to push aside the glass door. Flint was right behind her. Both of them nearly collided with Mike who was ambling toward the door from the inside, absently sorting through some mail. He looked up, nodded politely toward Flint and then smiled easily at Rani. There was the faintest of questions in his eyes.

"Hi, Rani. Thought I might have missed you today. Got time for an iced tea over at the café?"

Flint spoke before Rani could answer. "No, she doesn't." He gave

Rani a small push in the direction of the counter. "Better hustle, honey. I'm starving."

Rani dug in her heels and summoned up an apologetic smile for Mike. "Sorry, Mike. I really do have to hurry. I'm afraid I've made some plans for the afternoon."

"I see." Mike's mouth lifted with faint, good-natured acceptance of the situation. "Maybe some other time." He didn't look at Flint.

"She's going to be tied up for the rest of her stay here," Flint said coolly.

Mike kept his eyes on Rani's flushed features. "I get the picture."

"I'm sorry, Mike," Rani rushed to say, feeling warm and uncomfortable as she sensed Flint's quietly aggressive challenge. "I'm definitely tied up today, but I'll probably see you tomorrow or the next day when I pick up my mail."

"Get moving, Rani." Flint's voice was soft, but there was a definite hint of laconic command buried in the tone.

Annoyed, she turned her head to meet his gaze. "We're not in that big a hurry, Flint."

"I am."

"I don't know why. We've got the rest of the afternoon ahead of us." But she stalked off toward the counter, common sense telling her it would be best to get Flint out of the post office. He was difficult to manage under the best of circumstances. Faced with what he perceived as a challenge from another man, he might prove downright impossible.

"Hello, Mrs. Hobson," she said brightly. "Anything for me today?"

Mrs. Hobson peered at her over the top of her tiny glasses. The polished stone necklace she wore today matched the bracelet on her wrist. Her blue eyes were alive with interest. Rani knew she hadn't missed the small scene in the lobby. "Not much. A couple of letters is all. How are you doing today, Rani?"

"Just fine, thank you. And yourself, Mrs. Hobson?" Rani took the letters and briskly sorted through them. One was from a co-worker and the other from the neighbor who had volunteered to look after Rani's plants.

"Oh, not bad. John and I are getting ready for a trip to Arizona.

Gonna take the motorhome down there and park it for a while in the sunshine. It's gonna get colder and colder in these mountains. Winter's not far off.''

"That sounds lovely. More rock hunting?"

"You bet."

Rani grinned suddenly, glancing at the collection of polished stones in the case that sat near the counter. "What do you do with all the rocks you collect, Mrs. Hobson?"

"Keep the good stuff. Use the rest to decorate the front yard," Mrs. Hobson said with an amused shrug. "Nowadays I only bring back the best. When I first got started I brought home everything that took my eye. But you learn. When you've been collecting rocks as long as I have, you learn." But Mrs. Hobson had no intention of being side-tracked from her main interest at the moment. "Friend of yours?" She nodded toward Flint who was lounging against the high post office desk in the lobby. Mike Slater had disappeared.

"A handyman the Andersons hired to do some work around their cottages this winter."

"Funny time of year to do that kind of thing."

Rani wasn't quite sure how to respond to that. It *was* a strange time of year for repairs and gardening. "The Andersons probably wanted the work done now so that they could enjoy the place themselves next spring." It sounded a bit weak, but it was the best Rani could come up with on the spur of the moment.

"Well, he looks as though he ain't afraid of hard work," Mrs. Hobson offered by way of opinion.

"No, Mrs. Hobson. He isn't." Rani was aware of the firmness in her voice and wondered vaguely why she felt obliged to defend Flint. The man could take care of himself.

"Is he staying in the back cottage?"

"Uh, yes."

"What's your artist friend think of all of this?"

"Mrs. Hobson, I..."

"You city folks do live exciting lives, don't you?" Mrs. Hobson observed with satisfaction.

"I'll see you tomorrow, Mrs. Hobson."

Flint watched as Rani turned away from the counter and came toward him. She was frowning slightly, wearing that faintly belligerent expression she wore when she was being pushed. He wondered what the woman behind the counter had said to inspire it.

"Ready?" he asked.

"I'm ready. Where's Mike?"

"Gone."

"I can see that," Rani said with careful patience. "What did you say to make him leave so quickly?"

Flint gave her an offended glance. "Hey, he's an artist. Artists are temperamental. Who can figure them?"

"Flint…" she began firmly. Then she floundered to a halt.

Flint smiled. "Let's go get that boat. I can't wait to sink my teeth into that tuna fish sandwich."

She didn't argue. Pleased, and a little relieved, Flint swung the Jeep out of the small parking lot and headed for the tiny marina. There was a small park fronting the lakeshore, and he and Rani walked through it to get to the old wooden building with the dilapidated sign over the doorway that read Gibson's Boats for Rent, by the Day or by the Hour.

"Won't be many more days you can take a boat out and go picnicking on the island," the old man said as he fit the oars in the locks. "You know how to handle these?" he asked Flint.

"I can manage them," Flint said unconcernedly, helping Rani into the small, rocking boat.

"Yup, I guess so." The owner of the boat eyed Flint as he easily unshipped the oars and dipped them into the rippling surface of the lake. "See you in a couple of hours. Five bucks an hour if you go over the two hours you already paid for."

"That's a little steep isn't it?" Flint called back mildy. "Considering the time of the year?" As far as he could see they were the only customers that day.

"Take it or leave it." Gibson didn't appeared worried which choice they made. "Don't reckon you'll stay out more'n a couple of hours, anyhow. It'll start getting a mite chilly on that lake by late afternoon."

Flint didn't argue. He'd discuss the matter with Gibson when he got back. Right now he was more interested in getting on with the picnic. He felt the water's resistance against the oars and leaned into the long pull. Rani sat facing him, her eyes still reflecting the curious combination of uncertainty and acceptance that had been in them when she'd awakened that morning.

Flint searched for the right words, wanting to reassure her and at the same time let her know that everything was settled. He wanted to remove the last of the uncertainty. She was such a cautious, careful creature, he thought. He wanted to impress upon her that the time for wariness was past. All day long he'd been mentally planning what to say to her and how to say it. He gathered himself. "This might be a good time to talk about what happens when your vacation is over, Rani."

He was expecting a tentative response. What he got was an unexpectedly serene smile.

"Why?"

Flint pulled on the oars. "Because I know you'll worry about the future. I don't want you to worry, honey. There's no need."

"I know," she said gently.

A fierce satisfaction mingled with relief washed through him. It was far better than he'd anticipated. She had understood exactly what had happened the night before after all. Flint realized he was probably grinning like a fool, but he couldn't help it. It was going to be much easier than he expected.

"I was afraid you'd fight it," he said softly.

"Were you?"

He inclined his head, combining the action with another long tug on the oars. The boat was skimming swiftly along the surface. Flint glanced back over his shoulder to check the location of the tiny island. "I get the feeling you've been waiting a long time for some guy who fits your mental image of perfection. I wasn't sure how you'd feel when you found yourself in bed with me instead."

"Surprised."

He turned his head to look at her. She was still smiling that serene smile, but now he thought there was a trace of some other expression in the way her mouth curved, something feminine and secretive. "What?"

"Surprised is what I felt when I found myself in bed with you, Flint" she elaborated. "But I think, on the whole, it's going to be an interesting experience. You were perfectly right when you implied I probably hadn't taken enough risks in life. I'm thirty years old, Flint. It's time I took some risks. If I don't, life will pass me by, won't it?''

"Rani, what are you talking about? We're not discussing risks. We're talking about you and me."

She shook her head earnestly, warming to her theme. Belatedly it occurred to Flint that she had done a great deal of thinking on the subject during the day. "I know exactly what we're discussing. Don't worry, Flint, I'm not going to pressure you for a long-term commitment. I'm going to take what you're offering and live life to the fullest for the next three weeks. I've never done this sort of thing before, you know. I've never just jumped into the stream and let the river take me wherever it would."

"Rani…"

"When I woke up this morning, I was feeling confused," she went on candidly. "I was a little scared, I think. There you were, acting as though everything were settled for the next three weeks. Maybe I was a bit resentful at the way you just moved in on me. But I've had plenty of time to think about things and I've decided you were right. It's time I took a risk. I've spent years trying to protect myself, always trying to analyze the extent of a man's commitment before I gave anything of myself."

"Rani, that's what I'm trying to explain to you," Flint broke in, not liking the direction of the conversation. "You don't have to worry about that this time."

"I know. This time I'm just going to enjoy myself. I'm not going to even think about what happens when the vacation is over. I'm going to live for the moment." Her eyes brimmed with a new excitement. "I've probably missed a great deal all these years, Flint. No doubt I've passed up some wonderful experiences because I didn't see any future with the man who was offering those opportunities."

Now he was getting annoyed. "You haven't missed a damn thing, Rani. You were right to be careful."

She shook her head. "No, I overdid it. What's life without a few risks? That's how we grow and change, isn't it, Flint? Risks are what makes life exciting. Oh, I realize this is probably a cliché for you, but for me it's a whole new way of thinking. I feel free. I won't think beyond tomorrow for the next few weeks. Don't worry, Flint. I'm not going to be moody or temperamental. No scenes, I promise. I'm just going to enjoy myself.''

"The hell you are," he bit out. "Now listen to me, Rani Garroway. What happened last night was important. It changes a lot of things for us and it changes them permanently, not just for the next three weeks. Do you hear me, lady?''

She nodded, reaching down to fish around inside the black-and-white tote bag. "I hear you, but you can stop worrying, Flint. I feel quite capable of dealing with the situation. You don't have to pretend there's a long-term future involved here. In fact, I'd just as soon you didn't try. I'd rather keep everything strictly honest if you don't mind. I promise not to try to maneuver you into an extended affair or, heaven forbid, marriage, but in exchange I'd like you to promise you won't lie to me because you think that's a way of keeping me cooperative for the next few weeks. Let's agree to be honest with each other, Flint. We're adults. We can take our risks honestly.''

"Now just a damn minute," he began savagely, pulling so hard on the oars that the small craft almost leaped out of the water. "You're twisting everything around. I'm trying to talk about a future and you're acting as if you're only in this for the next couple of weeks.''

"We both know we're only in this for the next couple of weeks. Why pretend otherwise? Want a potato chip? They're the extra thick kind. They make them with the skins on, but I'm not sure how much real nutrition that adds. I mean, after you've deepfried a slice of potato and poured salt all over it, how much good is left in the poor thing? But it does taste wonderful.'' She munched cheerfully as she spoke, reaching out to put a chip between his lips.

"Rani, I'm trying to deal seriously with this.'' Flint ignored the potato chip she was holding quite close to his mouth. "I don't understand you today. What the hell has gotten into you?'' And then, quite suddenly, he did understand her. She was scared. She didn't want to talk about the future because she was afraid of it. Rani was hiding the fear behind a veil of feminine bravado. He understood completely, and he could hardly blame her. Giving her a lecture on how he intended to stick around wasn't going to reassure her. It would be best if he just backed off and let her adjust in her own way. Sooner or later she would begin to grow more certain of him. Then they could talk.

"Don't you want the potato chip?" she asked politely.

Flint opened his mouth and crunched the chip very forcefully between his teeth. "Are we going to eat the whole picnic lunch before we get to the island?" he asked softly.

"Nope. Just a few appetizers." She watched him, the anxiety almost hidden beneath the determined brightness of her smile. "Want another chip?"

"Sounds terrific."

The phone rang two evenings later, just as Rani was finishing the task of rinsing the last of the dinner dishes she and Flint had been washing. The past two days had been composed of homey scenes like the present one, interspersed with hours of such compelling passion that Rani had begun to wonder if her life were indeed real. She had never thought real life could contain such a spectrum of quiet happiness and intense excitement. As long as she didn't think about the future, she was free to enjoy it to the hilt.

"I'll get it." Rani tossed a cotton dish towel at Flint. "Here, you can start drying."

He took the cloth with a nod, and Rani headed quickly toward the phone in the living room. Flint had been quite agreeable for the past couple of days, ever since she had squelched his attempt to discuss the future. Perhaps he was secretly relieved at not having to pretend their relationship was of the long-term variety. The last thing she wanted from Flint Cottrell was lies, Rani thought as she lifted the receiver. She could handle anything except lies from him.

"Hello?"

"Miss Garroway, this is Charles Dewhurst. Have I caught you at a bad time?"

Startled, Rani hastily denied any problem. "Not at all, Mr. Dewhurst, but I wasn't expecting to hear from you. Has something happened?" The ring on her hand briefly caught the lamplight. She looked down at it, frowning.

"Not exactly," Charles Dewhurst said in an apologetic tone. "It's nothing really, just some trade gossip that has reached my ears. I thought I would pass it along, although I hesitate to alarm you."

"Alarm me about what?"

Dewhurst cleared his throat, obviously a bit uncertain about how to proceed. "Well, it's about your Uncle Ambrose, my dear. About the accident back East."

Rani's fingers tightened fractionally on the receiver. "What about the accident?"

"My dear, you must realize that one hears a lot of gossip after a man with your uncle's, uh, reputation, dies. The world of gemstones tends to thrive on mystery and rumor. Your uncle knew a great many people both here and abroad, and more than a few suspected he indulged his talents in, shall we say, somewhat shady ways."

"Please, Mr. Dewhurst. Tell me what the problem is."

She could hear Dewhurst taking a deep breath before continuing. "There is talk, my dear, that your uncle's death was not precisely an accident."

Rani went cold. She also went very still. "Not an accident?"

"Now, I've gone and alarmed you and I had no right to do that. I just felt you should know what sort of things are being said. It's all over now, my dear, and I'm sure there's no reason to be concerned, but when I heard the rumors I thought it my duty to pass them along. Please don't take them too seriously. I only mention them in the first place because you were the one who inherited the jewelry."

"But the jewelry is paste! Mr. Dewhurst, are you suggesting Uncle Ambrose was killed?"

"There is a rumor in the business to that effect, I'm afraid," Dewhurst said with a small sigh.

"But it makes no sense. If the jewelry I inherited is all fake..."

"It seems, Miss Garroway, that some people believe your uncle actually had the Clayborne ring in his possession at the time he died. They think he had not yet made the duplicate of the stone."

Rani caught her breath. "Someone believes the emerald is real? That my uncle might have been killed because of it?"

"That's what I have heard. Please, Miss Garroway, there is no need to get upset. You and I both know that if Ambrose ever did have the ring the original is long gone now."

"But what if someone believes I have it? What if whoever killed Uncle Ambrose doesn't know my uncle had time to make the imitation ring and get rid of the original?"

Dewhurst hastened to reassure her, obviously upset at having caused Rani to worry. "Please, Miss Garroway, don't be unduly alarmed. I have done what I could to squelch the rumor of the stone being real. I have a certain degree of respect in this field and I have let it be known that I personally saw the ring after you inherited it. I have also let it be known that the duplicate is one of Ambrose's finest works, but that it is definitely glass. With any luck my evaluation will become known to the person who may or may not have been responsible for your uncle's death. I'm sure there is little cause for concern. But since you are now officially the ring's owner, I thought it best that you be notified."

"Do your trade rumors indicate who might have been responsible for my uncle's accident, Mr. Dewhurst?" Rani was surprised by the steadiness of her own voice.

"No. There is only some speculative talk about a man who has been on the trail of the ring for years. Someone your uncle apparently dealt with at one time. I'm afraid I know nothing more about him. Please try not to worry, Miss Garroway. Perhaps I shouldn't have called."

"No," she interrupted quietly, "I'm glad you called. I appreciate your warning."

"I will do what I can to make certain everyone who might be interested in this affair is aware that I have ascertained the ring is a fake. If there is someone out looking for the ring, he is sure to hear of my assessment. That's probably the best defense under the circumstances. Surely no one would spend time and money continuing to pursue green glass."

"Thank you, Mr. Dewhurst."

"You will take care, my dear?"

"Oh, yes," Rani whispered. "I'll take care." She hung up the phone, not moving. Blindly, she continued to stare down into the green depths of the ring.

Rani didn't know quite when she realized she wasn't alone in the living room. She only knew that, when she turned slowly to find Flint watching her from the doorway, she experienced no real sense of surprise. She also knew from the look in his eyes that he had overheard her conversation with Dewhurst.

"Mr. Dewhurst says there is a possibility that someone killed my uncle because of this ring.'' She felt as if she were speaking in a dream. There was a sense of unreality pervading the room. She was trapped.

Flint slowly dried his hands on the towel he was holding. ''He's right.''

Eight

It was Zipp who broke the stillness. He ambled in from the kitchen and meowed loudly. Rani reached down to pick him up, holding him protectively. Then her eyes went back to Flint's face. She didn't say a word. Flint swore softly.

"I didn't want you to find out this way," he said.

"I imagine you didn't." Her voice was even but very remote. "Who are you?"

His gaze narrowed as he realized what she was thinking. "I'm not the man who killed your uncle." But he twisted the dish towel savagely, and the small violence drew Rani's attention. She stared at his hand as if he were holding a gun. "Did you hear me, Rani? I'm not the one who killed Ambrose."

"Then who are you?"

"I've told you the truth. I was a friend of your uncle's. I helped him trace the history of the ring."

"And now you want it for yourself." She looked down at her hand. The ring was partially hidden by Zipp's fur. "I don't understand any of this. It's just junk."

"Someone thinks it's real."

"The same someone who killed Uncle Ambrose."

"Rani, for God's sake, stop talking as if you were waiting for me to pull a gun on you."

"Where is your gun, Flint? It was certainly very convenient the other day in the woods when you scared off that stupid hunter." Clutching Zipp so tightly that he squawked mildly in protest, Rani edged back a couple of steps. There was an outside chance she could make it through the door before Flint caught her. He wasn't armed at the moment. She might be able to disappear into the woods before he could get his ugly handgun. It wasn't much of a chance, but in that moment she couldn't think of anything else.

"Please don't run away from me, Rani." His voice was low and harsh.

"You can have the ring," she said, struggling to remove it from her finger without letting go of the cat. "I can't imagine why anyone would want it. Believe me, I don't. Not after all this. Take it, Flint. You've worked hard enough to get it."

"The ring is yours."

It came free of her hand, and she tossed it toward him. Flint made no move to catch it, and it clattered to the floor. "Take it," Rani commanded softly. "Take it and get out."

"I don't want the damned ring. Are you going to sit down and listen while I explain this mess, or are you going to make some idiotic dash into the woods? Make up your mind, Rani. If you're going to run, go ahead and try it. Let's get that part over so we can start talking."

He was reading her mind, Rani decided. Flint knew exactly what she was thinking. But then perhaps he'd seen more than one person in this situation. She was shivering, she realized. Faint ripples of fear and anger flowed through her. She had to control both the fear and the anger or she wouldn't stand a chance. Zipp meowed again.

"You must think me a complete fool," she whispered. "I made it all so easy for you, didn't I? I gave you shelter, fed you and, to top it all off, let you into my bed."

He took a step forward but stopped when she instinctively retreated. Flint's expression hardened. "Do you really think I'd hurt you, Rani?"

She stared at him. She was feeling so disoriented that she couldn't seem to think properly. "You're here because of the ring."

"I'm here because your uncle was killed. He owned that ring and now you own it. I don't want the same thing happening to you that happened to Ambrose. Listen to me, Rani. I'm here to protect you, not hurt you.''

''I don't understand.''

''I know you don't. Stop figuring out how you're going to make it through the door and start listening to what I'm saying. I did not kill Ambrose. I had nothing to do with his death. But when I heard about the circumstances of his so-called accident, I realized it might have been an act of murder. And if he had been killed, I had to assume it was because of the ring.''

''Why should you assume that?''

Flint slung the dish towel over the back of a nearby chair. ''Because I knew the ring wasn't fake.''

Rani caught her breath. ''What are you talking about.''

His mouth twisted wryly. ''Oh, the stone you've got there could easily be paste. Most likely is, judging from what your uncle's jeweler friend has told you. I'm no authority on gems. But when Ambrose first came into possession of the ring, he told me it was the real thing. He also told me that he intended to keep it, not copy it. He said it was going to be the one perfect stone in his collection. It was too beautiful too valuable and contained too much history to be cut up and sold or the black market. The Clayborne ring was the one genuine piece in his collection. Don't you see, Rani? If I knew the emerald was for real, so did any number of other people. Ambrose sent me a letter shortly before his death telling me he was worried. Someone else was on the trail of the ring, and he planned to take precautions. He didn' spell out the precautions. I didn't get the letter for several weeks because I was in North Africa. By the time I picked up my mail your uncle was dead.''

''So you immediately came looking for the ring?'' Rani challenged

''I learned that whoever had arranged your uncle's accident hadn' gotten his hands on the ring. Your uncle's collection of fakes was being held by his lawyer, and according to the itemized list, a ring matching the description of the Clayborne ring was still with the rest of the stuff Ambrose had created when he died. The police went under the assumption the accident was for real. They didn't suspect murder I might not have either if I hadn't had your uncle's letter and if hadn't known that one item in Ambrose's collection wasn't a fake. I decided that if Ambrose had been killed whoever had done it might still be following the ring. I went looking for the person who had inherited Ambrose's collection of fakes.''

"I see. What exactly did you intend to do when you found me?''

"Keep an eye on you for a while. I wasn't sure if anyone would make another try for the ring, but I wanted to be around if it happened. I felt I owed it to Ambrose.''

She closed her eyes in brief anguish. "I certainly made it easy for you to keep an eye on the ring, didn't I? Why didn't you tell me all this when you arrived on my doorstep?''

"Because I wasn't even sure if Ambrose had been killed. I only suspected it. I didn't know at first where you fitted in. You seemed to be an innocent bystander in all this. I didn't want to alarm you. I just wanted to keep tabs on you until I knew for sure what was going on. I didn't even know if the stone in the ring was still the genuine emerald. Ambrose had said he was going to take precautions. He might have made a duplicate before he died and hidden the real emerald. Making copies was his profession. It would have been natural for him to attempt to protect the ring by creating a fake.''

"Since this is a fake, where's the real one?''

Flint ran a hand through his hair. "I don't know. There's no telling where Ambrose might have stashed it. My concern was that whoever was after it wouldn't know he was following a piece of glass. He still might be willing to kill to get hold of the ring.''

Rani shook her head in mute denial. "Why should you have felt obliged to protect me? You didn't know me. Why go through all this trouble just to keep an eye on whoever inherited the ring?''

"I told you, Rani, your uncle was my friend.''

"The way you move around, you've probably got a lot of acquaintances. Do you feel this sort of obligation toward all of them?''

His mouth thinned at her skeptical tone. "I said Ambrose was a friend. I may know a lot of people, Rani, but I don't have a lot of friends. Ambrose was one.''

"So you looked me up out of some noble sense of friendship?''

"Damn it, Rani, it *was* a sense of friendship that brought me here. If you want to know the truth, it was more than that. Maybe if I'd had that letter from Ambrose earlier, I could have kept him from getting killed.''

''It was guilt that brought you here then?'' She knew she was pushing him, but she couldn't help it. She felt hurt and angry and still somewhat afraid.

''I only knew I had to check up on whoever had inherited the ring. When I traced it to you I wasn't sure how to handle things. I thought it would be easier just to hang around for a while and see what developed. I told you I didn't want to scare you unless it was absolutely necessary. Like Dewhurst, I was hoping that word would spread the ring had been duplicated and the stone in this one was fake. That information should have kept you from being interesting to whoever had killed Ambrose.''

''All that talk of tracking down the ring because you were writing an article on it was just a convenient lie? You must have lied to the Andersons, too, to convince them to give you the job. Were all those lies and fabrications simpler than telling me the truth?''

''I've never lied to you. I am writing an article on that ring. I would have wanted to know what became of it even if I hadn't been concerned that someone might be after it. I never lied to the Andersons, either. I asked for a job and I'm doing the work.''

Zipp wriggled in Rani's grasp, demanding to be released. She hesitated because there was a vague element of comfort to be found in clutching him in front of her like a shield. But when he growled to show he was serious she slowly lowered him to the floor. Zipp trotted over to Flint, stroked his tail once or twice against Flint's jeans and then headed back toward the kitchen. The cat was clearly unconcerned about the small drama taking place in the living room. Rani watched him disappear, her mind whirling with confusion and hurt.

''I'll admit you're a hard worker, Flint,'' she said at last. ''The Andersons, at least, are getting their money's worth. All in all this probably rates as one of your better gardening jobs, doesn't it? Or is sleeping with the lady of the house a common fringe benefit in your line of work?''

Flint's eyes were shuttered and cold as he moved forward to catch hold of Rani. She sensed his intention, but she didn't have time to evade his grasp. His big hands closed around her upper arms as he orced her to look at him. "I'm sleeping with you because I want you and you want me. It's as simple as that. Don't drag our personal relationship into this."

She glared at him in open amazement. "Don't drag our personal relationship into this!" she repeated. "Are you joking? That's what his whole mess is all about, isn't it? You made what might have been a business relationship or a matter of obligation into a very personal relationship. Or don't you see it that way? I realize that you probably view our...our affair as a casual and convenient little romp but that doesn't mean I, at least, don't find it a very personal matter."

"Don't get hysterical on me, Rani."

"I am not hysterical, I'm mad!"

"You're hardly a woman scorned. Don't act like one."

She tried to free herself. When he wouldn't release her, she glanced pointedly down at his hands. He followed her look and reluctantly released her arms. When he dropped his hands to his sides, she stepped away, folding her arms across her breasts. She came to a halt in front of the window, staring unseeingly out into the garden at the front of the house.

"You should have told me the truth, Flint. Right from the start. It wasn't fair of you to let me think you were here only to write the article and pick up a few bucks doing repairs for the Andersons. I feel used."

"You have no right to feel used," he told her harshly. "I haven't used you and you know it. Maybe I should have told you the truth, but I've already explained I wasn't sure what was going on. I didn't want to alarm you. I just wanted to keep an eye on you and the ring for a while. If I'd walked in here that first night and told you there was a possibility someone might kill you for the ring, how would you have reacted?"

"We'll never know, will we? You didn't handle it that way."

"I'll tell you how you would have reacted. You'd have thought I was insane. You'd have been scared to death and you wouldn't have let me in the front door."

"The only difference now is that you're in the front door."

He came up behind her. "Rani, I didn't realize your friend Dewhurst would hear about the rumors surrounding Ambrose's death. I didn't know he'd call and warn you. Hell, I was hoping your uncle's death really was an accident. With any luck this whole thing would have blown over in a few months."

"And having done your duty, you could slip back out of my life the same way you slipped into it," she concluded bitterly.

"Stop it, Rani."

"What made you think you were qualified to protect me if I was in danger? You're a handyman, a gardener, someone who writes articles for treasure hunting magazines."

"I told you, I've done some work as a bodyguard," he said stiffly. "Some security work."

"Oh, that's right. I'd forgotten your varied résumé. Do all body-guards get to sleep with their female clients?"

Flint jerked her around to face him again. "That's what's really bothering you, isn't it?" he charged. "You're madder than hell because I had the nerve to take you to bed, not because I didn't tell you the whole truth. You've decided I took advantage of you."

"Well, didn't you?"

"Lady, we would have ended up in bed regardless of what story I told you the night I arrived."

"Not necessarily!"

"Want to bet?" He pulled her closer.

Rani's unstable mixture of emotions exploded. "No, I do not want to bet. Nor do I want you trying to prove how irresistible you are. What I want is for you to get out of here, Flint Cottrell. You say you're here to guard me, so, okay, start guarding. Go fetch that big ugly gun of yours and start patrolling the perimeter or whatever it guards are supposed to do. Go on, get out of my cottage. You can spend the night walking around outside watching for jewel thieves."

"I'm going to spend the night in your bed, damn it!"

"Not a chance."

Something that might have been desperation moved across his face. "Rani, honey, listen to me. I know you're angry, but the bottom line in all this is that nothing between us has changed. We're involved. You can't kick me out."

"Want to bet?" Deliberately she mimicked his own earlier challenge. "I'm ordering you out of this cottage, Flint."

"No." He shook his head firmly. "You can't."

She took a deep breath. "You won't leave willingly?"

"I'm not leaving. Period."

"In that case, I don't have much choice, do I?"

His gaze softened. "You don't want a choice, Rani. You want me to stay and you know it. Stop fighting both of us."

She ducked out from under his arm, striding down the hall to the bedroom. "You're bigger than I am, Flint. If you won't go on request, I can't force you."

"What the hell are you up to now?" he demanded, following her down the hall.

"If you won't leave, I'll have to do the leaving. I am not spending another night in this cottage with you." She opened the closet door, shoved aside his clothes and dragged out her suitcase. Tossing it on the bed, she began filling it with the contents of her side of the closet.

"Rani, cut it out. You're acting like a child."

"I thought you said I was acting like a woman scorned."

"You're being ridiculous."

She shrugged and reached for a stack of underwear. He put his hand out and shoved the drawer closed.

"All right, all right. If you're going to be this way about it, I'll leave," Flint said through gritted teeth.

She stood very still, waiting. "Goodbye, Flint."

"You're going to regret this, you know. You're hurting both of us."

"I, for one, will be far more hurt if I allow you to spend another night in my bed."

"Honey, that's just not true. When you've calmed down, you'll realize it."

"Get out of here, Flint."

He stood looking down at her for another moment. She saw the frustration and the leashed anger in him and wondered if it would escape. But in the end Flint controlled himself as she had somehow known he would. Without a word he turned and walked out of the room.

Rani stood where she was until she heard the kitchen door slam shut. Then she sank slowly down onto the bed and huddled into herself.

She concentrated her full attention on trying to keep the tears from escaping between her lashes.

Two hours later Flint gave up trying to sleep and swung his legs over the edge of the decrepit old bed he was using in the back cottage. He was still wearing his jeans. He hadn't bothered to undress completely because a part of him refused to admit he was really going to spend the whole night in his small cottage. For the fourth or fifth time he paced silently over to the window and stared out into the night. Rani's bedroom light had finally been switched off. It had been on a long time after he'd left.

She was lying there in the darkness, but he doubted if she was asleep any more than he was. She would be thinking of all that had been said that evening. What he really wanted her to think about was what had not been said. Had she realized the full import of that yet? When and if she did, would it make any difference to her? He had no way of knowing how she would respond even if she did admit the truth to herself.

Restlessly Flint turned away from the window and walked over to the refrigerator. It was humming noisily in the kitchen alcove. Absently he gave it a kick to quiet it and then he opened it to see if there was anything interesting inside. It was empty except for the last of the six pack. He reached for the beer and popped the top. Can in one hand he went back to his post at the window.

She couldn't be asleep. She must be lying there thinking about what she had learned that evening.

Flint felt a distinct sense of irritation toward Charles Dewhurst. he hadn't called with his belated warning, the present situation wouldn't have arisen. Flint could have told Rani the truth in his own time and in his own way.

She didn't understand why he hadn't been completely honest with her right from the start. Flint had to admit she had a point. His main goal had been to protect her without alarming her, but she didn't seem to appreciate that. Perhaps he should have just told her the truth. would have scared the hell out of her, though, and possibly with real justification.

There had been no proof that anyone had deliberately killed An brose. Flint was surprised the rumors of murder were strong enough to reach all the way to Dewhurst. Even the police hadn't been concerned about the possibility that the accident was anything more than what it seemed. Still, the fact remained that Dewhurst had heard it somewhere and had called Rani to warn her.

The whole thing had disintegrated into an idiotic mess because he'd mishandled everything that first night. Flint groaned and took a swallow of beer. He should have told her the facts right at the beginning.

But if he had done that she would never have felt comfortable or relaxed around him. At best she might have treated him like a professional bodyguard. She would have tried to keep the relationship on a businesslike basis. At worst she would have fled back to her safe, secure world, leaving him to chase after her and try to convince her to let him into her life. As a handyman-gardener who was trying to write an article on the side, Flint knew he was a lot less threatening to her than if he'd walked in the front door and told her he was there to protect her from her uncle's murderer.

Perhaps he'd taken the selfish route, but in retrospect Flint was inclined to think that, given the same situation, he would have done things the same way. He had known the moment she'd opened the door to him during the storm that Rani wasn't going to be just another job. He had known she was going to change his whole life.

When a man found a woman capable of changing his entire life, he probably didn't think as clearly as he would under normal circumstances. Maybe he'd behaved like an ass.

The real question tonight was whether Rani had settled down and really thought about the evening's events. Flint stood silently at the window, drinking the beer and reflecting on his own stupidity.

Rani was wide awake, lying quietly in bed and staring at the play of shadows on the ceiling when she became aware of the familiar figure of a man standing in the garden outside her window. Zipp jumped lightly off the bed and bounded up onto the windowsill. Ducking inside the sheer curtains, he pressed his nose to the glass and meowed inquiringly.

On the other side of the window, Flint didn't move for a moment. Then he put out his hands and calmly opened the window. Rani watched with a curious fascination as the window was raised. The Andersons really should hire a handyman to fix the broken lock, she thought.

"Hello, Zipp." Flint made no move to enter the room. He leaned inside the open window, letting chilled air into the room as he casually scratched the cat's ears. Zipp purred loudly for a moment and then something caught his attention. He dived through the window and disappeared. Flint continued to lean into the room, his elbows resting on the sill. "You awake?" he asked quietly.

"I'm awake."

There was a silence for another moment and then he said carefully. "I've been thinking."

"So have I."

"About the same things, I wonder?"

"I have no idea," she murmured. Rani felt as if she were back in the dreamlike atmosphere that had enveloped her earlier in the evening. Nothing seemed quite real except for Flint's inescapable presence.

"You're not going to make this easy for me, are you, Rani?"

"What do you want me to do?"

He exhaled slowly. "I'm afraid to ask. That may not seem strange to you, but it is to me. I can't remember the last time I was afraid to ask for something that was important."

He probably couldn't remember the last time he'd ever actually asked for something politely in the first place, Rani decided with a detached sort of amusement. Like Zipp, Flint was far more accustomed to simply taking what he wanted. "Why are you afraid this time?"

In the moonlight his bare shoulders lifted in a self-deprecatory shrug. "Because I'm nervous about the answer, I guess. Most things aren't this important."

Rani didn't know what to say to that. She sensed the honesty of his words, but she wasn't sure what to do next. All her life she had been careful. Only this man had the ability to make her reckless. From her point of view that represented a truly awesome power. The safe course of action was to keep him at a distance. But Rani wasn't even sure she had that option any longer. She had been doing a great deal of thinking during the past couple of hours and some conclusions were unavoidable. "Am I really that important to you, Flint?" she heard herself ask gently.

He looked at her through the shadows. "If you weren't important, I probably wouldn't have screwed things up this badly. Rani, I need to know if you've thought about what else happened earlier."

"I've thought of little else."

Flint hesitated. "Did you realize exactly what happened tonight after the phone call?"

It was her turn to hesitate. "I realized I didn't react the way I should have reacted under the circumstances," she finally admitted.

He nodded. "You were madder than hell and a little confused, but you didn't really believe I was the murderer."

"It did cross my mind initially," she managed to point out dryly. He wasn't going to have it all his own way.

Flint came through the window, slipping into the darkened room like a cat returning from an evening's hunt. "It may have crossed your mind, but you weren't worried about that aspect for very long, were you? Why not, Rani? It was the logical assumption. Dewhurst had just told you that someone was after the ring. You know nothing about me except what I've told you." Flint moved over to the bed and stood looking down at her. "So why didn't you call the cops the second I left?"

"Maybe it was nothing more than female pride that kept me from doing it," she retorted.

"Pride?" That took him back. It wasn't the answer he'd been expecting.

"I might not have wanted to admit to myself or the sheriff that I'd been having an affair with a murderer."

Flint sat down on the edge of the bed, his weight making a heavy impression on the mattress. He rested his elbows on his knees, his hands clasped loosely in front of him. "You really aren't going to make this easy for me, are you?"

"What do you want me to say, Flint? That I've been lying here realizing I couldn't suspect you as a murderer because of the way you make love to me? That I'm far too involved with you to let myself believe you're a danger to me? That all my feminine instincts tell me I can trust you? That deep down I believe you intended no harm, that you only wanted to protect me? Is that the sort of thing you want to hear me say?''

He inclined his head but didn't turn to look at her. ''Something like that.''

''Ah,'' she said knowingly. ''Perhaps that wasn't quite as much as you wanted. Maybe you wanted to hear a little more.''

''Such as?''

''Such as I'm probably falling in love with you and that's the real reason I couldn't possibly believe you're a danger to me?'' Her voice was a soft whisper of sound in the darkness. She wasn't sure he heard until he moved.

''Rani.'' Her name was a deep sigh of masculine relief. He came down beside her on the bed, gathering her into his arms and holding her fiercely against his bare chest. He buried his face in her hair. ''Oh, God, Rani.''

''You're cold,'' she heard herself say, touching him with a sense of wonder. ''What on earth were you doing running around outside without a jacket?''

''I was hoping you'd let me warm up in your bed,'' he said into her hair. He stroked her with his big, callused hand. ''Are you falling in love with me, sweetheart?''

''Does it matter?''

''It matters. I want you to love me, Rani. I want it very much. swear I'll take care of you.''

''You keep saying that.''

''I mean it.''

Rani sighed, relaxing against him. ''I know.''

''You trust me?''

''I don't seem to have much choice,'' she admitted.

''Maybe neither one of us has a choice.'' His mouth closed ove hers with a heavy, dark need. The deep kiss was both an act of claim ing and an act of gratitude.

She should be more afraid of the power he had over her, Rani tol herself as her lips parted beneath the pressure of his. But there was n way she could ever really fear this man, and she knew it now. It wa the unavoidable, inescapable conclusion she had reached as she ha laid alone in the darkness thinking about the evening's events.

She knew with a sure, womanly instinct that Flint Cottrell was th man fate had chosen to teach her about the reckless, uninhibited powe of passion and love.

Nine

The sun was forging an unsteady path between a coalescing mass of gray clouds when Rani stirred into wakefulness the next morning. She knew Flint was already wide awake beside her, although he hadn't disturbed her by moving. He was like Zipp in a lot of ways, she thought in sleepy amusement. There was a lazy alertness about him that seemed to be part of his basic makeup even when he was sound asleep.

She turned in his arms, and Flint stretched luxuriously. "What I'd really like to know," he announced, leaning over to kiss her, "is what Amors Dewhurst actually heard."

"That's not the first thing you're supposed to say in the morning."

Flint propped himself on his elbow and rested one hand possessively on her breast. He tilted a lazy brow. "No? What am I supposed to say?"

You're supposed to say I love you, Rani thought silently. Aloud she murmured, "Something along the lines of how cute and cuddly I look in the morning, I believe."

He gave her a slow grin. "How cute and cuddly you look in the morning!" he exclaimed dutifully. "Also sexy as hell." He moved his thumb on the tip of her breast and watched with interest as the nipple reacted. Satisfied with the firming peak, he slid one foot down the calf of her leg. Then he deliberately pushed his knee between hers, his eyes never leaving her face. His hand made its way over her breast, trailing slowly toward the soft nest of hair below her flat stomach. "Very cute. Very cuddly."

"So are you. She wound her arm around his neck and pulled his head back down to hers. Flint obeyed the summons willingly, his mouth closing over hers as his fingers snagged gently in the nest he had found.

She loved the feel of his big, callused hands, Rani thought as Flint bore her back against the pillows. Such strong, careful, gentle hands. Hands that could coax a garden into shape. It was hard to remember that once she had seen a gun in those hands. He was meant to grow things, not kill things.

"You should stick to gardening," she told him in a soft whisper.

"You think I'm good at it?" He touched her intimately until she sighed and lifted herself against his hand.

"You're very good at it. Oh, *Flint*!"

Zipp roused himself in disgust, jumped down off the bed and stalked off to the kitchen to find his morning spot on the windowsill. Humans had a way of getting their priorities mixed up. This was the time of day for breakfast and a nap in the sunlight.

It was a long while before Rani and Flint joined the cat in the kitchen. When Rani finally did start breakfast for the three of them she was feeling healthy, vibrant and very much alive. Her hair was in its usual knot, and she wore a brilliant coral shirt with her jeans. The ring on her hand glinted in the morning light as she flipped pancakes.

Sitting at the kitchen table, a cup of coffee in one hand, Flint watched her with a hunger that wasn't just for the pancakes. Rani could feel his eyes on her as she worked, and the sensation was a little disquieting. It was difficult to tell sometimes exactly what Flint Cottrell was thinking. He'd spent too many years learning to conceal his emotions.

"What was it you started to say about Mr. Dewhurst this morning?" she asked, deciding to get Flint talking.

There was a slight pause behind her. "I was just wondering how Dewhurst heard the rumors about Ambrose's death. Did he say who had told him?"

Rani shook her head. "Only that there was some gossip in the trade."

"Dewhurst is a long way from the East Coast where your uncle was killed."

"True, but he was a longtime business associate of my uncle's. If there was talk about a murder, it makes sense it might have gotten back to him. He said something about a man who had been on the trail of the Clayborne ring for many years."

Flint was thoughtful. "A lot of people have wanted that ring over the years. So far as I know, none of them has wanted it badly enough to kill for it."

Rani glanced down at the gem. "How valuable is it, Flint. If this was the real thing, what do you think it would be worth?"

"Hard to say what it's value would be to a collector, but Ambrose once told me that if the stone were removed, cut up and sold a man might get somewhere in the neighborhood of a hundred grand if he knew what he was doing. Cutting up the stone would devalue it. No telling what it's worth whole."

Rani swallowed. "That's a nice neighborhood."

"Whoever cut and sold the real stone would have to know what he was doing and who he was dealing with, Rani. Not everyone has access to that kind of skill."

"My uncle would have known what to do and who to contact." Rani sighed.

"True. But Ambrose told me this was the one piece of jewelry he wasn't going to duplicate. He wanted to keep the Clayborne ring. He was fascinated by the history surrounding it. It wasn't just another pretty trinket to him."

Rani piled the pancakes on two plates and carried them over to the table. "But he still might have copied it just to protect the original."

"That's a possibility," Flint agreed, accepting his plate with the enthusiasm he reserved for Rani's cooking.

There was no doubt that he liked having her cook for him, Rani thought with concealed humor. She was a decent cook but not a great one. She doubted it was her culinary skill that appealed so much to him. It was more subtle, more primitive than that. Rani sensed it had to do with the symbolic fact that she was doing the cooking for him.

He liked eating her food because in a nonverbal way it established a very distinct, very basic bond between them. Until now Rani hadn't realized just how basic cooking for a man could be.

"Assuming that he did decide to duplicate the ring, where would he have hidden the original?" she asked, buttering her pancakes.

"I don't know." Flint munched reflectively. "A safe-deposit box that we don't know about perhaps. Somewhere in his shop. The possibilities are endless."

"But he would have wanted someone to find the ring eventually," Rani pointed out. "He wouldn't have hidden it so that no one would ever find it."

"He may not have had time to set up the hiding place and the clues." Flint forked up another bite. "We don't even know for sure he was killed because of the ring. I told you, Rani, it's just a suspicion."

"One that Dewhurst shares, apparently."

"Yeah. I'd sure like to know how he heard that particular suspicion. Maybe he knows someone who could shed some light on this mess for us."

Rani put down her fork. "What do we do now, Flint?"

"The same thing I've been doing all along. Exercise due caution for a while. If nothing happens we can assume eventually that either no one really is after the ring or that whoever is after it has heard it's a fake and is looking elsewhere."

"How long do we exercise this 'due caution'?"

"Until things feel right," Flint said casually.

Rani stared at him in astonishment. "Until they feel right? What on earth does that mean?"

"It means I'm operating on a gut feeling that I can't really justify with evidence."

She frowned. "A feeling that something is wrong?"

He nodded. "Don't worry. I've been off base before when I've had this feeling. I could be wrong this time, too."

He looked up, his gaze locking with hers. "It's all I've got to go on, Rani."

Rani couldn't think of anything to say to that.

The pattern of the day fell into its normal routine, although Rani didn't see how that was possible. Surely, after the realization she had made the previous night that she was falling in love with Flint, something significant should have changed in the environment. But everything went on as it had for the past several days. Flint seemed to have accepted with magnificent calm what to her was a momentous discovery. It was rather irritating.

It was late in the afternoon when Rani decided to run into town to check the post office and pick up some items for dinner. She wandered out into the garden to find Flint. He was coiling a hose near a stack of gardening tools when she found him.

"Give me a minute to change my shirt and I'll come with you," he said.

Rani nodded pleasantly but secretly wondered if he were raising the intensity of the watch he had decided to keep on her. Perhaps Dewhurst's call had worried him more than she'd realized. She waited while he went into the main cottage and found a fresh shirt to replace the dirt-and sweat-stained one he'd been wearing. He came out of the front door buttoning it.

"We'll take the Jeep," Flint said. He glanced down at Zipp who was sitting in the doorway. The cat looked up expectantly. "You're going to have to stay here, Zipp. Keep an eye on things for us," Flint closed the cat inside the house and locked the front door. "What have you got planned for dinner?" he asked Rani, automatically checking the lock.

"Sometimes I think you have a one-track mind." She followed him to the Jeep and climbed in beside him.

"Two tracks," he corrected with a grin as he turned the key in the Jeep's ignition.

"Food and sex?"

"I like to keep life simple."

He guided the Jeep out onto the narrow road that led toward the town of Reed Lake. Rani liked his driving. He brought to it the same competent, relaxed skill he brought to his gardening. She studied him out of the corner of her eye as he maneuvered the vehicle along the twisting, winding road. There were so many things she still didn't know about the man. How was it possible that he had so easily captured her heart when she had guarded it so carefully for so long?

"What are you thinking?" Flint demanded, shifting gears for a curve.

Rani moved restlessly in the seat and glanced out the window. "That it looks as though it's going to rain this evening." It was only a small lie, after all. And it did look as though a storm were brewing. The sky had been gray and overcast all day. Now the clouds seemed heavier, and the wind was definitely chilly. She should have brought along a jacket.

Flint found a space in front of the Reed Lake Post Office and followed Rani inside. Mrs. Hobson looked at both of them with interest as she handed over Rani's small stack of mail.

"Not much today, I'm afraid. How are things going out at the Anderson place?" the older woman inquired cheerfully. She looked from one to the other, obviously trying to determine just what was happening at the Anderson place.

"Fine, thank you." Rani flipped through the letters, ignoring the woman's curiosity. Mrs. Hobson wasn't going to rest until she had established the facts of the situation. Let her guess, Rani thought. It'll give her something to do. She wondered if she and Flint were providing the chief source of entertainment and speculation for the folks of Reed Lake these days. There wasn't all that much to do in the town.

Mrs. Hobson was persistent, however. She smiled brightly up at Flint. "That's a nice ring, Rani has. Did you give it to her?"

"No." Flint's total lack of interest was barely concealed behind a semblance of politeness. "It's a family ring."

"Oh, I see." Mrs. Hobson's obvious satisfaction made Rani smile. The woman had been fishing to find out just how scandalous the situation was at the Anderson place. Now she knew the ring was not a symbol of an engagement. That would make whatever was going on that much more interesting. "It's a lovely stone," Mrs. Hobson observed.

"Thank you." Rani picked up her mail.

"Not real, is it? I mean, an emerald that large…?"

Rani chuckled. "No, it's not real. Nicely cut glass."

Mrs. Hobson frowned thoughtfully, her interest switching from gossip to something of a more professional nature. "Glass? Mind if I take a closer look? I wouldn't have guessed it was glass. Perhaps another sort of green gem. There are plenty of green-colored stones besides emeralds, you know. Few of them have such good color, though.''

Rani shrugged and slipped the ring off her finger. She handed it over the counter. Mrs. Hobson whipped out the jeweler's loupe, which she kept next to her collection of quartz. She popped it onto her glasses over her right eye and peered down at the object in her hand. ''Hmmm.''

''What do you think, Mrs. Hobson?'' Rani asked indulgently.

There was a long silence while Mrs. Hobson studied the ring. At last she looked up, frowning in concentration. ''You're quite sure this isn't an emerald?''

Rani's pulse suddenly picked up speed. Behind her she could feel Flint's almost palpable alertness. ''I was told it was paste.''

''Well, I'm no expert,'' Mrs. Hobson said, ''but I can tell you for certain this isn't glass.''

''Perhaps another sort of green stone?'' Rani suggested carefully.

''If I had to take a bet,'' Mrs Hobson said casually, ''I'd say it was a genuine emerald.''

Rani realized she had forgotten to breathe for a few seconds. Flint was silent. Slowly Rani extended her hand and took back the ring. 'Good heavens, Mrs. Hobson. If you really think there's a possibility it's genuine, perhaps I'd better get it reappraised.''

''Wouldn't hurt. Unless you're quite sure of the facts,'' Mrs. Hobson said with a quick nod.

''No, I'm not absolutely positive of the facts. As Flint said, it's a family ring and everyone just assumed it was fake.''

''I could be wrong, of course,'' Mrs. Hobson remarked. ''After all, my specialty is quartz. But it might be a good idea to have a real jeweler take a look at it.''

''Thank you, Mrs. Hobson. I believe I'll do that.'' Rani turned blindly and nearly collided with Flint. He reached out to steady her, his gaze intent.

''We still have to stop by the grocery store,'' he reminded her. ''Good-bye, Mrs. Hobson.'' He guided Rani outside where the smell of rain was now in the air. ''Don't look so shocked,'' he drawled. ''If the ring is real, it would explain a lot of things.''

''It doesn't explain why Charles Dewhurst told me it was paste.''

"No," Flint said thoughtfully. "It doesn't."

They stopped at the grocery store to allow Rani to collect frozen ravioli and the makings for a cheese sauce. It was starting to sprinkle by the time they returned to the Jeep. Rani sat on the passenger side, studying the ring on her hand.

"I don't see any green fire," she complained.

"What green fire?" Flint swung the Jeep back onto the road.

"Dewhurst said that in a true emerald the inner light was quite striking. He said it was like looking into green fire."

"Maybe a gem expert sees things in stones the rest of us don't," Flint suggested dryly. "Or maybe he lied."

"Yes. Maybe he lied." Rani turned her head. "But why would he do that, Flint?"

"I don't know."

"If he'd been after the emerald he could have stolen it when I gave the ring to him to be valued."

"How? As soon as you discovered the loss you would have known exactly who'd stolen it. How long did he have Ambrose's collection?"

"Not long. Just for one afternoon."

Flint thought about it. "He wouldn't have had time to duplicate the emerald. No, he didn't have any choice except to give the ring back to you."

"Why tell me it was a fake?" she demanded. Then she came up with an answer to her own question. "Unless he didn't want me to think it was valuable. That way if I should happen to 'lose' it, wouldn't make too big a fuss."

"Yeah. An interesting notion."

"Flint, I've got news for you. I don't find it interesting at all. I find it scary."

"You're not the only one," he responded grimly as he swung the Jeep around a curve.

"What do we do now?" Rani asked.

"I think we'd better see about getting the police involved. I'm not sure what they can do. There still isn't much to go on, but maybe they'll have some ideas. We're sure as hell going to get that ring off your hand and into a safe-deposit box."

The rain was beginning to fall in earnest by the time Flint pulled the Jeep into the driveway of the front cottage. "Wait here until I get the front door open or you'll get soaked waiting on the porch," he said, reaching into the back seat for one of the bags of groceries. "I've got to do something about that leaking porch roof."

Hoisting the bag in one hand, Flint hurried up the steps of the porch, flipped through the keys on his chain and shoved the appropriate one into the lock.

He stopped dead on the threshold, realizing that the key had found no resistance. The door was already unlocked.

The next thing he noticed was that Zipp wasn't waiting impatiently on the other side of the door. The third thing he noticed was the odd silence in the cottage. Everything felt wrong.

"Stay where you are, Rani," he called very casually. "I'll bring an umbrella."

She had one leg out of the Jeep and was waiting with a grocery bag in her arms to make the dash for the house. "It's all right, Flint, I don't mind getting a little wet."

"I said, stay there." This time he put enough command into the words to make her blink. Setting the bag down on the porch, he loped down the short flight of steps and over to the Jeep. When he grabbed her arm, she looked up at him in astonishment. She was opening her mouth to protest the high handed action, but he already had her out of the Jeep.

"Flint, the groceries!" The bag fell from her arm, falling onto the wet, graveled drive. A can of tuna fish rolled under the wheel of the Jeep. "What in the world? What do you think you're doing?"

Flint ignored the confused demands. He was already running, dragging her along with him into the shelter of the surrounding woods. "Don't argue. Just move, Rani."

He sent up a silent prayer of thanks when she closed her mouth and obeyed. Flint didn't slow until they were into a stand of old fir. Huge branches cascaded to the ground like the skirts of formal ball gowns. He sought temporary refuge behind one grand dame. Rani was panting as he brought her to a halt. She looked questioningly up at him, her eyes wide with a silent demand for answers. The rain was pelting down heavily. Both of them were already quite wet. There was no sound from the direction of the cottage.

"Zipp didn't come to the door," Flint said starkly.

"So what? He often doesn't come to the door when there are strangers around—" She broke off, looking shaken as the full implications came home to her. "Oh, my God. I see what you mean. But, Flint, he might be outside or something."

"In this rain? You know cats and rain. Besides, I realized when I put the key in the lock that the door was already open."

"I remember you locking it," she whispered. "Do you think someone's been inside the cottage?"

"I think there's a possibility that someone has not only searched it, but that he's still in there. That's why Zipp is in hiding somewhere."

She stiffened under his hand. "I've heard you're not supposed to walk in on burglars. They tend to panic and get violent. But, Flint, by now whoever's in there must know we're gone. Why hasn't he come out? Where's his car? Maybe he's already left."

"I have a feeling he's still in there." Flint could barely see the corner of the porch when he peered through the branches of the old fir. "Stay here, Rani. I'm going back to have a look."

"The hell you are," she retorted. "We're both getting out of here."

He felt a stab of amusement at the sharpness of her tone. "You're cute when you're giving orders. I like to think it's because you care."

"Flint, I'm not joking. We have to get out of here and get the sheriff if you think there's a chance someone's in the house."

"I want to make a try for something that, like an idiot, I left behind."

"What? The groceries? Don't be ridiculous, Flint."

"Not the groceries. The gun. It's in the Jeep."

"Oh, my God. Flint, I don't think that's a good idea."

He glanced at her, debating how much to tell her. There wasn't time to go into details, and if he told her what he suspected she would only be more alarmed than she already was. How could he explain that he didn't think whoever was in the cottage would allow them to casually walk back to Reed Lake to get help?

"I'll be right back, Rani. Don't move."

She tightened her lips but said nothing. Flint patted her hand a little awkwardly and then slipped out from the cover of the huge fir. Hugging the shelter of the trees, he approached the house from an oblique angle. He tried to avoid coming into full view of anyone who might have been watching from a window.

But the last few yards between himself and the Jeep were devoid of any cover. He had to choose between making a dash for the driver's side or giving up the project altogether. Silently Flint crouched close to the ground, studying the quiet house and wondering if he was the victim of an overactive imagination. There was no movement from within. It was the unnatural stillness that bothered him the most. It was a waiting kind of stillness.

A hunter's stillness.

Flint made his decision. He ran for the Jeep, heading for the cover of the driver's side. The rifle shot cracked overhead just as he broke cover. Whirling in midair, Flint threw himself back into the trees, hitting the ground hard.

So much for the heroic dash to the Jeep. There was no way he could cross that open ground without getting shot. Accepting the inevitable, he picked himself up and ran back to where he had left Rani. Behind him he thought he heard the front door of the cottage open.

Flint saw a splash of color before he saw Rani and groaned silently as he realized her bright coral shirt was as vivid as a beacon. She was waiting with anxious eyes as he came through the low-hanging branches. He paused only long enough to grab her arm and start running again.

Rani felt his fingers close around her upper arm and staggered awkwardly to her feet. "No gun?"

"No gun."

"I heard that rifle shot. It wasn't just a hunter's shot, was it?"

"It was a hunter, all right, but not the usual kind. Get that shirt off, Rani."

She glanced down at herself. "But, Flint…"

"You can see it for yards. Don't you have any neutral colors in your wardrobe?"

"No."

"Get it off."

She fumbled frantically with the buttons as she ran. "Where are we going? The road?"

"Too obvious. If there was more traffic we might stand a chance of getting someone's attention, but I haven't heard a single car go by since we got back here. Let me have the shirt.''

Mutely she tugged it off, vividly conscious of the lacy scrap of her bra. The rain was cold as it hit her bare skin. Flint took the bright shirt from her hand just as they topped a small rise and started down toward a tiny meadow filled with ancient, twisted manzanita shrubs.

They slowed, sticking to the edge of the meadow as they circled it. On the far side Flint stopped.

"What now?" Rani asked, glancing anxiously back through the woods. She could see nothing. Between the heavy rain and the thick stands of fir and pine, visibility was severely impaired. One could be grateful. "Do you think he's following us?"

"It's what I would do if I were in his shoes." Flint was arranging the coral shirt in the branches of a fir.

"Maybe he won't be able to figure out which way we've gone. This rain will make it hard to track us," Rani pointed out.

"We're going to have to assume he's a professional."

"A professional what?" she gasped. "Killer?"

"If he's not a professional, he'll be desperate. Either way, he'll be coming after us. He must realize by now that I'm not armed." Flint finished his work with the shirt and led Rani deeper into the woods. They crouched down in a small dip in the ground that was ringed by trees. Rani felt wet needles sticking unpleasantly into her bare skin. The small bra offered no protection from the elements or the terrain.

"Now what?" Rani asked again. She seemed to be asking that a lot today.

"Now we wait."

It occurred to Rani that the guy with the rifle wasn't the only professional in the vicinity. She cast a quick, curious glance at Flint's hard profile. He knew what he was doing and that was a frightening thought in and of itself.

"How long do we wait?" she asked quietly.

"Hush, Rani. Not another word." He pulled away from her, signaling her to stay put.

She watched as he slithered across the wet needles, realizing he was doubling back to the far side of the meadow. Holding herself very still

Rani tried to ignore the coldness of the rain and the way the green stone on her hand seemed to mock her.

The silence stretched out with unmerciful tension, broken only by the ceaseless drumming of the rain in the trees. The world seemed composed entirely of green and gray. Dusk was settling slowly, augmented by the weather. Visibility was becoming worse by the minute.

Rani was beginning to wonder if the horrible afternoon would ever end when she heard the crack of the rifle. The sound jolted her. She hugged herself tightly as another shot echoed through the storm.

The second shot was followed by a shout of mingled anger and surprise. Startled, Rani lifted her head and stared through the trees in the direction of the meadow. Two men were on the ground on the far side, twisting in a tangle of arms and legs. She knew at once what had happened.

When the gunman had paused at the edge of the manzanita meadow, he must have caught sight of the coral shirt among the branches. He'd gotten off two shots before Flint had jumped him.

There was an eerie absence of sound from the two men as they flailed savagely on the ground. Frantically Rani dashed forward into the meadow and across it.

She arrived in time to see Flint straddle his opponent and launch a brutal fist straight into Mike Slater's jaw. Slater's eyes rolled back into his head, and his body went very still.

Ten

"Don't say it," Flint ordered as Rani followed him out of the trees and back into the driveway of the cottage.

"Say what?" she demanded.

"That he seemed like such a nice man."

"Well, he did. A very pleasant, artistic type. I liked him, Flint."

"With one glaring exception, you've got lousy taste in men."

She grinned in spite of herself. "Who's the glaring exception?"

"Me."

"Oh, of course." She sobered thoughtfully. "Do you think he'll be okay tied up back there with our belts?"

"Are you afraid he'll drown in this rain?"

Rani thought of the unconscious man Flint had left secured in the woods. "I wasn't worried about that. I was just afraid he might get away."

"It would take him hours to work through those belts even if he wakes up in a condition to make the effort. We'll be back with the authorities by then." Flint glanced around the yard. He was carrying Slater's rifle with the same casual expertise he used to drive the Jeep or work in the garden. "I don't see Zipp."

"He probably hightailed it when Slater walked into the house. It might be sometime before he reappears." Rani straightened the soaking wet coral shirt she was wearing. "I'm cold, Flint. You must be freezing, too. Both of us need a shower."

"First I'm going to call the local authorities. There are a hell of a lot of questions that need answering. When Slater wakes up, I want those answers. You can take a shower while I'm on the phone." He shoved open the door and stood aside for her to enter.

Rani frowned up into his lean, lined face. "At least put on some dry clothing. I don't want you catching pneumonia."

A faint smile flared briefly in his green gaze. "Yes ma'am. Right after I call the sheriff's office."

She sighed and started down the hall. Flint could be as stubborn as Zipp at times. She was going to have to work at finding a suitable way of managing him. Currently her methods were too unreliable. Sometimes they worked and sometimes they didn't.

Rani rounded the corner of the bedroom and nearly collided with Charles Dewhurst.

He was clearly as rattled by the near collision as she was, but Dewhurst had a distinct advantage. He was holding a small pistol in one hand.

"Don't move!" he hissed in a sharp whisper, pointing the weapon at her as if it were a magic wand. "Don't move an inch."

Rani froze, her eyes going from the gun to Dewhurst's nervous but fiercely determined expression. "Mr. Dewhurst, I don't understand," she managed weakly. "What are you doing here?"

"Take a wild guess," he snapped. "Turn around and walk ahead of me down the hall."

"I'm getting sick and tired of guns being pointed in my direction."

"Shut up!" He prodded her with his gun as she reluctantly turned and started back down the hall to the living room.

There was no sound from the other room. Flint obviously hadn't had a chance to dial the sheriff's number yet. Even as she watched, he appeared silently at the far end of the hall, the rifle in his hand. She said nothing as Dewhurst prodded Rani again.

"I want the ring, of course," Dewhurst said tightly. He reached out and wrapped an arm around Rani's neck, pulling her back against him.

"Sure," Flint agreed quietly. "It was you all along, wasn't it?

You're the mysterious man on the trail of the Clayborne ring. Did you hire Slater to do the dirty work back East as well as here?''

"He was a fool. I thought he knew what he was doing. But he failed both times. Oh, he managed to kill Ambrose, all right, but he didn't get the ring. The whole point was to get the ring. But Ambrose had already taken care to see that it was safe. I was so close and he beat me again. For years Ambrose and I have chased the Clayborne ring. When I learned he had finally gotten his hands on it, I couldn't believe it. He didn't deserve it. He had no right to it. He made his living *copying stones*, for God's sake. He made fakes. *Paste.* When he held the real thing in his hands his only interest was in duplicating it and selling the original. The man had no ability to appreciate true gems. What right did he have to something like the Clayborne ring? He wasn't worthy of that beautiful stone with all its history.''

"After the screwup back East you had to bide your time, didn't you?'' Flint murmured.

"It was a long wait, but it was worth it when I convinced Ambrose' heir to bring the collection to me to be valued. She thought I was merely doing her a favor! I saw at once that Ambrose hadn't had time or inclination to copy the ring. Once I knew where it was again I could take my time planning a way to get it. Put down that rifle or I'll kill her, Cottrell. Go on, put it down.''

Slowly Flint lowered the rifle, his eyes never leaving Dewhurst. "When Slater told you I was on the scene you couldn't figure out what was going on, could you? So you played a wild card and tried telling Rani someone was after the ring. You hoped she'd get scared and assume it was me.''

"It would have been a logical assumption. As far as we could figure out, she didn't know much about you. After all, you're just a handy man.''

"Yeah, I'm supposed to be that, all right.''

Rani broke into the tense conversation. "Why did you tell me the ring was a fake, Dewhurst?''

"So you wouldn't panic and put it somewhere I couldn't get at it.''

"Somewhere like a safe-deposit box?'' she asked.

"Exactly. And you believed me. It was so easy. It was obvious you had no eye for the real thing. No appreciation for true beauty. You don't deserve the ring any more than Ambrose did. But I needed time to work out a way of getting it without drawing attention to myself. I thought at first the easiest thing to do was have Slater simply steal if from you. You'd never know who'd taken it, and since you assumed it was a fake you wouldn't get too concerned. But Slater said he was just setting up the situation, just getting close to you, when *he* showed up.'' Dewhurst indicated Flint with an aggressive movement of his chin.

''So Slater suggested staging a hunting accident,'' Flint concluded.

''That was Mike shooting at me that day in the woods?'' Rani was suddenly intensely angry.

''That incompetent couldn't even handle a simple hunting accident,'' Dewhurst raged. ''When he blew that, I decided I'd better come up here and take charge. We've been biding our time, Slater and I. Waiting for an opportunity. Slater was supposed to take care of this end of things but, as usual, he obviously failed. Luckily I was prepared for that contingency.''

Rani could hear the older man's breath coming too quickly in his chest. The arm around her neck was rigid with tension. She guessed he'd never been faced with dealing out real violence himself. It was a different proposition from that of hiring a professional such as Slater.

''Back up, Cottrell. Slowly. Back into the living room. Stay where I can keep an eye on you.'' Dewhurst hustled Rani ahead of him, still locking her close with his arm.

''It won't work, Dewhurst.'' Flint spoke calmly, as if discussing whether to plant roses or azaleas. ''Slater has made too much of a mess of things. Your best bet is to get out of here. If I were you, I'd leave the country.''

''There won't be any need for me to leave the country,'' Dewhurst said dangerously. ''And I'm not going anywhere without the ring. I've searched for it too long. Take it off, Rani. Put it down on the table.''

''I get the feeling you're going to kill us anyway, so why should I cooperate?''

''Damn you, you little bitch! Take off that ring. It's mine!''

Dewhurst tightened his hold around Rani's throat, shaking her in an excess of tension and fury. Rani staggered in his grasp. Dewhurst struggled to regain his balance. Out of the corner of her eye, Rani

caught a flash of movement down around her feet. There was a star-
tling screech that could only have come from an enraged cat, and
Dewhurst jerked backward in instinctive reaction. He had stepped on
Zipp's tail. Zipp dashed back into the kitchen where he'd been hiding.

Rani didn't hesitate. She could feel her captor struggling to rebal-
ance himself. It was the only chance she was going to get. She swung
her hand upward, palm out, and slashed the huge ring across the side
of Dewhurst's face. The man yelled, twisting his head to avoid the
painful swipe; Rani shoved at him and they both lost their balance.

The gun in Dewhurst's hand roared in Rani's ear, temporarily deaf-
ening her. She felt herself falling and then she was free of her tormentor's hold as Flint moved with lethal grace to end the chaotic
scene.

Rani looked up at Flint from her position on the floor. He was
pinning Charles Dewhurst's arms. Rani assayed a shaky smile that held
her bubbling relief. "You're very useful around the house, Flint."

It seemed hours before the mess was cleared up to a reasonable
extent. The authorities responded quickly enough, but it took time to
go through the paperwork and to explain the bizarre situation. Rani
and Flint did learn in the process that the man who had called himself
Mike Slater was also known as Lawrence Carmichael and was wanted
under that name in several states.

Rani and Flint had a late snack, which they shared with a disgruntled
Zipp and they fell into bed. There was no passionate lovemaking that
night. Both of them were asleep almost instantly. It wasn't until Rani
stretched languidly awake in Flint's arms the next morning that she
suspected something was wrong. He was wide awake, as usual, waiting
quietly for her to open her eyes.

"What is it?" she asked softly, sensing a different sort of stillness
in him that morning. She touched him lightly, aware of a tension within
herself.

"I've been thinking."

Rani closed her eyes, afraid of what was coming. It was much too
soon. Sooner than she had expected. But she would not cry. She had
known this moment would arrive sooner or later and *she would not
cry*. She had lived with the knowledge in the back of her mind since

e had met Flint Cottrell. You couldn't hold a free-ranging alley cat
he didn't want to stay.

"I guess I was hoping for later," she whispered.

Flint shifted to look down at her. She felt his fingers under her chin
ting her face. Bravely she opened her eyes, her lashes damp with
shed tears.

"You're crying," he accused softly.

"No. I told myself I wouldn't cry."

"Please don't cry, Rani."

She tried a tiny smile. "I won't."

"What did you mean, you hoped for later?" he demanded urgently.

"I was hoping that you'd choose to hang around a while longer. I
ew you'd leave sooner or later. I'd hoped for later."

He swore softly. "I knew it. That's exactly what I've been thinking
out this morning. Damn it, Rani."

"It's all right, Flint. I'm a big girl and I've known all along what
s coming. I was prepared for this when I took my risk."

"It is not all right," he snapped. "*I've* known all along you didn't
st me to stay. It's been driving me crazy."

"It's not a question of trust. It's a question of understanding," she
tested gently. "I do understand, Flint. Honest."

"The hell you do. Listen to me, Rani Garroway, and listen good.
 not leaving. I can't leave. I don't want to leave. Can't you get it
ough your stubborn little head that I'm home now? You couldn't
 rid of me if you tried."

Frantically she tried to stifle the flare of hope that was threatening
overwhelm her. "You're not leaving now that you've done your
y by my uncle?"

'Now you're finally catching on. Rani, I came here because of a
ling that I owed Ambrose something. I'd been too late to protect
, but I thought I might be able to protect his niece. But that's not
y I'm staying. I want a home with you, Rani. Now do you under-
d?"

She smiled tremulously. "Let's just say I'm more than willing to
convinced."

He sighed. "That's what I was thinking about just now. Convincing
."

"Oh, Flint, I didn't mean it that way," she said anxiously, terrif
that he'd misunderstood her tiny attempt at lightness.

"No, you're absolutely right. You deserve to be convinced."

"Flint, wait a minute, you don't understand."

He shook his head, leaning back against the pillow. Rani recogni
with dismay the stubborn, set expression in his emerald eyes. "I
going to take the time to convince you, Rani. According to the lege
of the ring, the other men who found themselves in my situation ev
tually took drastic action. They forced their women into marriage.
I'm not going to do it that way. This isn't a legend we're living he
it's for real. I want things done properly. I don't want to push y
I'll show you I know what I'm doing and that I'm here to stay.
prove you can trust me."

"How?" She was deeply wary now.

"We'll go back to Santa Rosa, your town, your neighborhood.
get a regular job. A nine-to-five job. Something with a real desk
an office copier. A job with benefit plans and retirement plans and
leave. I can find one. Hell, I can do just about anything. I'll show
I'm capable of taking care of a family and that I've got the deter
nation to stick around for the long haul. In a few months, when
settled into the routine and you're confident I'm not going to disap
in the middle of the night, we'll get married. In a year or two, w
you're really convinced I'm reliable, we can talk about having a
I'd like a child, Rani, but I realize a woman has to be sure of a
before she takes that kind of risk. All along I've wanted you to
a risk on me, but I know it's not fair of me to ask you to do that
I've given you some evidence that I'm going to make a depend
husband and father."

"Flint…"

"The thing is, Rani," he went on very seriously, "we re
shouldn't wait too long to have a kid. I'm getting close to forty
you've just turned thirty. Biological clocks and all that stuff, you kn
We won't be able to postpone it too long. Do you think it will
too long for me to prove myself to you?"

Rani leaned over him, her eyes very brilliant with her love. "F
there is absolutely no need to go through all of that. If you say yo

going to stay, that's all the proof I need. I love you, Cottrell. I trust you.'' She brushed her mouth against his, willing him to respond.

''I love you, Rani.''

His voice was husky and weighted with emotion. Rani could have sworn there was a trace of dampness in the emerald fires of his eyes. The thought fascinated her. She nestled close, offering comfort and love as Flint's big hand stroked heavily through her tangled hair. He kissed her with a deep need and a promise that filled her with hope and trust in the future. He did love her. Rani was certain of it.

''Can we get married now?'' she demanded teasingly as Flint slowly broke the kiss.

''In a few months,'' he said firmly. ''When you're sure of me.''

''Flint, please, there's no need for this.''

''This is the best way, Rani.''

''According to you! Flint, this is crazy,'' Rani said, knowing already she was virtually helpless against the stubborn streak in him.

''Trust me, Rani.''

''I don't seem to have any choice,'' she said unhappily. ''There's just one thing I won't tolerate, Flint Cottrell.''

He smiled crookedly. ''What's that?''

''No nine-to-five desk job for you. I can't see you behind a desk.''

''What would you suggest?''

''I suggest,'' she said, ''that you find a job doing what you do best.''

Two months later Flint pushed open the small wrought-iron gate and started up the garden walk of his new home. He examined the gingerbread trim around the windows as he climbed the porch steps. He'd finished painting it the day before and was pleased with the way it looked. The next step was the plumbing. A man could devote a lifetime to plumbing repairs if he wasn't careful. But women were fussy about good plumbing. He couldn't ask Rani to move in until he got the kitchen remodeled and the new shower installed. Another month or two would give him time to take care of the basics. Then he could talk seriously to Rani about taking the risk of marrying him.

The old Victorian house had been in a very dilapidated condition when he'd found it. The owners had given him an incredible deal, and

Flint had grabbed it. He was good at grabbing an opportunity when
arose. He'd moved out of his apartment and into the old house at onc

Flint liked the neighborhood. It wasn't far from Rani's place, ar
there was plenty of space around the house for a garden. He liked th
town, too. Santa Rosa was a good size but not overcrowded. Th
mountains were near, and San Francisco could be reached in an hour'
drive. A good town for raising kids and flowers. Flint stood on th
porch, surveying his domain with a satisfied gaze. Everything wa
falling into place very nicely. Soon, another couple of months at mos
everything would be perfect.

Rani had been persistent at first, trying everything from logic
tantrums to convince him to at least let her move in with him. B
Flint had stood firm. He had insisted Rani stay in her own place durir
what he called his trial period. True, he saw her nearly every evenir
for dinner and frequently spent the night, but he thought he'd manage
to keep the affair as free of outright coercion as possible. He wante
her to be sure of him. He wanted her to trust him completely befo
he took the final step. In another couple of months he thought sh
would have enough evidence of his new, domesticated ways.

Pleased with himself, Flint unlocked the front door, stepped insic
the hall and nearly tripped over Zipp. The cat sat on his haunche
meowing quietly in welcome. Flint stood stock-still, staring down
the big animal.

"What are you doing here, Zipp?"

Before the cat could answer, Flint caught an aroma of a rich fi:
stew wafting down the hall from the old kitchen. Curiously he walke
forward, Zipp at his heels.

"Rani?"

She looked up from the salad she was preparing on the cracke
drainboard and smiled brilliantly. She was wearing a loud crimso
and-yellow sweater over a pair of black trousers and, as always, sl
looked sexy and sweet. God, how he loved her, Flint thought even
he narrowed his eyes in a reproving frown.

"Hello, Flint." She dropped the spinach leaves and came forwa
to kiss him lightly on the mouth. Then she returned industriously
her salad. "How are things at the nursery?"

"Fine. The shipment of Christmas trees arrived from that suppli in Reed Lake,'' he said automatically. ''Just in time. And we got the fancy tulip bulbs from Holland today. I've got a long line of customers waiting for them.'' He directed his gaze pointedly at the salad. ''Rani, what are you doing here? We're supposed to have dinner at your place tonight. I just came home to change my clothes.''

She scanned his dirt-stained jeans. ''Yes, why don't you do that? You've got potting soil all over you.'' She began slicing mushrooms. ''I'll pour us both a glass of wine while you're washing up.''

He hesitated, aware of a distinct feeling of being gently manipulated. This was the first time Rani had cooked a meal in his new house. The place wasn't ready for her. Unable to think of quite what to do about the change of plans, Flint decided the simplest thing was to wash up as she had instructed. He went down the hall to the bathroom.

Stepping inside, he realized Rani had changed more than just the evening's dinner plans. There was a new toothbrush standing beside his own in the glass that sat on the chipped sink. When he opened the cabinet, he found an array of feminine items inside that certainly didn't belong to him. He stood scowling at a pink deodorant bottle and then slowly shut the cabinet door.

He washed the traces of rich soil from his hands. Running a large professional nursery was a dirty business, but the dirt was clean. Not like some of the dirt he'd had on his hands during his former life. He'd fallen into the nursery management job with his usual luck. A little fast talking and some convincing displays of his gardening skills, as well as his management skills, had persuaded the owner, Mr. Rodriguez, that he knew what he was doing. Once he'd been sure Rani wholeheartedly approved of the work and didn't find it ''unprofessional,'' Flint had launched into the job with enthusiasm. Now Rodriguez was talking about retiring. He had inquired that day if his new manager was interested in purchasing the business. Terms could be worked out. He was a flexible man. Flint hadn't hesitated, he'd said yes immediately. Owning the nursery would speed up the approach of the day when he would feel he had a right to ask Rani to marry and move in with him. His new life was falling into place the way he'd planned.

Flint realized he thought of his life in two segments now—BR and AR. Before Rani and After Rani. He didn't waste time dwelling on the BR portion of his existence. Rani and the future were all that mattered.

Flint rinsed his hands and eyed the rest of the bathroom. Rani's hairbrush was sitting on the counter along with a red plastic comb. He dried his rough palms on a towel and left the bathroom for the bed room. A suspicion was growing steadily in his mind.

When he opened the closet doors, he knew he was right. To the right of his drab collection of work shirts and pants hung an array of brightly colored blouses, skirts and blazers. Underneath them was a neat row of sandals and high-heeled shoes. Flint just stood there, star ing, until he sensed Rani at the doorway behind him.

Slowly he turned to look at her. "You've moved in."

She nodded once, her mouth set in a determined line, although there was a faint wariness in her eyes. She held the salad tongs in front of her as if in self-defense. "I've waited long enough. I decided to use your own technique and not ask for permission. If we do things your way we might go on waiting another couple of months. I'm not inter ested in waiting any longer. I love you, Flint, and you love me. It's high time we got married."

"I wanted you to be sure of me. I didn't want you to think you had to take a risk on me."

She smiled and stepped forward, putting her arms around his neck. "I suppose you could say that just living day to day is a series of risks. I've decided some risks are much more interesting than others, however. I've waited a long time to find a man who's worth taking a chance on. Now that I've found him, I'm afraid there's hardly any risk involved at all. You, Flint Cottrell, are a sure thing."

"Do you really believe that, Rani?" He wrapped his arms around her, aware that his hands were trembling slightly.

"With all my heart," she whispered.

"*Rani.*" He caught her face between his palms and kissed her with rough eagerness. "Rani, I swear I won't let you down. Ever."

"I know," she said simply. "I swear I won't ever let you down either."

When Flint lifted his mouth from hers at last, his emerald eyes were gleaming. Rani looked wonderingly into their depths.

"Green fire," she murmured.

'What are you talking about?'' he asked with sensual humor.

'Dewhurst said that in real emeralds there was a green fire that
tured anyone who looked deeply into the stones.'' She had to admit
'd never really seen anything that qualified as fire in the Clayborne
g that presently resided in a safe-deposit box, but when she looked
) Flint's eyes she believed what Charles Dewhurst had said. ''He
s right.''

Vhen spring arrived the old Victorian house was looking very
ased with itself. It had just about everything a house could want.
ere was a large cat who spent most of his time dozing on the freshly
ated porch, a man and a woman who filled the inside with passion
 love, and a truly spectacular garden. Neighbors always stopped to
e at the velvet lawn and the unbelievable wealth of plants and
vers. Everyone agreed that the Cottrell garden was the marvel of
 neighborhood.

he article Flint Cottrell had written on the Clayborne ring was
lished in the August issue of *Legends and Fantasy* that year. The
ular magazine hit the stands the same day that Amanda Jane Cot-
l was born. She didn't know it then, but her proud parents planned
jive her a very special ring when she grew up. It had a brilliant
:n stone in it that would match her eyes.

* * * * *

Secret Passions

A spellbinding new duet
by

Miranda Lee

Desire changes everything!

Book One:

A SECRET VENGEANCE
March #2236
The price of passion is...revenge

Book Two:

THE SECRET LOVE-CHILD
April #2242
The price of passion is...a baby

HARLEQUIN®
Presents

The world's bestselling romance series.
Seduction and passion guaranteed!

*Available wherever
Harlequin books are sold.*

HARLEQUIN®
Makes any time special ®

HARLEQUIN®
Temptation®

It's hot...and it's out of control!

This spring, the forecast is hot *and* steamy!
Don't miss these bold, provocative, ultra-sexy books!

PRIVATE INVESTIGATIONS by Tori Carrington
April 2002
Secretary-turned-P.I. Ripley Logan never thought her first job
would have her running for her life—or crawling into
a stranger's bed....

ONE HOT NUMBER by Sandy Steen
May 2002
Accountant Samantha Collins may be good with numbers, but
she needs some work with men...until she meets sexy but
broke rancher Ryder Wells. Then she decides to make him a
deal—her brains for his bed. Sam's getting the better of the
deal, but hey, who's counting?

WHAT'S YOUR PLEASURE? by Julie Elizabeth Leto
June 2002
Mystery writer Devon Michaels is in a bind. Her publisher has
promised her a lucrative contract, *if* she makes the jump to
erotic thrillers. The problem: Devon can't write a love scene to
save her life. Luckily for her, Detective Jake Tanner is an
expert at "hands-on" training....

Don't miss this thrilling threesome!

HARLEQUIN®
Makes any time special®

What is your secret fantasy?

Is it to have your own love slave, to be seduced by a stranger, or to experience total sexual freedom?

Enjoy all of these and more in Blaze's newest miniseries

Heat up your nights with...

#17 EROTIC INVITATION *by Carly Phillips*
Available December 2001

#21 ACTING ON IMPULSE *by Vicki Lewis Thompson*
Available January 2002

#25 ENSLAVED *by Susan Kearney*
Available February 2002

#29 JUST WATCH ME... *by Julie Elizabeth Leto*
Available March 2002

#33 A WICKED SEDUCTION *by Janelle Denison*
Available April 2002

#37 A STRANGER'S TOUCH *by Tori Carrington*
Available May 2002

Midnight Fantasies—The nights aren't just for sleeping...

*Sometimes a marriage of convenience
can be very inconvenient...
especially when love develops!*

Terms *of* Engagement

Two full-length novels from two favorite
Harlequin® authors—at one astonishingly low

KATE HOFFMANN
MIRANDA LEE

price!

HARLEQUIN®
Makes any time special ®

Visit us at www.eHarlequin.com

BR2TOE

ROCK
THE
BOAT

ORCA limelights

ROCK THE BOAT

Sigmund Brouwer

ORCA BOOK PUBLISHERS

Library and Archives Canada Cataloguing in Publication

Brouwer, Sigmund, 1959-, author
Rock the boat / Sigmund Brouwer.
(Orca limelights)

Issued in print and electronic formats.
ISBN 978-1-4598-0455-5 (pbk.).—ISBN 978-1-4598-0456-2 (pdf).—
ISBN 978-1-4598-0457-9 (epub)

I. Title. II. Series: Orca limelights
PS8553.R68467R63 2015   jc813'.54   C2014-906600-7
C2014-906601-5

First published in the United States, 2015
Library of Congress Control Number: 2014951650

Summary: Webb thinks he has what it takes to make it
in Nashville, but one shady music producer may have the power
to crush Webb's dreams.

*Orca Book Publishers is dedicated to preserving the environment and has
printed this book on Forest Stewardship Council® certified paper.*

Orca Book Publishers gratefully acknowledges the support for
its publishing programs provided by the following agencies:
the Government of Canada through the Canada Book Fund and the
Canada Council for the Arts, and the Province of British Columbia
through the BC Arts Council and the Book Publishing Tax Credit.

Cover design by Rachel Page
Cover photography by Corbis Images

ORCA BOOK PUBLISHERS   ORCA BOOK PUBLISHERS
PO Box 5626, STN. B   PO Box 468
Victoria, BC Canada   Custer, WA USA
v8R 6s4   98240-0468

www.orcabook.com
Printed and bound in Canada.

18 17 16 15 • 4 3 2 1

To the real Jim Webb—you rock!

One

ebb was desperate to come up with some great lyrics.

The dark air felt like sweet clover.

No.

The dark air tasted like sweet clover.

No. Neither of those images was right. He wasn't sure why. The verbs maybe? *Felt* was a useless word. How about *The dark air enveloped him like sweet clover?*

Nope. It wasn't the verb's fault. Okay, *enveloped* wasn't that great, but it was the sweet-clover comparison that hurt the phrase. And maybe it should be *dark night air*, because *dark air* by itself didn't convey the same emotional tone. Get shut in a closet and you're in dark air. Dark, dry, stale air. Not at all like the still night

1

air that surrounded him as he sat on the deck of the houseboat in a lawn chair with frayed nylon straps that had stretched with age. His butt was only a couple of inches from the deck, but he wasn't going to write lyrics about that.

So there he was, just before midnight on a Monday night, sitting in a saggy lawn chair in air that was heavy with humidity and may or may not have felt or tasted like sweet clover. He shook his head and rolled his eyes, mocking himself and his cheesy stab at the beginning lyrics of a song.

He reached over to a plate on a nearby lawn chair and grabbed a chunk of watermelon, telling himself to enjoy the moment instead of trying to find a way to express how the moment made him feel.

He had no problem admitting that he felt amazing.

Most nights he sat in the same lawn chair in the same spot in the same solitude, looking through a gap in the rocks that led out to the deep brown waters of the Cumberland River. When it rained, he sat under a big umbrella.

The houseboat was moored in a small harbor cut into the banks of the river. About three miles downstream was downtown Nashville, and when the occasional barge passed by, he thought about the crew's first view of the city skyline and wondered if the sight of it made them as breathless as it did Webb. Even after being in Nashville for weeks.

Nashville.

Webb thought it would be pretty cool if he could go back in time and visit the kid he was at thirteen—a kid playing the same J-45 Gibson acoustic guitar for the same reasons Webb played it now.

To get lost in the rush of music. To feel the scrape of the pick against nylon and steel, the pressure of callused fingertips against the frets, holding a chord the perfect length of time and letting the note of that chord meld into the next.

The difference was that thirteen-year-old Webb could only dream about Nashville. Seventeen-year-old Webb was there.

Webb bit into the watermelon and didn't care that juice dribbled down onto his T-shirt. He was thinking about chasing dreams. There was a song in that. But it had been done a million times. So the big question was, could he write a hook excellent enough to justify yet another song about kids who yearn for bigger things?

It wasn't just the still, scented air that made this moment amazing: it was the moon. Webb had been on the upper deck of the houseboat on dozens of nights, but this was the first time the moon had risen right in the gap in the rocks that led to the river.

It was kind of like Stonehenge, he realized. Mystical.

Warm night air. Chirping crickets. The slap of tiny waves against the houseboat. Slight swaying of the lawn chair as the water cradled the boat. The taste of watermelon juice drying on his lips. The aloneness that was bigger than loneliness. With that big, timeless moon creeping upward from the river, slowly pulling away from its reflection on the water as if even the moon was reluctant to leave Nashville and all that it promised.

Webb watched the moon and knew he'd never forget this feeling.

A swell of river water came from what seemed like nowhere, and the houseboat began to rock. That reminded him of all the times he'd heard the phrase "don't rock the boat." Like it was a bad thing to rock the boat. Because everyone wanted the boat to be safe and stable and predictable.

Well, Webb thought, he wouldn't be here in this moment if he hadn't been prepared to rock the boat. The moment he was living was one he'd remember when he was an old man. He didn't want to look back wishing he'd—

Then he had it. *Live in the moment.*

The whole sweet-clover thing wasn't working only because the *lyrics* were bad. The idea behind the song didn't work. Sometimes you had to try something that didn't work to find something that did. You had to rock the boat. Live life loud. Bring the roof down. Walk the high wire. Not look back and regret what you didn't try.

It wasn't a new concept for a song, but a fresh way of presenting it began to unfold in his head. He scrambled to grab his guitar, because he could already hear the melody to go with the lyrics that tumbled through his brain.

You have to know we're gonna walk the
  high wire
Maybe playing with some hot fire
We spell our names like trouble

But you know we're gonna love it.
Yeah, we're gonna rock the boat
That's the only way to know
We're gonna have to rock the boat
Yeah, that's the only way to go.

An hour later, long after the moon had climbed to the center of the sky, Webb had finished the entire song. He didn't need to write it down. He knew every word and every note.

And felt great about it. A feeling that didn't even last until noon on Tuesday.

Two

Performance-wise, Webb thought he'd killed the new song, but as the last chord echoed into silence in the studio, he did his best to keep a straight face. Webb didn't like telling other people what to think about his music, even through body language.

He looked across the studio, waiting for a reaction from Gerald Dean, the producer. Gerald sat in a chair behind the mixing board, leaning back, hands locked behind his head. It was a small room, but it didn't need to be big. Gerald had a couple of Mac Pros, some large computer monitors, and some high-quality speakers mounted on the soundproofed walls.

Webb tried to read what Gerald was thinking. Nashville was known for country music, but it had a strong pop and indie scene too, and Gerald was supposed to be among the better producers.

Gerald wore a dark blue silk shirt, hanging loose over faded jeans. Italian dress shoes, big watch. He was mid-thirties and clean-shaven, with dark hair. He talked in soft tones, never seeming pushy. Webb felt ratty in comparison. His well-worn T-shirt was emblazoned with the black-and-gold logo of the Hamilton Tiger-Cats, a CFL team. It made Webb feel less homesick.

Finally Gerald gave a *so-so* shrug, not even lifting his hands away from his head. "Needs lots of work. Lots. You're not thinking of putting it into production, right?"

This was the reason, Webb thought, that he chose not to make a big deal about something himself. It hurt a lot less and was a lot less embarrassing when someone shot him down. He'd been too excited about "Rock the Boat," too in love with his own song.

"Got it recorded anywhere?" Gerald asked.

"No," Webb said. "Like I said, it's something I wrote last night."

It was eleven in the morning. Webb had spent a few hours after he woke up practicing the song. Then he'd taken a bus to East Nashville, where Gerald had a studio in a small house in a run-down neighborhood. Lots of music people, especially indie producers, lived in the area. Music Row, close to downtown, was where the big labels took up real estate.

Gerald gave another shrug. "I know you don't want to hear this, but I wouldn't even record it on your iPhone and send it to a friend. Things like that get passed around, they can haunt you. Kind of like posting a bad photo on Facebook that goes viral."

"That bad?" Webb said. Man, maybe he knew absolutely nothing about music.

"Look," Gerald said "People in this town, sometimes they write fifty songs and only one is good. Don't beat yourself up."

Difficult not to, Webb thought.

"Thanks," he said, thinking it was crazy to thank someone for shooting him down. But Gerald was the producer.

Gerald scratched the back of his head and shifted in his chair. "Invoices came in from the studio musicians I needed for your songs. Higher than I expected."

"Any chance I can have a copy of the invoices for my files?" Webb asked.

"Sure," Gerald said. "I can look around and get them to you sooner or later."

Sooner or later?

Webb lifted his guitar off his shoulders and set it in its case. He needed to do something to avoid showing his anger. He snapped the locks shut on the case and straightened.

Gerald was still leaning back in his chair, hands behind his head. This made Webb even angrier, but Gerald had something Webb wanted— the ten songs Webb had already paid to have produced, three that he'd written and seven covers, including a remake of a seventies song called "One Tin Soldier" that he'd done for a friend. Unfortunately, that gave Gerald all the power.

"Um," Webb said, trying to sound as casual as possible, "I thought last week you said everything would be finished today. I didn't know anything about you bringing in studio musicians. I mean, didn't we talk about budget?"

For a while now, Webb had been trying to figure out if the producer was telling the truth or ripping him off. It had all started when Webb's grandfather—as part of his will—arranged for a producer in Nashville to work with Webb and prepaid for production. But the producer kept finding ways to drag out delivery and charge more money. Like now.

"Look," Gerald said. "I do high-quality stuff, okay? If you're going to pitch something to a label that comes from my studio, I have to stand behind it. I needed something to lift your songs to a decent level."

Webb understood the implication. The songs would have been crap otherwise.

He sucked in oxygen. "I need to understand this stuff clearly, okay?"

"Of course," Gerald said in his soft, reasonable way.

But then, Webb thought, it was that soft, reasonable way that had been stringing him along.

"All through December," Webb said, "I called to find out when I could get my songs, and then in early January you tell me that I'm still three thousand short."

"Demo quality versus finished-and-ready-for-production quality. We've been through this, but I don't mind discussing it as many times as you need to feel good about the process."

In the first week of January, Webb had been able to pay Gerald, thanks to an unexpected insurance windfall. Now, two weeks later...

Webb sucked in more oxygen, feeling ripped off all over again. "And today, the day you promised to let me walk out with the songs, you're telling me I owe even more?"

"Look," Gerald said. "You don't think I feel like crap? I wasn't expecting another three thousand in—"

"Three thousand!" Webb couldn't help himself.

Gerald sat forward. "Raising your voice doesn't change things."

"We had a deal," Webb said. "I mean—"

"I said I feel like crap," Gerald told him. "So I'll eat half of that. I take a $1,500 hit and you come up with another $1,500, and it's all yours. After that, you can do a CD run if you want to stay independent, or try to chase down a label. Me, I'd go independent. A CD costs maybe ninety cents to produce. If you do five hundred at a time, you can sell them for ten bucks. Start a website for

your band—what was it called, mile oneTwelve—
and go from there."

Webb realized the side of his jaw hurt from
clenching it. "Fifteen hundred."

Gerald said, "That's the price of quality. And
you understand, from a business point of view,
I can't release anything until the check clears."

Sixteen hundred and seven dollars was all
that Webb had left in his bank account.

There was a knock on the door.

Gerald stood. "Hey, that's my noon appointment. Just let me know when you're coming
back, right? And think about wearing a different
shirt. That tiger is an eyesore."

Gerald walked past Webb and opened the
door to a girl about Webb's age. Dark hair, red
sleeveless T-shirt, snake tattoo running up the
inside of her left wrist.

She flicked him a quick look and said, "Hey."

"Hey," Webb said, still trying to comprehend
what had happened.

Then Gerald pointed at the door, and Webb
walked out.

Bad day, this Tuesday.

Three

Walking through an alley, guitar case in hand, Webb was in a can-kicking mood. But there weren't any cans on the pavement. There were lots of wind-swept pages from a copy of *The Tennessean*, Nashville's daily newspaper. Pieces of bent and broken grocery carts. Even an abandoned couch, green and tattered. But no cans to kick. Not in this neighborhood when there was money to be made collecting cans and bottles for recycling.

Webb was furious and discouraged, a new combination for him, and that made him feel something else—helpless.

How was he going to move forward? He was in Nashville because he'd wanted to be where music was made. The deal his grandfather had arranged seemed solid because Gerald Dean did have good credentials. But once Gerald had learned there was only Webb—that Webb's grandfather was dead—it seemed like he figured he could take advantage of someone young and alone in the city.

In four months, all Webb had really accomplished was to write the lyrics and music of a few songs that Gerald had said were worth recording along with the covers. And now Gerald was holding those songs hostage for a final payment of $1,500.

If he wrote a check for that amount, he would have only $107 left. He was living rent free, so he'd expected he could make his money last a while, at least until he got his green card and could work legally in Tennessee. It would be tough to be down to the last hundred. That wouldn't last long enough for him to get a job— it wouldn't even be enough to get him back to Canada. Busking was fun and brought in some money, but he couldn't depend on it.

Obviously, Gerald Dean was trying to rip him off, taking the songs and essentially holding them hostage for the $1,500. But did Webb have a choice?

Maybe what really hurt was the producer's reaction to "Rock the Boat." Did Webb know so little—was he so untalented—that what he believed was good was just the opposite?

He looked again for something to kick. A can. A box. Anything.

Instead, he saw a sign on a pole: *Hungry? Free dinner. All are welcome.*

Webb snorted. That'll be the day, he thought. Then he remembered. One hundred and seven dollars. That's all he would have left after he wrote Gerald's check.

Why not share a meal with a bunch of homeless people? The way he felt, he couldn't get much lower.

Four

The sign led him to a gathering of people beneath an overpass just outside the downtown. A dozen or so long plastic tables had been set up with plastic chairs. A temporary kitchen was protected by the overpass in case of rain. A handwritten sign said *Welcome to Under The Overpass. Every Tuesday night.*

Webb stood at the back of a long line. He guessed there were maybe thirty people in front of him. He had expected a bunch of old-looking men in filthy overcoats. He knew all too well from his time on the streets of Toronto how living rough could make a middle-aged person look ancient, and how important it was to have a long, heavy coat that could serve as a blanket in winter and a mattress in summer.

But here, there was little of the tangy smell of men who had not bathed in months. Some people were dressed as if headed to watch a Saturday soccer game. There were mothers with young children. Some people met his eye, some looked away. Some stood with shoulders bowed, some with chins high and backs straight.

Seeing the children shook away some of Webb's self-pity. They were reaching up to hold their mothers' hands, bewildered by all the people around them.

When Webb reached the front of the line, an older woman with short graying hair and a dark vest over a purple shirt gave him a smile that looked genuine.

"Glad you could join us," she said. Nothing in her tone or manner suggested she scorned him for needing free food. "You decent with that guitar?"

"Some days," Webb said, watching as she scooped potato salad onto a paper plate for him.

"Well," she said, "if this is one of those days, I bet a couple of the kids would be a little less anxious if you played for them after the meal. It's really hard on kids when their mother has to get them away from a bad situation. Some of the other folks here, well, they'd be in a hospital if they could afford it. Music might make them forget that, even if just for a little while."

She plunked a hot dog in a bun onto his plate. "Fixings at the table."

Webb saw a little girl already sitting at a table and thought about why he'd been homeless for a while. He and his mom had needed to get away from his stepfather, who was hurting them. But his mom hadn't left. Not then.

The girl had badly cut dark hair, and she was clinging to her mother's hand. Even though there was food on the table in front of her, comfort was obviously more important to her right now.

What a schmuck he was. Moping around like his world had just ended, thinking it was the lowest of lows to accept a handout.

The little girl was the one with real problems. Her mother too. Webb figured it wouldn't take much convincing to get them to trade places with him. His problems were nothing compared to theirs.

Webb didn't have to look into a little girl's face every morning and wonder in desperation what the day might bring. Webb didn't even have to worry about money if he didn't pay the producer. He had $1,607 in his checking account. He could use it to get on a bus and go to Toronto, move home with his mother and live a great life, find a job and think about saving up for university. He had choice, and he had freedom. No one was making him live in Nashville.

The girl and her mother, on the other hand, probably had neither choice nor freedom. Nor did the people who needed medical care they couldn't afford.

Yup, Webb concluded, he was a real schmuck.

As soon as the meal was over, he took out his guitar and quietly started to play. Not in a way that made it look like he was trying to put on a show to make money. As if he was just trying to pass the time with some tunes.

He played songs he knew people would like. No sense bringing out one of his own songs, like "Rock the Boat." According to one of Nashville's top producers, that would be a bad idea.

One of his favorites was "One Tin Soldier." Webb hadn't written it, but it was going on his album.

It was not the right song for this situation, though, with its lyrics about the horrors of war.

Instead, Webb played "Drift Away." He loved singing the chorus: *"Give me the beat, boys, and free my soul..."*

He looked up and saw the little girl smiling and singing along.

Oh yeah, Webb thought. Nothing like getting lost in a song.

Five

Music Row, just southwest of downtown Nashville, was where you went to find the offices of the major labels, publishing houses, video-production houses and music-licensing firms as well as all the businesses that supported the music scene in Nashville.

The big trees along the sidewalks provided gentle shade. Some of the houses, long converted into offices, had been there a century. Others, like the Sony building, shiny with reflective glass, spoke of power and wealth.

These were the buildings where the legends had cut songs. These were the sidewalks those legends had once walked as unknowns, guitars on their backs, just like Webb.

But Webb wasn't walking these streets today to pitch his music.

He was here to kick producer butt.

The name of the law firm was etched in the glass of the door: *Bing and McGee.*

Webb took the elevator to the tenth floor. He'd done some online research and found a firm that specialized in music law.

He felt nervous. This was a new type of journey for him. He was a long way from home. The only real friend who could have helped—a Vietnam vet named Lee Knox—was on a two-week vacation, and Webb wasn't going to call and bother him on the beach. Maybe if he couldn't resolve the problem himself by the time Lee came back, Webb would ask for a favor. Nor was he going to call his mom in Canada. She'd get worried but wouldn't be able to help him, so why add stress to her life? For now he was alone. If he didn't do this, who would?

Webb pushed open the door and stepped onto a rich-red plush carpet. The room was hushed. There were empty straight-backed chairs on one side of the room. They faced floor-to-ceiling windows that looked out over Music Row. At the back of the foyer, behind a burnished-wood desk, sat a woman about his mother's age. She wore cat-eye glasses, and it looked like her hair had been styled just before he opened the door—not a wisp was out of place. She gave him a neutral smile.

He took a couple of hesitant steps forward. The name plate on her desk said *Ms. Planchette.*

"My name is Jim Webb," he said. "I called and set up an appointment for this time."

"Yes," she said. "It's nice that you're prompt."

It didn't seem to bother her that Webb was young. Or that he had a guitar with him. Of course, in this business, some musicians his age were already brand names. She'd probably seen plenty of types come through the door.

"Stampeders?" she asked, eyeing his red-and-white T-shirt.

"Long story," Webb said. Wednesday. Different day, different CFL team.

"Attorneys love long stories," she said. "Not me. If you don't mind, I've got a form for you to fill out."

"I only have a couple of questions for Mr. Marvin," Webb said. "It's about—"

"Ms. Marvin." Ms. Planchette's voice grew distinctly cold.

"Ms.?" The law firm's website had listed Jordan Marvin as one of the attorneys. When Webb called for a morning appointment, Jordan Marvin was the only one available.

"Yes," she said. "Ms."

The implication was clear. Webb was a caveman for assuming the lawyer would be male.

But Webb wasn't in a mood to be pushed around. He'd already let Gerald Dean do that to him. For weeks.

"Really?" he said. "You're going to bust me for assuming that Jordan was a man's name? Because it is, you know. I bet I'm not the only one who has made this mistake."

That thawed Ms. Planchette a little. "Maybe."

"You mentioned a form?" Webb said.

"Also," she said, "we'll need a retainer. Credit card or certified check. Cash too, I suppose, but..." She let her voice trail away, as if only drug dealers would deliver cash.

"Retainer." Webb took a breath. "Would you mind explaining that?"

"Ms. Marvin's hourly fee is $250. We need a minimum deposit to cover her first two hours of billing."

"Five hundred dollars."

That would leave him with $1,099, because he'd already spent eight bucks on some Kraft Macaroni & Cheese and milk, as well as bus fare.

Doing more simple math, he realized that if he paid a retainer of $500, he wouldn't have enough money to get his music from the producer. He'd be gambling on being able to legally force the producer to give him his songs. And if he gambled wrong...

"Um," Webb said, "all I need to find out is whether Ms. Marvin can help me with this. I'll explain what's happening, and if she thinks she can do something, how about I pay the retainer then?"

Ms. Planchette leaned forward as if she were going to speak confidentially, even though it was only the two of them in the office.

"You seem like a nice kid," she said. "Are you new to Nashville?"

Webb nodded.

"And you don't have a car, right?"

Webb opened his mouth to ask how she knew, then hefted his guitar case as an answer.

"Exactly," she said. "You're not here to audition. This is a law firm. So why bring up your guitar unless you don't have a car trunk to keep it in."

Her voice was growing more sympathetic. "And you don't have an agent or a manager. If you did, they would have made the appointment on your behalf and fought your battles for you. Which means..."

"I'm a kid without a car, and I don't even have a contract anywhere. Otherwise, someone else would be here for me."

"Exactly," she said again. "Fast learner. Which means the firm is going to need a retainer as the first step. Otherwise Ms. Marvin might as well sit in a coffee shop and answer questions for anyone who doesn't understand the business."

"A producer ripped me off," he said. "I just want to—"

"Believe it or not, I'm trying to help you," Ms. Planchette said. "From your perspective, you *think* a producer ripped you off. It's going to take someone like Ms. Marvin to tell you whether that's true from a legal perspective."

"What he did was—"

"I'm not an attorney," she said. "Telling *me* won't get you anywhere. You're going to need legal advice."

"How do I even know if I have a chance of getting my songs unless I explain the situation and ask a couple of questions?"

Ms. Planchette said, "The answers you get from Ms. Marvin *are* what would be considered legal advice. To repeat, I'm not trying to mess with you here. I'm just trying to give you a clear understanding of the situation."

Webb said, "I thought some legal firms gave a person a chance to find out if it's worth hiring the lawyer."

"Sure," she said. "Legal firms who have lawyers who are desperate for clients. And those kinds of lawyers are often very happy to string you along so that they can bill you for an hour or two anyway. At Bing and McGee, our attorneys don't need to play those games."

Webb gazed out the window. Sony seemed a lot farther away than across a mere strip of pavement on Music Row.

Paying the retainer guaranteed he wouldn't be able to pay the producer. In the short term, that meant he'd have to give up on getting his music. In exchange, there was only a possibility the lawyer would tell him he could claim his songs in the long term. And even if the lawyer said he had a chance, it still meant he wouldn't get his songs anytime soon.

That's what it came down to, he decided. Weighing a certainty against a possibility. If he wanted those songs, he'd have to pay. This was something Gerald Dean had no doubt known all along.

"Well," Webb finally said to Ms. Planchette, "I appreciate your help with this. I won't waste your time by filling out the form."

Six

D espite telling himself he shouldn't whine about his situation, Webb was in a bad mood when he reached Nashville's downtown core after about a forty-five-minute walk from the law office. He stepped off the curb across from the Bridgestone Arena, where the Nashville Predators played, and realized that affording a ticket to watch a game live was an impossible dream at this point. He reminded himself he should at least try to enjoy the weather and maybe make a few bucks while he played music.

Late January, and it was T-shirt weather. He peeled off his jacket and hung it over his shoulder. He was wearing a red T-shirt with a white horse logo—the Calgary Stampeders. Each day he chose a different team. At first he'd done it because he liked being reminded of Canada as he chose his shirt for the day, and that was still a good enough reason. But he'd also noticed that it helped with his busking in the downtown core. Lots of the tourists were Canadian, and they liked being reminded of home too. It put them in a better mood, and that bumped up the amount of money they threw in his guitar case.

Webb needed the money, of course. He'd cover some classics, because that paid the bills, but every fourth or fifth song would be one of his own.

As people streamed past him on the sidewalk, he didn't immediately look for his own corner. His first stop was always a guitar store with hundreds of guitars; the people who worked there were passionate about guitars. They didn't put pressure on anyone to buy and were happy when people came in and treated it like a guitar museum.

Webb walked inside, guitar on his back, and made a beeline for the Gibson section. He stood in front of the guitars and just soaked up the vibe, imagining great guitar players from decades ago with their Gibsons, wondering about all the places the instruments had been, all the beautiful sounds they'd produced. Yeah, Webb liked his Gibson J-45, but it would never hurt to have more than one.

He had needed to be recharged, and when he stepped back outside again, he vibrated with energy. There was a spot on 2nd Avenue he liked, across from a bar called Coyote Ugly, where he could stand in the late-morning sun. He considered it a prime place to play.

Long before he reached the spot, however, he saw an older, gray-haired man putting his guitar case down exactly where Webb always did.

Webb didn't see the guy as competition, though, and felt no irritation. The guy was wearing a ballcap—Nashville Sounds, the city's baseball team—low on his forehead, and it covered most of his face, like he was embarrassed at his age to have to busk. He looked scruffy enough, with his long hair and thin corded arms, that Webb wondered if maybe he had alcohol problems. In theory, someone of this guy's age should have a decent job to keep him busy during the day. If he didn't and needed to make money busking, times probably weren't good for him.

Webb knew the bottle was often an escape for someone like that. He'd rather give the man food than money.

Remembering how it had improved his mood the afternoon before to help someone else—when his playing had put a smile on a little girl's face—Webb made a detour into a bagel shop and ordered a cup of coffee and a breakfast sandwich with cheese to go. It hurt to dig into his cash, but a little busking would cover it sooner or later.

When Webb was on the street again, coffee in one hand, breakfast bagel in the other, the old guy was playing some amazing riffs. Nobody needed to feel sorry for this guy, Webb decided.

He felt his chin bobbing to the rhythm of the guitar riffs as he stepped closer to the man.

Nobody else was around yet.

The guy was leaning against the wall as he played. When Webb's shadow hit him, the man played a few more chords and then looked up. Only a little. The shadow from the ballcap still hid most of his face. He flicked his eyes up and down, examining Webb but still hitting the tune. Webb liked the guy's guitar, a black-and-white Fender Stratocaster. At least things weren't so bad that the guy had to pawn his guitar, Webb thought.

The man, who was wearing an Elvis shirt, squinted at Webb.

"Early to be headed for a gig in one of the places around here," he said. "Were you looking to busk somewhere too?"

"Sooner or later," Webb said. He leaned down and set the bagel and coffee beside the man's empty guitar case. "Lots of times I've been busking, people bring me food. Figured you wouldn't mind if I did the same thing."

The guy snorted. "Yeah. Never hurts." He nodded at Webb's guitar. "You any good with that?"

It wasn't said like a challenge but as friendly conversation.

"Don't think I can hit that complicated riff you did in the middle there." Webb hummed the piece. "How exactly did you do that?"

"Here," the man said. "Let me show you."

Seven

"Harley," the man said, arching an eyebrow as he strummed a simple riff. "You?"

"Webb." He set his guitar case down, opened it, pulled out the J-45, straightened, dropped the strap over his left shoulder and shifted the guitar into place. He casually flipped his guitar case shut. Nobody else was nearby, but Harley had chosen the spot, and Webb wanted to make it clear he wasn't here to compete for money.

Webb ran his left-hand fingers up and down the frets, picking, not strumming, with his right-hand fingers.

"Early Lou Reed," Harley said. "I like it."

"Loved Velvet Undergound," Webb said.

"You know what they say about the debut album," Harley said. "Commercial failure. Only sold thirty thousand copies. But every single one of us who bought the album started our own bands."

"Mile oneTwelve," Webb said. "That will be the name of my band At least, someday..."

Webb dipped his head and kept playing. Harley picked up on the riff, slipping into some of the open places.

Webb grinned and held up his right hand, stopping Harley mid-riff. "What was that thing you did?"

Webb recalled the chords Harley was playing when Webb walked up with the bagel and coffee. He played the first few riffs, stopped and played them again, satisfied he had replicated that much, then stopped again.

"It was right after that," Webb said. "Something..."

Harley hit the notes. Quick and hard. A four-on-the-floor beat.

"Yeah," Webb said. "That."

"Here," Harley said. He slowed the tempo. Webb watched the man's fingers on the strings.

"Aaah," Webb said. "This."

He played it at half speed a few times, fumbled it, found it and picked up the pace.

"Aaah," Webb said again, playing the entire riff. Harley joined in, chasing him.

A five-dollar bill floated into Harley's guitar case.

Webb glanced over, not losing any of the chords. He hadn't even noticed the approach of a middle-aged couple. She had shiny hair and an even shinier smile. She held hands with a balding man wearing brown pants and a light orange sweater; a camera hung from a strap around his neck.

The man was doing a kind of turkey bob with his chin to the beat.

Webb grinned at the couple. Harley hadn't noticed them. His eyes were closed.

"Whoo-hooo!" the man said. "This is what it's all about."

Yup, tourists, Webb thought.

Harley opened his eyes and grinned. "Yes, sir. This is what it's all about. Kid's not bad, is he?"

"Can't be," the man said. "He's a Stampeders fan."

Webb shrugged. But Harley was right—this *was* what it was all about. Music brought people together. Even if it was a street bum, a kid from Canada and some guy probably visiting Nashville for a plumbers' convention.

Webb hit a few new chords. Harley arched an eyebrow. Not a questioning eyebrow, but a *hey, let's see where that goes.*

It was the chorus of "Rock the Boat." Webb throttled into it, and it didn't take Harley long to fit in. The woman started tapping her toes, and Bill the Plumber kept up the turkey bob. Webb couldn't help himself: he lit into the vocals.

> *Yeah, we're gonna rock the boat*
> *That's the only way to know*
> *We're gonna have to rock the boat*
> *Yeah, that's the only way to go.*

Webb had his head tilted up, looking at the tops of the buildings, at the clouds drifting in the blue sky. It felt great. This was what it was all about. Chasing dreams.

> *This is the time we're living*
> *Let's live it so loud*
> *This is the world we're given*

Let's bring the roof down
And we won't be looking back
Only wishing that we had
This is the time we're living
The time of our lives.

"Whoo-hooo!" Bill the Plumber said again. His wife winked at Webb. Webb hung his head, suddenly shy.

Bill the Plumber pulled up his camera. "Let me video this. Play the chorus again, okay? The two of you. So when you're famous someday, I can prove I was here with you on the first day of our vacation."

Harley kept his head down and joined in as Webb replayed the chorus.

"You guys are awesome," Bill the Plumber said.

His wife nudged him, and he caught the hint. Before they walked on, he pulled out his wallet and dropped another bill in the case.

"Look at that," Harley said, pointing at the bottom of the guitar case. "Dude must have really loved us."

The bill beside the original five showed a different number: 100.

"Or he's Canadian," Webb said. The couple was almost to the corner. "He knew the Stampeders logo on my shirt."

"And that means?"

"Fives up there are blue, hundreds are brown. Down here, all the same color. Easy to make a mistake."

"You willing to turn down an easy fifty bucks?"

"None of it's mine," Webb said. "This is your gig."

Harley laughed. "The guy's sweater looked like it was made in the last century. She's got a home perm. They look like they can throw out hundreds?"

"Your gig," Webb said.

"Would you take it if you were me?" Harley asked.

"Nope."

"Me neither." Harley put a couple of fingers up to his mouth and whistled hard. The husband and wife turned at the same time. Harley waved them back.

By the time the couple reached them, Harley had the money ready in his fingers. Bill the Plumber had a puzzled look on his face.

"Kid here thinks you're from Canada," Harley said. "Thinks you might have mixed up some currency—unless you meant to drop a hundred. Neither of us wants to steal from you."

Bill the Plumber's mouth formed a wide O.

"That's what I thought," Harley said. He handed over the bill. The man's fingers were trembling as he accepted it. "You folks have a good weekend," Harley said.

"Wow," Bill the Plumber said. "Yeah. We will. Thanks. Thanks a big bunch."

"Give them your card," his wife said. "Case one of them is ever in Moose Jaw and needs a favor."

"Yes," Bill the Plumber said. "Most definitely yes. You ever get to Moose Jaw and need new tires, we're not hard to find."

He pulled out his wallet, carefully extracted a business card and threw the card onto the velvet.

"Yes, sir," Harley said. "Next time I'm west of Regina, I'll make sure to stop by."

"See, honey?" Bill the Plumber said to his wife as they walked away. "People down here know where Moose Jaw is."

"Impressive," Webb said. "Not many people know Moose Jaw. You made their day. First the money and then the Regina thing."

"Used to travel some," Harley said. "Now, it's just this."

"Music is music," Webb answered. He wondered what downhill path had led Harley to busking to get by but decided it wasn't his business to ask.

"Yup." Harley cocked his head, thinking something over. "Tell you what. I've got some buddies. We get together Thursday nights in an old warehouse at the river. We just jam. Sound good? Any time after seven thirty."

"Sounds good," Webb said.

Harley wrote the address down on the back of the business card.

Webb tucked it into his wallet but not before flipping it over. *Ward Auster*, it said. *Tires and Services.*

Yeah, Webb thought. That would have been his second guess. Ward the Tire Guy.

Eight

In the early afternoon, he walked through the doorway of Gerald Dean's studio. Webb was officially down to six boxes of Kraft Macaroni & Cheese, and once the check to Gerald for $1,500 cleared, he'd have $99 in his bank account.

He just didn't think he had much choice. He needed those songs. They were going to be his calling card. With his remaining money, he'd buy a twenty-dollar package of blank CDs and transfer the songs. He'd go from label to label, dropping off a CD, and maybe someone would listen to it and want to talk to him. And he'd upload the songs to iTunes, selling the music as an indie artist while he hoped for a break in Nashville.

Still, the thought that Gerald Dean was ripping him off was enough to set Webb's teeth on edge. He realized that showing his anger would not help him in any way, so he reminded himself to be polite.

Gerald was in the recording room, behind the glass. He saw Webb and held up his index figure, giving Webb the classic wait-just-one-minute signal.

Webb saw through the glass why Gerald hadn't jumped up from the mixing board. Sitting behind the mic, guitar across her lap, was the girl he'd seen the day before. Webb's age. Dark hair. Snake tattoo on her inner wrist. She had her head tilted as if hanging on to every word from Gerald Dean.

Webb remembered doing the same thing. Cutting a song meant doing the vocals forty or fifty times, and Gerald had interrupted constantly, requesting a slightly different pitch or tone.

Webb hadn't expected that. He'd thought he'd play a song all the way through and try to get all of it right, figuring he might have to do it five or six times.

But a producer would take the best word in one line of vocals and mix it with the best couple of words in another line of vocals, cutting and pasting to get an entire vocal near perfect. That was before the fine-tuning. Produced songs were without blemish.

Webb preferred a more organic approach. He liked it when a song came alive between him and the audience, creating an almost mystical connection. Webb didn't want to be a studio musician. He wanted the process to be more like busking, where a song possessed you and the audience until the last notes.

Gerald's promised one minute became ten. It began to irritate Webb. He'd learned to hide his emotions—letting someone else see them gave that person a degree of control. That had been one benefit of having an abusive stepfather, learning that lesson.

Webb wandered out of Gerald's sight. No sense standing right in front of the window like he had nothing better to do. Even though he had nothing better to do.

A new poster on the opposite wall caught Webb's attention. It was an audition poster. A band needed a lead guitar and vocalist. There was an email address for setting up a time slot. Webb wasn't thinking of trying out. He was just killing time.

He turned away from the poster as Gerald finally stepped out of the booth. The usual silk shirt and blue jeans. This time the silk shirt had a paisley pattern.

The girl followed Gerald out of the studio.

She gave Webb a decent smile. He returned the same.

Gerald didn't make introductions, as if Webb were invisible.

So Webb kept smiling like it didn't bother him, reached out his hand and said, "Hey, I'm Jim Webb. Nice to meet you."

"Charlene," she said. "Charlene Adams."

Gerald coughed.

Charlene gave a half-hiccup kind of laugh that Webb thought was cute.

"Sorry," she said. "Elle McWilliam." She shrugged. "Gerald thinks it's a better stage name."

"Cool," Webb said. He liked the thought of her as Elle. "I'm mile oneTwelve. That's my band. Even though I don't actually have a band yet. But that's the name going on my CD."

"Mile oneTwelve?"

"Long story," Webb said. "It's a place on a trail up in the Arctic. Has significance for me."

"The Arctic." She leaned closer. "Like polar-bear Arctic?"

"Grizzly," Webb said. "Definitely grizzly."

"Sounds like a cool story." Her smile grew wider. "But that T-shirt. Really?"

Webb grinned. "Football team. One for each day of the week."

"Like branding yourself, huh? People don't forget you."

"Either that," Webb said, "or a message that I'm not the kind of guy who gets up and spends the first hour of his day blow-drying his hair and buffing his fingernails."

She laughed.

Gerald said, "Hate to break in, but time is money."

Webb paused. "So is paper."

He handed Gerald an envelope.

Gerald didn't open it.

"You got a link for me?" Webb asked. "I'm looking forward to hearing the songs."

"When the check clears," Gerald said.

Webb said nothing. He was too angry.

Probably to break the awkward silence, Elle said, "You were looking at the audition poster?"

Webb felt the tightness in his jaw. He was staring at Gerald, thinking he'd like to push the guy up against the wall. *When the check clears.*

Webb felt a touch on his arm.

"I said, are you going to the audition?"

"Wouldn't be a good move, Webb," Gerald said. "Hate to say it, but it's true. They are going to need someone with some skills. Live performance is different than studio performance. I mean, in the studio I can make you sound good. But I wouldn't want you embarrassing yourself at the audition, walking in wearing a horse T-shirt. The tiger yesterday wasn't bad enough?"

What was going on here? Webb wondered. Two months earlier, Gerald had gone on and on about how amazing Webb was on guitar and vocals. Oh, right, that was when Gerald was trying to milk a bunch of money from Webb.

Webb moved his stare slowly away from Gerald and tried to relax and smile naturally at Elle.

"Yeah," Webb said. "The audition. I'll be there."

Nine

T he road ran parallel to the murky brown of the Cumberland River, climbing away from downtown into a district of low faded-brick buildings with peeling painted signs for tire sales and oil changes and used furniture. The signs must have been shiny new at about the time soldiers were leaving town to fight in World War II, Webb guessed

He coughed away diesel fumes as the bus left him curbside, giving him a view of the downtown core and the football stadium where the Tennessee Titans battled each year for a shot at the playoffs. The stadium was placed squarely where, a hundred years earlier, dock men and grifters had wandered the warehouses, and the wharves held steamboats.

As Webb took in the blue sky behind the Capitol building at the far side of downtown, he held his face to the sun, closed his eyes and told himself it was great to be in the moment on a beautiful January day.

Thursday morning. Time for his audition. Feeling good in a vintage Edmonton Eskimos T-shirt. Green and yellow. Big *EE* for a logo.

Then he thought about his immediate future. He squinted at his iPhone to double-check the street map on the screen. He was close to the right address, but this didn't look like a place where guitars and dreams could take someone to a place on the charts. Not like Music Row.

A sign on a building across the street promised coffee. Webb had forty minutes to kill before the audition, and the thought of a bone-white china mug filled with liquid black enough to soak up the miseries of a soul seemed attractive, even if it would take another couple of bucks. He told himself he would make it up by busking later.

As he took his first steps across the street, Webb adjusted the strap of the guitar case on his back and shrugged to make it as comfortable as possible. But really there was no way to get a guitar case to fit the contours of your back. The only place a guitar belonged was out of the case, hanging from a strap around the shoulders and cradled across your belly.

That's where it would be when he proved that he deserved to win the audition.

Jim Webb.

Ten

nside the coffee shop, Webb found a table in the corner and set his guitar case on a chair.

As Mumford played from invisible speakers, Webb wandered to the counter, where gleaming silver espresso machines contrasted with the brown-painted concrete blocks of the walls and the nicked and scarred hardwood floor. There was a place for a band to set up, with a chalkboard announcing live music on Friday nights. Speakers and wires and cables were plugged in and ready to go.

This had once been a warehouse, obviously, now converted to the kind of trendy café that drew the kind of people he saw around him. Long hair. Tattoos. Earrings and pierced eyelids. Thrift-store clothing made chic. Funky hats. He knew he was catching a few glances, as if people were wondering if he was lost.

His hair was almost preppy short, and he wore his CFL shirt, blue jeans and black Blundstone boots. It wasn't a look that fit in a place where the baristas wrote the names of organic coffee beans in pastel chalk on a blackboard, but the glances Webb got didn't bother him.

The coffees listed on that trendy chalkboard weren't cheap. The era of selling tires and used furniture in this neighborhood was long gone.

All he wanted was a simple cup of coffee and a bagel, but now it looked as if he'd have to drop close to six bucks for it, more by the time he put some change in a glass tips jar at the till.

Webb didn't have to count the money in his pocket. He knew exactly what he had in bills and loose change. Six bucks that would buy plenty of macaroni and cheese at the grocery store near the marina. It would also go a long way toward a can of ground coffee for the filtered stuff he could make in the morning.

Webb turned away from the counter and nearly stepped on the foot of a girl carrying an uncased guitar across her back.

"Sorry," he said.

It was Charlene. From Gerald Dean's studio. Or, rather, Elle—he told himself to think of her as Elle.

She gave him a dark scowl he knew would sting for a while. What had he done wrong?

He couldn't think of anything to say, so he tried a smile. Her scowl deepened, so he took the hint and moved past her to get his guitar case, passing a guy in a suit standing behind her.

Normally, that was the thing about guitar. You could be the skinniest, dweebiest, nerdiest guy in the world, but get a guitar in your hands and rip a couple of chords, and you were transformed from someone girls scowled at into a chick magnet.

At least, that's what drew some guys into guitar.

Not Webb. His Gibson J-45 was a legacy from his father. And so was Webb's love of music. Every time Webb held his J-45, it took him back to those years of joy and innocence when his real dad was alive and patiently showing Webb where to put pressure on the frets, how to make his fingers move with silky magic and draw sound out of the guitar as if it were a mysterious creature with a soul of its own.

"Great decoration, a guitar like that," Webb heard as he lifted his case from the chair.

He turned and straightened, thinking someone was talking to him.

He was wrong.

The comment was directed at Elle. It had come from the guy in the suit—maybe late twenties, probably owner of the silver BMW that hadn't been parked in front of the coffee shop when Webb first walked in.

Suit Guy sounded like he was kidding around, trying to engage Elle's attention. If so, it worked. She turned around, and her eyes locked on his face.

But it was the wrong kind of engagement. Suit Guy wouldn't understand. A guitar wasn't like a BMW. You didn't have one to impress other people. You didn't even own guitars; they owned you.

Great decoration, a guitar like that. Webb had no doubt that Elle thought of her guitar as more than decoration. Just like he thought of his J-45 as more than polished metal and burnished wood.

Even from the far side of the small café, Webb could see there wasn't any playfulness in Elle's eyes. But Suit Guy, standing so close to her that he could have reached across and pushed a lock of hair off her forehead, wasn't reading her correctly.

"Looks good on you," he said.

"Like a Beamer looks good on you?" she countered.

"Something like that." He'd taken it as a compliment. "You noticed, huh?"

"When you nearly ran over me outside," she said. "Not good at paying attention, are you?"

"What do you think I was distracted by?" he said. He paused. "The guitar, of course. Like I said, great decoration."

Webb could see both of them in profile. He could see Suit Guy's grin, like he was thinking he was sharp and witty and she was totally into him and his BMW and his implying that he'd been looking at her butt but was charming enough to say it was her guitar. Like saying "nice pair of... sunglasses" to a girl with cleavage and thinking she'd dig you for it.

Elle reached up to her guitar strap and with a deft movement spun the guitar around from her back and into her hands. She walked to the band area, plugged in and did a test riff to make sure she had sound. Then, without taking her eyes off Suit Guy's face, and definitely without any hint of humor, she ripped into the opening chords of Deep Purple's "Smoke on the Water," riffed on a Coldplay tune, settled into something haunting, intense and totally original, and finished with an amped-up version of Chuck Berry's "Johnny B. Goode."

When the last chords faded into silence, spontaneous applause broke out from the trendies scattered through the coffee shop.

Elle unplugged and spun the guitar around and onto her back again.

"Dude," she said to Suit Guy, "if you could drive your decoration half as well as I play mine, you'd be NASCAR championship material. But I doubt you can even parallel park."

Elle pointed at Webb.

"And you," she said with that scowl. "I wouldn't bother to cross the street for the audition."

Eleven

The band was set up in a large, open warehouse. The walls were painted black. Lightbulbs dangled on cords from the ceiling.

At the back of the room, a low stage had been constructed from four-by-eight-foot sheets of thick plywood resting on concrete building blocks. Drums were at the back, stage left. Microphones rested on stands. Cables with quarter-inch jacks snaked across the plywood, giving band members easy access to plugging in their instruments. Monitors were placed in front of each chair so the band members could hear the sound mix as they played.

The band consisted of a guy on drums, a young woman at a keyboard and another guy on bass guitar. All three wore black T-shirts showing the name of their band, Deus Ex Machina. Off to the side, a soundman stood in front of a mixing board.

The bass player riffed on his guitar. While not a melody, the sound was not unpleasant.

The drummer watched Webb and Elle approach.

"You guys sent in emails about the audition, right?" he said, touching a drumstick to his head and raising it in salute. He had a round face, short ginger hair and a goatee. "Then you're our last two."

"Last one," the bass guitarist said. "Just the girl."

He was skinny. Not skinny weak, but the kind of skinny that had grown up learning how to fight in alleys. He stared at Webb. "Sorry, dude. This won't be your gig."

"I've got the email giving me the audition time," Webb said. "So if the spot isn't filled—"

"Won't be by you." The bass player crossed his arms.

"Is the spot open?" Webb said. "I mean, if you're giving her a shot, I don't understand."

"Maybe return those guitars to Gerald Dean," the bassist said.

Webb squinted in confusion, but the guy was already looking past him.

"Come on up," he told Elle. "Let's hear what you have. Dean said you rocked."

She shrugged and without looking back at Webb stepped onto the stage. She plugged in her Stratocaster.

"Give us a solo," the bass guitarist said. "Then we'll try you with a couple of our songs. You gave them a listen, right? Or do you want charts?"

"No charts," Elle said. "Up-tempo solo?"

"Dean said you were working on something that had a lot of potential. Said if we did it right, the song could take us all a long way. He said something about getting a label behind you and taking us along for the ride."

Elle grinned. Webb had to admit she had a great grin. Lots of charisma.

"Just a little something we're batting around," she said.

"Dean sent us some charts, and we've had a chance to rehearse. How about we give that a shot first? If you sound as good as he promised, that's all we're going to need. We can break for lunch and all of us can get to know each other a little better."

"Cool," Elle said.

The bass guitarist looked at Webb. "You still here?"

"Yup."

"Why?"

"I'm wondering how you know you have the best guitarist before you hear both of us."

"They know," Elle said flatly to Webb. "Trust me. Even if they didn't, who would want you anyway? Gerald told me all about you."

Told you what? Before Webb could croak out the question, the bass player set down his guitar and took a step toward Webb.

"Take a hint," he said. "You're not welcome here."

Webb's face burned. He'd received an email invitation to audition, but now it seemed rigged. He'd done nothing to deserve this hostility. Or the humiliation. But clearly, nothing he could do would help the situation.

He picked up his guitar case to leave.

The bassist spoke to the woman behind the keyboard. She had a pinched face and blond hair in a long straight ponytail.

"How about you get us started?" he said.

She gave a quick nod.

"Then," the bass guitarist said, turning to Elle, "you jump in with guitar and vocals. You know the song better than we do, so that should be simple."

"Ready to rock," she said.

Webb was halfway to the door when the first simple notes of the piano reached him. Catchy beginning, he thought. Clean and simple.

He was almost at the door when the bass guitar and drums kicked in, and he reached it as Elle jumped in on guitar and hit her opening vocals.

You gonna have to know we're gonna mess up
You gotta know we might wreck stuff

Webb froze. Those were *his* lyrics.

He didn't turn, but listened.

You're gonna see us learn our lessons
But it's gonna be our best of...

Webb felt blood rush to his face again. This time it wasn't from embarrassment or humiliation but from anger. Those were *his* lyrics.

He spun around, anticipating the chorus, and the white heat of his anger took him back toward the stage as he heard, feeling a combination of disbelief and certainty:

Yeah, we're gonna rock the boat
That's the only way to know
We're gonna have to rock the boat
Yeah, that's the only way to go.

Webb kept marching. He stopped in front of the stage. He didn't flinch as the bass guitarist put up a hand to stop the music.

"What's it going to take for you to figure out you're not welcome here?" the bass player said. Once again he put down his guitar and took a threatening step toward Webb.

"Step off that stage," Webb said, "and you're going to regret it."

Something in the coldness of his voice must have sent a clear signal. Webb was in no mood for anyone to mess with him.

"That's my song," he said to Elle. "My lyrics. My music. Every note, every word, every chord."

"Shocker," she said. "Like the two Gibsons missing from Dean's studio were yours too?"

The bass guitarist held up his cell phone. "Check it out. I'm five seconds away from calling 9-1-1. You've been asked to leave, and you've threatened us with physical violence. When the cops come, you're going to have to explain a lot more than missing guitars."

"That's my song," Webb said again.

Elle shook her head, her face laden with scorn.

"Go away," she said.

So Webb did.

Twelve

Webb felt his blood surge as he walked into the recording studio and stared at Gerald Dean, who didn't bother to get up from his chair behind the mixing board.

Yet Webb did his best to show no emotion.

"So," Gerald sneered, "I hope you're here to make things right."

The sneer nearly drove Webb beyond control. He wanted to break Gerald's nose and smear the blood across Gerald's lips. Webb had had training in martial arts. It seemed like a lifetime ago, but his body hadn't forgotten the moves.

He took deep breaths. He wasn't going to let Gerald control him.

"Absolutely," Webb said. "I'm here to make things right. That means—"

Gerald cut him off. "Let's start with the bounced check then. I got a call from my bank. Your check didn't clear. So I'd like it in cash. Plus fifty more bucks for bank charges."

Webb had five hundred bucks in his back pocket. The first thing he'd done after walking out of the audition was hit a bank machine and withdraw the cash.

"That's not going to happen," Webb said. "When I realized you were cheating me, I wanted the check to bounce. What we're going to do to make things right is—"

"You're going to bring back my guitars?"

Webb felt his nostrils flare as he sucked in more air. His forearms trembled with desire to lash out at the man in front of him.

"Maybe you could explain that to me," Webb said. He moved closer and stood over the mixing board. "That's another reason I'm here. You're telling people I stole from you?"

Gerald responded by pulling out his iPhone and pointing it at Webb. Gerald spoke loudly. "Sitting here in my studio. The guy in front of me with a stupid yellow double E on his green shirt is Jim Webb. Rip-off artist who looks like he's on the verge of becoming violent. I'm videoing this as proof for possible criminal charges if he attacks me."

Webb didn't back away, but he did stop.

"Keep the video going," he said. "I'm here because you're the rip-off artist."

"Two of my best guitars," Gerald said. "Gone. I'd like them back."

"Then talk to the person who took them," Webb said. "And stop spreading rumors about me."

"Sure," Gerald said. "When I see my guitars. Back in my studio."

"That's not the issue," Webb answered. "You know it. And I know you know it."

"I'd say ten grand's worth of missing guitars is a major issue."

"Not as major an issue as you ripping off my song." Webb lifted his right hand and slowly and deliberately pointed at Gerald. "Yes. You. Producer. Ripping off my song. 'Rock the Boat.'"

Webb dropped his hand and stared at the phone that was videoing him.

"What's going to happen," Webb said, looking past the phone to Gerald, "is that you are going to send me a link to the songs you produced for me. You're going to take out a pen and paper and write that Jim Webb wrote the music and lyrics to 'Rock the Boat.' If you do that, I won't go out there and tell people that you ripped me off."

"Go ahead," Gerald said. "And please keep track of the people you tell. Slander is a serious issue. I'll be able to use them as witnesses when I see you in court."

Webb couldn't help himself. He slammed the board with an open palm. Hard enough that Gerald flinched.

"You're telling people I stole two of your guitars! That's slander!"

Webb regretted his actions immediately. Slamming the mixing board and raising his voice. He had just lost control.

Gerald smirked.

That's when Webb realized Gerald had been goading him, hoping for something that verged on violence. Something on video.

When Gerald spoke, however, there was no trace of a smirk in his voice. As if he knew it wouldn't sound good on the video.

"You don't understand what slander is," Gerald said. "What I've told people is that two of my guitars are missing. I've also told them I left you alone in the studio. And that later I noticed the guitars were gone. I didn't once tell anyone that you stole my guitars. However, I do find the coincidence troubling, and I would like them back. If you can arrange it."

"Unbelievable," Webb said. "You're going to hear from Jordan Marvin, my attorney at Bing and McGee. You're not going to get away with this."

"What's unbelievable," Gerald said, "is that you are here, clearly making slanderous charges. You. Someone who hasn't yet paid for the production work I did. Someone who bounced a check. The same someone who was alone in the studio the day my guitars disappeared. And *you* are accusing *me* of being the rip-off artist?"

"I played you that song. In this studio. You told me it wasn't worth producing. You asked me if anyone else had heard it or if I'd recorded it anywhere. You told me not to bother because it would embarrass me. And then I hear it at an audition. Played by an artist that you are developing."

"No," Gerald said. "You've been in my studio. The same studio where you stole guitars. You heard the song. And now, after failing to pay for my production, you're trying to run a scam on me."

Gerald put the phone down and stood. He looked directly into Webb's eyes.

"Dude, whatever game you're playing isn't going to work. And you shouldn't have made me mad. When you leave, I'm going to erase every bit of music I produced for you. I suggest you leave here and never return to Nashville. It's a small town. I'm going to make sure no one is going to work with you. Ever."

Thirteen

An hour later, Webb was back at Bing and McGee.

"Hello, Mr. Webb," said Jordan Marvin. "I'm glad I was able to fit you in on such short notice. It's nice to meet you."

Webb decided that paying $250 an hour for someone's time also earned you the right to be called mister.

Jordan stepped out from behind her desk. Her office was down the hall from the reception area. Unlike the foyer, with its floor-to-ceiling windows, her office had one small window that showed the backside of a brick building across the alley.

And unlike the motherly receptionist who had carefully counted Webb's five hundred dollars and as carefully handed him a receipt, Jordan Marvin was tall and slim and wore a dark blue pantsuit that managed to seem both feminine and businesslike.

"It's nice to meet you too," Webb said. He still couldn't get her fee out of his mind—$250 an hour. No wonder it was nice for her to meet him.

She pointed at one of two leather chairs in the corner of her small office. There was a coffee table between the two chairs. On it were a notepad with leather binding and a pen. Beside the notepad sat a white carafe and two white coffee cups on saucers. Nice china.

"Coffee?" she asked.

Webb nodded.

"Cream?"

Webb nodded again.

She poured the coffee and added cream. The coffee tasted great. But then again, when a person was paying—

Webb told himself to get over the cost. He had decided to spend the money and come here, so there was no sense whining, even if it was silent whining.

Jordan picked up the pen and notepad. She opened the pad and lifted the pen, poised to take notes.

"I understand," she said, "that you believe a music producer named Gerald Dean has not fulfilled his legal obligations to you?"

"My grandfather made a provision in his will for Gerald Dean to be paid to produce some of my songs," Webb said. "When I asked Dean why he hadn't finished it by the time he promised, he told me he'd hired studio musicians who charged him more than expected and that I owed him more money. When I asked to see the invoices they gave him, he dragged his feet. I still haven't seen them."

She jotted down a few sentences. "You have a contract to show me?"

Webb dropped his head. "No. My grandfather set it all up before he died. Dean said it was cool. Told me he had lots of references. That I didn't need to worry."

She tightened her lips.

Irritated at Webb? Or irritated at the producer? Or both?

"It gets worse," Webb said. "That's why I knew I had to come back here. I played a song for him earlier this week. On Tuesday morning. A song that I wrote. Music and lyrics. In his studio. This morning, an artist he's developing played the song at an audition I was at and said the two of them wrote it yesterday."

Saying this brought back the emotions, and Webb had to set his coffee cup down because he felt an urge to throw it through the window.

"You have my sympathy," Jordan said. "This is a difficult situation. Can you prove you wrote the song? Lots of musicians make rough demos. If you did, and the time stamp on the electronics shows you wrote it before Mr. Dean says he wrote it, that will go a long way toward solving this legally."

Webb shook his head. "It was just something that came to me on Monday night. I was so excited about it, I wanted to play it for someone, so when I was in his studio on Tuesday morning, I played it."

"Just to confirm. You played it live. Not from a demo tape."

"Yes."

"Tell me the time."

Webb did. She wrote it down.

"And to confirm, you said you heard it at an audition two days later, and the artist told you that she and Mr. Dean wrote it."

"That's right."

Jordan tapped her front teeth with her pen. Webb noticed a smudge of red lipstick on one of her teeth. "The difficulty is that it's going to be your word against his."

"You need to believe me," Webb said. "That's the way it happened."

She gave him a grim smile. Webb noticed the lipstick smudge was now gone.

"It doesn't matter whether I believe you," Jordan said. "What matters is what we can prove."

Webb noticed that she dodged saying whether she believed him. That mattered to him. But he didn't push her on it.

She spoke again. "It's even more complicated than you think. Just before you showed up this afternoon, our receptionist received a letter from a law firm across town. They are representing a producer named Gerald Dean who wants to initiate a legal action against you."

"What!" Webb leaned forward.

"Because our files did not show you as a client, there was some confusion," Jordan said. "Our receptionist, however, cross-referenced all our recent calendars and realized you had come in yesterday. So she gave the letter to me, as you had set up an appointment with me. You'd given us your cell number when you made the initial appointment, so I was going to call you as a courtesy. Then the receptionist got your incoming call to set up this appointment. And since you've engaged me with the retainer, with your permission I suggest we deal first with the legal action about to be taken against you. After that we decide what to do against Gerald Dean."

Webb stood. He had to. He really wanted to go into Hulk mode. Rip, destroy, crush. But that wouldn't do him any good. He paced to the window and back to the chair.

Jordan hadn't moved. "Gerald Dean's legal action is to ensure you don't make any slanderous statements about his integrity."

Webb couldn't help himself. He thumped his thigh with his fist. "I'm the innocent one."

"Please sit," she said. Her voice was so calm that it served to calm Webb. He sat.

"Let me explain the situation. Do your best to see it from a legal perspective, not a personal one. Unless we can prove your accusation against their client, you can expect a lawsuit for slandering his reputation if you make that accusation anywhere public."

"But—"

She held up a hand. "It will not go well with you in front of a judge. I took the liberty of making an informal call to my colleague at the other law firm. He says the check you made for payment bounced."

"I took money out of my account so it would bounce," Webb said. "I thought that would be easier than trying to get it back."

"Heard of a stop-payment request?"

Webb had no answer.

"That makes you look bad, as you can see. And he says his client has a video of you physically threatening him, and that on the same video you clearly make the slanderous accusation."

"It isn't slander. It's true!"

"Not to an impartial judge." She paused. "You need to hear me out on this. Gerald Dean has also hired that law firm to take you to court for the bounced check and to get a restraining order against you. Legally, you appear to be in a bad position."

Webb leaned back in his chair, suddenly exhausted by the unfairness of this.

"It's going to be expensive to fight," she said. "You should know that up front."

"I'm the innocent one," Webb said, "but it's going to cost *me*?"

"That's how the legal system determines who is innocent. And if you lose, they are seeking damages of $50,000. Plus his legal expenses."

"I don't have the money," Webb said. "To fight or to lose."

She spoke softly, as if to lessen the blow. "Their offer is that if you formally sign an admission that Gerald Dean is the writer of the song and lyrics titled 'Rock the Boat,' no further legal action will be taken."

She paused. "And they have given you until noon tomorrow to sign the admission."

Fourteen

For Webb, when things were as bad as they could be, there was only one way to escape. Music.

He found a street corner in downtown Nashville. He set his guitar case on the ground, pulled out his acoustic, left the case open for donations, sat down and leaned against the wall behind him. The brick was warm from the afternoon sun, and Webb tried to focus on the pleasantness of that feeling.

It was difficult, however, to think beyond what he was facing. He had written a song good enough for a producer to steal for another artist, yet it looked like he had no chance of proving the song was his. He needed thousands of dollars to fight Gerald's legal action against him, and he'd need thousands more if he lost. As Jordan Marvin outlined the situation, no judge would side with Webb. He'd have to sign over the rights to the song—*his* song—just to be able to leave Nashville with the last of his money in his checking account. And the same producer who was stealing that song from him refused to deliver all the other songs that Webb had not only paid for already but also put in endless hours recording in the studio.

Webb closed his eyes. Yup. That about covered it.

Only one song would help him disappear into the music. "To Get Here." About a journey to get to someone you loved. It was one of his originals for the album, and one of the studio songs he'd spent so much money and time on, only to have Gerald Dean take it from him in the end.

But Gerald Dean couldn't steal the song from Webb's heart.

Webb kept his eyes closed. He didn't need to look at his guitar to find the frets and strings and chords. He hit the strings hard.

Spinning wheels over dotted lines
You're a moving picture in my mind
And I keep on looking round the bend
For that sweet, sweet moment I see you again.

Hold on, baby, let me catch my breath
From seeing you smile, it's as good as it gets
And every step felt like a year
But it would have been worth a thousand miles,
Oh, to get here.

He was so lost in the song that when a strange noise broke through, it took him a few moments to realize that it was applause from half a dozen people who had stopped in front of him and his guitar case.

Webb gave them a half smile. He wasn't doing this for them. He was doing it for himself.

There was another song he'd worked on with Gerald Dean. Not one he'd written himself but one he'd wanted to record for a friend who loved the song. The song about war and peace. About valley people attacking mountain people in an act of greed and hate. That seemed to fit the situation too.

So Webb played and sang his remake of the song, shifting some major chords of the original to minor.

More people stopped. Dollar bills floated into his guitar case. A couple of fives and tens too.

"You rock!" someone said.

It was a decent balm for his soul—except for the phrase "You rock," which reminded him of "Rock the Boat."

Then it occurred to Webb that when he wrote the song, he'd really believed what he was saying. Want to reach your dreams? Live life loud. Bring the roof down. Rock the boat. Make sure that when you look back, you have no regrets.

And now he was feeling sorry for himself. So sorry he was thinking about signing that piece of paper in the lawyer's office and taking the safe and sure way out?

Forget that, Webb told himself. He wasn't going down that easily. It was time to rock the boat.

So he hit the opening chords hard, shifted into the up-tempo portion and leaned into the vocals, grinning widely as he played the chorus.

You gonna have to know we're gonna mess up
You gotta know we might wreck stuff
You're gonna see us learn our lessons
But it's gonna be our best of.

Yeah, we're gonna rock the boat
That's the only way to know
We're gonna have to rock the boat
Yeah, that's the only way to go.

The small crowd was clapping to the beat, and when he reached the chorus for the third time, some people sang it with him.

Great moment. No, awesome moment. Wasn't this what it was all about?

Webb noticed someone had pulled out a phone and was shooting a video.

And that's when he realized something he should have thought of a lot sooner.

The realization felt like a current of electricity running from his guitar and through his body. It was such a strong bolt of inspiration that he almost jumped to his feet without finishing the song. But there was the clapping and the singing, and no way was he going to break the amazing

83

connection the music had created between strangers.

So he forced himself to play the song to the end, even though he felt embarrassed by the hollers of appreciation.

When he stood and the crowd moved on, he reached into his guitar case and pushed past the bills for the small compartment where he'd put the business card with Harley's address on the back.

It was Thursday. He hadn't planned on accepting Harley's invitation to go hang with some of his friends for a jam session that evening, but Webb's bolt of inspiration had changed all that.

Yup.

Tonight Webb was going to find Harley and definitely rock the boat.

Fifteen

"Hey," Harley said when he answered the door. "Great to see you. Come on in and meet my friends."

Harley paused, taking in Webb's shirt. "Edmonton today? Aren't they, like, Calgary's biggest rivals?"

"I rotate through the league," Webb said. "No favorites."

He was surprised at Harley's knowledge of CFL teams, just like he'd been surprised that Harley knew where Moose Jaw was.

Then again, Webb had been surprised when he was down on the street pushing the intercom button for Harley's place. When Harley had said he and his friends jammed in a warehouse, Webb had pictured a few guys getting together in some empty, long-abandoned building with broken windows and maybe an empty oil drum in the center with burning wood to provide some heat—a movie cliché, but Webb hadn't been able to help himself.

This building at the edge of the river, east of downtown and close enough to the core to be in the shadows of the skyscrapers, was in an area of upscale coffee shops and intimate cafés.

And calling it a warehouse was accurate only in the sense that, yes, at one time it had been a warehouse.

As Webb stepped through the doorway and followed Harley into his loft, he saw a huge space with living quarters at one end, hardwood floors and large windows that overlooked the Cumberland River. Only someone with money could afford a place like this.

Harley had set up the center of the open area as a stage, complete with monitors and speakers. Four guys were hanging out there, chatting quietly as they tuned their instruments. None of them looked like the homeless people Webb had known when he was living on the streets in Toronto.

Two of the guys had guitars. Webb tried not to show any reaction as he realized the guitars were top-end Telecasters. A third guy was riffing quietly on a drum set. And a fourth sat behind a keyboard, eyes closed, smiling.

Crap, Webb thought. Have I gotten myself in over my head?

Then he noticed the framed records on the walls. Framed gold records.

Crap, he thought again. Who exactly *is* Harley?

"Guys," Harley said, "this is Webb. He's the one who fed me the other day when I was busking."

All of them laughed. It was good-natured laughter, not mocking laughter.

"Cool," one of them said. "You made Harley's day. He was telling everyone that he wouldn't have made it through the day without that kind of generosity."

The guy at the drums—middle-aged, earrings on both sides, goatee—hit the snare with the kind of *ba-rump* that follows a punch line.

"Well," Webb said, thinking of the gold records on the wall, "he was playing his guitar so bad I thought he'd starve otherwise."

That earned another *ba-rump* from the drummer and more good-natured laughter from the other musicians.

"That's right, Harley," the keyboard guy said. "Remember, you can't eat a Grammy."

This was heavy-duty stuff. A Grammy?

Webb leaned close to Harley and spoke in a low voice. "I had no idea. Really. But you play on the streets to keep the music real, right?"

"The industry can wear you down," Harley said. "That's why all of us hang out here on Thursday nights. To get away from managers and lawyers and agents and enjoy the music."

Those words sunk in. *Managers and lawyers and agents.* As in musicians who had deals and needed managers and lawyers and agents.

"Maybe," Webb told Harley, "I could just sit in a corner and listen?"

Harley looked at his friends. "The kid just wants to sit in and listen. Not a chance."

He put his hand on Webb's shoulder and pushed him toward the stage. "Plug in and give us that great song you played on the street."

"About that," Webb said. "Something has been happening, and I've got a question or two."

"Business?"

"You could say that," Webb said.

"Rule one here," Harley answered. "No business. Just music. Come on. Plug in and play. They don't know the song, but they'll jump in like I did."

Fresh from playing it on the street, Webb was in a great mood for "Rock the Boat." Harley joined in immediately, but the bass guitarist froze and stared at Webb until Webb stopped, just after the first chorus.

"I mess up somewhere?" Webb asked the openly hostile face.

"Yeah," the bass guitarist said. "When you ripped off those guitars from Gerald Dean. And his song."

Sixteen

"Hang on," Harley said. "Everybody stop playing and come and sit down."

"Huh?" said the drummer.

"Rule one. When we're playing, we don't discuss business."

Harley pointed to the far end of the loft. At the easy chairs and leather sofa that formed part of the living area. "Let's grab something to eat and drink, and settle in and talk about this."

The drummer was the first to move. The others followed.

Harley stayed back a few steps and put his hand on Webb's shoulder.

"Straight up," Harley said. He spoke in a low voice to keep the conversation private. "That your song?"

Webb said, "Yes."

"You steal Gerald Dean's guitars?"

"No."

"Then I've got your back."

To Webb, those words felt like the first rays of sunshine penetrating fog.

At the other end of the loft, Harley made a point of grabbing a can of soda and handing it to Webb with everyone already seated and watching.

"First thing," Harley said. "I invited Webb here as my friend. Someone's your friend, you give them a good hearing if someone else makes accusations against them, right?"

"Stealing someone else's music is a big deal in this town," said the bass player.

"Let me ask you this," Harley responded. "How many great songs has Gerald Dean written?"

Silence.

"How many not-so-great songs has he written?" Harley asked.

Again silence.

"See what I mean?" Harley said. "The guy's a decent producer. We all know that. He's not known as a writer."

Harley kept going. "When I was busking with this kid, a guy accidentally threw a hundred into my guitar case. Kid said no way we should take it. Does that sound like someone who'd steal a guitar?"

Harley turned to Webb. "This is putting you on the spot. But I'm thinking any guy who brings breakfast to someone he believes is living on the streets has a code that would keep him from ripping someone off."

"It's my song," Webb said. He reached into his back pocket and pulled out the papers he'd been given at the law office. "I came here to show you this and ask about—"

Harley held up a hand, smiling. "We're music people. Not agents or managers. If you wrote that song, no way is it your first song. So I'm okay doing this to you: play us something else of yours."

Webb understood where this was going. He went back to the center of the loft and stood alone among the cords and speakers. He picked up his guitar and strummed it a few times to be sure it was still in tune. Of course it was, but this was something he did automatically.

Webb didn't see any point in playing another up-tempo song like "Rock the Boat." Harley's challenge was simple: show us you *are* a songwriter, because we know Gerald Dean is not. Webb would demonstrate some range and give them his favorite slow song. About a girl he missed—a girl whose smile he missed.

"Tuesday Afternoon."

Webb started slow and kept it slow.

In my favorite spot on a Tuesday afternoon
With a coffee pot and a window to the world
Where my thoughts seem so much smarter
And my heart beats that much harder
For you...

Webb had spent some time with a girl from Alabama, who had come up to Nashville to visit. Not enough time. She'd left to go to college in California, and he'd spent long hours thinking about what might have been.

Did you leave me because I wasn't what you
hoped for?

Wish you would have told me something
  I could do
But there's some things you can't change
The way that I can't change
That I love you...

As he sang and played, he went back in time. He was sitting in the houseboat with Ali Hawkins, watching rain streak the windows and spatter the calm water, listening to her say she was going to California and it wouldn't make much sense for either of them to wait for the other while they were on opposite sides of the country.

The sadness and longing must have filled his voice, because when he finished the song, it was so quiet that the ticking of a clock somewhere seemed to echo across the loft.

Finally the bass player stood. He gave a single clap of his hands. Then a few seconds later, another clap. He spaced the claps far enough apart that his applause served as an ovation. The others stood and joined him.

Webb lifted his guitar strap off his shoulders and set down his guitar. He was just realizing how important this moment was. He didn't know who these guys were—it was killing him not to go over and check out the gold records—but they were obviously a tight-knit group of Nashville insiders who believed first in music. "Tuesday Afternoon" had been make or break. If he'd messed up, he'd have been out the door.

His legs wobbled on the way back to the sitting area. He sensed that whatever had just happened was far bigger and better for him than if he'd landed a spot with the band at the audition earlier that day.

Harley met him halfway, put an arm around his shoulder and walked him the rest of the way to the guys.

"All right," Harley said to them, his left arm still across Webb's shoulders, "I'm thinking maybe we should put out some feelers and find out what's really happening with Gerald Dean these days."

Seventeen

S
hortly after eleven the next morning, Webb stepped into a restaurant called the Pancake Pantry. Harley said it was one of the great breakfast places in Nashville. For the occasion, Webb was wearing the Saskatchewan Roughriders logo on his chest.

On the walls were the standard head shots of celebrities and musicians who had stopped by the Pancake Pantry over the years. Webb grinned when he saw one of Harley. Who knew the guy had been a major country star a generation ago?

Webb scanned the restaurant and saw Gerald Dean sitting with Elle and a man he guessed was Elle's father.

Time to rock the boat, Webb thought. He stepped forward amid the din of conversation in the crowded restaurant.

There was an open chair at the table, and Webb stopped and said, "Hello. I'm Jim Webb. I hope you don't mind if I join you for a few moments."

"Yes," Gerald said. "We do. We're waiting for someone."

Elle scowled at Webb. "Daddy, this is the guy from the audition."

Elle's father was large in the shoulders. He wore a plaid shirt and blue jeans. He looked exactly like his picture in the online advertisements for his chain of lumber stores in Minnesota. Webb had done his research before going to the Pancake Pantry. This was Steven Adams.

"The guy who stole the guitars from the studio?" Steven said.

"Since that's just a rumor," Webb said, "I'd appreciate a chance to explain myself."

"No," Gerald said. "We've got a guy coming from A&R. This is an important meeting.

Now that Elle has a band to back her up, we've got a deal memo to discuss."

A&R. Artists and Repertoire. The division of a label responsible for signing new talent.

Webb looked at Steven. "As best as I can tell from what I read about you online, you built your business on being fair. I'm just asking for a chance to be heard. Five minutes max. If I'm right, it will ensure that your investment in Elle's career makes sense."

"I hope you're not implying that I'm trying to buy her a career," Steven said. His tone suggested he was sensitive to the accusation.

"I've heard Elle play and I've heard her sing," Webb said. "I don't think anyone would ever make that accusation. She's too good. Word around town is that she's going to be the next Taylor Swift. Someone with a lot of talent who did things right with a lot of savvy investment and help from a father who knows business."

Steven grunted, satisfied by Webb's answer. He pointed at the empty chair. "You have five minutes."

Gerald tried to speak. "But—"

"Five minutes," Steven said. "There's no downside to giving this kid a chance to tell his side of the story."

Gerald glared at Webb.

There was a coffee cup on a saucer in front of Webb. He turned the cup upside down so the server wouldn't offer to pour coffee. This too seemed to relax Steven. Elle, on the other hand, kept giving Webb dark looks.

"I also understand from a musician friend," Webb began, speaking to Steven Adams, "that you and Elle went around town to some of the best producers in the business. You promised a great bonus and a percentage of future earnings for the producer who could help her break in."

"That's no secret," Steven said. "I approached this like an investment."

"We don't need this," Gerald said to Steven. "We need to be preparing for the A&R guy."

Webb went steely cold and spoke to Gerald with a restrained fury that made the man shrink. "You, sir, have made a public accusation that I stole guitars from your studio. If you aren't man enough to give me a chance to defend myself, tell all three of us right now and I'll leave."

Gerald blinked and looked away.

Webb turned back to Steven. He exhaled, finding calmness again. "And one other thing I've heard. Ahead of time, you asked each producer to come up with an idea for an original song to write with Elle."

"Yes," Steven said. "That's just good business. The artist needs to be a co-writer—otherwise he or she loses out on a big percentage. It doesn't make sense to cut songs if most of the money goes to the label and to a writer."

Webb said to Elle, "I know you think I'm scum. But I hope you'll still answer a question. The day before the audition, when you wrote it with him, how much did you come up with and how much did he suggest?"

"I'm a 40 percent writer on it," she said.

"But did you *write* 40 percent of it?" Webb asked.

Her silence was enough of an answer.

To break the silence, she looked at her father. "Gerald was on a roll. Inspired. I didn't want to get in the way. And he said it didn't matter because I'd still be listed as co-writer."

"It happens a lot," Gerald told Steven.

"Mr. Adams," Webb said to Steven, "I've heard from a few sources lately that Mr. Dean has a habit of recording everything that goes on in his studio. What would it do to your daughter's career if people learned that he ripped that song off after I played it for him earlier? Because as co-writer, Elle is also listed as the primary witness in a legal action filed against me. She will be required to testify that the song was written on a specific date at a specific location with her. And that I was not the writer. So when I prove it was written before that date—"

"Court action?" Steven's voice was a threatening rumble as he glanced at Gerald. "Court action? That never plays well in the media. And music is a media-driven game."

"It won't make it to court," Gerald said. "That's why I had my attorney initiate the legal action. And because it won't go to court, I didn't think it was anything you needed to worry about."

"Why wouldn't it go to court?" Steven asked, clearly unhappy. "This is not a relationship where you hide things from me."

"It won't go to court because he knows I can't afford it," Webb said. He pulled a folded paper from his pocket. "It's all right here. A legal request from Gerald's attorney for me to sign over the rights to the song. My attorney said I'd have to spend thousands to fight it and spend thousands more if I lost. I don't have that kind of money."

Dean said, "This kid can't go around town making claims that Elle and I stole the song from him."

Steven looked at Webb. "You are down to one minute."

"The same musician friend of mine said this seems like a heavy-duty kind of thing to threaten somebody like me with, being new to town and with no connections," Webb continued, "as if Dean wants to make sure I run away as soon as possible. My friend said it made him wonder why Dean is so anxious to get rid of me."

"Gerald?" Steven asked the producer.

"I will repeat. This kid can't go around town making claims that Elle and I stole the song from him. I'm trying to protect her reputation as much as mine."

"Or," Webb said to Gerald, "maybe once you heard her sing, you knew exactly how much it would be worth to you to be the producer to take

Elle to A&R. And maybe you didn't have a good song idea until you heard me play 'Rock the Boat.' I remember exactly what you asked after I played it for you. You asked if I had recorded it or shared it. When I said no, you told me it would be a good idea not to let anyone else hear it. To save myself the embarrassment. I think you knew that if you pretended to write the song with Elle—"

"Slander," Gerald said.

"Not if it's true," Webb said. "That's why I invited my musician friend to join us."

"We really are waiting for someone from A&R," Steven said. "I'm not interested in a he-said/he-said argument right now. And frankly, even if Elle didn't do the lion's share of writing, she was there as they came up with it. You should probably take your attorney's advice."

"Mr. Adams," Webb said, "my musician friend is a good buddy of your A&R person, which is why I knew where to find you. My musician friend also asked your A&R person to show up a little late. Really, it is for your benefit as much as mine if you listen to him."

Webb lifted his hand as Harley walked into the restaurant.

Harley walked over to the table. "Hey, I'm Harley Hays. Nice to meet you."

Steven stood so quickly that he almost knocked his chair over.

"Harley Hays?" Steven said. "*The* Harley Hays?"

Eighteen

"Nice of you to show that kind of enthusiasm." Harley grinned and pointed at Webb. "Some kids these days don't remember the go-go years of country music in the nineties. Mind if I join you?"

Steven responded by pulling a chair from an empty table and setting it in place for Harley.

"You okay if Elle takes a photo of me with you?" Steven asked.

"We'll do better than that if you like," Harley answered. "Next Thursday night, why don't you and Elle join me and my friends at my loft for a jam session? Webb says Elle is a spectacular guitarist and singer, and I'd love to have her sit in."

Steven couldn't even speak as a grin split his face.

"Thing is," Harley said, "I love music. Not one for the business side myself, but I know it's a necessity. That's why me and the boys get together when we can. And every once in a while, just to keep my sanity, I dress scruffy, put on a ballcap to hide most of my face, and I sit on a street corner and play, with an open guitar case in front of me. I'll tell you, that's when you sink or swim. Everywhere else, for someone with a bunch of gold records, it's like that story about the emperor with no clothes. Fans are going to tell you that you sound great even if you stink. When it's me and my guitar and nobody knows me, I don't have to deal with people who think they need to kiss my keister."

"You couldn't play badly if your hands were taped," Steven said.

"And I believe you just proved my point." Harley grinned to take the offense out of it. "Not that you were trying to kiss my keister. It's pretty clear people in the music business these days want to keep you and your daughter happy. My buddy in A&R raves about Elle."

Steven looked at Webb. "This is the musician friend you were just talking about?"

Webb shrugged. "Thought he needed breakfast one morning."

"Yup," Harley said. "I'm busking and this kid comes up and gives me a bagel and some coffee, like I'm a homeless person. I was cool with that and glad he didn't know me. He had his own guitar, so we jammed some, and it turned out the kid could play."

"In the nineties," Webb said to Steven, "the iPod didn't even exist. Neither did iTunes. How was I to know who this guy was?"

Webb grinned at Harley. "But I did know Lou Reed."

Harley grinned back at the jab.

"I loved it," Harley said to Steven. "And I loved how Webb sounded. Reminded me of me when I first moved to Nashville. So I figured I'd mess with him a bit—ask him to come up to my loft and jam with the guys in my band, then enjoy the expression on his face when he figured out who we were."

"They managed to keep up," Webb said to Elle. "You won't have to teach them much when you get there."

Steven groaned.

Harley grinned again.

Elle looked like she was still trying to figure out what was happening.

And Gerald Dean sat upright and stiff, exuding anger.

"The reason I'm here," Harley said, "is that when Webb was jamming with us, I asked him to play the song he'd played on the street with me. That's when it got real quiet. I had no idea what was happening to the song, and that's when one of the guys said he'd already heard it. Said the word was out there that some kid from Canada was trying to rip it off from Gerald Dean. Said Dean was telling everyone the kid stole a couple of guitars."

Harley turned his gaze to Gerald. "Not cool. You should have proof before you tell people someone stole guitars from your studio. It's a small town when it comes to the music business. You know how important reputation is."

Gerald sputtered, "You have no right to—"

"Shut up," Steven told Gerald. "If Harley Hays is here, there must be a good reason for it."

"I didn't know anything then about the legal action," Harley said. "But I gave Webb a chance to prove he really was a songwriter. He knocked it out of the park with something called 'Tuesday Afternoon.' For me, that was almost all I needed if I had to choose between whether Webb wrote it or Dean wrote it. But, of course, that wouldn't do any good in court."

Harley paused, as if he wanted to make sure Steven was listening closely. "I've been around long enough to know a thing or two about the business end myself. Reputation means a lot, not only in music but also in life. The advice I gave Webb was not to push this legal business any farther or harder. Mud-throwing spatters everybody. Webb does want all the legal stuff to stop. It's good for your daughter, it's good for you, and it's good for Webb."

Harley nodded at Webb. "Where's the other paper? From the attorney?"

Webb pulled a second paper from his back pocket and unfolded it. "This will officially assign rights to the song. I've signed it where I need to."

"Would you mind giving it to Dean then?" Harley asked.

Webb passed it across. Gerald had begun to smile.

As he read it, however, Gerald's smile turned to a frown. "This assigns rights to you!"

"It's my song," Webb said. "There's a place at the bottom to sign, and if you do, there won't be any more legal action. My attorney will confirm that with your attorney. My attorney will also expect a check from you to cover the legal expenses to this point. It might not be a lot to you, but it is to me."

Webb let that hang a couple of beats. "And oh yeah. You're also going to write a certified check to refund me all of the production money I spent on the songs you never delivered."

"But—"

Webb cut Gerald off. "You really don't want to go to court, do you? The amount you were going to sue me for is about what we'll ask from you. It's going to be a lot simpler if you just sign the paper. And you've got a deadline of five minutes to think it over."

Steven said, "Elle, you told me you wrote the song with Dean that afternoon we met with him."

"I'd never lie about something like that," Elle said. "I hate liars as much as you do."

They both looked at Gerald, but Harley spoke and drew the attention back to himself.

"Mr. Adams, I'd hate to go to court too," Harley said. "Because as it turns out, I'd be a primary witness along with Elle. And what the judge would hear from me is that at about the same time Gerald was pretending to begin to write the song with Elle, Webb here was playing it on a street corner with me."

Gerald blurted, "You are making this up. You have no proof."

"Actually," Harley said, "we do."

Harley snorted as he spoke to Webb. "Moose Jaw, right? Of all places."

"Moose Jaw?" Steven said.

"A town in Saskatchewan," Harley said. "I remember touring through it once. Turns out a guy named Ward from Moose Jaw took a video of us as Webb played the song. I've already tracked him down, and he's emailed it to Webb's attorney. Time stamp and all. Plus the guy is ready to fly down from Canada any time and testify. I'm sure a judge will give that kind of evidence a lot of weight."

Steven leaned across the table and stared directly at Gerald Dean. "I strongly suggest you sign that piece of paper. And give him all his money back. Because if it comes to a legal fight, I'll back this Jim Webb kid as long as it takes. And I suspect my pockets are a lot deeper than yours."

Nineteen

John McMullen was wide and blocky, just like his face. He had thinning red hair and lots of charm in his Irish grin.

He was also the A&R director who had signed Elle to her deal. And now he was sitting on the houseboat patio with Webb, who was wearing the big white *W* of the Winnipeg Blue Bombers.

Ten in the morning. Lots of sun. A cup of coffee each, the third for both of them. It had been a great hour for Webb, sitting with McMullen and talking music and music dreams.

A short silence had fallen between them, and McMullen broke it, grinning as he spoke. "Ugly shirt. Harley told me about this CFL thing you have going on. I've been waiting all morning to ask. You going to stick with it?"

Webb grinned back. "I'd be happy to buy a new wardrobe. Long as it's with someone else's money."

McMullen laughed. "Like the label's marketing money?"

"As long as I don't have to blow-dry my hair to match something frilly, you get me shirts less ugly and I'll wear them."

"I'll make note of that," McMullen said.

The boat rocked slightly as swells came in from the river.

"And you're good with the rest of what we just discussed, right?" McMullen said. "If so, I'll leave you with the deal points. It's essentially a legal commitment from the label that we will proceed with you according to those deal points. We'll record three or four songs, work it up with a band, showcase it for the label and from there get a full record deal. We're bound to you, and you won't accept offers from another label."

"I'm clear," Webb said. He didn't want to do anything goofy like pinch himself to see if this was a dream. Harley had told Webb to play everything cool, as if whatever McMullen offered was a little less than Webb deserved. That was part of the game.

"Great," McMullen said. "You and I get to step away from the legal details now. Leave the painful part to the lawyers. Your attorney will work with our attorney, and they'll do the usual posturing and fighting to make it look like they're working hard for each of us and then go out for dinner after and talk about their kids and school and stuff and count all the money they make off pretending to fight each other. Along the way, it makes sure everyone has a fair deal."

Webb smiled.

"I know you had a producer who tried to mess with you," McMullen said, "but in this town, it hardly ever works to play it that way. Reputation means a lot around here. You're not going to see much of that guy in town anymore."

"Thanks," Webb said, thinking of Harley and how Harley had been able to open so many doors just by being someone trustworthy. And, of course, by being someone who could do amazing things with guitar and vocals. It wasn't just one or the other. You had to combine both. Business. Music.

"Speaking of fun," McMullen said, "you mentioned you might have an idea for a music video for 'Rock the Boat.' I'm in no hurry to leave this little oasis you have, so run it past me, if you don't mind."

"You remember I said that sometimes people tell you not to rock the boat because they like things the way they are?" Webb said. "And that if you want to make changes in your life or around you, sometimes you have to take chances and ignore those people?"

McMullen nodded.

"I know lots of videos have been done about trying to achieve your dreams," Webb continued, "so I was thinking maybe the video starts like that. You have a musician in the video who—"

"You mean you're the musician in the video."

Weird, Webb thought. Planning out a mini movie where he was the star.

"Okay. The video opens with me busking, and you see people throwing money in the guitar case. That's true to my life. And then you see me at such a low place that I'm lining up to eat with other hungry people at a kitchen some organization has set up under an overpass. Except people need more than just food. They need music. So I'm standing in line, and people around me are dejected. A guy is behind me, shoulders drooping. A little girl looks sad. Maybe there's a shot of me sitting down after I eat, quietly playing guitar."

"So far, so good. I can picture all that."

"Then I get on a bus, and the highway signs show that I'm headed to Nashville. I'm in the studio, recording 'Rock the Boat.'"

"Let me jump in here," McMullen said. "When I offer a criticism, it's not meant to be negative. It's meant for evaluation, something to consider. And this is as good a time as any for you to understand that. You're going to be working with experienced people, and their input will be valuable. So don't take it as insult but as a legitimate desire to help make your music or your record or your video even better."

"Great advice," Webb said. "So what are you thinking?"

"Feeding the hungry is great. But the bus to Nashville and a kid pursuing his dreams is, well, overdone."

SIGMUND BROUWER

"I totally agree," Webb said. "But if you take a cliché and twist it, does that make it worth using the cliché?"

McMullen cocked his head, thinking. "Tell me more."

"Then the kid gets back on the bus, like he's failed. Leaves Nashville. You see him busking again, and the camera zooms in on the guitar case with a sign that says *Feed the hungry*, and you assume that the musician is broke and needs food. But then the camera zooms in a little more, and you see the mile oneTwelve CD cover in the guitar case—"

"Good advertising, by the way."

Webb grinned and continued. "It's your first hint that maybe the musician didn't fail. Then you see him back where he started, under the over-pass, except he's giving all his busking money to the organizer to help feed the hungry, and you see that the little girl now has a toy, and when the mile oneTwelve band is playing, you understand he went back to give a concert to the people who helped him when he was down."

"Not bad," McMullen said. "Anything else you want in the video?"

"Would it be too much of a cliché to end with a homeless person flashing a peace sign?"

"World could use more peace," McMullen said. "We could use more people helping other people. As long as it doesn't look too cheesy."

"Thanks," Webb said. "I'll make sure of that."

McMullen stood, a clear signal that the meeting was over.

Webb stood with him.

McMullen glanced at the channel that led to the river, then back at Webb.

"You know this is a great place to be," McMullen said. "Right?"

"Worse places to spend a night," Webb said. McMullen might have been talking about the houseboat, but Webb was thinking about all of it. What it had taken to get here, where it might lead.

All you needed to do was rock the boat.

Acknowledgments

Enormous gratitude to Cindy Morgan and Jeremy Bose, two of Nashville's great songwriters and musicians. Thanks for giving me insight into music and the music industry. The songs you both created for *St. Lola in the Fields* are always in heavy rotation on my playlist.

SIGMUND BROUWER is the bestselling author of numerous books for children and adults, including *Rock & Roll Literacy* and titles in the Orca Echoes, Orca Currents and Orca Sports series. Sigmund is the author of two previous books about Jim Webb: *Devil's Pass*, part of Seven (the series), and *Tin Soldier* (The Seven Sequels). Visit his websites, www.rockandroll-literacy.com and www.sigmundbrouwer.com, for information about Sigmund's books and school presentations. Sigmund and his family divide their time between his hometown of Red Deer, Alberta, and Nashville, Tennessee.

To hear the songs that Webb played in this story, and to learn more about the music and the video, go to www.mileonetwelve.com.

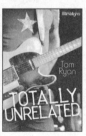